D0586611

EL MACCA

EL MACCA

Four Years with Real Madrid

Steve McManaman
and Sarah Edworthy

SIMON &
SCHUSTER

London · New York · Sydney · Toronto · Dublin

A VIACOM COMPANY

First published in Great Britain by Simon & Schuster UK Ltd, 2004
A Viacom Company

Copyright © Steve McManaman and Sarah Edworthy, 2004

This book is copyright under the Berne Convention.
No reproduction without permission.
All rights reserved.

The right of Steve McManaman and Sarah Edworthy to be identified
as authors of this work has been asserted in accordance
with sections 77 and 78 of the Copyright, Designs
and Patents Act, 1988.

1 3 5 7 9 10 8 6 4 2

Simon & Schuster UK Ltd
Africa House
64-78 Kingsway
London WC2B 6AH

www.simonsays.co.uk

Simon & Schuster Australia
Sydney

A CIP catalogue record for this book is available
from the British Library

ISBN 0-7432-5684-0

PICTURE CREDITS
1, 2, 4 © Action Images; 3 © Empics
5, 41 © Sporting Pictures; 7, 12, 28 © Offside; 29 © swpix;
all other photographs are from the author's
private collection or Real Madrid

Typeset by M Rules
Printed and bound in Great Britain by
Mackays of Chatham plc

SMc: To Victoria for her love and for always being there for me. Without her none of this would have been possible. To my family for their support, especially my mother whom I adored and my father who was, and still is, my biggest inspiration in football.

SE: To Rory, Isabella, Alexander and Emily, and my parents.

Contents

EL MACCA

Prologue

'That's his car,' says Steve, always the first to emerge from the
training-ground dressing room with hair still wet from the shower.
('He's the fastest guy in the world,' laughs Míchel Salgado. 'I think
he leaves still dripping, with his trousers wet. He'd be showered and
gone in five. Now you see him, now you don't. Bang! He's gone.')

McManaman emerges from one building only to go into the press
Portakabin, which is parked unceremoniously between the two
dressing-room exits. Swinging his head out of a rear door before he
takes his turn in front of the microphones and cameras, he points
along a row of sports cars and showroom-clean off-road vehicles.

'Stand by the driver's door and don't let him go! I've reminded
him you're here. The cafe's closed. He'll probably take you into the
TV interview room inside that door.

'He may be a while, though,' he warns with a grin, Scouse humour
intact after four years in Spain. 'He's having a rub. He's very old, you
see.'

Friday 20 June 2003

'Twelve noon. Hierro. Training ground.' The diary entry for Friday
is written triumphantly, then crossed out, later reinstated with both
a question mark and an exclamation mark. To reflect . . . what

exactly? A *mañana*-ish acceptance, perhaps, of what has come to be a familiar arrangement: a meeting with one of Steve McManaman's Real Madrid teammates, set up verbally across the open-plan dressing room.

To fix this, I imagine Steve jesting in loud accomplished Spanish with his club captain, the dark, gangly-lean Fernando Hierro, throwing in a casual word about his book, about whether an interview on Friday after training would be OK, followed by more laughter. It will be an agreement forged in semi-dressed camaraderie, surrounded by damp towels, discarded kit and boots, in a fug of scent from aerosols and hair gel. Míchel Salgado, the ultra-competitive right-back, will be brooding over losing to a debatable goal in the five-a-side. 'He's a psychopath in training,' moans Steve as if feeling the bruises. Iván Helguera is ribbing goalkeeper Iker Casillas. Ronaldo chants words from American rap songs he has made Macca – as Steve is known to all the players – painstakingly transcribe for him on a piece of paper. Kitmen pick up the morning's scarcely dirtied shirts, players flip-flop through to the physio beds or saunter from the gymnasium towards the showers. A team doctor wanders through the forest of athletic limbs that is his professional domain. Sheafs of paper, the day's delivery of fan mail and personal requests, are piled high in compartments left ajar at the bottom of each player's locker next to car keys, sunglasses and deodorant. The ever-playing radio competes with mobile phones now they have all been switched back on after training. There is a television too, but it won't be on. 'Not unless something very important is happening, like the Champions League draw,' says Steve. 'Or some matador stabbing some bull.'

And on that premise, of teammate trust granting access where the etiquette of the outside world does not (you don't get far with an official faxed request to interview a *galáctico*), I will get up at dawn and travel the eight-hundred-odd miles from London to Madrid in order to be standing, waiting, fingers crossed the player's still on for it, next to a silver Audi in the Ciudad Deportiva car park.

However, that is not the case this time. The crossing-out and reinstatement reflect the week's billowing drama. Sunday 22 June marks the last day of the domestic season and the city vibrates with tension. Real Madrid (on 75 points) will play Athletic Bilbao in a league title decider. Real Sociedad (73 points), the other championship contenders, are due to play Atlético Madrid at home in San Sebastián. The capital city is the highly charged backdrop for the contest between two Reals. Atlético, so the conspiracy theory goes, might not put up too much resistance if the reward is witnessing the humiliation of their overbearingly regal neighbours. Meanwhile a host of competitive, political and emotional reasons give Bilbao the will to beat Real Madrid. The situation is more finely balanced than the maths suggest. Bilbao are still vying with Barcelona for a UEFA Cup place. Earlier in the week their coach Jupp Heynckes (himself a former European Cup-winning coach with Real Madrid) had feistily announced he would not be renewing his contract, attacking the club's directors and fans for not supporting him and his players in the manner he expects. The very next day club president Javier Uria died of throat cancer at the age of forty-one. 'We'll be playing for Javier and want to win for him. It was his dream to see us back in Europe,' says Bilbao striker Ismael Urzaiz.

It is going to be one hell of a tough game, right down to the small print. Under Spanish League rules, if the two contenders end on equal points then Real Sociedad will take the trophy because the club from San Sebastián have better results in the head-to-head contests against Real Madrid.

I was coming to see Hierro to talk about McManaman's four years at Madrid, before the match Steve thought could be his last in the famous white shirt. The two met when playing against each other in Euro 96 and their friendship and mutual respect will count as one of those intangible trophies players take away from a fulfilling stint abroad. If Steve left for Spain pigeonholed at home as one of England's most enigmatic talents, he has earned a different status at his new club. Hierro, the ultimate teammate's teammate, values the way the versatile Englishman works for the team. Far from being the flaky embodiment of style over substance, as his critics had suggested, McManaman has proved there is far more to his game than crowd-thrilling dribbling runs down the wing. He protects Roberto Carlos when the left-back bombs up the pitch; he covers for the Zidanes and Figos; he adds fluidity and allows everyone to play to their strengths. He is, as Johan Cruyff wrote in the Spanish sports daily *Marca*, 'everyone's partner'.

'It's an age thing,' Steve says. 'We've got a lot of youngsters in the squad, but there are a group of us who remember each other in Euro 96 or World Cups. We've played four years together here, won two European Cups. We've reached ten or eleven finals together. That experience creates a bond.' For his part Hierro says that Steve is 'the most fascinating, most fantastic person I've ever met in a dressing room. The day he leaves we'll all miss him immensely. He's integrated perfectly and his Spanish is fine – we all understand him. Mind you, we'd understand Steve in English.'

Fortunate timing (from my point of view) or typical drama (from a club haunted by the 'Tenerife syndrome', named after the club to whom they have lost twice on the last day of the season, in 1991–92 and 1992–93, thus surrendering the league title to arch-rivals Barcelona), it has added a potential twist to Steve's last game. Who better to discuss this tightly poised league situation than Real Madrid's long-standing captain? To win a league championship is a triumphant achievement in itself, but for the lyrically touted team of 2002–03 – a 'butterfly collection of the world's most exotic talent' – victory simply represents a covert rescue package. The European Cup is Real's great obsession. Their record nine victories define the club. The handles of the glass doors to the city centre merchandise shops form two halves of the distinctive trophy; players carry a European Cup-shaped key ring. However, this season they have come up short in the elite competition, even in the Copa del Rey, the Spanish domestic cup competition. Victory on Sunday, and a record twenty-ninth Liga title, will redeem a season tarnished by failure to reach the Champions League final. Will Hierro explain how it has come to this, a last-gasp display of swagger required from the team and the roll-call of stars everyone can recite – Raúl, Figo, Zidane, Ronaldo and Roberto Carlos?

Meeting Hierro will be a privilege in itself, for it is impossible to overestimate the authority carried by the thirty-five-year-old Grand Old Man of Spanish football. Talking to him will surely generate more than the usual few sentences that are typically expanded upon to fill pages of the Spanish sports dailies. I wonder how he interprets the mood of brash change, orchestrated by the acquisitive president Florentino Pérez, sweeping the club he has served for fourteen years. A senior player during the presidential terms of Lorenzo Sanz and Pérez, Hierro is the link between Real Madrid's turn-of-the-century presidential terms of office.

So that was the plan, the noon appointment scrawled in a diary.

Tuesday 17 June 2003

That *was* the plan. However, just three days beforehand everything had been thrown into jeopardy. With implausible timing even for a club at ease with putting their players under immense pressure, Real Madrid announce they have reached an agreement with Manchester United to sign David Beckham. The interview with Hierro, which was to have concentrated on the captain's friendship with Steve, now has a further dimension. The Beckham signing is confirmation that events at Real Madrid have taken a fascinating turn. Those beginning to see Real Madrid as the Harlem Globetrotters of football are calling it the culmination of the revolution initiated by Pérez, whose three-year reign has been witnessed from day one by McManaman. 'What fun! Beckham too,' these people say. Others darkly claim this latest action by Pérez, one of the hardest men in football, represents the sacrifice of the club's soul on the altar of commercialism, that Real Madrid have 'Gone Hollywood'. Players are valued according to the number of shirts they sell, i.e. they have to be pin-up forwards, superstar creative spirits, not combative midfielders or battle-hardened defenders with the less glamorous roles. Resentment is brewing over how the *galácticos* are hailed to the detriment of other players. The colourful debate imbues Hierro with a certain frisson of influence, not so much trade union shop steward now, but something more akin to Gandalf, Tolkien's white wizard, poised to protect his fellowship of men from the merciless machinations of the moneymen. The season that began with controversial attempts to offload dressing-room favourite Fernando Morientes ends with the addition of another star midfielder the team surely does not need.

After weeks of speculation and persistent rumour that failed to be quashed by an unprecedented verbal 'never, never, never' denial to the BBC (and an 'official statement' posted on the club website which read: 'Contrary to speculation, Real Madrid does not have any intention to negotiate the hiring of Mr Beckham'), after weeks of smokescreens and bare-faced lies, of fuzzy photographs of Real and United officials meeting in Sardinia, of Naomi Campbell confiding to gossip columnists how her friend Victoria is looking at houses in Madrid, of promises to the players that transfer talk would start only once the season had ended, after all of that comes the declaration that shakes Hierro's dressing room. The deed is done.

A short statement is posted later on the club website as the third of three items, listed in order of importance. The first is a lengthy essay on *Parallel Ligas*, dwelling on the similarities of this championship-deciding weekend with the ultimately victorious 1979–80 season. The second trumpets another potential record for Raúl, one goal away from becoming Real Madrid's fourth all-time top scorer in la Liga. But that third item is composed with forceful language. The agreement with Beckham is 'definitive' and was made possible through 'David's strong and unmistakable determination'. All the way through the statement is a repetition of 'will' – 'England's captain will be playing for Real Madrid from next season' . . . 'the signing will take place next July 2nd' . . . 'the signing will make our club a more competitive squad' – not so much future tense as statement of intent. Is it too fanciful to say it reads as an attempt to nip in the bud an anticipated uprising?

Within seconds of the bombshell, Beckham mania grips Spain. Despite daily drip-feeds of speculation since March, despite the fact it has come as a surprise to no one, the reality is a huge story. Pérez's 'never, never, never' *was* president-speak for *sí*; his 'Neverland' is like Peter Pan's – a fantasyland for those who believe in enchantment. The sports dailies *AS* and *Marca* fill twelve pages each on the signing of Madrid's sixth *galáctico*. Every minute of the personal promotional tour of the Far East undertaken by David and Victoria Beckham is beamed from television sets into local tapas bars. Fans flock to the training ground to chant Beckham's name, to the club shop to enquire about his shirt (not yet available). Young girls show off their midriffs with Beckham's name inked in an arc over tummy buttons, boys adorn plain white T-shirts with the word 'Welcome' and a silhouette of the double-decker ponytail. Adolescent girls are overcome with emotion, sobbing as they clutch magazine pictures of the new *guapo*, or handsome, addition to the most adventurous squad on earth. Madrid shopkeepers sell out of white suits and chunky fake diamond studs. Gossip columnists speculate on what shops and restaurants the celebrity couple will frequent. In Britain photos of Beckham appear everywhere from the *Times Higher Education Supplement* to front-page pictures of his image adorning the back of a Tokyo bus. (How powerful now the Beckham image, to re-work the old saying about looking like the back end of a bus.) Viewers watching a Sky News live broadcast of Prime Minister's Question Time see a red 'News Flash' pointer alerting them to hold for a Real Madrid press conference. What is of more interest to the public: war in Iraq or Beckham in Madrid? Whose words carry more weight, Tony Blair's or those of Jorge Valdano, Real's general sporting director?

And Steve – even laidback, philosophical Steve – sounds like an adrenalin-charged embedded reporter filing from the front line. 'It's been unbelievable. Getting to work was horrific this morning,' he says. 'We've all had reporters outside the house, cameras sticking out of hedges, photographers up ladders, hordes at the training ground banging on the car window, people shouting questions into the air hopeful for any old answer about what we think of Beckham or what life is like for a player in Madrid. The players are very, very upset about it. Raúl's wife was doorstepped at home – she's a well-known model, they're always in the celebrity magazines, but they're treated with respect, never doorstepped. That's never happened before. A few other players' wives were approached too and were more than unhappy. The press who have arrived have broken all the unwritten rules. It's very off-putting. In the last two years Zidane and Ronaldo arrived with nothing like this fuss.

'Everyone is uneasy. No one can understand why the news of the signing has come out a matter of days before our title decider. Distraction is the last thing players need going into the last game. For us to lose out now would be nigh-on catastrophic. For a club who set such store by Champions League success, to have missed out on that, and the league championship, would be disastrous. The overwhelming feeling is that the whole Beckham furore shows a lack of respect for players who are still trying to win a league. That's what everyone feels very strongly.'

You can see affront in the body language at the training ground. Hierro, Raúl, Roberto Carlos and Guti, the four *capitanes*, or senior professionals, are said to have met Valdano ten days ago and been given assurances about being kept informed of the club's transfer plans. So why the 'shock' announcement now? Why in the week building up to a match that could render the season a success or an embarrassing failure? Why this insulting notion that, *finally*, Real Madrid is huge, because David Beckham is coming? The phrase that seeps from under the dressing-room door is 'lack of respect'. Hierro refers to Beckham curtly, and anonymously, as a 'reinforcement'. '[He] is more about marketing than playing,' says Casillas, while Guti is more emotional: 'I don't think it's fair that we are reaching a climax of the league and the front pages of the papers are only about Beckham.' Roberto Carlos calls Beckham a girl. 'He can eat my balls,' he shrugs dismissively.

'It was just the timing, it had nothing to do with the player individually,' Steve recalls later. 'It had been a long, long season and suddenly this bombshell happened and all the press materialised from nowhere. It was not the usual Spanish press or the sports journalists, it was the huge, huge influx of garbage press who came over. The pressure of that was what the players became pissed off about, not about Becks, because he had nothing to do with it, he was on the other side of the world. He had signed for Real Madrid, which was fair enough. All of us in the dressing room had done that in the past. It was just that the timing precipitated this horrendous press intrusion in the week we least needed to be distracted. People were coming in to work and saying to me, "I had English people outside my house all morning and they want to speak to my wife. What on earth's going on?" And I'm like, "Oh, I know, it's murder. That's what they're like, I'm awful sorry."'

For Victoria McManaman, unfamiliar with dealing with the press, it was difficult to get on with her own professional life as a lawyer lecturing in Spanish universities. 'There were lots of people at our gate every day for a week or two,' she says. 'They kept ringing the intercom and asking to speak to us. The sound of the doorbell nearly drove us mad. I either pretended I was Spanish and couldn't understand them or in the end we just ignored it and tried not to walk past any windows so they'd think we were out! I only spoke to them once and that was through the gate intercom – I took the polite, guarded approach and made it clear I didn't want to talk about the Beckhams, so they asked about life in Madrid, learning the language, if we liked the city et cetera. Of course when it was written in the paper they turned it all around so it looked like I'd *only* been talking about the Beckhams. For example, I had said, "Yes, the shops are great," and they printed that I couldn't wait to take Victoria shopping and that I thought she'd love the shops. I never even mentioned her name. I was so annoyed because I'd said nothing of the sort, and it made it seem as if I had nothing better to do than shop. Somehow several members of the British press had got hold of my mobile number and were pestering me for interviews, insisting they were interested in Steven and his life in Spain. As I pointed out, they had not been remotely interested for the last four years and I was not going to help fill their pages now. The other wives and I discussed the situation at the last few games. They were so fed up. They lead really private lives. Now all of a sudden they were being followed and asked questions about a player they had hardly heard of. They couldn't understand the fuss and thought it disrespectful to their husbands and the club as they still had games to go to win the league. Being English, I felt embarrassed that it was English reporters who were pestering the other families. They had only heard of Beckham because of the games against Man U and they didn't understand the scale of the fuss.'

Steve chips in: 'And all the players were getting that. That was the thing. You'd leave home with that and then get to the training ground, walk out of your car and again there'd be cameras shoved in your face, microphones in the window. "What food will Becks eat, please?" It was so frenzied. Everyone was looking for a comment. If you stopped and talked to one of the Spanish football journalists who you speak to every day, then all the newcomers would crowd in and jot down whatever they could overhear. It was all quite tacky. It went downhill fast. So it was important, the fact Valdano came in to speak to us the next day.'

Wednesday 18 June 2003

Valdano, insistent there is no choice in the timing of the announcement as Manchester United are stock-market-listed, goes into feather-smoothing action. Steve recalls: 'I think the club knew the reaction they were likely to get and they wanted to nip it in the bud. That's why Valdano took the unprecedented step of coming in and speaking to us. The reaction was such that he had to come in and give us reasons why. People were not happy.

'He came into the dressing room just before we went out to training. We all sat down on the benches under our lockers, which are in two lines opposite each other – some of the world's most famous players sitting like schoolboys. He stood at the top of the two lines. No one said anything, but you could sort of tell everyone was reassured by him coming in to explain what was going on. He confirmed we'd bought him, and said he would be treated like everyone else. Then he said he and Hierro were going to do a press conference so that the waiting journalists could take away official comments. He warned us not to answer questions about Beckham, not to mention him at all. No one asked questions of Valdano. We all listened, and thought, "Great, it will soon die down." So in that respect it was fine. I came out and said to the hordes, "Look I'm awful sorry, I'm not allowed to speak about it. We've got a big game on Sunday," and that was it.'

It was, and it wasn't. At Valdano's press conference – let's leave Tony Blair and go live to Madrid, as they were saying on Sky – the subliminal message rang out. The urbane former captain of Argentina stressed the significance of Beckham's signing for the club's status and future direction. 'As a club we will have a better presence and image. As a player, it means we can count on another megastar joining a very powerful side. It is a quality boost which will just make us better,' came the translation from Spanish. Only after the marketing reasons came mention of Beckham's potential contribution on the pitch. Was his signature more about marketing than playing, as Casillas had claimed, or as much about marketing as playing? It was a fine distinction. The Beckham furore moves on to a debate on whether the England captain is a more convincing central option than those already at the Bernabéu, and what his arrival might mean for the large number of existing squad members listed under midfielders, particularly for Figo (who had earlier been rumoured to be part of an exchange deal with Manchester United) and Guti.

Most players' minds may have been put to rest by Valdano, but the twenty-four hours of disgruntlement picks up a momentum of its own. Doing the rounds are stories that Raúl is livid about the violation of his family's privacy and the anticipated continuation of the media circus that accompanies the Beckhams everywhere. The fear is that it could open up players' private lives to the *prensa rosa*, the malicious Spanish gossip industry. Up until then players could happily fall out of the city's legendary nightclubs at 4am and no one would report it. There is consternation that Beckham is said to have demanded the No. 7 shirt worn by Raúl since he was a teenager. There is sympathy for Guti, a homegrown talent dubbed the 'Becks of Spain' thanks to his hair and fashion adventures, who has shared his anxiety about his future status. 'I was doing well in midfield and they bought Zidane. I was doing well further forward and they go and buy Ronaldo. Now Beckham. There is no place for me,' he pouted, with good reason. When Florentino Pérez buys a *galáctico*, he expects him to play. Every game. Whatever his form. It has become an unwritten rule. In the big games, the big names always start. The 'must-play' globally recognised star – the player who has signed over his image rights to the club – is a controversial feature of Real's new commercially switched-on era. That is fine if you are talking Zidane, who plays like a god, or Raúl, the undisputed King of the Bernabéu, or Ronaldo, who arrived as the World Cup's golden boot. But Beckham? Is he one too many? As of June 2003, where was the respect for the player who was invisible in the first leg of United's Champions League quarter-final against Real, who started from the bench in the second leg, who was considered by Madrid's demanding fans to be a one-trick right-footed crosser and deadball artist? Wasn't he just a pretty boy worried about how good his hair looked? The word – from a source purporting to be close to Luis Figo and his wife – is, that if Beckham brings his celebrity baggage because he (and/or his wife) courts it, he won't receive an over-friendly reception in the dressing room. Players don't like that.

'There was a bit of anger in there, but it was nonsense to think we were all standing around saying, "Let's be horrible to him when he arrives,"' said Steve. 'I think the fact that our lads had played against Manchester United in the Champions League [meant] they had an opinion of him as a player. The first game was in the Bernabéu, Real Madrid won quite comfortably and Beckham had a very quiet night. In the second game, Becks was on the bench. They see a lot of English football on the television. There was a little bit of anger, not against him as a person, but it was his name they'd had pushed at them all week. People were just sick of it. Even when the Spanish players were preparing for the Spain v. Northern Ireland game, they kept fielding questions about Beckham and they'd had enough. There was definitely frustration there.'

Later that day came an apology from the Beckham camp. 'I want to apologise to the Real players because all this has not been caused by me. I did not want it to detract from their last game of the season. They're fighting to win the league. I didn't want to upset that. I wish them good luck.' And more: 'I would never think of taking that number off Raúl. He's the king of Real Madrid as far as I'm concerned. I'll take whatever number they want to give me.'

'The lads appreciated that,' conceded Steve. 'It was on the front pages. Statements like that go down well without a doubt. He meant it because he was now a Real Madrid player and you certainly don't want to upset your teammates. PR-wise, it was a shrewd thing to do because Raúl is king. As much as we all thought those stories about Becks's demands were nonsense, it was good to have them quashed straightaway. If he had been given the No. 7 it would have marked a massive change of policy. It's like Ronaldo. Ronaldo is always No. 9, isn't he? He's got a sponsorship with boots as R9. When he does his autograph signature, he always puts R9 underneath because that's his thing. He has his number now, but when he first joined Real Madrid he wasn't No. 9. Fernando Morientes was. The club have always had the same attitude, regardless of who they signed. The new player will always be treated as another player and you'll get a number that is free. That's always been the case.'

For the dressing room, that twenty-four-hour period was another pointer towards normality, but to the outside world the sense was still of a rattled group of players. The Friday noon appointment with Hierro is definitely more exclamation mark than question mark – an interview with the man who leads a dressing room that has faced turmoil in a week it cannot afford to be in psychological disarray. He may be bound not to mention the B-word, but this is a time to observe the captain in his legendary role. As Ronaldo is to tell me later: 'He is a leader, and having a leader in a team is really important. He has the trust of all the players. We knew he would fight for us on the pitch and he had our interests at heart off it, too. He would always fight for our rights.'

Friday 20 June 2003

High noon, the appointed hour. It has been a frantic rush to get from the airport to drop bags at the city-centre hotel and go on to the Ciudad Deportiva training headquarters on time, especially on a day when Vicente Del Bosque is likely to have cut short his players' workout because of the heat. But training is only just over, the last of the players have trailed back into the dressing room. Salgado and the goalkeepers will be having their moan about debatable goals; Helguera will be acting prankster; Ronaldo, Roberto Carlos and Steve will be laughing and joking; César will be switching off the Walkman of anyone who is not open to joining in the fun; Raúl and Zidane will quietly be going about their serious business of warming down. Guti, I imagine, will be doing something to his hair in front of a mirror (though later I learn it is Salgado who is most punctilious about his appearance. 'Because I need to, much more than all the others, ha, ha,' he laughs).

Now the ongoing daily theatre starts. Between noon and almost 2pm, players re-emerge one by one from the unprepossessing doors, each individual greeted by a bespoke clamour from fans behind grey steel-bar fencing. For the few metres each player must walk to his car, it is semi-catwalk, semi-goldfish-bowl nonchalance. Shrill hysteria for local boy Iker Casillas as he flip-flops to and from the press Portakabin, wild chanting for Ronaldo who looks as if he wants to disappear in a hurry – his car is the only one parked rear-in for a quick exit – but Ronie ends up giving time to everyone proffering pen and paper, shirt, poster or ball. Time and again he puts his arm around strangers' shoulders and silently stares into a camera lens with that set, buck-toothed smile. There are respectful cheers for the introspective Zidane, characteristically in open-necked black shirt, jeans and ridiculously exquisite leather trainers, staring at the ground as he walks to his car, mobile phone to his ear. Luis Figo – black leather jacket as sleek as his slicked-back hair and Fonz-style sideburns – inevitably carries off a slightly over-coordinated up-to-the-minute designer look with a presence as big as he has on the pitch (he owns the Guess jeans concession in Portugal). Close your eyes, and you can play the game of identifying each player from the tenor of his reception. It can be a long wait.

Today it is also hot. Thirty minutes earlier, in the city centre, the stone pavements around the Puerta del Sol radiated stifling heat. Red neon digitals on electronic information boards declared the temperature at 35°C, and set to rise. Reporters and television crews huddle in a corner of shade, but the extraordinary thing is the emptiness inside the secure area. Where are the Becks-trivia hunters? Where are the hordes who have been staking out the Real Madrid players? The normal player-to-fan theatre plays on, but the media circus has packed up and left. 'It's weird, isn't it? So quiet. Yesterday this whole area was packed. Someone said everyone's gone to the Intertoto Cup. Strange,' muses Steve, who has re-emerged from speaking to the press, and wonders if I have spoken to Hierro yet.

I haven't. But with the help of Oscar Soler Vázquez, a young Spaniard who has come to act as interpreter, we are casing both possible places from which Hierro might emerge: the medical-centre exit and the dressing-room doors. Quiet it may be in Beckham-mania terms, but there are enough people to swamp an individual from view. Inside the fenced-off area there are the usual battalion of television crews and the usual array of radio, agency and newspaper reporters. There is also a considerable bustle of loitering fans. Given the strict security checkover you get even when you have a bona-fide appointment, it is training-ground mystery number one how so many pass muster every day. (Mystery number two is Raúl, whom few have seen emerge from training. 'He's last out. He takes his time, then gets a long massage, he'll come out when he's ready, probably when everyone's gone,' Steve explains.) So Oscar and I stand sentry at our posts, with mobile phones poised to summon the other immediately, sensing somehow that it is going to be a long wait.

Valdano's instruction not to mention Beckham is followed to the letter. A Spanish radio journalist tells me Hierro arrived this morning saying tetchily, 'I don't want to talk about Beckham. I don't see how he can help us win the league.' The heat is stifling and the siege mentality adds to the sense of players taking umbrage. Now Míchel Salgado stalks to his car, the same businesslike gait with which he operates on the right of the pitch, but a much less refined vision out of his white team kit. 'From now until Sunday night, David Beckham does not exist,' he says with a shake of lanky mousy hair. His T-shirt is cut off at the shoulders and an arm with a band tattooed around his biceps reaches for his car door handle. Guti comes out, and stands looking disconsolate in a plum-coloured fashion disaster. He is not going to say anything, but just as on the pitch, his body language says everything. If anyone is going to lose out on Beckham's arrival, it will be him. He knows it, and he is not ready to accept it, and he seems to want everybody to know the whole scenario is horribly unjust.

And so Oscar and I continue our wait. We have never met before, but he was recognisable the instant he walked into the car-park melee, having talked his way through the security guards. He is kindly taking a few hours out from his work in the offices of Madrid & Beyond, a travel agency set up by Englishman Nigel Hack, in which he is a partner. His office civvies of crisp white shirt and dark blue trousers set him apart from the crowd wearing designer-distressed jeans and up-to-the-minute leather trainers. He is not a Real fan. Born in Barcelona, his father registered him at birth as a member of Espanyol – 'the poor club', he smiles. 'As a child, I hated this club. Real Madrid were rich, they always won, they were so perfect. I liked to suffer with my team . . . But this . . .' he nods, watching Ronaldo putting his arm round yet more fans to a chorus of cheers – 'this is, wow . . .'

Time ticks by. The sun scorches down. Everyone – even the Spanish and Brazilians – has corralled themselves into the decreasing area of shade, gulping from mini-bottles of mineral water. More uproarious cheers and whistles signal the sighting of other players . . . Javier Portillo and Francisco Pavón. The two local boys walk past in team shorts and flip-flops, their gazelle-thin legs a reminder that they have years yet to grow physically, and symbolically. If they have only now been released from the physios, how much longer Hierro, who is more dependent on physical attention to maintain his fitness? Steve's quip about his age sinks in further than intended. The icon I have come to see – whose trophy cabinet, centrepiece three European Cup-winners' medals, would require an official inventory from Sotheby's – is lying prone, an ageing mortal on a massage table. Pérez's Never-Never Land fantasy may make Peter Pans of supporters who inhabit a world of perpetual football enchantment, but not of players, who are all too subject to the real-time process of waning powers.

At the beginning of the season Hierro was indubitably a giant figure, the spirit of Real Madrid incarnate: 'The defender with a forward's soul' as Santiago Segurola of *El País*, Spain's leading sports writer, once beautifully described his emblematic approach to the game as perpetrated at the Bernabéu. And 'the daddy of the dressing room' as Steve noted on his first day at the club in 1999: 'Hierro is the spokesman, absolutely nothing gets done without his say-so. He's been around so long he's held in awe by everyone.' On the taxi ride to the training ground this morning we skirted the imposing towers of the Estadio Santiago Bernabéu. Set back off the main boulevard, the architecture is grey and startling in its steep facade, the site slightly shabby with its sand-and-gravel car park. But what prompted a tingle down the spine were the giant banners billowing down from the upper levels. Each bore the same phrase, 'Solo Un Idioma', 'only one language', and above that line the same rear-view image: Hierro, in the white shirt bearing his No. 4, slumped to his knees in the ecstasy of victory. Yes, players at this club can be that big. But how big is he now, after a season of increasingly biting criticism?

I had mentioned his name to the taxi driver, knowing Madrid supporters are nothing if not demanding and pragmatic. 'His legs have gone, he's too slow,' he gesticulated unsentimentally, suggesting that Iván Helguera, a natural midfielder, has been running his socks off as the other centre-half to cover for his captain. After defeat in the Champions League semi-final, cruel headlines pinpointed Hierro – 'A man destroyed' – as if it were solely his failing legs that caused Madrid's defeat by Juventus, the game that ruined the dream of a record tenth European Cup. *AS* described his performance as 'horrible', adding: 'Some footballers are incapable of admitting they are finished.' Hierro was cast the villain, though crucially Del Bosque had no Claude Makelele or Ronaldo because of injury, Luis Figo had a soft penalty saved, and Raúl had begged to return prematurely after his appendectomy operation. The general consensus is that Hierro has become a liability in defence and needs to be replaced. However, it is said he has a verbal agreement to remain at the Bernabéu, possibly for the next two seasons.

Steve will not hear a word against him, especially malicious whispers that he is a brooding presence around the training ground. Hierro is one of the players he admires most. 'I think he's the most wonderful player. It's just the way we play sometimes leaves him vulnerable. That's all it is. He is the greatest centre-half I'll ever play with by far . . . his distribution, his passing. He can play anywhere. He's won everything. He's the most decorated player. He is not self-promoting about how much he's won and stuff, but real football people know how good he is . . . the rest don't matter. Some fella off the street, if he thought he was crap on the strength of a few games and some horrible headlines, well that's immaterial.'

There is a great roar from the fans behind the wiring. Suddenly I see Hierro's head above a sea of shoulders. The neat, short black hair, the slightly stooped shoulders of a tall, lean athlete, the ears – as someone jestingly said – shaped like the handles of a trophy. In pristine white T-shirt and faded jeans, he is moving towards his car surrounded by a sea of outreached hands clamouring for his autograph. Oscar and I have joined forces and try to catch his eye. I sense he has clocked us, and he duly indicates that we should follow him. For a minute he is caught by his car door, but all he does is remove something from the door pocket and scribble his auto-graph on an official photo-card. That finished, he beckons us to follow him through the crowd towards the interview room situated inside the players'-entrance doors.

With its shabby peach-coloured walls, high windows, bare table and chairs, and two vending machines, the immediate impression is of a prison interrogation room, but Hierro sits down, very much at ease. He has warm eyes and even via the interpretation process, he shows a friendly receptiveness and sense of humour that clashes with his battle-hardened, referee-challenging on-field image. Before we start, he has a concern which he explains with one forefinger held on his watch face. (We are in that linguistic zone where, even with an interpreter present, the protagonists speak with exaggerated body language.) He has been told that he is due to go to the Bernabéu to launch the new Real Madrid shirt and he will have to leave in fifteen, maybe twenty minutes. If we start now, he wonders, would we be able to return tomorrow, at the same time after training, to continue our interview? I am stunned – a professional footballer who is not rejoicing at an opportunity to curtail an interview . . . I am thrilled on Steve's behalf, that his captain, the player of such iconic stature, is so willing to give time to talk of his part in the Real Madrid team of 1999–2003. As Michael Robinson later tells me in his distinctive, stream-of-consciousness crescendo: 'If you had been writing almost anyone else's book, you wouldn't have been received like that. It is not known in England, of course – Spain? You must be living there in penitence? – but Steven has a reputation in Spain that transcends his generation. He will always be important to the Real Madrid family because he made it clear his only ambition was to play for the club. "He scored a goal in a European Cup final. He gave us glory and he was overridingly a gentleman." That's what they say. Steven McManaman now forms a part of the history and the legend of Real Madrid Club de Fútbol. That is within the reach of very few human beings, and that is what Fernando Hierro was honouring in his friend.'

And so we start. Hierro recalls his initial impressions of the player who entered the dressing room in the summer of 1999. 'Steve has a personality that everyone likes. When you first meet him, whether you speak the same language or not, the first impression you get is very good and positive. His personality is genuine; he is the same with everyone. As time went by I realised that possibly out of all the professional footballers I've come across, he has the best character, irrespective of whether or not he's in the team. He's happy when he's playing, even if he gets on for only thirty, ten or two minutes, but even when he's not playing, he remains the same. He doesn't take any worries about playing or not being picked into his daily life or the dressing room, and that is a shining example. And something you don't see very often . . .'

He continues talking, answering questions, recalling incidents and games the world over, while through the window the choruses greeting players still emerging from the dressing room explode periodically. An official comes in, glances at Hierro, indicates by tapping his watch that he had better go soon for the shirt ceremony. We are at the stage where Hierro is considering the images he holds in his mind of Steve representing Real Madrid on the pitch – not a great time for an interruption – and Hierro is hurried into opting for one.

'For me it has to be his performance in the Champions League final in Paris. Not only did he score a goal, but he also had a great game, a fantastic game. He ran the show. In that respect it was probably his finest moment in a Madrid shirt. I was on the bench and apart from scoring the goal I remember thinking as every minute went by what an extraordinary game he was having. That was his most influential time on the pitch.'

A pity it was three years ago, I half-mutter to myself, certainly not for Oscar to offer an official translation. He doesn't, but I look up and Hierro is nodding, agreeing, with a warm, knowing smile. He understands his friend's frustrations.

I want to ask Hierro about the notion of Madrid's must-play players, the unwritten policy which has latterly kept Steve on the bench. Even if Figo is in poor form, or Zidane is returning from injury, Del Bosque has not been in a position to ask either to sit it out. They are the stars, the men Spaniards call 'cracks', the players who are the currency in Real Madrid the worldwide brand. Fans pay money expecting to see them play. Their names are inked in on the team sheets; the manager is not expected to subject them to tactical rests or psychological gee-ups. Both Hierro and McManaman predate this era ushered in by President Pérez. Could the captain describe the differences in atmosphere under the different regimes?

'Differences?' he queries, clearly indicating there should be none. 'I think the future should simply be about the game of football.'

He pauses: 'There are people who want to focus the future on marketing and merchandising. With Lorenzo Sanz, the team were champions of Europe on two occasions in three years without quite so much of a show as we have now. With Florentino Pérez possibly we are much more financially stable. We have signed top-quality players of the highest profile. But only time will tell whether the team being put together since the arrival of Florentino Pérez will match all the achievements of Lorenzo Sanz.'

The official is back, and hovering. We double-check the arrangement about returning tomorrow. Hierro stands up, apologetic about breaking off. I say we understand, it is a big week, what with all the end-of-season business and the Beckham distraction.

'I'm not worried about the team being distracted by that,' he says firmly. 'We're about to play the most important ninety minutes of the season. We can't think about anything other than winning the game. We can't think about any other subject, whether it be David Beckham or anyone else. Nothing matters other than winning the game on Sunday. That's the one and only thing on our minds.'

As we prepare to walk towards the car park he is chatty about the excitement of the title decider – as far as anyone as competitive as he goes in for 'chat'. 'The difference is that Real Sociedad will have played thirty-nine games, one in the cup and thirty-eight in the league, while we have already played seventy. I think there's a huge distinction when you have one team, a good team with good players only playing one game per week. And then when you look at us, there have been busy periods when we've had Champions League fixtures and international call-ups week after week. That's my point of view as a player, but as a supporter I think it's great that the Spanish League is going all the way to the last weekend.

'This club and this team are all about winning, and so when we don't win, things are always difficult. We are used to winning and it's a bad day whenever we lose. Before a game I always think we are going to win, I never predict a defeat. One thing for sure: we know that if we win, practically everything will carry on as normal without any problem. But if we don't win, there will obviously be situations where things, possibly, might not run as smoothly as they should. But there you go.'

And with that he is off – to launch the new shirt at the Bernabéu, a shirt that with Beckham's name would sell a million times over by December, a shirt Hierro would never wear.

Saturday 21 June 2003

Oscar has a family wedding to attend outside Madrid and is unable to act as interpreter for the second noon appointment at the training ground. He and Nigel Hack have conjured another friend with perfect English – Juan Ramón Martín-Portugués, a *Madrileño* and Real Madrid supporter who is working in the marketing department of Porsche. We meet outside a hotel in the Plaza de San Martín – he is tall, wears his office white shirt-sleeves rolled up and bears a strong resemblance to the former *EastEnders* and *Holby City* actor Michael French. We walk across the square and down an alley to the Puerta del Sol, past advertising posters of a grinning Roberto Carlos, and hail a taxi. Again, it is a wilting 40°C.

Oscar had been impressed with Hierro. On the taxi ride back the previous afternoon he had marvelled at how different the Real Madrid captain was from his hard-man image. He was not the first to point out that Hierro means 'iron' in Castilian. 'The conversation with him was brief but enough to gain a good, genuine impression,' he said. 'Here was a person who has been repeatedly bad-mouthed. I had formed the idea that he was an inaccessible person, even unpleasant, and yet all these images were quickly dispelled as he exuded friendliness, patience and, above all, courtesy.

'Don't be too impressed with his courtesy in stretching the interview to the next day, though. He *is* the captain of Real Madrid.'

I repeat the gist of Oscar's observations to Juan as we go down the Gran Vía and skirt anti-clockwise past the Cibeles fountain, the traditional gathering point for Real Madrid victory celebrations. His excitement at the prospect of meeting Hierro is tangible. Knowledgeable about Real Madrid, the history and players as characters and soap opera, he is keen to know whether I have yet asked him about the 'Tenerife syndrome'. Emilio Butragueño, the former star striker El Buitre, 'The Vulture', now Valdano's assistant, will later tell me that Valdano, who was coach in those two last-day surrenders, was indeed 'very anxious, very concerned' about a repeat of that humiliating scenario. To lose in that way twice as coach, then a third time as sporting director . . . no, that would not be good.

We arrive early at the gates of the Ciudad Deportiva. On the pavement strewn with sunflower seed husks and cigarette butts there are even a few fans shuffling towards the ticket kiosk to watch the last half-hour or so of training. Once more the banter with the security guards, once more the prolonged walkie-talkie conversation before they allow us through; once more the same scenario with the guards at the gate to the players' car park. But we're well in time to watch the player-to-fan catwalk begin again.

Oscar had observed the players to be 'reluctant' rather than indifferent performers in their daily circus. He was uncomfortable with the way fans simultaneously show a lack of respect to those whose very celebrity they have come to respect. 'For example, as Casillas tried to sign autographs for an impatient horde he received what appeared to be a very serious, personal telephone call,' he said. 'Far from respect their hero's privacy and intimacy, and provide him with some distance, the hunters pressed ever closer, jockeying for a better position to pounce again as soon as he hung up. Witnessing all this from a very neutral perspective – as a fan of struggling Espanyol! – it certainly provided a moment to reflect on what Real Madrid is, or, more precisely, what it has become.'

Juan, on the other hand, looks mesmerised and bemused by turn. I warn him it will be a long wait, but time passes swiftly. Del Bosque, Juan informs me, lives in an apartment just over there. He points to a building a few hundred yards away. The manager has always been part of the club furniture since he finished as a player. When he was youth coach he would often say that he could look over and see which of his players turned up early for training.

Juan asks about Beckham and why the English deride his technical accomplishments. I explain it is perhaps more to do with people being fed up with his 'celebrity', the Beckham 'brand' overshadowing Beckham the footballer. By chance, today's *Telegraph* has published a thumping old-style reader's letter, which illustrates the point. I show him.

'Sir,' writes Eugene Harkin of Bolton, Lancashire. 'The effects of David Beckham are truly amazing. After weeks of constant media coverage of his transfer, I could bear it no longer. Instead of buying my morning paper on my daily rail journey into Manchester, I sought solace and comfort in Evelyn Waugh's *Put Out More Flags*. I was not alone. I noticed that everyone near me in my carriage was reading a book. The person next to me had actually reached page 268 of Dostoevsky's *Crime and Punishment*.'

Juan furrows his brow, and shakes his head, as if the English are even more incomprehensible than he thought.

We wait and wait until surely we have counted out most of the Real Madrid senior squad and many unrecognisable faces from the youth team. Suddenly a blue-shirted official walks towards us and asks if we are waiting for Fernando Hierro. He explains Hierro has had a family emergency and has had to leave by an alternative route. 'But Fernando is very concerned you have been waiting. He knows you are here but he had to go very suddenly. He asks me to pass on his apology and suggests you go to Gate 50 at the Bernabéu at noon tomorrow, and he will continue the interview then.'

Gate 50, tomorrow? The day of the title-deciding game?

'Yes,' nods the official. 'That is where he will see you.'

Juan and I walk back to the gates, past a stone-grey painted polystyrene statue of the goddess Cibeles riding her chariot. Chunks of painted polystyrene have been removed for souvenirs, giving the replica of the Cibeles statue an even tackier appearance. I am marvelling aloud again at Hierro's courtesy, this time to invite us into the inner sanctum on the day of such a crucial match. Juan, I note, dismisses it with the same line as Oscar: 'What else would you expect of the captain of Real Madrid?'

Sunday 22 June 2003

Gate 50. It has just gone twelve when Juan, in shades, the very embodiment of *mañana*, saunters down the pavement on the east side of the stadium. I have been window-shopping in the upmarket shopping mall that adjoins the Bernabéu for a good twenty minutes. We compare the after-effects of a typical long night out in Madrid, and report to the security guard. After consulting a clipboard, he motions us to stand inside the gate on the concrete ramp that runs for about fifteen metres from the gate towards the stadium.

A sports car whooshes through the gates and up the ramp past us. It is Guti, his blond gel-tufted hair recognisable through the window. Dressed in jeans and a short-sleeved shirt, he gets out, hands his keys to an official who will park the car further down ready for the player's departure after the game, and walks into the shadows towards the lift that will take him down. This is the first season that players have not had to spend the night in a hotel before a home game, but they go through the routine on autopilot. Guti goes downstairs into the dressing room, changes into pre-game kit that will have been left out – shorts or tracksuit – and hangs up the clothes he will put on again after the match. He joins the other early arrivals and waits until everyone has rolled up before being taken by bus to the team hotel a few blocks away. There they eat, catnap, eat, have a meeting and come back to the stadium. The final flourish is to throw the pre-game kit on the floor, where it will be collected, before donning match kit and heading towards the little television room to watch, invariably, football. 'There is *always* football going on somewhere,' as Steve says. A few prefer a massage or a little game of football to warm up.

Hierro, Guti, Steve and the others are still a good eight hours from that stage. Casillas has now arrived, and a stadium official beckons Juan and me towards the lift. He then motions us to stop and wait again – the usual game of Grandmother's Footsteps with security. As we stand around and glimpse the pitch being prepared for tonight, Luis Figo drives in behind the wheel of a silver Mercedes with two men I recognise as his father and a mate. Clearly it is odd to see anyone unattached to the club standing in this pre-match sanctum. Figo, relaxed and smiling, walks over, greets me with a kiss on both cheeks and asks how I am getting on with Steve's book. I explain we are here to talk to Hierro and introduce Juan to Figo. We all laughingly agree there is no need for introductions the other way around. We wish him luck and he is off, down the lift. 'White teeth!' comments Juan.

César arrives, a low-key presence in jeans and faded brown T-shirt. This time the security guard motions us to follow him into the lift and we go down a level squashed into the tiny space with the reserve goalkeeper. Emerging on to a corridor, César goes one way and Juan and I are led through a door, turning back on ourselves to go up some marble stairs to the reception area of the stadium offices. We wait again. Suddenly the doors swing open and Hierro appears in shorts and T-shirt, carrying a wash bag. He smiles as if this is any old day in any old season, as if he has all the time in the world, and sits on the blue sofa to talk for another half-hour about the teammate he has valued for four years . . .

Real Madrid v. Athletic Bilbao. 9pm kick-off

The thirty-eighth and last game of the season; the last game, it would turn out, for Steve McManaman in a Real Madrid shirt. And the first time in those four years that Robbie Fowler has been able to fly out and see his mate in action at the Bernabéu. While Victoria is at the airport collecting Robbie and his cousin Paul, Steve is leaving the team hotel, filing onto the bus for the dramatic end-of-season finale. Had Del Bosque sent them off with a great, inspiring oratorical address? You can only ask that wryly, knowing that for Real Madrid players, even half-time – the time for managers of Gettysburg tendencies to vent their stuff – is normally fifteen minutes of regular watch-checking after Del Bosque has said all he needs quietly and within seconds. ('He never had much to say. He never raised his voice, ever. At half-time we'd come in, listen to him for a minute, get a drink, sort out our boots, chat to the physios, go to the toilet and, even then, keep having to look at the clock to see if we could go back out yet.')

'God bless us, no. He didn't say anything,' says Steve. 'We had had a great victory the week before against Atlético, 4–0 in the local derby that we had to win. We could have effectively lost the league at their place but we went there and spanked them in good style. At home we're normally very, very strong. With eighty thousand people in the Bernabéu and the players we've got on the pitch, you couldn't have a bet on Real Madrid losing, could you? We were always mad odds-on favourites to win. For Del Bosque it was just another day in the life of a Real Madrid manager: you know, the furore, the big game, the big new signing, where is he going to fit him in the team. He'd had it all before. When we were all saying we had to focus on winning the game, we didn't do anything different. No way. We didn't talk about their players, we didn't watch videos. Christ, no . . .'

The atmosphere on the pavements around the Bernabéu is festive. The two-hour period before kick-off is ripe for that fast-action photographic treatment reserved for blooming flowers or hatching eggs. One minute the pavements of the expensive residential-cum-commercial neighbourhood are empty except for the odd businessman and smartly dressed staid couple. Then the momentum changes, and minute by minute people decked in white and purple scarves flock towards the tapas bars dotted along the avenue between the women's lingerie shop, the smart children's clothing boutiques, men's fashion store, florist and bijou toy shop. They stroll from the Metro station, family groups across every generation and the odd distinctive posse of international supporters, mostly Japanese. The normal home-game rites, the familiar setting, the uniting garb of matching scarves and flags seem to calm nerves. Tens of thousands of individual anxieties have merged into a collective safety blanket of pre-championship excitement on a sticky summer night. As Butragueño would later recall, 'People here [inside the club's administrative offices] were very nervous, very concerned about the game,' but they knew that they had given the fans something to celebrate in signing Beckham. For this is also the last game Real Madrid play before the England captain arrives. Beckham shirts in home and away colours hang from stalls outside. There is no number on the white home shirt, but traders have gambled on the No. 11 on the black away strip, the theory being Ronaldo will switch to the No. 9 worn now by reserve striker Fernando Morientes. No runaway sales there though. Tonight is a stirring occasion for the 2002–03 squad.

Inside, the stadium fills up with loud chatter, the smell of cigar smoke, people spitting out sunflower-seed husks, munching on popcorn and foil-wrapped chorizo and *jamón* sandwiches. The stadium is a patchwork of white shirts, ribbons of white scarves held aloft together. 'La Liga is in your hands' reads a giant yellow banner which unfurls across the width of the pitch from the south side of the stadium. There are more banners than usual: the biggest of games demands a big show. Perimeter advertisements for *Marca* reflect the week's drama: 'BECKHA*MARCA*', with *Marca* in the paper's trademark red letters.

The team are announced to a tumultuous chorus of cheers. Steve is named among the substitutes with César, Morientes, Flavio, Portillo, Solari and Pavón. Emotionally charged, the Bilbao team do not cower in their task, proudly determined to win and gain a UEFA Cup place. It was their late President Javier Uria's great desire to see his club in European competition. The captains of both teams, Hierro and Bittor Alkiza, lay individual wreaths – white flowers from Real Madrid, red from Athletic Bilbao – in tribute. Then it is time for quick team photos, a minute's silence, and the game begins under a balmy summer night sky.

Within nine minutes of the kick-off, three of Real Madrid's brightest *galácticos* combine and start the celebrations that electrify the Bernabéu stadium. Luis Figo threads a ball down the left to Roberto Carlos who crosses to Ronaldo for the simplest of tap-ins.

1–0. 'O-lé olé olé olé. O-lé. O-lé!' The stadium resounds. Next to me a spectator's glasses are knocked flying by a scarf twirled by a frenzied teenage boy.

Twenty-six minutes later, nerves tauten as Bilbao midfielder Alkiza scores from outside the area when Casillas is unsighted by the leaping form of Hierro whose head fails to meet the ball. 1–1.

Radios around the ground keep up with Real Sociedad's game in San Sebastian. Minute by minute the intensity grows. Bilbao play with composure, proudly fielding eleven Basques (including Aitor Karanka, who won three Champions League medals with Madrid) against a Real team with their celebrated foreign imports. Carlos Gurpegui tries to restrain Zidane; Makelele has to fight with all the grittiness in his armoury to win the battle in central midfield. But on the stroke of half-time, a foul on Ronaldo gives Roberto Carlos the chance to score a bullet free kick. 2–1. My Spanish neighbour, glasses found but frames now wonky, grins and nods his head.

The second half begins with wave upon wave of attacks. After fifty-five minutes the news, via hand-held radios, that Sociedad have scored fails to dampen the spirit. Victory is sealed six minutes later when Ronaldo charges on to a ball laid on by Zidane, and notches his twenty-third league goal of the season. 3–1. And just like Zidane the previous season, when the French genius scored that unstoppable volley in the European Cup final in Glasgow, Ronaldo, the newest *galáctico*, had stamped heroic authority on the most important game of the competitive year.

And Hierro? The captain plays a magnificent game. As the club website, with its comical automatic English translation, later captions a picture of him bringing the ball out of defence: 'Iron [Hierro] was impeccable during the party [game]. The great captain received a great ovation.' Del Bosque had taken Hierro off five minutes from time. Did he know what was afoot? Was it a conscious gesture to ensure Hierro had a memorable farewell that night?

The full-time whistle is the cue for unbelievable celebrations. Against a backdrop of meteoric fireworks – 'that illuminate the stars which are in the sky', as opposed to the ones on the pitch, as a magazine caption later waxes – great bursts of metallic confetti flutter slowly down onto the pitch, the floodlights transforming them into a million glittering flecks that make the Bernabéu pitch an image of the starriest night sky. Dancers wielding flags that would do justice to an Olympic opening ceremony leap from the tunnel, followed by a line of white-clad figures who lay out an enormous white silk circle bearing the triumphant title, CAMPEONES 29, champions for the twenty-ninth time. The players jog around the pitch, hands held above their heads applauding the supporters. Some wear their match shirts, others have already thrown on the commemorative *Campeones 29* T-shirt. An exultant Figo holds up a huge silver replica trophy. And the sound system blares out the anthem that already wallpapers the club's trophy room during visiting hours: the inevitable Queen, 'We are the Champions'.

After one lap of honour the players go down the tunnel. Photographers charge onto the pitch and gather at the place where the team disappeared. There seems to be some confusion, an expectancy around the tunnel exit. Outside the stadium a white open-topped bus slowly inches into position outside Gate 50, decked out in full *Campeones 29* regalia (where would they have hidden that, had they lost?). Supporters slowly start to leave, reluctant to relinquish hold of the scene, this stirring culmination of the week; soon they flow out like a white lava stream heading with frenzied intent down the Castellana to join the waiting throng around the Cibeles fountain. Traditionally the players climb up on the statue itself – the goddess of the city – and drape it with club scarves. The local authority cut off the water supply to allow them to perform a ritual that is Real Madrid's equivalent of reaching the summit of Everest and hoisting their flag to mark their achievement.

After hanging around for an hour, the players – including Robbie Fowler and his cousin Paul, a painter-decorator from Toxteth – emerge to board the open-topped bus that takes the victory route down to Cibeles. 'Robbie and his cousin were hanging around for ages because we took an eternity to get ready,' says Steve. 'So I told them they might as well come with us on the bus. I gave them two

T-shirts, which they put on, and the bus moved off. It was quite funny having Robbie alongside all the players celebrating the Spanish league championship, but it wasn't a problem. All the players made a fuss of him. I did tell them not to get off the bus at the fountain because that would have looked a bit strange. The hilarious thing was, when the bus stopped to let us off at the fountain, there were a load of English lads right by the railings, right on the side where Robbie was and they were all shouting "Rob-bie Fow-ler".'

Not all the fans are at the fountain. Those who want to scrutinise the players' faces watch on TVs in hundreds of bars dotted around the city. In the Sarao bar close to the north-east corner of the stadium, two teenage boys sing, 'Olé, olé, olé, olé, olé,' while one waves his flag like a matador to bait the other. The dark grey walls are crammed with photographs, including Steve captured as the ball leaves his boot en route for the back of the net in the 2000 European Cup final. In the corner above three empty metal beer kegs a small television, hanging precariously from a bracket, shows the scenes at Cibeles. Helguera first on to the platform . . . players singing on the bus and swinging scarves, their turn to play fan . . . a grinning trio of Hierro, Raúl and Morientes performing a conga, arms aloft, waving, singing . . . Ronaldo and Roberto Carlos laughing . . . horns tooting, a great sea of upturned faces as far back as the eye can see in every direction. It is a vision of untroubled joy, a tremendous mass release of emotion despite the feeling that the town-hall officials have sanitised the show by building a sort of Perspex protective box over the monument. Over the last few days it has been an object of derision – the platform, constructed around the fountain, complete with sponsors' logos, floodlights and the legally required protection for the stone statue. Unable to perform the spontaneous, age-old rite, they simply do an impromptu dance around the circular platform.

As a unit, the players look to be in genuine celebratory mode. The outside world has no idea that the very fountain that is the centre of a historic celebration has, in fact, become the focus of bitter resentment. Who would guess, observing the scene of noisy jubilation, that a raging argument between dressing room and boardroom was in midflow?

The story is that Hierro and Valdano had a bust-up after the players had retreated into the dressing room following their parade lap. Valdano relayed the message that the president wanted the captain to lead the players out for a second lap. However, by that stage, the tunnel exit was a massed scrum of photographers, cameramen and reporters. The players didn't want to go out again. Valdano insisted they return to the pitch; Hierro said no. One report has Valdano punching Hierro, another the other way around. A further story pits Pérez against the captain, with the line: 'You are a cancer in this club. I am going to cut you out.' It seems unlikely that either Pérez or Valdano would be crass enough to use that kind of language, or that Hierro would have punched either of the men in suits, but the two Fernandos, Hierro and Redondo, had four years previously been dubbed by one columnist as a 'cancer at the heart of the dressing room'. There was endless, overexcited speculation on the radio and in the papers. The basis was that Hierro and Raúl had led a dressing-room revolt. It is said they had such a strong argument with Valdano and Pérez that afterwards some players did not even want to go to celebrate the championship with the supporters at Cibeles. The conclusion was it was a very unpleasant episode.

'We were all celebrating noisily in the dressing room,' recalls Steve. 'I think people wanted us to come back out, and there was talk that maybe we ought to go out again, but the press had run on and it was chaotic. We said no, we've done one victory lap, we've been photographed in the special T-shirts carrying the trophy, we're not going out again now. We've done all that. The president did come into the dressing room and spoke to Hierro in the corner but there certainly wasn't a full-scale argument. There were various issues to discuss about the next day. We were supposed to go for a civic reception at the town hall in the Puerta del Sol, but a few players refused to go because it was the town-hall officials who had insisted on covering the Cibeles fountain with a Perspex platform around it so we couldn't climb up and hang scarves on it as had been the custom. They felt that it was all silly bureaucracy, and pretty stern measures to stop us putting on the traditional celebration for the supporters.'

Del Bosque did not see the fiery argument: 'I can't shed too much light on events as I was a little bit on the edge of all the celebrations. I didn't go into the dressing room after the game, I went straight to my own changing room. I think there was some kind of scene with the director of sport, but I don't know what happened exactly. Then there was apparently another bust-up in the Txistu restaurant at the official celebration dinner, and again I wasn't there because it had blown over by the time I arrived. The director of sport and the president were sorting it out, and I didn't have anything to do with it. It wasn't for me to get involved in a non-football issue. It was all about whether we were going to go to the town hall, and to the church – to present the title to La Almudena, the female patron saint of Madrid – or not. The players didn't want to go. Hierro and Raúl are the ones who know most about this. It was all non-football stuff, our work had finished out there on the pitch. The arguments were more about the image of the club.

'The mayor and the local authority hadn't wanted anyone to climb on to the statue of Cibeles as many people living and paying taxes in Madrid [Atlético fans!] didn't want to see their statue damaged by the Real Madrid team [a bit of an arm had been broken off the previous year]. And the players didn't want to go to Cibeles without going up on the statue . . .

'But we did go to Cibeles, eh! And with Robbie Fowler on the bus, ha, ha, ha. Fowler was just like any other member of the squad. We had spoken so much about him for years that it was like he was part of the squad!'

After the trek to the fountain the players once again boarded the bus, still bearing Robbie Fowler and his cousin, and returned to the stadium where they reclaimed their individual cars and went to the Txistu restaurant for the official celebration dinner. 'I went for a drink first with Ronaldo and a couple of the other lads, Robbie, his cousin and Victoria, and then we went on to the restaurant designated for our meal,' says Steve. 'The entire place had been taken over for the players, wives, staff, directors, manager – plus about thirty seats around four or five tables in another room where friends could go – like Robbie, who sat near a lot of Zizou's family. That's when the fun and games started . . . That's where we had all our meetings and arguments.'

The supper of champions, it is billed, but the atmosphere hanging over the pale-green table cloths, the exquisite flower arrangements and the staid restaurant furniture draped with white silky '29e Liga' flags and posters was – as Del Bosque later tells me – 'like a funeral'. Raúl broodily confides his resentment to his wife, Mamen, in a black silk dress. (He had screeched 'Ring the mayor!' at a policeman at the fountain.) Ronaldo, unusually a picture of introspection, reads the headlines of the first editions of the newspapers. Roberto Carlos is on his mobile. Flavio, Figo, Hierro, Salgado, all the players are casual in T-shirts; the majority of their wives are in backless or strappy silk dresses. There are bottles of red wine on the table and a vast array of food to pick at – *jamón ibérico*, chorizo, *lomo*, grilled prawns – before everyone is served fillet steak. Pérez stands to raise a toast; his wife sits next to him, one hand raised with a glass of champagne, the other hand glumly supporting her cheek, elbow on table. Every couple looks self-contained, there is no communal sense of partying.

'The atmosphere was horrendous. There was a lot of tension in the room, a lot of the players weren't happy. It was as if we had lost,' recalls Victoria. 'Steven and I were sitting with Raúl, Figo and Hierro and their wives, and everyone was very sombre. Del Bosque was extremely quiet. All the players kept withdrawing to a room to speak to Valdano. It was all politics. A few of the players were arguing with Valdano and Pérez in public. The president had a face like thunder at the dinner. The rest of us were all annoyed as the players kept leaving for long periods. We didn't understand what was going on and we were angry that they had won the league after a long hard season and we weren't celebrating. Also, by this stage, it was very late. We didn't sit down to eat until 2am and we wanted to move on to somewhere with a better atmosphere where we could celebrate.'

Steve concurs: 'It was very subdued. I was trying to enjoy myself, but it certainly wasn't a happy "we've just won the league" meal. We had had our food and were drinking when suddenly all the players were called into a room with Valdano to hear the plans about the following day. He said we had to go to the town hall, and the "voices in the dressing room" said no. We were there for a while. Then we all went back out to where our wives were and it certainly wasn't a party atmosphere. We were discussing issues at 3 or 4am, and we were called back in again. Three times we were called back in with Valdano and Butragueño. On one occasion we were in there for about an hour.' Iván Helgeura cites 'lots of reasons' for the *mal rollo*, the bad atmosphere, between club and players. 'We normally get fifty tickets for each game; that game they only gave us twenty. We didn't know if they were going to let us climb on Cibeles, which is an important symbolic celebration with the fans, and if the council did not allow that, we didn't want to go to a reception at the town hall the following day. The club, not Del Bosque, had wanted us to be *concentrados* [in a hotel the night before the game]. We had wanted to do a lap of honour around the stadium but the journalists jumped in immediately. We couldn't run, or walk; we couldn't move, we were hit by cameras. People wanted to get to Ronaldo and they'd battle with other players to get to him. It was the same old thing, the *galácticos* thing but multiplied and made physical. They, the club, demanded we do a lap of honour and we refused as long as the scrum stayed out there. It was important for the players to speak as a collective, to show we are football players, not there just to promote the club commercially.'

Eventually the majority of players left to celebrate. 'Victoria had been waiting for an hour by herself, so we went to a discotheque with Robbie, his cousin and met up with more friends and players and tried to party,' recalls Steve. 'The likes of Raúl and Hierro stayed on discussing the situation further. When I left the Txistu restaurant the civic reception was all off. At about seven in the morning – and this is my memory after a night of partying – I think Raúl came into the nightclub and said it's all back on again.'

Monday 23 June 2003

So President Pérez and Jorge Valdano won the argument. By 11am players, dressed in blue-grey team suits, start arriving at the Ciudad Deportiva to go on the victory parade and take the trophy to the city council and to the Catedral de Santa María de la Almudena. Raúl is first to arrive. Roberto Carlos struggles in at 12.40, followed by a jaded Helguera who had just left Ronaldo and McManaman. The party had continued at Ronaldo's house with Robbie Fowler, his cousin, Victoria and her friends. 'I was with them and left an hour before,' smiles Helguera. 'I was ringing Macca and Ronie, saying, "Don't forget you've got to be there . . ." and they were both going [affects dopy voice] "Yeah, yeah, I'm there, man." I kept ringing when we had to be there, but they never answered and they never quite made it there. The significance of their absence was exaggerated as the club has an obligation because the council helps Madrid *muchísimo*, but it didn't matter. They had simply overslept. The club fined them both and that was that.'

As Steve recalls, 'Ronie's house is always crazy. You'll walk in and there'll be people he's sort of collected – everybody from judges and doctors to street musicians. He's not bothered. Usually I'll let myself in, grab a beer and wait. Once I went round, there was a guy with a shotgun aiming pellets into the hedge while a line of women sunbathed. It's mad! But the party continued there, with Ronie acting DJ behind his decks in his massive party room.'

'It was quite surreal,' adds Victoria. 'There were two huge terrapins, or tortoises, in the pool. My friend, who is a great animal-lover, noticed one was in distress. It was on its back, gasping for air. There was another walking solemnly by the pool too. I asked Ronaldo about them and he said he'd bought them last week, and they were free to go where they wanted, but they kept falling into the pool. That was it – my friend dived in to the rescue and the next thing I know we're attempting to resuscitate a tortoise in the small hours of the morning!'

Two buses leave the training ground. The first carries the players, the coaching staff, doctors and physiotherapists; the second conveys Florentino Pérez, the board of directors, Valdano, Alfredo di Stéfano and Butragueño among others. First stop, the town hall, where a smiling Raúl, Hierro, Pavón, Morientes and Roberto Carlos lead the players out on to the balcony. Below thousands of fans gather in the precise geographical centre of Spain, chanting 'Champions, champions'. Figo wishes Zidane a public happy thirty-first birthday while Raúl enters into a spirited chat with Alberto Ruíz-Gallardón, mayor of the city, about the now-infamous Cibeles fountain. There are speeches, presentations and the fans chant 'Del Bosque, Del Bosque.' He is about to leave and they know it. Next stop is the municipal seat of the government. Raúl starts proceedings again by shouting 'Champions, champions' through a microphone. Roberto Carlos makes matador gestures to suggest it is a two-way achievement with the supporters. The crowd call out to Guti to win it again. Salgado dedicates the championship to the public. As they leave, Figo, Flavio and Roberto Carlos take over the microphones and sing 'We are the Champions'.

On to the cathedral. Five hundred people receive the players. After a brief homily Hierro and Raúl offer flowers and the League trophy to the patron saint. Members of the squad go up to the altar to pay tribute to the Virgin of the Almudena. Prayers are said on behalf of the team by the resident dean with a rosary blessed by Pope John Paul II on his recent visit to the city. Outside, Solari, Casillas, Figo and Salgado sign autographs. The retinue returns to the training ground where the players are officially wished a happy holiday.

'Later on that day it came out – I was actually flying to Mallorca on my holidays – and it came out that Del Bosque had been sacked and

Hierro hadn't had his contract renewed,' recalls Steve. 'It was a huge shock, a massive shock to everyone. No one could believe it.'

Victoria said: 'We were all disgusted. All the fans and everyone at the club thought it was disgraceful behaviour and should have been handled much better. If it was going to happen, the president should have toasted them the night before and thanked them for their hard work and service. He wouldn't even have had to say they were being sacked the next day – but he should have acknowledged all they had done for the club and how long they had been there. Everyone was so shocked. The manager and the captain, it was as if the club had turned upside down. When we arrived in Mallorca, people telephoned to say the fans had turned against the president. There was offensive graffiti at the stadium, the training ground and I think even at his house. The thing is, no one was given the chance to thank them or say goodbye, and when Del Bosque went so did all his coaching staff. It really left a bad taste in the mouth. When I think back to how depressed Del Bosque seemed at the dinner, it was as if he knew what was coming. He is a lovely man and didn't deserve to be treated so shoddily.'

'Unbelievable! Del B sacked. Hierro out,' texts Oscar.

'It is amazing,' says Juan, numb disbelief detectable via a satellite link. 'After winning la Liga, the captain and the manager are sacked. *Madrileños* are talking of nothing else. I believe it's true that Hierro and Raúl, as captains of the team, led a dressing-room revolt. The only difference between them is that Raúl is untouchable at Real Madrid. It is as simple as that. A lot of things are being said about last night but nobody really knows what happened. Can you ask Steve?' he pleads.

What was it Hierro had said on Friday? 'One thing for sure, we know that if we win against Bilbao, practically everything will carry on as normal, without any problem.' He had been calling on an instinctive feel for the nature of a club he had served for fourteen years. His prediction was wrong. He had found himself, suddenly, out of tune with the way his club worked. It was proof, indeed, that Real Madrid was gradually changing, evolving, so that Sunday 22 June 2003 represented the end of an era – a significant period in the club's history, which Steve as both insider and outsider had witnessed from day one. The week had begun with a simple arrangement to talk to a captain about a teammate. How touching, now, to consider that on his last day in a Real Madrid shirt, on a controversial end note of a triumphant career, Hierro had given so freely of his time to put on record Steve's value to the club's family. Mere hours after he had discussed Steve's tactical versatility and laughingly recalled how regularly the dressing room was regaled with news of the Macca & Growler string of racehorses, Hierro was to lead a dressing-room revolt, which, rumours insist, culminated in his sacking.

As Steve mused: 'It was a massive shock. The whole winning-the-league celebration was a bit odd, but what hurt most were the departures. They had done it right at the end of the season, so we all had four weeks to get our heads around it. We came back and no one mentioned it that much. You know what it's like, the start of a new season, all the build-up, the new signings . . .'

Season One

1999–2000

The Bosman ruling was a threat to Spanish football, but not for Real Madrid. Steve's arrival coincided with the beginning of the philosophy of combining a successful youth policy with signing star players. That's to say, almost 50 per cent of the Real Madrid first-team squad was made up of players who had come through the youth scheme. Steve was very much one of the 'big name' players who the club continue to sign to this day. In fact he was the embodiment of this. He was extremely highly rated in Spain at that time – after Euro 96, of course, but first and foremost because of what we knew of him from Liverpool, a club greatly admired, not only for their successful history but also for their exciting style of play.

—Vicente Del Bosque, Real Madrid manager, 1999–2003

'You know what it's like, the start of a new season, all the build-up, the new signings . . .'

Four years earlier Real Madrid's high-profile signing was McManaman himself. 'Macca strikes gold in Spain'. 'Macca hits the jackpot!' 'I'M A REAL MAN'. 'MY £15m REAL DEAL!' 'MACCA'S SMACKERS!' It is 30 January 1999, the day after his advisers and the Spanish club shook on a five-year contract, and the Liverpool and England midfielder woke up to find that his first transfer had earned him bigger headlines than almost any game in his career. As the first household-name British player to be allowed a free transfer under the Bosman ruling, his milestone moment had the tabloids competing for witty emphasis in ever increasing point size, as if to mirror his impending accrual of wealth. 'There was this assumption that someone arrived in my house with a wheelbarrow and said, "Here's all this money," and that was it,' he recalls wryly.

Steve flew to Spain twenty-four hours later to sign a pre-contract that committed him to joining the then European Cup-holders the day after his contract with Liverpool expired on 30 June. Shadowed by Spanish reporters, jostled by backward-scuttling cameramen during every step and handshake of this formality, he was bemused by the reception. 'I came through the terminal doors and was hit by a wall of cameras. I remember grabbing someone's coat and them leading me through the sea of bodies to a car . . . they were literally cracking each other round their heads with cameras and falling all over the place. It was absolute chaos,' he recalls, shaking his head at the memory. However, the minute-by-minute details of this brief trip and photo-opportunity were not relayed home in the way they were broadcast in Spain, where it was almost reality television. 'White and radiant' ran the headline on the front page of *AS*, the Spanish daily sports paper, with pictures of a bewildered McManaman in an unmarked black tracksuit. 'Macca Yes' screeched rival tabloid *Marca* in English. Both confirmed how Madrid had tracked the English winger for more than a year, ever since a mooted deal with Barcelona in September 1997 had fallen through embarrassingly as Steve waited in a hotel in the Catalan capital (Barça had secured a last-minute £18m deal with Rivaldo, their interest in Macca having spurred Deportivo La Coruña to drop their price for the Brazilian).

The following day *AS* began the first of a series of double-page features celebrating their new signing's Liverpool world. The first set out *su estadio*, his stadium – Anfield, with a picture of the wrought-iron stadium gates and the motto, You'll Never Walk Alone; *su coche*, his car, a Mercedes 500 coupé, with details of price in euros (90,152); *su casa*, his house, illustrated by a postcard image of Albert Dock 'by night' where Steve had a flat; and *un pub*, the Albert, close to Anfield, and an establishment in which he had never set foot. Above a mini-biographical section on other English players who had played for Real Madrid – Arthur Johnson (1902), John Fox Watson (1948) and Laurie Cunningham (1979) – they even reproduced in full, complete with the newspaper's logo, his most recent monthly *Daily Telegraph* column. Heaven knows what the Spanish readers would have made of his musings on Tottenham and Wimbledon. The following day *AS* homed in closer to Brimstage Road, a street of terraced houses in Walton. No. 21 had been the McManaman family home from 1985 until December 1997. They captured local children posing on the pavement in Real Madrid and Liverpool shirts, talking about Steven, '*el héroe de Brimstage Road*'; Laura Jones, a former neighbour, was snapped in her school uniform and commemorated as the girl Steven occasionally babysat for. In clasping McManaman to the bosom of the Real Madrid family, the semi-official Madrid press warmly embraced his entire background, early Evertonian idols, St John's Primary School, his younger brother's best friend and all.

Back home, a preoccupation with the financial aspect of his transfer – £15m over five years, which translated into a weekly wage of approximately £60,000, making him the richest export in British football history – dismayed Steve. This was the lad who despised the stereotype flash lifestyle associated with Premiership players: at the start of a night out, he used to supply his best mate Gordon, a supervisor in a Docklands factory, with a wad of cash so he wasn't seen buying all the drinks. When Stan Collymore, plus Channel 4 film crew, once turned up in a white stretch limo on Albert Dock, to spring an unwelcome surprise on his teammates enjoying an evening out in the Pumphouse, McManaman was the first to the exit. Of the so-called Spice Boys, he was the one who never accepted the offers to model for Armani or Top Man. 'He always said to me, "I'm not going to sell my soul,"' says Victoria. 'He's always avoided commercial self-promotion.' Yet the implication was, his sole criterion for moving clubs was money. In an earlier *Telegraph* column he had written of being demoralised by 'a concerted campaign' against him once it had become clear he was prepared to let his contract run down, and leave Liverpool as a free agent. 'I'm not one to whinge about criticism, but it annoys me that some outrageous claims have been made, and not once has the person doing it had the decency to check whether there is the remotest bit of truth in it,' he wrote. 'Every week the figures bandied about have gone up. I'm demanding £110,000 a week? God bless us, are you having a laugh? I know Liverpool supporters are not gullible; they know that sort of stuff is nonsense. Anyone who knows me at all will vouch that money is not the issue. I have been criticised for underachieving in my career, and it is a criticism I want to counter. When some of the biggest clubs in Europe come calling, you have to be flattered. I have ambition to test myself on the highest stage. I want to make myself a better player. I feel now is the right time to take up the opportunity offered.'

The obsession with the 'big-money' element also shrouded the inherent challenge of playing abroad. Steve's decision to move entailed exactly that; a move, or, more accurately, an uprooting, from the place of his birth to a city almost a thousand miles south of the familiar Merseyside skyline, to one of the most energetic capital cities in Europe which, in true holiday-brochure parlance, offered a different culture, climate, language, lifestyle and attitude. At that time Ian Rush's comment on his return from Italy – 'It was like a foreign country' – summed up English players' aptitude for absorbing new cultures. There was not a single British player in Spain's top division. The last English player to sign for Real Madrid was Laurie Cunningham, twenty years earlier. Even Anfield hero Alan Hansen admitted he simply could never have put himself through the language barrier to pursue his career abroad. For a one-city, one-club player like McManaman, the local lad from a Kirkdale council house, signing for the aristocrats of European football was in every sense as big and bold a move as the tabloid headlines.

'The whole business had an aura because, without being egotistical, I was probably the first big name to utilise the Bosman ruling to go from one very big club to another,' he says. 'Everyone had an opinion, mostly money-orientated, which saddened me, because that was ultimately not the choice I was making. The offer from Liverpool was incredibly generous, a hell of a lot of money. When the choice is between a hell of a lot of money and a hell of a lot of money, the difference between the two sums, in reality, is not enough to sway you one way or another. I wanted to play abroad, full stop. The prospect of that challenge was always in the back of my mind. When I joined Liverpool as an apprentice I was training with the Barneses, the Beardsleys, the Hansens, Steve McMahon, Steve Nichol, Ronnie Whelan, stars who had won everything. I was a small kid of sixteen, but I remember hoping I could emulate them and carry on that winning tradition. Collecting trophies was a habit for Liverpool Football Club then. The fans were programmed for glory. I got into the team with these stars, but then suddenly it seemed five, six, seven, eight of them finished or retired. For Graeme Souness, as manager, the timing was awful. From 1991 onwards, it was such a transitional period. The older players were too old and the younger players were too inexperienced. There was nothing in the middle. Whoever had come in as manager when Kenny Dalglish left would have had problems. Souey probably got rid of the experienced players too quickly. He got a lot of stick for a variety of reasons, but in Premiership football terms he was ahead of his time. After his experience in Italy, he introduced a healthier, Continental diet. He developed Melwood as a training ground. We brought players in, had a few good youngsters come through, and eventually regrouped under Roy Evans.

'At the time you think you're just as strong. We probably weren't, at least not strong enough to clear that final hurdle and pick up the trophies. I have always maintained, though, and I always will, that we had a very good, very skilful team. From Dalglish to Souness to Roy Evans, the philosophy of attacking play never changed. We were exciting to watch, we played some excellent stuff. Roy Evans's record speaks for itself – we finished 1995 in fourth, '96 in third, '97 in fourth, '98 in third. Every year we would have been in the Champions League as it works today. People talk now of this magical fourth spot to qualify. Christ! Back then you were vilified if you weren't in the top two. Nigh on every year Roy Evans took us to third or fourth . . . so he would have been this great successful manager instead of being labelled, along with many individuals in his team, as "underachieving". Evo's departure from the club was another factor in my decision to go. As much as I'd been in two minds about leaving, the fact he did go swayed me. It added to a certain end-of-era feeling. I got on very well with him. I thought he was an excellent manager who had received a lot of unwarranted criticism.

'Winning trophies is what we're in this business for. From the day I signed professional forms, wages escalated out of all proportion, but top teams have always paid very well. Of course, as in any line of business, you become conscious of how much you earn compared to your peers. I signed schoolboy forms at fourteen, joined the YTS scheme at sixteen, turned professional at eighteen, and took up a four-year contract at the age of twenty-three. I've always seen it as climbing rungs on a ladder. Each time, you'd get a bit more money and another year on your contract. When you've been at one club all your career, of course you notice people come in and they're earning three or four times more than you. It's like any business, it's far more lucrative to be headhunted than promoted internally. But that said, the deep-seated motivation has always been to be successful, to win every game, every trophy on offer. It had always been my dream to win the league championship with Liverpool, but it hadn't happened. I was approaching twenty-seven, and I found myself wondering more and more what I could achieve if I left. Eighteen months prior to that I'd had interest from Barcelona. I was playing very well, so I was attracting the right kind of teams who would offer me the chance to play in the Champions League. That was important. I had never played on that stage. My first Champions League experience came with Real Madrid. The move enabled me to take a massive step up. Maybe if Liverpool had finished second and qualified for the Champions League I might have thought I could get everything I wanted at Liverpool, but at the time we kept missing out. I would see the Champions League on the television, the whole mystique of it, and pine for it.

'Psychologically, I was more interested in Spain than Italy. When you're dealing with clubs of a similar stature in different countries, it boils down to which league appeals to you. That's all it was. I wish I could be a football romantic and say I remember Real Madrid playing Liverpool in the European Cup final on a fuzzy black and white television and it made a huge impression on me . . . but I can't. I just fancied the football in Spain more than in Italy.'

Shortly after signing the pre-contract, Steve would meet up with Michael Robinson, the cult Spanish television pundit, and former Preston, Manchester City and Brighton forward who, in 1983, had been signed by Joe Fagan as a third striker behind Kenny Dalglish and Ian Rush. That season, Liverpool won their first treble – the First Division Championship, Milk Cup and European Cup. After two further years at Queens Park Rangers, Robinson moved to Spain and won the hearts of Osasuna's fans, and the Spanish football world at large, by voluntarily terminating his career-twilight contract. He declared it was unfair to take a salary from the small Pamplona-based club while he was injured and unable to do what he was paid for. Robín, as he is known in Spain, is now arguably the most famous face on Spanish television, having pioneered a new approach to the traditionally staid Spanish sports broadcasting. He deals in emotion, the pulse of human endeavour, all relayed to his audience with what he describes as his 'interesting descriptive Spanish. I have a strange terminology with a foreign accent'. Legendarily good company, especially over his trademark goldfish-bowl-sized gin and tonics, he is a fitting frontman for the soap opera that is Spanish football. Flying in that February to Liverpool, accompanied by a Canal Plus camera crew eager to interview Real Madrid's new Scouse signing, Robinson felt a bond as they walked around Anfield together and wandered through the museum. He detected that extra per cent of ambition that was propelling McManaman to Spain.

'When we first met I remember Steven giving *me* too much reverence because Liverpool won a European Cup in 1984 – *even though* I was among their squad! I could not have laced Steven's football boots he has so much talent, but he'd say, "Don't, I've still not won anything!"' Robinson relates with dramatic self-deprecation. (Steve, in riposte, says: 'He's barmy, Michael. He puts himself down. How can he feel he wasn't worthy to play for Liverpool – he won all those medals and scored as many goals as Kenny Dalglish that season?')

'Steven's innate competitiveness, his ambition, gets overlooked because he is so wonderfully easygoing,' says Robinson with almost paternal insistence. 'Easygoing, in a sporting environment, sometimes gets translated into "I don't give a monkey's. I'm a great friend to have around, but I'm not going to dig us out of a trench". That is a great misinterpretation of Steven's character. His body language always projects a happy-go-lucky, relaxed character – even when he's talked to me about how he felt a failure at Liverpool because as soon as he was a first-team regular the club didn't win European Cups any more; even on the eve of his first European Cup final with Real Madrid, I could see that behind the joking manner he was nervous, excited, scared out of his brain. He left Liverpool because he needed to satiate his desire to be successful. Steven landed at Liverpool Football Club as an Everton fan, and rose to prominence at a club who had seemed from generation to generation, almost by accident, to win league championships or the European

Cup. When that cycle of success came to an end, it hurt him. He felt himself to be a very good player with a thirst that would be quenched only by winning the big trophies. Therefore Steven took a very deep breath, squeezed his nose and jumped off the highest springboard into a tremendous adventure. I remember speaking to Steven on many occasions about this "exam he never quite passed". He had played for his nation many, many times. He had played for a wonderful football club, Liverpool, but only won minor cups. That "exam he couldn't pass" meant he had to challenge himself by going somewhere else to practise his profession, somewhere he could share his dreams. That "somewhere" contained an awful lot of inconvenience: an alien language, lifestyle, the responsibility of bringing a companion, eating and sleeping at funny times, making new friends. He went for it and he found what he was looking for, because he was able to interpret the challenge.'

Somewhat less loquaciously, Souness, manager at Anfield from 1991 to 1994 (and the lynchpin around which much of Liverpool's success in the eighties had evolved), agrees: 'Macca was always a wee bit different from the rest of the young lads. He was very much one of the boys, and accepted by everyone, but he kept his thoughts to himself. He joined in the banter and took part in everything, but there was something about him that made him a bit different. He's laid-back, but he always had the determination to do well. I think the fact that he was prepared to let his contract run down and take the criticism that went with it showed a certain determination, a single-mindedness, a certain "This is what I've decided and I'm going to see it through".'

Steve had started preliminary contract negotiations with Liverpool on numerous occasions. 'I had had frank discussions with Gérard Houllier, and told him I wanted to go. I told him well in advance, and I kept him informed so he could search for his own player to replace me. Our relationship was good. We were very straight with each other. As he said, it would be unfair of him, a Frenchman working in England, to criticise a player who wanted to test himself in another

European league. He helped me out during that period. You have to sign a pre-contract in January, which leaves you in a tricky limbo situation, but Gérard was very positive about my decision whenever he spoke to the press. He could have come out and said, "It's a disgrace," or dropped me completely from the team, but he was sensitive to my circumstances. You could get injured and then be out for a year or two, which could feasibly happen. It happened to Rob Jones, a very good friend of mine. We both left Liverpool at the same time, both on free contracts. I signed for Real Madrid. He suffered a bad knee injury and has since retired. But Gérard was very supportive. It coincided with Evo leaving, so Gérard was in a difficult situation too; he didn't need unnecessary ill feeling. I had a lot of niggling injuries in my final season, which was frustrating, and fuelled the people who were saying, "Oh, he's not playing, he doesn't care, he's this, he's that," but Gérard always quashed any of the bitterness, anyone trying to make a meal out of a situation.

'There was one awkward episode. The news that I had agreed a contract with Madrid came out in Spain on a Friday and on the Saturday Liverpool were away to Coventry. I had a knock at the time and was on the bench, but the news had broken. In Spain nothing is kept a secret. Real Madrid had gone out of the Champions League, they were sixth in the league, they needed some good PR and they announced my signing straightaway. [In the Saturday edition of *AS*, Alfredo Relano wrote: *En medio de la tormenta, el Madrid puede ofrecer una buena noticia: el fichaje de McManaman* – In the midst of the turmoil, Madrid can offer good news: the signing of McManaman.] It was awkward in that it was confirmation to the fans that I was leaving this club they all adored, and yet I was still playing for them for another four months. I was an important member of that team, but I'd had a terrible year with injuries, an Achilles problem, a horrible ankle injury. When I wasn't playing the team invariably suffered. Roy Evans had gone, we missed him a hell of a lot. We weren't doing well and we would end the season a dismal seventh in the league. I came on against Coventry and scored, and I could sense the fans didn't know whether to cheer or jeer. It was weird: I could literally hear them humming and hawing. But I had kept Gérard very much informed. I had told him my advisers were in Spain speaking to the club so he certainly didn't view it as a bombshell that put him in an embarrassing situation. That evening, when I got off the coach, I went and had a chat with him. He congratulated me, as did a lot of the players. The chairman David Moores did too, which was lovely, and a couple of the directors who always travel with the team. They wished me all the best. It could have been very different, because I wasn't leaving for three or four months, and when I did it was for no money. The situation was always going to be difficult – few clubs had experienced the ramifications of the Bosman ruling – but I wanted to leave on the best note possible, and I did, I really did. Liverpool were very, very good about it, and I'll always remember that. I respect them so much. The chairman is a wonderful man.'

A philosophical Houllier emphasised the door would be left open for Steve to return. 'I respect his decision and he will leave here with my good will,' he said at the time. 'I understand why he is leaving and I will do my best to make sure that all the Liverpool supporters understand as well.'

It was not easy, especially after Simon Fuller, the image-maker behind the Spice Girls, had become McManaman's chief adviser. At the time when Mel C, a.k.a. Sporty Spice, was making the most of being a Liverpool fan (wearing a McManaman shirt) and of being a friend of Jason McAteer, the press were quick to dub him and his bright young Liverpool peers Robbie Fowler, David James, Jamie Redknapp and McAteer 'the Spice Boys'. The subsequent involvement of Fuller, negotiating a football deal for the first time, was deemed slightly risible. 'Anyone looking to criticise made a big hoohah out of Simon Fuller's involvement because he is associated with music and showbusiness, but in the end solicitors did everything because Simon was not a FIFA-designated agent,' says Steve. 'When you're dealing with Spanish law and English law everything is done by solicitors anyway. Regardless of whether I used my father or the woman behind the bar, I was always going to warrant a lot of money because the best club in the world were after a player in his prime at one of the biggest clubs in England. They were not going to offer me less than I would have got at Liverpool. It wasn't rocket science to realise I was going to get a hell of a lot of money. Because of the interest in the implications of the Bosman ruling, everyone was bandying figures about, but occasionally it did feel personal. I remember driving into training, switching on the radio and a local DJ was conducting a poll . . . "Macca's been offered £40,000 a week, do you think this is right?" I listened to people ringing up, the crazy outraged ones, and the earnest ones saying, "He's getting that and nurses only get this much a week – it's outrageous." That comparison is awful, of course it is. But someone rang in and complained, because the debate was taken off air within minutes. The emphasis was all on the money. From then on, if Liverpool had a bad result – and it did turn out to be a poor season – it was my fault and the press would bandy around the figures, you know, the lad who is going to earn blah, blah, blah played badly or whatever . . .

'But, saying that, to my face I didn't have any bad words off anyone. I am a Liverpool lad, and I would be out in town, walking around and seeing people, and everyone would say, "Well done! We're so proud, a local lad done well." "The whites of Real Madrid, di Stéfano, fantastic for you." I experienced so much local pride. A Kirkdale lad, who started off in the Sunday league team, was off to play for a glamour club like Real Madrid. I look back now and can honestly say I left Liverpool exactly the way I wanted to leave it. It could have been so different, but I tried to conduct myself appropriately, give the club their due respect. They conducted themselves great as well. I left on a very good note and they always make me feel welcome going back.'

Sunday 11 July 1999

Striding along the wide corridors of Terminal 1, Heathrow, in the one-way flow of passengers bound for Gate 48, a few of the less self-absorbed airport transients might have noticed a certain tall, whippet-thin athletic figure with trademark unruly hair. Like anyone accustomed to life in the public eye, Steve tends to scurry through airports. But July is a rare football-free month in the domestic calendar, and few antennae were alert to an England player, dressed in summer clothes, travelling casually with his girlfriend. As he prepared to board an early morning flight to Madrid, he instinctively absorbed the odd unspoken hello or flicker of startled recognition from a stranger, and that was it. In virtual anonymity – as he had planned it – Steve McManaman sloped off on the most exciting adventure of his career.

Of the typical departure-lounge scenarios on which airport television programmes run and run, Steve represented one of the rarest in late twentieth-century travel. He was a successful young man about to leave the country and ply his trade abroad. He was not walking out one midsummer morning with a song in his heart like Laurie Lee; nor was he a cocooned celebrity with an entourage primed to ease every detail of his transition. After twenty-seven years of living and working in the city where he was born, he was hurling himself into the unknown. He had always wanted, needed, a challenge, but the decision to accept an offer from one of the Italian and Spanish clubs – Barcelona, Juventus, both Milan clubs and Lazio – who had chased him doggedly was not easy, professionally or personally.

Ever since the bigger lads in his Kirkdale neighbourhood came knocking to get the gifted five-year-old to come out and play in the street, Steve had practised his exceptional ball skills and jinking runs on Merseyside turf or tarmac. Then it was school teams, representative City of Liverpool teams, the Sunday league, schoolboy forms and a YTS place followed by a professional contract at Anfield, and all the time a passionate Evertonian: his footballing stock was Scouse through and through. 'You can't take Liverpool cheek out of the boy, and there is some doubt whether you can take him out of Liverpool at all,' was the conclusion of one interviewer three months before Real Madrid succeeded in doing exactly that.

Steve spoke of his 'tough' and 'sad' decision to leave the club, the city and its magnificent fans. Resolutely private, he did not divulge another deeply personal grief. In the same period that his contract with Liverpool was coming up for renewal, and speculation about his future became rabid, his mother Irene was seriously ill with breast cancer. The decision to move abroad proved emotionally agonising, but he had the support of his family. 'We talked a lot, my whole family. I needed some good advice and maybe some kind of "permission" as well. I got that. My family have always given me fantastic support and I wouldn't have gone if they felt it was the wrong decision.' Steve remains exceptionally close to his immediate family – his father David, who he calls one of his best mates, his older sister Karen, her husband Peter and two sons Luke and Jacob, and 'our kid' – his brother David, nine years his junior. He was especially devoted to his mother, who passed away on 19 May, less than eight weeks before he joined his new club. Even when he owned a flat in Liverpool's cool Albert Dock development, he preferred staying at his parents' home in Brimstage Road, and later in the new house he bought them in Crosby, enjoying his mum's warm company, his dad's milky coffee and the talk about family, football and the horses. 'She was always very, very close to him, and he to her,' reminisces his father. 'I think a bit of it was because she didn't know about football, and he loved that. The first time I took her to see him play, she turned to me after twenty minutes and said, "Which way are they kicking?" Steven loved that. So that was another thing he had to deal with too, starting a new life, when he had just lost his mother, all in a couple of months.'

Coming to terms with his mother's deterioration in health was distressing, although the perspective on life it gave him may have helped numb the sting of criticism that came from spurned supporters. Where Steve's pre-Liverpool FC life, 1972–1990, almost exactly coincided with the club's glory days, his emergence as a compelling, homegrown entertainer happened at a time when those well-gorged fans, replete with European honours and domestic glory, were struggling in the novel, alien, post-Dalglish environment of football frailty. Under the down-to-earth old-school approach of Roy

Evans, an older generation of fans who had grown up on the Kop, dodging the muggers behind the Anfield Boys Pen or relieving themselves down a rolled-up *Liverpool Echo*, saw in the passing and running of the young McManaman, Fowler, Redknapp, McAteer, Jones, Stevie Harkness, Dominic Matteo, Jamie Carragher and Michael Owen glimpses of the Liverpool Way. In McManaman, the waif-like twenty-year-old who sprang to attention when he started in place of John Barnes and opened up Sunderland with menacing runs in the victorious 1992 FA Cup final, they saw a player whose touches can turn a game. In the Coca-Cola Cup final three years later, he provided a cameo to treasure with two virtuoso goals and a Man of the Match performance against Bolton. There was the sixty-yard run at Parkhead, a trademark burst that resulted in a trail of dizzy defenders and an exquisite low-shot goal during the UEFA Cup clash against Celtic on 16 September 1997. Weeks later at Highbury, he unleashed a stunning volley from a Stig Bjornebye throw to defeat Arsenal 1–0. Supporters still dwell on his debut against Sheffield United in 1990, the Hat-trick that Wasn't in October 1994 against Sheffield Wednesday, his first senior goal in a 2–1 loss to Manchester City at Maine Road, his Merseyside derby bust-up with Bruce Grobelaar and so on. Steve would leave Anfield to a standing ovation after his final appearance in a red shirt against Wimbledon, but he would leave without the club claiming the benefit of a substantial transfer fee for one of their brightest youth products. Some fans were indignant, of course; but the majority, over a pint, would cheerily admit that given the chance to ply their particular trade in sunny Spain for five years, they too would be off like a shot. For Liverpool is a city of football purism as well as partisanship, as typified by Steve's brother-in-law Peter, whose football allegiances are strictly Everton and Barcelona . . . but who was thrilled for his wife's brother, a Liverpool player, to be sought out by Real Madrid.

'Most of us at least understood his decision,' says Jim Burns, a lifelong Liverpool supporter. 'His move was at a time when Madrid were only just emerging from a Man Utd-style twenty-year slump and had yet to adopt fully their now famous *galácticos* policy. We thought it was a sideways move for a combination of a bigger salary (it was assumed then that all foreign clubs paid more) and, more importantly, a change of culture. There was a certain pride in that one of our own was wanted by a big foreign club. Even now it is rare for British players to move abroad and here was a beanpole Scouser being courted by Barça, Lazio, Inter and Madrid. To sum up, I would say most people felt: "Thanks for the good times, now make us proud as you still represent us (you jammy bastard!)."'

Whatever, Steve resolved to carry on as if life was normal, as his mother wanted, and thus he followed his impulse. 'I talked to Gazza, Chris Waddle, Paul Ince and David Platt. They all said the opportunity to go abroad was not to be brushed off lightly. Even if the playing side did not prove particularly successful, the experience would be fantastic and they wouldn't have swapped their spells abroad for anything. I made up my mind. Later, I was watching the FIFA World Player of the Year ceremony on television and it struck me that the three players up there in the nominations – Zinedine Zidane, Davor Suker and Ronaldo – were all playing in countries foreign to them. I knew it was the right thing for me to try. It is the challenge every ambitious player wants: to succeed in a foreign environment.'

Before that sunny July day, Steve had only visited the Spanish capital twice, to sign the pre-contract, and again in March when he flew out for his medical. Both had been typical footballing visits, an eighteen-hour stopover with every minute scheduled: 'All you see is the inside of a car or bus, a hotel room and a quick impression of a stadium.' Now accompanied by Victoria Edwards, his girlfriend of five years, he was on a reconnaissance mission to find a house and initiate the settling-in process in the city he intended to make home. He had thought through the move in detail: he was determined to learn the language and find a house as soon as possible. Life in a hotel, even for a few months, would not allow him to relax away from the rigours of a big club's training and travel schedule. He wanted to be installed domestically, to have a house that felt like home and to welcome visitors from England. Having grimaced over Spanish hotel breakfasts on those earlier visits, he needed a few ex-pat props like Frosties, a fridge stocked with Anchor butter and pasties, and satellite television to keep up with Premiership results and the Racing Channel. Once nested, he would feel ready to throw himself into pre-season training and concentrate on making the most of his opportunity to wear the famous shirt of Los Blancos.

'I was a bit nervous that morning at the airport. You set off hoping that you will find a nice house in a suitable area and that the paperwork will all be sorted easily. It sounds crazy, but for most people house-hunting is something that takes weeks or months. We had to organise everything in a few days,' he recalls. 'I was conscious of wanting to keep a low profile. I realised from my medical that the Spanish press are mad, mad, mad. Back then a crowd of cameramen and news journalists hung around for me at Madrid airport. They were there early the next morning to follow me from the hotel to the clinic where I had the medical, and to film me crossing the road from one part of the clinic to another. They followed every single step of my day. It was bizarre. The last thing I wanted was to be followed around like that as Victoria and I made private decisions about houses and things. That's when you have to be wary of organising things through your club in Spain. Word leaks out.'

So they set off quietly, certainly not expecting red-carpet treatment. In fact they had no expectations at all, other than the understandable presumption that Real Madrid would provide an interpreter and local guide to help with basic orienteering and relocation advice, as they had observed Liverpool officials help the assimilation process for players like Patrik Berger. They took their seats on the plane chatting together, Victoria with a bundle of newspapers and magazines, Steve bowing his head to fit in under the overhead lockers. Footballers tend to be recognised by their gait and body language. With his distinctive frame and on-pitch air of laddish conviviality as good as stowed away with his luggage, McManaman was unlikely to be recognised . . . except by another footballer of international repute. Victoria recalls looking up as a tall, dark-haired Italian with a floppy fringe falling rakishly across his left eye greeted

Steve warmly before taking up his own seat. It was Christian Panucci, the young Italian right-back who had followed his mentor/manager Fabio Capello from AC Milan to Real Madrid (and would join him again at AS Roma). 'He'd been to London for a weekend with his girlfriend,' Victoria said. 'He came over to Steven and the funny thing was they couldn't communicate because he doesn't speak English and Steven didn't speak Italian, or Spanish then, so they sort of acknowledged each other, but in a friendly way. After their exchange, Steven turned to me and said it was a shame because Panucci was leaving Madrid, so he wouldn't be there when he started.'

Steve had no worries about the wisdom of his transfer to Real Madrid. Had he needed the tiniest reassurance though, the figure of Panucci embodied the reasons he was on the plane. At twenty-five, the Italian was known for his winning mentality and the collection of silverware he had accumulated, first at his home club and then, more prominently, from his move to Madrid. To his 1994 European Cup-winner's medal with AC Milan, he had added another in 1998 with Real Madrid; to two Serie A medals with Milan in 1994 and 1996, he now boasted a 1997 la Liga medal, and a 1998 World Club Cup winner's medal. He was young, stylish, cosmopolitan in outlook, and relishing the challenges and lifestyle that Spanish football afforded him. Like Panucci, McManaman had started winning things at his first club. Now he was leaving Liverpool to join the club where Panucci had consolidated his reputation alongside stars like Raúl, Fernando Redondo, World Cup Golden Boot winner Davor Suker, free kick specialist Roberto Carlos, Clarence Seedorf, European-Cup scorer Pedrag Mijatovic and Fernando Hierro, a club where success was not so much an aim as an expectation. As Steve had noted, the cynics who doubted his resilience and survival potential had keenly repeated the mantra that of the very few English players who had tested themselves abroad, even fewer had succeeded. But why should that lack of heritage be a gulf when the unspoken camaraderie of the dressing room had extended out so readily from Panucci, giving two like-minded players a facility to communicate even without words?

Heaven knows what fellow passengers thought of their pantomime exchange. 'Oh yeah, you have a lot of those sort of "conversations",' says Steve, giving a punchy recitation in his rich Liverpudlian accent with accompanying wild gestures: 'It's "Hello, OK, OK, OK, yeah, OK, yeah, well, bye then," with a lot of grinning, a few thumbs up, and the odd slap on the back.' If McManaman was even subconsciously grateful for that chance encounter with Christian Panucci on the British Airways Airbus, how much more grateful was Victoria when they saw him next.

'Those first few days were very difficult. We were staying in the Ritz, and I remember feeling apprehensive and a bit depressed at the way things were progressing,' says Victoria.

'We had flown out to look for houses. The plan was to find one, go back home to collect our belongings, and come back again so that Steven could go right into pre-season training. I thought it would be straightforward, but the biggest shock was that nobody from the club was available to help us. I was used to seeing foreign players come to Liverpool. There was a good support system for them and for their wives. There was always a translator, always somebody who would take them around to look at accommodation and make sure they were taken care of and feeling at ease. Rather than put you in a hotel, Liverpool had apartments and houses where you could stay, even for a few months, so players and their families were made to feel part of the fold. I expected the same kind of treatment from Real Madrid, because it's such a big club. So when we arrived and there was literally no communication with the club whatsoever, we didn't know where to turn.'

The Ritz, which is next to the Prado Museum, proclaims itself the most aristocratic and dignified hotel, not just in Spain, but in Europe. It stands between two impressive plazas, La Lealtad, filled with green elms and old magnolia trees surrounding an obelisk, and Neptuno, dominated by an ornate fountain and a statue of the mythological horses of Neptune's chariot. Its rooms and suites are decorated with antique furniture and 'individually designed Spanish knot rugs' – as the glossy bumf boasts. So, on one level, there were Steve and Victoria cocooned in the kind of stifling luxury a five-star hotel offers with a near-obsequious level of attention. On another level, they were unable to venture out for a feeling of utter helplessness and lack of guidance. The exciting prospect of a new life at Real Madrid remained just that. The reality awaiting them was a total vacuum, a zero welcome.

'We didn't speak a word of Spanish then. Very few people in Madrid speak English. That was a shock, because in the more touristy areas of Spain you can usually just about get by, but we soon learned that is not the case in Madrid,' continued Victoria. 'Steven had started having Spanish lessons in England but put them on hold to spend more time with his mother. So it was really, really hard. No one could understand us. We couldn't understand them. We didn't know where to start looking for estate agents. We didn't know how property "worked" in Spain. We didn't know what the working hours were: everything closes down from lunchtime to 5pm. We kept meeting all these strangers and the fact the club did absolutely nothing was infuriating. Being in Steven's position in a foreign country makes you very vulnerable. You don't know who you can trust and who you can't, and who is trying to take advantage.'

A call to Steve's London-based advisers, Simon Fuller's 19 Management, resulted in the arrival of a driver called José and an interpreter who had been briefed on likely estate agents. An intense whirlwind trawl through available flats and houses began, all surveyed in the sapping July 40°C heat. Steve remembers looking at about a hundred places, including numerous 'five-bedroom flats over one floor that you could get lost in'. Victoria recalls houses that were too big, too isolated, too far from the airport and training ground.

At this point one should mention that while Victoria, then twenty-two, looks every inch the well-known player's glamorous consort with her glossy blonde hair and immaculate style, she is as far removed as possible from the shallow 'Chardonnay' stereotype enforced by ITV1's far-fetched drama *Footballers' Wives*. She comes from Mossley

Hill, a smart suburb in south Liverpool, where her parents run a family publishing business. Her maternal grandfather, James Ross, was twice Lord Mayor of Liverpool, thereby enriching the family stock of stories – Victoria's mother dined with the Prince and Princess of Wales, the young Victoria met the Queen, and was photographed turning on the Christmas lights with Les Dawson. At the Penny Lane field, where a certain young Steve McManaman once trained, there hung a huge oil painting of his future wife's grandfather. True, Victoria met Steven – as she and his family always refer to him – in a nightclub when doing her A-levels at the private Belvedere School. This in itself would have had many a girl chuck in the academics and make a beeline for a life of champagne, nail extensions and the charms of multiple in-store credit-card spending sprees. But Victoria persisted with her long-held ambition to go into law, doing a four-year degree in English and German law at the University of Liverpool, which involved living in Berlin for her third year while she attended Humbolt University. She finished university with a 2:1 and went to Bar school, the Inns of Court School of Law in London, and was a member of Lincoln's Inn. As she modestly jotted in a note, 'Got scholarship so lived in the Inn . . . quite amusing when Steven used to come and visit!' She was free to accompany her boyfriend to Madrid because the pupillage she had been offered by 14 Castle Street Chambers (the chambers of Adrian Lyons, now Andrew Edis) had, to her immense gratitude, been deferred for a year. In other words, she is independent and feisty, a girl with a can-do attitude to life, who speaks fluent French and German; not the sort of unadaptable, narrow-minded girlfriend to drag a partner down with homesickness. Which only reinforces her description of the bewildering elusiveness of 'Real Madrid, the world's most famous football club' as, together, in those few days they desperately sought a sense of belonging . . .

'It was so bad Steven didn't even know when he was meant to sign in for pre-season training. They had his numbers but there was no communication from the club at all, so the girl who arrived as an interpreter was calling the club, but they were so disorganised they just kept passing her on to someone else. No one inside the Bernabéu stadium office could help. All we wanted to know was when he was expected to go in. It was incredible.

'The heat in July was unbearable, and we looked at so many houses and flats, but nothing was suitable. The final house we looked at was in a residential area called La Moraleja. The moment we saw it we knew it was the one. It was so ironic because who would be walking out of the door about to catch a flight for Milan? Christian Panucci. He said, "Do you want it?" And we said weakly, "Yes, it's perfect." I can't describe the relief. We signed for it literally in the last hour before we had to leave. As Panucci was going out of the door, rushing to catch his flight, he shouted back to say the removal men were coming later that morning to take some of his furniture away. Did we want him to leave it?'

Panucci cancelled the removal men and Victoria erased her doubts about life in Madrid. As they headed back to Liverpool for the turnaround trip to scoop up their belongings, Steve realised that the name La Moraleja had a familiar ring to it. He had, in fact, been driven hastily through the discreet, mazy complex of villas with high hedges and higher security gates on one of his previous eighteen-hour whirlwind tours. It was where Karembeu, Seedorf, Robert Jarni and a lot of other players lived, ideally situated between airport and training ground. Despite their good fortune, one valid lesson had been reinforced: the need to learn the language. As Victoria lamented: 'If only Steven and Panucci had been able to chat and understand each other on the plane, the house issue might have been raised and solved there and then.'

Relief that things had fallen into place meant that the couple could laugh at the press ambush awaiting them at Madrid airport. They may have arrived on the sly, but by now word had leaked out: they would not leave without the full treatment. As Michael Robinson had warned: 'What Steven has to realise is that when he becomes a Real Madrid player he is more important than a cabinet minister. The pressure on a Real Madrid player is immense. They are gods and there will be little peace for him.' The following day McManaman's *viaje secreto*, secret trip, to Madrid covered four pages each in *AS* and *Marca*. Snapped in the departure hall, the photographs of a carefree Steve and Victoria were printed as if taken on arrival. The *AS* team had whipped out a Real Madrid shirt at check-in, and begged him to put it on. This sacred act was reproduced on the page in sequential shots: the seven stages of the first time Steve McManaman pulls on the white shirt of Real Madrid. (Sensitive to the Kop, he had resisted all offers to pose in the shirt while still a Liverpool player.) *Marca*, not to be outdone, put a superimposed image of Steve in weatherman pose next to an enlarged map of Madrid on which he proudly indicated with a pointer the precise route his house-hunting trail had taken him. If only they had known the truth. Their visit to De María restaurant for lunch was fulsomely reported – table booked for four, orders taken for *jamón*, spaghetti with tomato sauce, chocolate pancakes and a further selection of desserts. The paper left readers with this speculative thought for the season: did McManaman have a sweet tooth?

Tuesday 21 July 1999

Steve reports for his first official day of work as a Real Madrid player. Contact had eventually been established with the club. At 9am he was to be at the Ciudad Deportiva training ground, a complex for Real Madrid football and basketball clubs, a block or so beyond the city's northern gateway, the Plaza de Castilla.

'Some man – I have no idea to this day who he was – sent a message to say I had to be in to give blood samples at 9am. I took a taxi to the Ciudad Deportiva and met him. He then introduced me to the security guards so that they would recognise me in future and wave me through the gates every day. He'd said nine o'clock so, of course, I got there at quarter to nine. The place was deserted. No one else appeared until gone half-past ten. I soon learnt that if they said nine o'clock, you come in anytime from quarter past ten onwards. That's Spain. But I didn't know that then. I was eager, anxious to do things right. David Beckham was the same. On the first day of the 2003–04 pre-season, I came in and had a laugh when I found Becks sitting there twiddling his thumbs. Sure enough, he'd been told to be in by 9am for a blood test, and he'd been there for hours before any of the rest of us rolled in. And I'd warned him!

'I arrived feeling nervous, excited, anxious, with butterflies in my stomach, having had a bad night's sleep – everything you can imagine. I knew I was walking into a strange dressing room and that to begin with I wasn't going to be able to converse with anyone. I had prepared myself for that, but it was daunting none the less. This team had won the European Cup the year before last, they were in the Champions League. I knew the squad was littered with superstars, and the stereotyped image was of volatile egos and in-house fighting, a lot of *protagonismo*, a revolving dressing-room door that regularly spat out foreign players. So I was nervous on two counts. First, on a social level of arriving and fitting in – being accepted, really – and secondly, because of the expectations on me to perform. I knew I had to gain professional respect. When I joined, a big fuss had been made, and it had been emphasised that I was a "superstar" signing. Real Madrid had not won a major trophy that 1998–99 season, whereas when I first started negotiating with them they were effectively European and world champions, having won the 1998 European Cup and, in early 1999, the Intercontinental Cup. The fans demanded signings. I came in on this big blaze of glory, with seven other new players: two Spaniards, Míchel Salgado, who was signed from Celta Vigo, and Iván Helguera who came from Espanyol; the Cameroon star Geremi; the Bosnian forward Elvir Baljic – everyone thought we were the spitting image of each other; Brazilians Julio César and Rodrigo Fabri, and Congo who comes from Colombia. We all sat together at a massive table and testified solemnly that we would repay President Lorenzo Sanz's investment of 9,000 million pesetas by winning every title on offer. We even paid a goodwill visit to the offices of the newspaper *Marca*. It was amazing how many people tried to talk to me about Liverpool, about how Liverpool's history was on a par with Real Madrid – about the game when

Liverpool famously beat them in the 1981 European Cup final – but mostly about the Beatles. I actually had to pose for photographers striding across a zebra crossing outside the Bernabéu as if I was the fifth Beatle. It was as if I had landed from Planet Success, not the other way around. In England, new players are given time to fit in. Allowances are made for them adjusting to the weather, the food, even for their wives to make friends. Not in Spain. You have to perform from day one. Reporters write up every training session. You have to fit into the football and at Madrid that means playing with a certain style. It's not enough to win or play well, you have to do it with panache and excite the fans.

'To arrive in a similar situation is more relaxed now, the culture is totally different. There are people to welcome you, show you around, escort you everywhere, sort out your house for you. But when I arrived it was under the last president, Lorenzo Sanz. It was "We've signed you, you're in at nine o'clock", boom that's it. Gus Hiddinck was manager when I signed, but I never met or spoke with him. I knew John Toshack had been called in to take over towards the end of the previous season when Madrid had slumped to seventh in the league and Champions League qualification looked doubtful, but I had had no contact with him. I wandered in that day like a little lost boy, you know, what do I do? Where do I go? Where do I sit? I remember lots of bare white walls, a very lived-in space. I wouldn't say it was shabby; there were new lockers, new sinks, but it was not brand spanking new. There was nothing on the walls, nothing to suggest the space was unique to Real Madrid, nothing that indicated it was the daily dressing room of the most famous team in the world. Everyone was meeting up again after the summer break and they were hugging each other, and asking after their families, telling anecdotes from their holidays. I felt totally invisible. Someone – again I haven't the slightest idea who – came over and greeted me, and pointed to my locker. Each player's number is on top of his locker, and the lockers are arranged in numerical order. Having been given the No. 8 shirt, I was between Raúl (No. 7) and Elvir Baljic (No. 9), with Fernando Redondo next but one (No. 6). My kit was hanging ready, and my towels were there. I changed and then followed everyone out onto the pitch.'

Given the fact that insiders at Real Madrid had for years watched head coaches 'come in and out like Henry VIII's fiancées', as Ian Hawkey of the *Sunday Times* put it, it was unbelievably fortunate for McManaman to find his new manager was a former Liverpool man, even if the manager had been having a difficult time sorting out a dressing room riven with petty jealousies. 'Not only had John Toshack worked with people I knew and respected, like Roy Evans and Ronnie Whelan, but every exercise we did in that first morning of training was familiar from Liverpool,' he chuckled. 'As a manager, just as a player, you take with you elements you have experienced under different coaches and regimes. So, on my first day at Real Madrid, I found myself perpetuating the Anfield heritage, if you like, but with Raúl, Roberto Carlos, Redondo, Manuel Sanchís, Hierro, Christian Karembeu, Clarence Seedorf and Fernando Morientes. That really helped: it was one important central element of my new life which was not a seismic culture shock. On the surface, players go through the same routine all over the world: you train, you undergo conditioning, you prepare for games, you play. But you cannot underestimate the demands of doing that in an alien environment, when you're still getting your bearings, assessing the mentality, sussing out the dynamics of the dressing room.'

According to Toshack, the coaching philosophy he espouses is the same that helped Swansea climb from Fourth Division to First in five years, that steered Real Sociedad to their first Spanish Cup victory in 1987, that propelled Real Madrid to the 1989–90 league championship as his side scored 107 goals (a record that still stands) and so on. 'Everything I learnt in football management, I learnt from Bob Paisley and Bill Shankly,' he says. 'Every club I've been with, we've done the same work from Monday to Friday that I did winning championships with Liverpool as a player. The basis of the coaching work is a way of trying to keep possession, a way of passing, a way of playing the game in a certain style. So Steve settled in easier because that was second nature to him.'

McManaman had no problems with Toshack. 'I found him all right. There was always that friendly face to help you out. Training was conducted in Spanish, as I expected, but if I didn't understand something specific, which I didn't always in those first few months, he would pull me to one side and tell me in English. It is a bit like Beckham experienced with Carlos Queiroz, who had been number two to Sir Alex Ferguson at United. To have a familiar figure helps you through. Toshack's presence was a safety net. In a quiet, paternal way, he explained the pitfalls of being at a club like Real Madrid. He warned me where the bullets would come from and he advised me, if I did get any hassle, to keep quiet, perform well, say the right things and stick to my guns. I felt he was someone I could turn to in case things went horribly wrong.

'On that first morning I recall a haze of faces, but very soon, with the intensity of pre-season training, I realised the Real Madrid dressing room was similar to Liverpool's or England's in that there are always the loud, crazy lads; the few who are the butt of their jokes; the ones who prepare quietly, others who rush in late. Hierro and Sanchís, the senior players, stood out initially. They were both obviously held in awe. People seemed to seek out their opinion. I'd seen a picture of Sanchís once in a magazine sitting on the floor surrounded by the hundreds of trophies he's won. It was astonishing what he'd won. He was a lovely man who helped me on my way. And so modest. I never knew until after I left that his father, also Manolo, was in the side that won Madrid's sixth European Cup. He was always first in every morning. He'd drop his kids off at school, get in and sit with a coffee reading the economics section of the papers. Roberto Carlos was a ball of energy, loud in manner and in his lairy Versace clothes. His style was great: whatever you'd think is naff, he'd think incredibly cool. That's what I loved about him. And he's always on the telephone. He's one of these fellas who has about six mobiles; he always has the latest gadgets. Karembeu, it was clear, was always, always, always late. Morientes, Iván Campo, the new boy Helguera, were all up for a laugh. Helguera was the comedian, very funny – as far as I could tell through the language, anyway!'

After training Steve met up with Victoria in the city centre. They returned home to find the now-familiar good-natured press ambush waiting at their gates, poised to capture the official welcoming of *el crack inglès* to his new home in Madrid – a welcome farcically prolonged by the failure of their electric gates to open. The detail in *Marca*'s subsequent four-page spectacular on this debacle was hysterical. What might have been a snatched photograph and a comment through the car window turned into a drama that afforded much investigative time to the reporters. The time taken for Augustín – a club *delegado* who looked after Panucci's house and who was to become a good friend – to arrive and fix the fault with the remote control allowed much snooping and subtle interviewing of workmen while Steve and Victoria sat in their air-conditioned car. The following day's report was trivia supreme: the house is 'like a mansion from *Falcon Crest*'; eight people, industrial cleaners and gardeners, have been working to get McManaman's house ready to rent; while Steve *y su novia* Victoria shopped in Marks & Spencer (which then had an outlet in Madrid) and ate lunch in sandwich bar Pans & Company, Mario and Gabriel were sorting out an automatic garden-watering system, working on the facade of the house and revising electric installations. Cue a picture of a thrilled Mario pushing his lawnmower. 'Despite five bags of rubbish and three full dustbins, McManaman is still happy,' read the bizarre final line.

The newly garnered squad of 1999–2000, of whom so much was expected, flew straight to Switzerland on a pre-season tour. Cocooned together for two weeks, it was in theory the best way for the only Englishman in the group to assimilate. 'I'd been in Spain for twenty-four hours when I was whisked off for two weeks with a load of guys I couldn't talk to. It was a nightmare. Half of enjoying your football is the banter with your mates. Whatever problems there were in adjusting, football-wise or socially, they were going to happen there,' he recalls.

'I concentrated on settling in on the pitch. We played five hard games and returned undefeated. As much as you want to do fantastically well, you would also think there wasn't a care because the games didn't mean anything. But the scrutiny was intense. You are judged from your first training session, even on pre-season. For me, training has always been like having a good game of football with my mates. Here were all the press seriously reporting on our training games and we were expected to speak to them every day. I was trying to find my way into the team, trying to know people's names, learning how they run. I really enjoyed it: I was head of the running, and the fitness assessment, stupid things like that. I remember watching Salgado, who I'd be playing in front of, and trying to learn his way of thinking. He's a completely different right-back from anything I've experienced before or since. Like Roberto Carlos, he does whatever he wants. On the pitch I felt comfortable until I suffered an annoying cut on my foot which was deep enough to reveal bone, and was not going to heal overnight. Off pitch was another matter, because it was July, notoriously hot and stuffy, and we were staying at the Beau Rivage, in Nyon, a very average hotel close to UEFA headquarters. The rooms didn't have air conditioning, so that was horrific. When I heard we were due to return there a year later, I called up in advance and asked them to put a fan in our room. I was sharing with Santiago Solari, and we were the envy of the rest of the squad – the only room in the hotel that had a big massive fan, on permanently!

'That first pre-season I roomed with Manolo Canabal, the Spanish forward who left later that autumn for Malaga. We couldn't speak a syllable of each other's languages, but we got on brilliantly well. I had this little phrase book – with lists of useless lines like "I want fruit" – and our gestures were hysterical. We didn't say a word to each other, except swear words obviously. To this day he knows all the English ones, and he taught me the Spanish ones. He drew a picture of a dick and a pair of bollocks and said, "Right, Macca, that's a *polla* and these are *cojones*." It continued from there. We didn't know the meaning of the words we were teaching each other, but we made each other laugh. He used to wake up every morning and his first word would be "Bollocks!" Or "Shit!" I would retaliate with a Spanish swear word I had no idea the meaning of. It was stupid, but it started the day with a laugh.

'I was sitting there like an idiot most of the time, but those weeks gave me time to absorb how a few things worked. Whenever we ate, for instance, there tended to be two tables, one for the Spanish players, and another for the foreigners. It wasn't an "us and them" attitude, merely a matter of sitting down next to your mates, somebody you could speak to. Clarence Seedorf's English is great, so he was friendly, very gregarious and forthright. He stepped in as my interpreter when I was called to do a press conference in Switzerland. When we returned to Madrid, and realised we both lived in La Moraleja, he was always picking me up and dropping me off to include me in whatever was going on. Christian Karembeu was another whose English was excellent, which speeded up the bonding process. I soon discovered that fellow new-boy Míchel Salgado has an English sister-in-law from Yorkshire. He once spent a month in Margate on a school exchange, and loved practising his English.

'Yeah, I bet Macca's never been to Canterbury to see the sites of Chaucer's *Tales*,' laughs Salgado. 'In Switzerland, the new boys were a group and the established players another. Macca and I would be wandering around on our own, we'd go and have a drink or pop to the shops. He was the only one who would speak English with me! We'd arrived at a club where there are lots of heavyweight players who have won everything and are well known in football. For me, it was a radical change in every way – in terms of the team, the city, media repercussions. You have to know how to adapt, how to live with all that. I came from a modest team, Celta, whereas Macca came from Liverpool, a huge club, but he had to adapt to a new country. So it was just us, finding our feet together, for a bit. The big plus with Macca is that he made an effort. He can separate himself a bit, but he is a very open guy. If we said, "We're going to wherever," Steve would be there. That's why he won people over so quickly. And being English, he was unusual. He'd wander around the hotel in bare feet [Salgado starts laughing], he did a load of things that aren't normal . . . he'd be ambling about bare-footed, doing whatever he felt like, a very happy bloke, easy-going, relaxed, nothing bothered him . . .'

'Steve's bare feet really struck all the players,' recalls Iván Campo. 'We'd say to ourselves, what's he doing, this hippy? The other hotel guests just stared at him. We had a word with him and explained he couldn't come downstairs like that because it didn't look good for Real Madrid's image.'

Without the English speakers, Steve admits he'd have been desperate. 'For huge chunks of the day I felt lonely. I read a lot, spent a lot of time bantering on the phone to Victoria and mates in Liverpool, and watched any channel I could find that was English-speaking. Apart from the jokes with Canabal, I didn't want to be boring some Spanish lad by getting out my phrase book and trying to make conversation. I did feel uncomfortable. Things like dinner time would be announced to us in Spanish and you'd be like, "What time was that?" "What did they say?" That's when rooming with someone is great because they'll say, "Come on, let's go and eat."

'At that stage I hadn't absorbed the impact of changes in lifestyle as a player – the late-night games, the amount of time we'd spend in hotels before home as well as away matches, the constant travel – but what did strike me was how much the players were left to be responsible for themselves. We were treated as adults and expected to look after ourselves. There were no rules. Most of the greatest footballers are players of instinct. You have to, literally, let them be. The unofficial line seemed to be: If you're that good on the pitch, you are allowed to function as you will off it. After training you went out and had a beer, or a coffee, in the bar. On the bus, and on the plane, we had beer. We had red wine and beer with the meals, lunch and dinner. Roberto Carlos doesn't drink Coke or water, he'll always have a beer, but he won't necessarily finish it. He is the first to have a beer on the flight home; he probably has one for breakfast. And he's one of the fittest men alive. In England, show players beer and they'll have ten. In Spain, they have one or two. On that trip to Switzerland there was no curfew. It wasn't like, "It's ten o'clock, you've got to be in bed, you can't do this, you can't do that." There is a lot more trust.

'By the end of the second week I still couldn't speak the language but it was clear I was trying my best, making an effort. When I wasn't greeting someone with a swear word, just for a laugh, I was probably making hundreds of howlers. Even when I could regard myself as fluent, months later, I knew I made mistakes – probably excruciatingly embarrassing ones – so I turned it into a big joke from the start. All the interviews I did then in Spanish, you see people curling up laughing, bent double. Christ knows what I've said literally, but I think the players got the gist. Whenever the lads sat down for a beer or two before dinner in the hotel, I would go and sit with them, and smile and laugh even though I didn't understand a word. I was trying to join their company even if I couldn't join their conversation. I think they appreciated that. Every morning I'd say, "*Buenos días, como está?*" – hello, how are you? – with a smile on my face. I think they thought, "he's all right, he's laughing and having a joke with us."'

Iván Helguera remembers him 'standing out a mile' straightaway: 'With Macca, just saying hello, you could see something, the air he has, the feeling that he's a good guy, that he likes a joke. He's very loveable, very natural. In the world of football, with so much money, so much vested interest, he's one of the very best people there is.' Raúl, a key senior professional to impress, agrees: 'When someone new turns up it's normal for it to be difficult for them because Madrid is such a big club and first impressions can really impact upon people, but Macca won our respect and affection unusually quickly, because apart from being a great footballer he is a very happy, loveable person.'

In contrast to his sense of personal awkwardness, he was pictured at ease in affectionate press coverage. 'Sensación McManaman' ran a front-page *Marca* headline, describing how 'the new white player becomes an idol on his first day'; how he is the player most sought after by fans; how hundreds of Liverpool shirts arrive daily for signing. '*La estrella de McManaman no ha tardado en brillar*',

McManaman has not been slow in shining. He is *un personaje*, a character; his punctuality, his patience . . . he is an English gentleman. It was ridiculously flowery stuff. Concern about his foot injury prompts conjecture he may have *ampollas* – blisters – which necessitated a graphic of a foot showing three possible ways to lance a blister. A recurring feature is the resemblance between Steve and Baljic, with never an opportunity missed for a *¿Quién es quién?* photograph. As semi-official outlets for the club, *AS* and *Marca* both embraced Steve as a new member of the Real Madrid family. Desperate to beat others to an 'exclusive' knowledge of his off-pitch hobbies, too, *Marca* photographed him next to a motorbike (he couldn't understand why at the time) and devoted hundreds of words to the Englishman's passion for two-wheeled speed machines. '"Motorbikes are a passion of the Englishman",' a bemused Victoria would recite from the paper. 'No, they're not!'

Meanwhile, back in Madrid, Victoria was working hard to make Panucci's bachelor pad their home. The experience of a 'terrible year' in Berlin meant her second move abroad was undertaken with apprehension. 'I had my pupillage in Liverpool, and initially I found that difficult to put on hold because it was everything I had worked towards, but I didn't want Steven to have to go to Spain alone. His mum had just died and I knew it would be incredibly hard for him. He didn't speak the language. He hadn't lived away from home before. I had a meeting with my chambers, who were absolutely fantastic. They told me it was an amazing opportunity and they would defer my pupillage. The decision was made: I was going too.'

Victoria's year studying German law in Berlin could be a Hammer Horror script and ominously the horror sprang from accommodation issues. It started with the discovery that the halls of residence designated for the Liverpool University students were not only a two-hour journey from the lecture halls, but were also graffiti-covered grim concrete blocks, with windows that were either freshly smashed or repaired with yellowing newspapers. 'It looked like a POW camp.

One of the other students had gone out there early and she was in tears down the phone. That was a shock because she was a tough cookie.' So Victoria and another student, Charlotte, searched for a flat in the city. 'There's no culture of student accommodation, so we were literally looking in newspaper ads. We eventually found a horrendous flat, which turned out to be in the red-light district, opposite an S&M club. We looked out of the window on to a dummy in a gimp suit, zips over the eyes and mouth. Next to us on one side was a brothel and on the other side a gay club. We never set foot outside without two rape alarms. I couldn't stop crying. I was a complete baby. I was really homesick, missing Steven and my family. Then it turned out the landlord – who had once burst in on us like a psycho when Charlotte was in the bath – was illegally renting the rooms. We had to be out that minute. We found another flat in East Berlin, again a grim block with one light bulb swinging in a dingy hall, but owned by a beautiful Thai family who were going travelling for a year and were happy to let us look after their home.

'University life was awful, there were no sports or drama clubs or any student societies to join. Despite the fact I spoke German fluently, no one was friendly. So we decided simply to bury our heads and study. Then, when we only had one week to go, and we'd spent our final day revising for the last exam, Charlotte and I decided to have a chill-out evening. We put on pyjamas, had a glass of wine, I remember speaking to Steven who'd been playing Paris St-Germain and was about to fly back to Liverpool, and then I smelt burning. We were six floors up with only a wooden staircase and a fire had broken out – below us. Initially we thought the fire was in our flat so we opened the door onto the hall, and whoosh, the lights blacked out, flames roared up. We'd caused a backdraft and suddenly we were stumbling around in the jet black, struggling to breathe through the heat and thick smoke. I'm asthmatic, it was like having cotton wool stuffed down your throat. I remember feeling my way to a window, opening it, leaning out as far as I could balance on the thin ledge. I glimpsed fresh air and I was going to jump into it. All rational judgement had gone, I was desperate for that clear air. Below the firemen were starting to inflate the landing mat you jump into, but that would have been too late. Charlotte literally rugby-tackled me to stop me from leaping and they eventually managed to raise the ladder extensions on the fire engine. We ended up hurling ourselves about two metres out from the ledge, in our pyjamas, into the arms of a fireman. I had a panic attack, and had to be strapped down in the ambulance. We both looked like chimney sweeps, we were laughing and crying hysterically, and then the hospital was like a dark, filthy asylum from Victorian Britain. We both had serious carbon-monoxide poisoning and had to stay in for a week. My heart had gone into panic, the rhythm had become irregular, and my eyes were spookily dilated from the trauma. They stayed that way for three months. We couldn't even call home because the hospital wouldn't let us make a foreign call . . . and we couldn't leave the country for another two weeks. The fire had been caused by illegal immigrants and we had to participate in an official investigation.

'So my only experience abroad was so consistently awful, I couldn't imagine I was going to truly enjoy Spain. That is probably why I was unnerved initially by the difficulties of finding a house. But I felt at home as soon as we moved into our own place. There is a real mixture of people who live in La Moreleja: embassy staff, bullfighters, sports players and so on. The neighbours keep to themselves, but always smile and wave. Next door is a family with lots of sons so we hear them splashing around in the swimming pool in the summer. The Spanish are such a courteous, warm people. If you get into a lift in a shop or a hotel, complete strangers say hello, how are you. If you return to a shop, they greet you like a long-lost friend. Of course they adore the football players, but even without Steven I was treated very well wherever I went.

'The house was perfect in that it was big enough for our family and friends to visit, but not too big for me to be in on my own. It was a typical marble-floored spacious villa, with five bedrooms, terrace and swimming pool. It wasn't necessarily furnished in our taste, but its only real eccentricity was upstairs: a bizarre maze of dressing rooms and hanging space hidden by ruched pink silk curtains – I think a previous owner had been a fashion designer! After that mad, last-minute Panucci encounter, we went back to England, picked up our belongings, came back, then Steven literally had one day here and he went away for two weeks' pre-season training. I was in the house alone. We only had the bits and bobs Panucci had left. We had never lived together before. Steven, even though he had a flat in Liverpool, was at his mum and dad's, or my mum and dad's, all the time, so we didn't have things like cutlery. We didn't have a teacup. I had to go shopping to get all the domestic basics, which was a nightmare because of the language. My mum came over to help and we tried to get everything sorted quickly because we felt the longer we were in a transitional period, the longer it would take to settle in to the whole way of life. It was an exasperating two weeks. Everything was a major frustration. It was so hot. Mum and I would go out and we'd be fainting by eleven o'clock in the morning. And where to go? When we first arrived in Madrid the management company in England had organised a chauffeur for us to our hotel. Not speaking any Spanish, and the driver not speaking English, we spoke in French and he was charming. His name was José and we got on well. When my mum came over, he was our driver again and we'd say we need furniture shops today and he'd take us where he thought was best, usually El Corte Inglés, the biggest department store. Michael Robinson's wife, Chris, also contacted us to see if we needed any help. She was away on holiday, but she gave me a list of places to go to. I was so grateful to her for being so thoughtful.'

As Chris Robinson points out, footballers moving to Europe between seasons arrive at the worst time. 'It is a nightmare trying to set up home, especially abroad, but to do it in July or August in Madrid is absolutely impossible,' she says from experience. 'The city shuts down for the summer. It's not only stifling hot, it's a ghost town. You could have £20,000 to spend, and a shop will send you away saying, "You have to wait for September." Either that, or there is no stock because they have had sales. Victoria is a very strong, independent lady, but she was understandably getting stressed out. I warned her not to panic. When you come to live in Spain, you need a vaccination against *mañana* . . . If you think you can sit in and wait for a delivery you'll go crazy. You have to spell that out to people. And they had no help from the club. I couldn't sit back and think of someone going through that, so I helped put her in touch with Teresa, an English teacher, and a cleaning lady and gave her a list of suggestions. She was very positive, absolutely determined to get it sorted for Steve. She did really, really well.'

Laughing about it in retrospect, Victoria recalls how she encountered all the inconveniences Spain could throw at her in those two weeks. 'I had a power cut in the house, and then it struck me I didn't know any of the numbers, the police, I didn't know how to call an electrician. When I succeeded in hailing an electrician, I didn't know what to say to him in Spanish. I quickly had to learn cultural differences. For example, that the morning in Spain ends at 2pm, not twelve noon, and then everything closes for three hours. At first, I would ring shops five minutes past twelve o'clock and say, "You said you would deliver in the morning . . ." and they wouldn't understand that I was sitting there, waiting for them! We had an assistant who was supposed to help us, but she had never driven in Madrid before and we kept getting lost for hours on end. It was one of those situations where if you didn't laugh you'd cry. It made me more determined to become independent as soon as possible. Steven came back after two weeks of chaos and everything was in place, as if by magic. We had a bed, and bedding. We had cutlery. We had sofas and Sky TV – that was the most important thing for him. So that was very nice for him, but it nearly killed Mum and me for two weeks.'

If the tag of underachievement had propelled Steve to Spain, he started his career in la Liga with large ticks down the column in which Souness, for one former manager, had put a question mark – namely, 'scoring, frequency of'. 'During his time in England the general perception was that the end product was not there. That was the only thing missing from his game,' says Souness. 'He had wonderful individual ability, wonderful, wonderful skills, but he didn't score enough goals. For someone who possesses so much ability, you would like to think they could get to double figures every year. That's the one criticism I'd put at his doorstep and I think he would agree with that.'

The first game of the season was against Real Mallorca. Steve did not start, but came on and made an immediate impression. 'We were losing 1–0, and I brought Macca on,' recalls Toshack. 'He came on and made the difference. We scored twice towards the end and it was a great result – the first time Real Madrid had won in Mallorca.' After that, whenever he played, he scored – in a friendly against AC Milan ('Now his *ampollas* aren't hurting!' trilled one headline), in the game against Numancia, and with a great effort against Athletic Bilbao when he picked up the ball on the right, jinked around defender after defender, played it off to Savio before sprinting forward, arm outstretched to demand the quick return ball, which he then lashed into the top right-hand corner of the net. 'It was a super goal,' said Toshack. 'Again, he made a difference. After an hour with ten men we ended up with a 2–2 draw. I recall that game clearly because Macca had a very good match and I had thrown Iker Casillas into the side for his debut.' Commentators made much of the Englishman who had shone against the club, in the heart of the Basque country, who are considered a throwback to the British influence on the game's introduction a hundred years ago. 'Sir Macca' and 'Big Mac!' were typical headlines for the player consistently picking up *AS*'s *el dandy* nominations for the most skilful player on the pitch. 'It was great to have scored at San Mamés, a notoriously difficult place, a typical English stadium as people kept saying to me. We came back after a 2–2 draw, and I was the club's top scorer,' he recalls with a hint of incredulity in his voice.

Before his move the English press had speculated about Real Madrid being overburdened with players of McManaman's ilk, implying he would find it impossible to win a regular role. However, he was soon ensconced on the right side of midfield. The previous season Seedorf had manned that flank in a stop-gap measure, but the Dutchman preferred a central role. 'Starting off by scoring goals relieves the pressure on you,' Steve reported in his *Telegraph* column. 'They are so quick to judge in the Bernabéu. You can sense it every time you touch the ball when you're new. It is a fantastic stadium, you feel you are there to put on a show – and it better be good. I guess it's the matador factor. And goals endear you to the crowd. Admittedly I am not going to score all the time, but if you're obviously trying then the fans appreciate that.'

In the first weeks, too, came Steve's first taste of Champions League action. In his response to playing Olympiakos, in Greece, you could register the depth of that pining for top-club competition he had spoken of before his move. 'It was exactly how European nights should be,' he enthused. 'A hostile atmosphere, a loud and vociferous crowd throwing all sorts of rubbish onto the pitch. Despite the buffer zone of a running track around the perimeter, missiles still reached the pitch when we were taking corners. A couple of times the game was held up. If you needed reminding, it makes you realise what is at stake in top-level European competition.' In the 3–3 draw, he put in another creditable performance, hitting the post and forcing an excellent save from the goalkeeper. 'As long as I keep going like this I'll be pleased,' he said. *Marca* went into gushing overdrive: 'He has become the most talked-about player and shone with his own inner light in a team weighed down with stars.'

Come October, though, the momentum was lost. McManaman tore a thigh muscle an hour into the Champions League game against Porto. 'It's the first time I've had a problem with my leg muscles. In fact, it's the first time I've been aware I had leg muscles, I thought I was just skin and bone,' he said wryly. The injury ruled him out for six weeks, which included the showcase domestic games – the *gran clásico* clash between Barcelona and Real Madrid, and *el derby* against Atlético. It also prevented him from participating in the England set-up during the cliff-hanging European Championship qualifiers. That pained Steve. He had recently broken his international duck, scoring twice against Luxembourg at Wembley. Already conscious of a potential 'out of sight, out of mind' syndrome, he was determined to continue his involvement with England. Nor did he want to become a peripheral injured figure at his new club. 'I felt I'd started very well, then bosh, this injury, it was unbelievably frustrating. I was isolated from the action, but not from the company. I'd go into the training ground and see the lads every day because the physio's room is part of the open-plan dressing room. When they'd go out to train, I'd be lying on the treatment table. Jesús, the main physio, spoke English well which was great as my Spanish didn't stretch to anatomy and the various nuances of "ow!" I got to know him and the other physios, Antonio and Emilio, well. I still call them for a chat.'

Steve was back to feature in a game against the third Madrid club, Rayo Vallecano, and fly home fleetingly for Lee Dixon's testimonial. However, during an England training session before the frenzied, hyped-up Lionhearts v. Bravehearts European Championship play-off against Scotland, a twinge in the same thigh sent McManaman back to the treatment table for a further six or seven weeks. Personal disappointment coincided with Real Madrid going through a horrible patch. The team endured humiliating league defeats – 3–1 at Atlético, where Jimmy Floyd Hasselbaink scored a couple, and, embarrassingly, 5–1 at home to Real Zaragoza, which prompted angry fans to sing, '*Nosotros encenderemos vuestros Ferraris*,' we will burn your Ferraris, as the scoreline recalled the utter humiliation twenty-five years earlier when a Johan Cruyff-fired Barcelona stifled Madrid 5–0, Real's worst ever home defeat. Injuries stacked up. The supporters continued to taunt the players – but McManaman's name was not associated with any of the mess. He was not on a losing Real Madrid side until April, which made him something of a talisman to the Spanish press. 'It was weird because when we were getting beaten, and I was still getting fit again after my injury, there'd be times when I'd be training on my own. After the 5–1 defeat, the team came out and the fans shouted obscenities and I'd jog past by myself and they would all cheer me, clap and ask when I was back. Football is so fickle. You win two games and everyone is happy again. It's that, and more so, in Spain. Toshack was unlucky. He had got the team pretty much as he wanted it, but the injury list was crazy. The picture was replicated among all three Spanish teams in the Champions League.

We were all doing well there [at least until Valencia played Manchester United], but struggling in the league. In November, we lost all but one league game and Barcelona lost all of theirs.'

Toshack was on his way out. In the summer he had urged the club to buy a new goalkeeper, but the club had ignored his request. Ten matches into the new season and he had called upon three goalkeepers. After blunders by Albano Bizzarri had given Rayo Vallecano a 2–0 lead in a November league game, from which Real battled back to reclaim 3–2, Toshack pointed out: 'We are in trouble if our defence and keepers keep making mistakes.' The goalkeeping coach took offence, even though the Argentine Bizzarri, standing in for injured German first-choice Bodo Illgner, had made many glaring mistakes in big games. Asked by President Lorenzo Sanz to retract that criticism, Toshack asserted his authority to speak out as the person in charge of the team by translating an English idiom into grammatically sound, but nonsensical, Castilian: 'There's more chance of seeing a pig flying over the Bernabéu than me retracting my words.' There being no such equivalent figure of speech in Spanish, a slapstick misunderstanding ensued (not encouraging for observers in the early stages of learning the language: speak it fluently, and it is still possible to be catastrophically misinterpreted). Sanz, incensed at being linked with the image of a pig (the front page of *Marca* showed a cartoon of a pink-winged pig fluttering above the stadium), summoned Toshack to verify his statement. Toshack said he had indeed used that expression. Unamused, Sanz had his secretary type up the Welshman's resignation letter.

The treatment of Toshack showed where the bullets come from. Club observers argue that the 'flying pigs' saga was merely an excuse to dismiss the coach and create a scapegoat. Toshack was known to be fond of idioms translated into Spanish – the media had learned to smile at the mention of 'headless chickens', 'water off a duck's back' and the ball being 'a hot potato'. Real Madrid had won two games in four days, both away from home: they had won 1–0 in Norway, without Raúl and Morientes, playing five or six reserves to go top of the Champions League group; and they had come back from a two-goal deficit to beat Rayo Vallecano with ten men. Toshack had rid the dressing room of its so-called bad apples, the foreign stars who had lost their discipline after the 1998 European Cup triumph. And, in an unbelievable stroke of fortune – 'it was an accident really', he says – he had discovered the depth of Iker Casillas's talent. The goalkeeping situation was suddenly resolved. But just when Toshack had a solid dressing room to rally and build on, he was out.

There was speculation that Jorge Valdano, the former Real Madrid striker who captained Argentina's World Cup-winning side in 1986, would return for another spell as manager. In the meantime, for the third time in his coaching career, Vicente Del Bosque, a loyal backroom club man who oversaw Real Madrid's youth squad, quietly stepped in to the breach as temporary head coach. Steve, still frustrated on the treatment table, made a statement that would be unbelievable if applied to any other club (except, perhaps, Atlético). 'Whoever the new manager is, it won't affect the players at all – they've had so many managers over the last couple of years.'

Whether it was Del Bosque's calm, understated presence, or the fact that injuries cleared up, or the fact that Seedorf, the last of the so-called bad apples, had decamped to Inter Milan, the change of management would soon bring about a swing in fortunes. But first there was the inaugural World Club Cup Championship, the one that caused so much controversy in England when Manchester United were coerced into participation instead of defending the FA Cup. Real should have done better. They finished a lacklustre fourth and also had three players, Guti, Roberto Carlos and Christian Karembeu, sent off in the group game against Raja Casablanca. Anelka missed a crucial penalty against Corinthians and suffered a knee injury. Steve missed a penalty in the third place shoot-out. 'The trip to Brazil was a weird disruption to the season. It was farcical from beginning to end,' he says. 'In order to go there, and collect another trophy for the greater glory of the club et cetera, we were given a bye to the quarter-finals of the Spanish Cup. Which is mad. How can you get a bye to the last eight of a cup competition? That's the sort of allowance that gets made for Real Madrid. That dispensation allowed us to travel to

Brazil for a couple of weeks. It was a long, long journey. We were based in São Paulo and it either poured down with rain or was horrendously humid. Against Necaxa it was almost impossible to breathe. There was no atmosphere at the games. We were playing to near-empty stadiums. Spanish and British TV wanted the kick-off times to suit their schedules so we played in the worst heat of the day. It was the strangest competition. Roberto Carlos is from São Paulo but there was no chance of him showing his European teammates around his home town – the minute we landed, he was off like a shot with his friends. Most of them anyway. Two others, two strange fellas, used to come around trying to sell us watches. One was a little fella called Banana, honest to God. He looked like the fella from *Fantasy Island* and he'd unravel this bag of Rolexes and leave us little notes at the hotel desk. Geremi bought one; I didn't. We were drowning in rain in São Paulo, but on the television, we kept seeing the Manchester United lads on the beach in Rio de Janeiro, sunbathing all in a row. As a tournament, it was a disaster for us. We finished fourth – it was all a waste of time, to be honest. Our backroom staff have different memories, though, because when we moved to Rio, and were in the same hotel as Man U, a lot of friendships were forged. I remember one night we were all having a drink in the hotel bar – Paddy Crerand with a group of Man U people and me with Raúl, Chendo (a former Real star who now works at the club) and some of our physios. We were all singing footie songs, all the crazy Real Madrid ones as Paddy and his lot were blasting out the Man U ones. It was a great night, and when the two clubs met in the Champions League quarter-finals a few months later, and again in 2002, those friendships were renewed.

'When we came back we were down to seventeenth in the league because we had missed games. Before going to Brazil we were mid-table, maybe tenth. When we returned we were near the bottom. Then we had to play eleven games in twenty-five days, something completely ridiculous . . . but the strange thing was, we came back and we were fantastic. We shot up the table, everything seemed to click, the team gelled. It was like a new pre-season, an exercise in living together, helping us bond as a unit. Before Brazil, even in the Champions League games we had been hammered. We were beaten by Bayern Munich in both group games, home and away. We came back from Brazil and suddenly – though we still had injuries, Sanchís was out, Hierro was out – every game we played was fantastic, every minute was thoroughly enjoyable. There was an incredible spirit about the team.'

The end of the stuttering period came when Real Madrid scraped through their Champions League group to reach the quarter-finals. 'We had to go to Rosenberg and get a result,' recalls Steve. 'It was freezing, snow everywhere, horrible Norwegian weather. We had Aganzo Mendez, a young kid of nineteen, playing up front with Raúl – again we were struggling with injuries – and we were 1–0 up. Then Guti was sent off, and we had to play sixty minutes with ten men. We were under the cosh. They had John Carew up front, the six-foot seven-inches fella, and they were lumping the ball up to him. We were battling to hold on. But once through, we were a transformed team.'

As Del Bosque concedes, it was a season of two halves. 'It was a case of Before and After the World Club Cup Championship, and Macca was a little bit like a man with a Before and After too, in the sense that with that unlucky injury in the autumn he'd struggled to make an impact. I think the thigh-muscle injury was a strange experience for him because he is such a fit lad. Afterwards we moved him a little more towards the centre of midfield to help out Redondo. Tactically, he was the man who helped Redondo enormously. They had an excellent understanding, and with that partnership we arrived at the team as we ideally wanted it. Up to that point everything had been very grey, almost like we hadn't got a team, but that changed from February or March onwards, and it had a lot to do with the return to form of Steve McManaman alongside Fernando Redondo in midfield.'

It was as if someone had swept a magnet under a tray of iron filings. Real Madrid bristled with creativity with Redondo as chief conductor. 'It worked because Redondo was a fixed reference point, getting the ball, and Macca did what he does: he enjoyed himself getting between lines, running all over the place,' recalls Iván Helguera. 'When the team was in trouble, you'd give the ball to Macca because he was always there to support, on one wing or the other, he always had an option. It's very like Zidane now. Macca doesn't have as much ability as Zidane but he creates discomfort, confusion in the other team because he is all over the place.' In Salgado's view, the confidence Del Bosque showed in Steve was crucial. 'Del Bosque was a manager who really liked Macca in any position. He defined Steve as a player who is, simply, very good at football, who uses his intelligence to play in any situation. In following seasons, even though on lots of occasions he couldn't call on him [because of the unwritten pecking order enforced by the *galácticos* philosophy], he wanted Macca.'

One common misconception of Del Bosque is that he was as avuncular in his stewardship of his stars as he is in manner. A big, endearingly gentle-mannered man, with a baggy face, serious eyes and heavy moustache, he looks every inch the typical tapas-bar owner doling out the expected fare without a flicker of emotion. But as a head coach he consciously set out first and foremost – to borrow his favourite phrase – to reintroduce basic values to dressing-room life. Allergic to the limelight, Del Bosque, who comes from a family of railway trade unionists, talks in terms of a collective backroom team effort. 'When I was appointed temporary coach we tried to create a feeling of harmony in the dressing room, a stable, healthy atmosphere where everyone got on well. I'm not saying it wasn't like that before, but we did try to "humanise" the set-up,' he explained four years later, sitting in his local cafe bar, Helen's, which boasts a window seat dedicated to Alfredo di Stéfano. Typically modest, Del Bosque shunned that for a less prominent seat in the corner at the back. 'Our idea was that the dressing room should shed its image of having too many "stars" and be more down to earth, made up of people who play football for a living, get on well with each other, and are unaffected by fame. It proved successful because the players understood what we were doing. Karembeu was excellent, Seedorf was magnificent, Redondo was a lovely person and a natural leader, Raúl . . . I could go on. They are all very courteous, real gentlemen. Macca was always an extremely spontaneous and natural leader. Some players are leaders because of their global superstar status – like Zidane, Figo or Ronaldo – and some are more "off the cuff" leaders. Macca was great for us in the dressing room, and Geremi too. They were both players who could get everyone fired up, who brought together the various groups within the dressing room, both the youngsters and the established stars. Macca, in particular, was really important in this. He never had any problems with anyone, whether it was the physio, the kit man, the manager, his teammates . . . never! He's an extremely honest person. Without a doubt, a valuable person to have in your dressing room.'

'I got the sense Del Bosque understood me, personally, very well,' acknowledges Steve. 'He has a very good brain in assessing what kind of footballers his players are, what kind of people we are, how we all work together. He is scrupulously fair-minded. I doubt even Raúl, Guti or Iker Casillas, who he had worked with as schoolboys, have the feeling he is looking after them individually, protectively or trying to motivate them particularly. He looks at us in terms of how we work together. He is not at all self-promoting. You see some managers winning things and shouting from the rooftops. He doesn't, and that is another reason why he's a wonderful fella. The Real Madrid job is the hardest job in the whole world. In reality, it's out of your own hands, isn't it? You pray that the football team are good, that's all you can do. The skill is in trying to get the balance with all the strong personalities. You can't go round telling Raúl or Roberto Carlos, Redondo or Hierro to do this and do that, because it won't work. You'll get sacked. It's all about balance. His skill is in subtly weighing up how the team could tick. He tried hard to make everyone feel they had a special role.'

In one aspect Del Bosque's subtlety was such that Steve did not realise he had been entrusted with a special role. Today, when the former manager considers McManaman's contribution in that 1999–2000 season, he is quick to bring up the 'important issue' of easing Nicolas Anelka towards acceptance. 'Steve played an outstanding role with all his playmaking qualities on the pitch, but off it he was invaluable in helping us to improve our relationship with Nicolas. It was Macca's character and personality that gradually helped Nicolas himself feel more a part of the team.' This was crucial, as it was the surly French striker's timely return and potent contribution – a semi-final goal at home and, another, away in Munich, where Madrid have never beaten their snarling rivals – that ensured Real Madrid reached the Champions League final. Because of their domestic problems, failure to make the final would have meant they would not qualify for the following year's competition. The socially reconstituted Anelka averted disaster.

Lorenzo Sanz had bought Anelka in September for £23m, describing the purchase as 'a beautiful madness' (to Arsenal fans, it was 'good riddance, great fee'). There followed plenty of madness, and little beauty, as the Frenchman failed to fit into the dressing room. A moody prima donna, a rebel with a materialistic cause, a paranoid self-obsessed sulker: the twenty-one-year-old's undoubted talent was imprisoned by his bad reputation. His brothers Claude and Didier, who acted as his agents, did nothing to alleviate the off-pitch issues. 'Life is a jungle,' declared Claude. 'If many people say we are parasites, and make trouble – it's up to us.' Within days of turning up, Anelka crudely attempted to promote his personal sponsor Puma by wearing a chain and pendant showing the company's logo at a time when Real Madrid were desperate to keep their kit sponsors Adidas happy. He soon found himself alienated. He did not bother trying to communicate, preferring the company of his Sony PlayStation. The players most threatened by his arrival were forwards Raúl and Morientes, both at the Spanish heart of the squad. Anelka was not going to earn the respect of his teammates easily, yet his price tag ensured his name was always on the team sheet. Desperate to prove himself after a fractious end to his stint at Arsenal, he complained self-righteously to the press about his treatment. Every time a microphone was held under his nose he would say the Spanish players didn't pass to him. In protest against Del Bosque's tactics, he started missing training. 'In reality he made a rod for his own back,' says Steve. Anelka was so critical of his teammates that the club suspended him for forty-five days, during which he had to train by himself. He returned at a time when injuries meant the team had a competitive, though not an emotional, need for his presence. Opening his locker on his first day back, it was like a scene from an American high-school TV drama: piqueishly some of his teammates had removed all his belongings. McManaman, genial to everyone, helped establish an entente cordiale, as Helguera – keen to disassociate himself from 'the Spanish players' – testifies. 'I think Del Bosque hoped that Anelka would be as outgoing, and keen to integrate himself as Steve,' he says. 'When the situation became impossible, he encouraged Steve as a sort of link in communciations, a go-between. I think what he hoped was that some of Steve's personality would rub off on to Anelka.'

Up to a point, it did, recalls Raúl. 'Anelka didn't adapt. There wasn't much communication between him and the others. Macca, who had a greater ability to transmit ideas, became the reference point to bring people together. And, in the end, it worked. Macca's role was crucial because Anelka was important for us in winning the eighth European Cup.'

'It was difficult for Nicolas because the Spanish lads didn't take to him,' concedes Steve. 'I tried to help by treating him like I treated everyone else. I had only been there two months before he arrived. He was quiet, very shy and only spoke French. There was an overall stink about the way the deal was done. Arsenal caused a furore about agents meeting behind backs in London. Details were leaked about how much money Nicolas's brothers got. It was nasty – not the blaze of publicity you want to arrive with. But he'd played in the Premiership. It was natural to go and ask him about Arsenal players, and chat about how he was settling in. He was only twenty-one years old and he'd been to three big clubs in as many years. Three countries, three languages. It is hard, and he is an introverted personality. I wasn't going to ignore him.'

Del Bosque's subtle manoeuvrings helped Anelka, and thus

helped Real Madrid gain attacking potency. Who would have thought that after all the censure, fans would gather one weekday night at the Cibeles statue, between Champions League semi-final and final, simply to sing Anelka's praises? The head coach's faith in McManaman gave the Englishman another signal that he had truly integrated as a Real Madrid player.

Rather like finding John Toshack was his first manager, drawing Manchester United in the quarter-finals of the Champions League was a timely link with the familiar. The night of 5 April 2000 would not only be the first time Steve had laced his boots in anger to play an English side since leaving Liverpool, it was an opportunity to take stock, and to catch up with family and friends he had missed. 'I'm still trying to accept the fact I can't jump in my car and drive round their houses,' he said. His Spanish was developing well, but not fluently enough yet to have established mobile-phone relationships with teammates. He and Victoria had progressed beyond the stage of going moo, moo or oink, oink in restaurants to clarify the meat on offer on a menu, as they had been forced to do in the smart hush of one establishment – much to the mirth of fellow diners – when celebrating Victoria's call to the Bar. Getting by is one thing, enjoying an easy chat another. For the refreshing joy of speaking without mentally translating it first, they socialised occasionally with Mark Draper, the former Aston Villa midfielder who spent a few months at Rayo Vallecano. If Steve wanted a good chat he would call his mates from Liverpool, or Paula and Karen, the receptionists at Anfield, or Anne and Paula, the ladies who cooked at Liverpool's Melwood training ground, or Sheila, the manager's long-serving PA. 'My confidence in the language is still subject to fluctuation,' he agreed. 'You learn the basics but Spaniards speak very quickly, and there are different dialects, and lots of slang. One minute you think you've got it, the next you feel like you're on another planet.'

Even Victoria, who picks up languages easily, had her problems. 'A carpenter and his assistant came to build a cupboard and some drawers,' she recalls. 'They were typical Spanish workmen, small, fat, cigarettes dangling from their mouths, ash going everywhere. I was speaking well by then, so I was chatting away, then I thought I'd get down to business and very confidently announced that what I'd really like is two big *cojones*, drawers, and I emphasised the size with my hands. The carpenter looked appalled, then his assistant burst out laughing. I should have said *cajones* – *cojones* is slang for testicles. It was just one vowel wrong . . .'

Steve was desperate to play against United, but a battered calf, suffered against Real Sociedad in San Sebastian at the weekend, threatened to sideline him. Fortunately, Del Bosque was determined to deploy him. 'Macca was an important player for that night because the Manchester United supporters saw him as their former local rival! And vice versa. It was a conscious decision to put him in even though he was returning from a slight injury,' Del Bosque confirmed. 'Besides, Macca's always been a lucky player for us, and that's important. He's got a very professional big-game temperament, and a way of putting things in perspective and taking things in his stride. He's exceptionally level-headed.'

Manchester United arrived in Madrid having battered West Ham 7–1 a few days before; Real Madrid, on the other hand, came into the encounter after another unconvincing league performance, a 1–1 draw against Real Sociedad, a scoreline which remained respectable thanks to the brilliance of goalkeeper Iker Casillas, still only eighteen. Del Bosque's switch to playing five at the back was much commented upon. Míchel Salgado and Roberto Carlos were to push on adventurously as ever, right and left, with Aitor Karanka, Iván Campo and Iván Helguera standing firm in the middle of the defence; Redondo and McManaman controlling play in the centre, Savio Bortolini in front of them, with Fernando Morientes and Raúl the strikers. Ever modest, Del Bosque describes his tactics in the first-person plural: 'We were afraid that the width Beckham and Giggs provided could open us up, so we went five at the back. Of course, it was not our usual formation but on that occasion it was ideal. It wasn't a system we would employ for ever – we kept it until the final, yes – but the following season we went back to our more tried and tested formation.'

Steve cites 'our famous back five' as the perfect example of Del Bosque's underappreciated tactical flexibility. 'He made us play in a formation we hadn't played in before. The players who played there hadn't played much football that year, or in their positions. Yet it worked. The players didn't moan, they played very well, and his tactic brought great success. Iván Campo probably didn't play a lot of football that year, yet in the quarter-finals, semi-finals and the final of the Champions League, he was outstanding. The same with Karanka. That is the thing, finding the right balance using players who may not have been playing particularly well, but were needed when the likes of Hierro and Sanchís were injured, and were happy to slot into a role. It caused comment because it had a makeshift feel about it. Because we had barely scraped through the group stage, we were the underdogs – so much so that *Marca*'s front cover repeated the line, "We're not scared of Manchester", over and over, in a mantra of self-convincing. United were the defending champions. Dominant from the start of their campaign, they were undeniably favourites. It was always going to be an intense test for us and we were united by that challenge. That spirit fired us up, as individuals and as a team.'

The first leg was at the Bernabéu. The atmosphere in both cities was stomach-churningly electric, recalling the earliest encounter between these two teams in the competition, in the 1956–57 semi-final. More than a hundred and twenty-five thousand people had packed the Chamartín Stadium when José Villalonga's team prepared to defend their inaugural European Cup victory. Matt Busby fielded young David Pegg and Eddie Colman, though it was touch and go, as both had fallen sick through nervous excitement. 'I didn't think I would be able to play them,' Busby said later. 'But eventually we went to the field with them, but it was quite an occasion for anyone in Madrid that day, let alone young players.' Bobby Charlton, then a United nineteen-year-old reserve, was an awed face in the crowd. 'I was right up in the gods, way above the pitch, and to be honest I was terribly pleased I wasn't playing. I saw di Stefano and these others, and I thought to myself, these people just aren't human. It's not the sort of game I've been taught.' Busby had claimed that United would win easily; the Spanish were delighted to prove him wrong.

Back in April 2000, Steve recalls a game in which both sides acquitted themselves well. 'Mark Bosnich was inspired – Man of the Match. He saved great efforts from Savio, Salgado, Raúl, Morientes, Roberto Carlos and Baljic. I had several chances, and should have scored late on in the game, but nothing was going to beat Bosnich that night. It ended 0–0, but we had performed well, the fans had been entertained, and of course United were then favourites to win at home. I remember it was considered almost a certainty that United would win, but I genuinely fancied our chances. I always enjoy playing against United. Their attacking philosophy, countering ours, means you can find yourself with lots of space on the pitch, with lots of time on the ball. The football is free-flowing. They are fun games, they always are. To look forward to playing them in a Real Madrid shirt added an extra buzz for me. They always give you chances, just as Real Madrid always give the opposition chances. I knew it would be a great game.'

19 April, Old Trafford. 'Coming over to England was crazy. It wasn't merely the media demands, I had friends who wanted tickets, people I hardly knew who wanted tickets, family I wanted to see. Robbie Fowler came down to the hotel the night before the game. We have dinner at nine o'clock the night before a game, but for an hour beforehand the lads would always have a few drinks. Robbie came round to the Marriott at Worsley Park with my sister Karen and some friends. He went to reception and someone told him I was at the bar. When he walked in he saw about fifteen of our players, and the management staff, sitting down with pints of lager in front of them. Of course in Spain if you ask for a lager, you get a little glass or a bottle, but someone had been up to the bar and ordered lager in pidgin English and got all these pints . . . He walked in, the day before we were playing the biggest game against Manchester United, and all the lads were staring into huge pints of lager. He couldn't believe it. We obviously played very well against Man United, and

when Robbie went back to Liverpool, they were having a squad meeting and one of the coaches said, "Right, Robbie, tell us, what were Real Madrid like, how do they prepare?" And deadpan Robbie said, "They all drink massive pints of lager" – and the coach paused, then said, "Well, they're not doing very well in their league, are they?"

'It was a huge, huge game. To win it 3–2 and get to the semi-final was the most important thing. Of course it was gratifying for me to play well, but as a Liverpool lad I was thrilled. We'd knocked out Manchester United, the defending champions!'

Salgado rates this game for himself, and maybe for the fans, the most *bonito*, beautiful, game in the European Cup. 'That night we were two great, great teams. For Macca, being from Liverpool, I think that was his most beautiful moment for Real Madrid. From then on he gained even more in confidence.'

For a Spanish lad, the injured captain Manolo Sanchís, the game had special resonance too. Though he sat out the match on the bench, he took familial pleasure in despatching United from the competition. Back in 1968, the year United went on to win the European Cup against Benfica at Wembley, Manolo Sanchís Sr., as tenacious a defender as his son, played and marked George Best. United had been 3–1 down at half-time but, in a decisive six minutes in the second half, they scored twice. It was Best who jinked past Sanchís and provided the cross from which the unlikeliest of scorers – Bill Foulkes – claimed the equaliser that took the English club through to the final on aggregate. Paddy Crerand expressed incredulity at Foulkes's positioning. 'I know people have talked about providence being involved, about fate evening things out for what happened to the club 10 years earlier. You cannot know about things like that. What I do know is that Nobby Stiles put a big note in the collection when he went to mass on the morning of the match. Maybe he sold his soul. Or maybe Someone decided we should win.' His reference to Roman Catholic practice within an English team conjured another tiny bond to add to the shared experience that was starting to build between these two giant clubs.

'It is one of those games you remember flashes of . . . Roy Keane's own goal after twenty minutes . . . Ryan Giggs fizzing at the centre of United's surges forward . . . the crowd going "NOOOOOooo" as Cole misses after a Beckham cross . . . me breaking down the wing and passing to Raúl who scores our second. Everyone remembers Redondo's brilliant backheel outwitting Henning Berg, from which Raúl scores again. Beckham gets one back . . . then I foul Roy Keane in the box and give a penalty away. I jump in when I shouldn't have, in the eighty-ninth minute, and that brought them back in it so there was a frenzied three minutes of additional time. I remember we got clapped off, I bowed to all the Man United fans who were giving me the fingers-up, of course. Alex Ferguson was doing his press conference, saying Redondo's ball-winning abilities were such he must "have a magnet down his pants". I changed quickly and went to the players' lounge. Roberto Carlos was about to get on the bus, but he came and had a drink with Robbie and a few of my mates – quite amusing as his English is non-existent. It became very boisterous, we were feeling quite cocky. We celebrated all the way home, chatting, drinking, partying on bus, plane and bus again. At Madrid airport there were loads of people to greet us even though it was about 4am – you'd have thought we'd won the trophy already. I'll never forget that reception.'

With the defending champions out, it was roll on the previous season's beaten finalists, Bayern Munich, for the continuation of one of Europe's tetchiest grudge matches. Out came all the 'beauty against the beast' clichés for this rare cross-border rivalry that started in the 1976 European Cup semi-final when a Madrid fan attacked the referee and Gerd Muller. If the purists in Spain have little respect for the snarling Teutonic 'kick-and-rush' game, conversely, for Bayern, Real Madrid are poseurs, clowns, purveyors of reckless art-for-art's-sake quality. Another arch confrontation loomed but, for this semi-final, Anelka was back. He had apologised to club officials early in his exile, but the club were adamant he had to serve his forty-five-day ban, even though Savio and Morientes were struggling with ankle and toe injuries. He came on during a Spanish Cup tie against

Espanyol, started and won a penalty in a league game against third-placed Zaragoza . . . soon the fans would adore him.

'Again, the semi-finals were excellent games,' says Steve. 'Bayern had hammered us in the group stage so it was a measure of our improvement that we came through so strongly. At home we played ever so well. Nicolas scored a goal in the fourth minute, which had the stadium buzzing and meant his teammates had to go and hug him! Before half-time we were 2–0 up courtesy of a Jens Jeremies own goal. We then went to Germany knowing that if we got a goal that would be it, because we'd restricted them to nil. The Olympic Stadium is an awesome arena; the pitch is sunk deep below ground level, the noise swirls around you. It's not hostile, but it's a heated, edgy atmosphere.

'They scored very early on, after eleven minutes, from a cross to the far post that went bouncing all over the place . . . Carsten Jancker, the massive tall fella, was the scorer and he went, "Aaarrrggghh," celebrating right in my face. I thought then we were on for a bombardment, we were going to get thrashed, but twenty minutes later Nicolas scored a great header from a Savio cross, an absolutely crucial goal that made it 1–1. That was it then, we were cruising because they had to win 4–1. They scored again early in the second half, but after that we guarded possession. The referee was Graham Poll and we were under pressure, not crazy, but he booked me for fouling someone or wasting time. I was saying to him, "Hurry up and blow the whistle," laughing and joking. We ended up winning the tie quite comfortably. When the game goes that well, time speeds by. When you're leading by that margin, you're taking more chances, you have more time on the ball, you pick out your passes more creatively. I'll always remember it as fantastically enjoyable football. With Raúl, Morientes and Anelka up front, I was playing more of a pivotal controlling role with Redondo. In style and appearance we were chalk and cheese. He had the neatest hair cut in the world. He was very meticulous. He'd come into work absolutely immaculate. He'd have the jewelry on, cream everything, the short hair with that precise parting. He looked like he'd walked out of a fashion show.

The personnel situation dictated the positioning, but pairing me with Redondo, who was on stunning form, worked well. Off the pitch I wasn't that friendly with him to be honest, only because the Argentinian accent was well-nigh impossible for me at the time. But on the pitch we communicated well. I was comfortable on the ball, I didn't get flustered. I had never enjoyed myself more on the football pitch. I had always said there was more to my game than being a winger.'

As Matt Dickinson commented in the *Times*: 'Those who said Steve McManaman had gone to Real Madrid simply to line his pockets would be advised to stay clear of Paris on May 24. The Scouser will be laughing last and loudest.'

The Champions League final

24 May 2000

The inaugural decade of the Champions League has produced a cavalcade of glittering memories but, asked by UEFA to nominate the defining moment of the first ten years, there can be only one.

There have been magnificent matches to cherish, glorious highlights to replay, heroics to salute and dramatic finales at which to thrill. But when it comes down to the single split second of time, which crystallises all that the supreme competition in club football means, that moment belongs to Steve McManaman. It came, as if preordained, in the first Champions League final of the Millennium, on the warm damp evening of Wednesday, May 24, 2000 in the Stade de France. It happened so fast that not even the scorer of that goal of goals saw it. Steve McManaman admits he shut his eyes as he fired the shot, which rang out from Paris and reverberated around the world. 'I closed my eyes as usual,' he says of his volleyed strike of genius at Valencia's half-clearance of a Roberto Carlos throw. By the time he opened them again he had made his indelible footprint in history with what he recognised instantly as 'the greatest moment of my life'. It was an instant to last for all football time. It came in the 67th minute. Real Madrid were leading 1–0 through Fernando Morientes and Raúl was to make it 3–0 before the finish. But it was McManaman's goal, which helped the vaulting traditions of Real to leap through the turn of the century.

What made it so thoroughly contemporary was that the legacy of the Spanish aristocrats of the European Cup should be given renewed life by a son of the mother country of the game. England's footballers had been the last and the most reluctant to join the free movement of players around the continent. As the first English player to win club football's supreme prize with a foreign club, McManaman broke down the final barriers and made the European family of football complete.

By doing so in such stunning fashion, Liverpool's ambassador to the Spanish League hoped to establish himself as a force majeure in England's European championship team. That ambition was not to be realised but he has one huge distinction, which no national team manager can ever take away from him: the McManaman moment, which the beautiful game will never forget.

—Jeff Powell in 'Ten Years of UEFA Champions League'

For almost eight months of the 1999–2000 season, the notion that Real Madrid would lift the European Cup for a record eighth time was almost inconceivable. Persistent rumours that the club's estimated £170m debts, if unresolved, would preclude them from future European competition, stories of boardroom strife, taunts from fans at the so-called Ferrari boys, the run of unacceptable results under John Toshack, a dressing-room split over the Anelka saga, the drafting in of a caretaker manager . . . no one could harbour the dream that the team variously captained that year by Manolo Sanchís, Fernando Hierro and Fernando Redondo would attain the highest goal in club football. Real Madrid had been on their knees: 'Meltdown in Madrid', 'Bernabéu Blues' screeched typical early spring headlines. 'We had been down to seventeenth in the league. We'd had fans shouting obscenities,' recalls Steve. 'Imagine if we had lost that game in the snow in bloody Norway and not progressed through to the last eight in the Champions League! We'd have got back and they'd have shot us.'

The *séptima* – Madrid's seventh European Cup, won two years earlier in Amsterdam – was symbolically a bigger game. Until then, the club had not claimed their beloved trophy since 1966: never on colour television, as Barcelona fans liked to gloat (not that you needed colour to see white ribbons decking the trophy, was the *madridista* riposte). Since the era when Real Madrid had won the first five successive European Cups with the legendary collection of cracks, Alfredo di Stéfano, Raymond Kopa, Paco Gento and Ferenc Puskás, the *madridistas* had watched while Barcelona, the detested Catalunyans, had grown into the exciting glamour team who attracted the world's best players. The skills of Johan Cuyff, Maradona, Romario and Rivaldo were showcased in blue and burgundy striped shirts. Barça had not just been racking up consecutive league championships, they even won the European Cup, when Ronald Koeman's free kick sealed the 1992 final at Wembley. More galling still, they billed themselves the Dream Team. The *séptima* redressed that. It launched the sale of thousands of replica shirts in the name of Pedrag Mijatovic. The Yugoslav's simple finish decided the 1998 final and made him only the ninth player to score for Real Madrid in a victorious European Cup final, after di Stéfano, Héctor Rial, Marquitos, Gento, Mateos, Puskás, Amancio Amaro and Serena. After thirty-two agonising years, the European Cup had come home. Madrid are a club with an obsession, and with that victory over Juventus, club loyalists Fernando Hierro and Manolo Sanchís felt purged of a troubling fixation. Hierro rates the minute he was entitled to kiss that huge piece of silverware in 1998 as his greatest moment on a football pitch. 'It was unforgettable,' marvels Raúl. 'The fans' reaction was amazing, wonderful.'

So with a potential *octava* to be won in the contest with Valencia, Real Madrid were back in the business of making history. It was the first Champions League final between two clubs from the same country. Iker Casillas, born the week before Del Bosque played on the losing side against Liverpool in the 1981 European Cup final held in the same city, was the youngest goalkeeper ever to play in a final. Casillas, a *Madrileño* with a Basque first name, had made his first team debut in September 1999 against Athletic Bilbao when Bodo Illgner was injured and Albano Bizzarri out of favour. Oliver Kahn had loftily said: 'I wouldn't play a kid in goal for Real Madrid.' But *el niño*, the kid, was not fazed. He never was. At the age of sixteen, and a member of the Real B team, he had been eating a sandwich during a school break when a member of Real's technical staff appeared and asked him to pack his bags: he could be playing in a Champions League game in Norway in forty-eight hours. 'Oh sure,' was his response. 'Must finish eating first.' The official convinced him he was not joking. Less than two years later John Toshack hailed him as 'a kid with the brain of an old man'. He still had fluffy hair, still came to train on the Metro or bus, still bore the brunt of the older players' jokes – 'He's very naive, gullible and probably doesn't have the wages of the other lads so we wind him up about his car,' chuckled Steve – but Casillas had claimed his shirt by the spring of 2000. 'Bodo was injured, Bizzarri made a lot of mistakes, they had to give the third-choice, very very young goalkeeper a go. And he was outstanding. That was it then, they had found a homegrown superstar. He had to play all the time. Against Manchester United he was excellent. Ditto Bayern Munich. It was an incredible season for him.'

Incredible, too, for Steve McManaman, the first Englishman to play for a foreign club in a European Cup final since Chris Waddle for Marseille in 1991. He was poised to achieve something that had eluded Waddle, Kevin Keegan at Hamburg, Laurie Cunningham at Real Madrid and Steve Archibald at Barcelona: namely, become the first Englishman to win this competition playing in a foreign team's colours. In the pre-match build-up, ITV viewers saw an uncharacteristically self-contained McManaman concede it was, it hardly needed saying, the biggest game of his career.

'You go into the trophy room at the Bernabéu and every European Cup victory is given the momentous, reverential treatment. Every goal, from every triumph, is replayed on a continual-play mechanism, with the commentators going mad each time. "Di Stéfano! Rial! Gento! Puskás!" It is hard to go in there now and match the result with the approach we took to achieve it – we were so relaxed it was ridiculous,' he recalls.

'You would never think we were preparing for the biggest game in club football in those three days before the final. There was a tremendous sense of calm, togetherness, and quiet excitement – even though we were up against a team we hadn't beaten in the league that year. Everywhere we went there were hundreds of Real Madrid people all hugging and kissing, the way the Spanish do. Roberto Carlos was always being collared by old fellas. He would diplomatically listen to their advice, speak down their mobile phones to give their friends a thrill. Del Bosque seemed happy, and proud I think that the season had turned around this way. That is when the history of the club helps. At some points in the season the expectation of success weighs down on you as players; but once you've reached a big final by playing consummately well, the expectation becomes less a pressure, more a feeling that we're where we should be. All we had to do was go out and play football the way we'd been playing football. For me, personally, I was taking a massive step up in my career. For the club, they'd been at this stage so many times before. History says the trophy is theirs, almost by divine right. It is always said the European Cup can find its way to Madrid by itself as if it has an in-built satellite-navigation system. You get a sense sometimes of how things might turn out, and I knew – or I suppose I just really, really hoped – that night in Paris was going to be special. Our team spirit was undentable. I flew out eighteen friends and members of my family to share the occasion with me. All those months agonising about moving abroad, those months of trying to get into the culture and learn the language, and there I was, lining up to play in a European Cup final at the end of my first season. It was unbelievable.

'I remember thoroughly enjoying the preparation and build-up. It is incredible how carefree we were. On the Sunday beforehand, for instance – May 21 – we were due to report at the stadium by midday. It felt like dawn. Outside the streets were dead quiet. You could hear birdsong, not the traffic which is Europe's worst noise pollution. A few diehard fans hovered around Gate 50. Roberto Carlos arrived late, wagging a finger in jest at stadium staff. Inside, we all changed for a light training session. Campo, Redondo and myself were messing around as we jogged out on to the pitch. Casillas, nineteen years and one day old, was rolling on the ground doing torturous goalie stretches. Sanchís and Raúl emerged from the tunnel together, the senior captain and the golden boy. Del Bosque stood hands clasped behind his back on the sidelines and all we did was warm up gently – high-step jogging in one direction, loping back the other way. We didn't even break into a sweat, then it was back in to the showers. It was the last opportunity for all the stadium staff to wish the travelling squad good luck. Hierro got away only after a multitude of back-slapping embraces. I remember going to have a coffee with Christian Karembeu, who was in this crazy, all-white outfit. As usual he was walking about with a big grin, as if trying to sniff out some fun. He knew all the restaurants in town, he owned his own bar. He was like a mobile party. We signed autograph after autograph with everyone milling around as if this happened every day.

'On the Monday we had a morning session at the training ground which was like a cartoon workout. Everyone was laughing at each other's attempts at sit-ups and press-ups. Then we had piggy-back dodgem races. I'm carried by Roberto Carlos and we're crashing into Morientes and Savio. Campo is playing the goof, stomach-surfing on to the ground as if in celebration . . . but really to take his turn at press-ups. He completes two, and curls up laughing like a hyena. It is a closed training session – no press, no fans – but for some reason Salgado must have forgotten that, as he dashes on autopilot from dressing-room door to his car, mobile phone clamped to his ear. Casillas, who has only recently passed his driving test, drives off in a dusty old car with a nasty rattle. Someone ought to sort him out on the car front! Then by 4pm, we're back, wearing our team suits, though Roberto Carlos, not a lad whose physique sits easily in a suit, arrives in black T-shirt, carrying his shirt and jacket on a coat hanger. We're on our way to the airport. On the bus, players clap and sing along to trashy Spanish pop music. Redondo sings with mocking heartfelt emotion, Campo bangs his hands to add dodgy percussion and drives everyone mad blowing huge bubbles with his gum. We exit to a bank of TV cameras and go through the normal check-in-to-final-call procedures on an Iberia flight to Paris Charles de Gaulle. Our plane is swarming with fluorescent-jacketed airport workers, surely more than the plane's official allotted number. They've all found a spot of the plane to polish or inspect in order to wish us luck as we walk up the steps to board. It is a short flight, but Guti is fast asleep within minutes. Raúl, too. Karembeu, still sniffing out potential fun, throws his newspaper across three rows of seats then hurls himself down horizontally to hide from someone's outraged reaction. Helguera and Morientes have the trays down and play a game which involves positioning geometric shapes on a magnetic board. A shirt is passed around to sign. We probably sign our name a hundred times a week, but you could not accuse anyone of taking a slapdash approach. Everyone has their little trademark style. I always sign my name in full, then write "MACCA" above the signature. The call comes to fasten seat belts. "Ten minutes to landing," the captain informs his crew. It is forty-eight hours before we will land Real Madrid an eighth European Cup.

'At the Hôtel Trianon, outside Paris, we went for walks, played tennis, had the odd beer, video-ed each other mucking around, received messages from friends. It was like being on holiday.'

Tuesday 23 May 2000

Five-star hotels don't have flies on their walls, of course, but a rogue one would have heard laughter all day. In the morning the Spanish players – Sanchís, Hierro, Raúl, Morientes, Salgado, Helguera, Campo, Guti and Casillas – spend time talking on a terrace, lolling over white wrought-iron furniture, eating nuts and crackers, shaving off pieces of cheese from a platter, drinking beer from the bottle. Campo, mad curly hair everywhere, is chief buffoon, making helicopter and gun noises, which has everyone bent double. Strolling in front of the hotel, Karembeu informs Steve there are fans from Liverpool at the main entrance gates. He goes off to sign autographs and enjoy some Scouse banter. Everyone is so stress-free that while banks of the world media are gathered for a press conference – asking about Valencia's psychological strengths, the threat of Claudio López and Miguel-Angel Angulo's pace, the fact they are the form team above Madrid in the league – Raúl and Roberto Carlos giggle while their utterances are translated earnestly, line-by-line, into English. Over lunch a still-cherubic Emilio Butragueño, another embodiment of Madrid success from the eighties, greets players with his surprisingly deep voice. Casillas, eating an apple, is caught by a fan for a photograph. He smiles mid-chew, then resumes once the picture is taken. Stuck into a photo album somewhere in Spain is a picture of the goalkeeper, arm around a fan's shoulder, hand holding a red apple with one very large bite taken out.

Wednesday 24 May 2000

'No photo, no photo,' protests the security guard accompanying Roberto Carlos and fellow Brazilian Julio César on a walk around the hotel grounds.

'*Sí*, photo!' grins Roberto Carlos, giving two grateful teenage boys high fives as well.

Back inside the hotel, McManaman, Karembeu and Campo cut an incongruous scene, jesting as they somewhat preposterously pour themselves tea from ornate silver pots while sitting in tracksuits, under chandeliers, on a silk-upholstered Louis-something gilded sofa. Macca is receiving last-minute messages from Robbie Fowler and Jamie Redknapp. The England squad are together, ready to watch the game at Burnham Beeches.

The players retire for an afternoon sleep. A few hours later they gather downstairs, and then, in grey suits, white shirts and azure-blue ties, they file one by one onto the bus, suddenly intense, lost in deep thought. The bus journey is strangely hushed. At the Stade de France, an empty dressing room awaits them: kit neatly folded on the bench, boots, flip-flops and shin pads meticulously lined up underneath. Outside, Madrid fans greet them with twirling scarves and resonant songs, a sea of white shirts and purple scarves mingling happily with fellow Spaniards in orange wigs. The door, *Entrée Joueurs*, beckons. It is 7pm and players mill around a huge, echoey, soulless dressing room in front of beechwood lockers with louvred doors. The room is strange to them, it's as if they don't quite know what to do with themselves. Hierro looks around, hands in pockets, an air of excited expectancy in his upturned face, as if he was being shown around a property he just might buy.

Paris is overrun by Spaniards. A great exodus has crossed the Pyrenees for a football fiesta. Confusingly, neither club are in their traditional strip – Real Madrid in black, Valencia in orange – although Casillas's dark-blue kit fits the matador theme, with its bright yellow stand-up collar and braid-like stripes across the shoulders and down his sides. His white socks, pulled high, complete the effect. The stripping of normal identity adds to the tension. For ninety minutes, at a neutral venue, there is no hiding behind history for Real Madrid or behind the media-decreed label of 'form team' for Valencia. Lining up for the anthems, Steve stands between Morientes and Salgado. It is impossible to read any emotion. From face to face, each man looks blank, though it is fair to imagine nerves are being wrestled, even in the four Madrid players who had won *la séptima*: Redondo, Roberto Carlos, Morientes and Raúl. They harbour confidence, too: Raúl and Morientes's shirts both cover T-shirts bearing photographic images of their baby sons, Jorge and Fernandito, ready to thrust towards the world's cameras should they score. In that huge stadium – new but already historically infused with drama, especially for Roberto Carlos following the pre-match commotion over Ronaldo at the 1998 France v. Brazil World Cup final – superstars standing to attention are reduced to vulnerable human beings, tiny dots on an expanse of grass surrounded by eighty thousand buzzing spectators. 'Before we'd gone up to the pitch to play, we'd gone into a huddle in the dressing room,' recalls Steve. 'But words are immaterial at that stage. It didn't matter what Redondo, Sanchís, Hierro or Raúl said, it was just noise really to gee us up as a unit.'

Real Madrid line up with their back five as before, with McManaman and Redondo in the centre, Raúl in front, tucked behind Morientes and Anelka. 'That's very bold team play,' says Terry Venables admiringly on ITV. 'They've got three at the back to stop Claudio López and Angula, and the threat of their pace. They're saying, "If you want to defend, defend this . . . we'll give you Anelka and Morientes right up front, with Roberto Carlos and Salgado pushing up, and Raúl, Macca and Redondo in the centre. We're going to play, probe, put you under pressure. Yeah, you're going to break on us now and again, but we're set up." It's very bold. The thought process shows a winning mentality.'

A hushed rustle of anticipation circles the stadium like an aural Mexican Wave, then it is kick-off. From the first move it is evident television will have problems fitting in the action replays. It is mesmerising counter-attack after counter-attack. The full-backs persistently surge up the flanks with swashbuckling flair; Redondo and McManaman link beautifully with Raúl, the trio maintaining an elusive electricity on the pitch. Anelka's slipperiness and pace terrifies Valencia's defenders. With every move Campo is endearingly courageous; Karanka and Helguera, too, play out of their skins. After the season's off-field problems, the injuries, the early lack of unity, here are Del Bosque's men – his down-to-earth family of honest workers who play football for a living and get on well – conjuring a spine-chilling show of sublime creativity.

'On a magical night for Steve McManaman, Real Madrid and the European Cup, the watching world was treated to a magnificent display of attacking football at Stade de France,' wrote Henry Winter in the *Daily Telegraph*. 'Real, inspired by McManaman, who had never played better, were sensational, defensively disciplined, industrious, inventive and absolutely clinical in front of goal. It was fantastic to behold.'

Statisticians sum up the match thus:

39′: Morientes goal. A Roberto Carlos free kick (won by Anelka) finds Salgado on the right of the box. He passes out to Anelka who works hard to keep possession and taps back to Salgado, who gets in a toe and flicks the ball back across goal – a perfect present for the head of the flying Morientes. 1–0.

67′: McManaman goal. A Roberto Carlos throw-in is knocked away by defenders. The ball takes a long time to come down but McManaman volleys it with the outside of his right foot. 2–0.

75′: Raúl picks up a ball from Savio inside the Madrid half, runs a mile and beats the goalkeeper. 3–0.

'My goal will always be the goal they show on television when they interview me. I never mind seeing it again. I decided to go in off Roberto's throw-in. One of their defenders headed it clean to me. The eyes were shut and the volley went in past Santiago Cañizares,' Steve coolly half-joked. 'I don't normally go crazy celebrating goals, but that one I celebrated a bit. I ran over to where my family were and had a very good scream.

'We played much better in the first half than the second. It was odd, the way the threat Valencia posed failed to materialise. Héctor Cúper is one of the shrewdest coaches around, but his team didn't turn up. All season they had been thrashing everyone whereas we'd been scraping through. We'd had two very hard games against them in the league, losing at home 2–3 and finishing level 1–1 at the Mestalla stadium. I'd also played against them for Liverpool, the previous season, when Paul Ince and I were sent off (my first red card), along with Amadeo Carboni in a decisive UEFA Cup tie. They were always well organised, strong at the back, creative in midfield and in Claudio López and Gaizka Mendieta they had two great players. We anticipated a very, very close contest. For us, the motivating thing was we absolutely had to win in order to qualify for the Champions League. The game, I've said a thousand times, felt very easy. Once we went 2–0 up, that was it, we didn't feel under pressure. Here we were on the biggest of stages and it felt like a stroll. The third goal from Raúl was ridiculous – Savio put him through from our own box. Then it was farcical. They started taking more and more chances and we were showboating more, passing the ball around. I had lots of space to run around, I can't express how much I enjoyed myself. It's easier to play football when you're playing with the greatest players on the planet, of course it is. Great players think quick, pass quick, give you more time on the ball. Someone worked out I'd run more than anyone else in a European Cup final that night, ten miles or something. I ran all over the place. When you're loving it, you don't feel it. When you're under pressure, you feel tired, because you're anxious and the adrenalin is going, but when everything is going well you can play for two or three hours. When you're enjoying yourself like that, you don't want the game to stop. The European Cup final! In my first year, to win the cup, this prized bloody Holy Grail of club football, to win it and score. I was asked a million times in the build-up whether it was the biggest game of my career – what a stupid question, of course it was – and in retrospect I view it as probably my best game for Madrid.'

England's elite, armchair spectators at Burnham Beeches, saw one inspired Englishman doing what he had set out ten months earlier to achieve: succeeding at the highest level in a foreign environment. 'Give me the big stage. Give me the ball. Let me play against Europe's best,' Clive Tyldesley was theatrically putting imaginary rhetoric to McManaman's actions. Ron Atkinson, imbued by McManaman's ubiquitous presence, kept using the phrase 'Even Steven' in his commentary. After the medal ceremony Venables declared Macca his man of the match. 'He must have been on the ball more than anybody in his team,' he commented. 'His passing was crisp and weighted. Everything was good about his game. He worked hard. He tackled for his team. He really enjoyed himself and I am so happy for him.' Alex Ferguson was equally impressed: 'McManaman, Redondo and Raúl just controlled the match, they were the top men. McManaman is not renowned for his goal scoring, but he threatened all the time. He gave penetration from midfield, and he was everywhere. He's blessed with marvellous stamina, the boy.'

Interviewed coming off the pitch, Steve agreed with the comment, delivered as an exclamation of near incredulity, that his teammates *really* trusted him with the ball. 'The battle when you come abroad – as well as the language, and the settling in, of course – is to gain respect from your teammates, the Spaniards. You have to gain their confidence. You have to show that you can play. That's a big battle and thankfully I've done that,' he said evenly.

Des Lynam queried McManaman's nonplussed demeanour. 'That's his way,' said Venables with a grin. 'Macca's a low-key guy. If you didn't know the result, you wouldn't know from his expression, but there's a lot going on in that mind of his.'

There was a lot going on in two pockets in the huge main stand – in VIP seats where Victoria, her family, Steve's father David, his younger brother David and sister Karen watched the family name flash up as scorer on the electronic scoreboard of a European Cup final; and on the very back row of the section of seating stretching behind them where a party of eighteen lager-fuelled friends of the McManaman family were celebrating feverishly. 'I will never forget that final. It was fantastic. We partied until eight in the morning and our flight was leaving Paris at nine!' laughs Steve's father. 'It was brilliant. I took eighteen friends: mates I'd grown up with, who'd known Steven as a child, and some of Steven's mates. I'll never forget his goal. It was the best – it wasn't just a goal in the Champions League final, it was the one which effectively sealed the match. I'll never, ever forget the sight of him running over to celebrate in front of us. I was thrilled for him, and very, very proud.'

'It was a fantastic way to finish my first season, brilliant, even if the celebrations afterwards were a bit crap to be honest,' recalls Steve, phlegmatic after all these years.

'Christian Karembeu had warned me that two years before in Amsterdam the official party was very formal, very staid. After the game I couldn't see Victoria, my dad, my family or friends. I had loads of messages on my phone. There was that much security, no one could get near us. Hydrant-sprays of champagne greeted us back in the dressing room. Sanchís was charging around dousing everyone to chants of "Campeones, Campeones, olé, olé, olé!" We all went mad drinking champagne from the trophy in various states of undress. The floor was awash with empty plastic water bottles, pools of champagne, dozens of oranges lying on trays. I remember seeing Anelka, in shirt and white pants, looking the happiest I've seen him as Hierro anointed his head with champagne. I'd hugged everyone and danced around, but there reached a point when I suddenly felt on the periphery of jokes, the slang, the throwaway remarks. We'd thrown the president Lorenzo Sanz in the bath, we'd thrown Del Bosque up in the air. You can be totally in tune on the pitch, yet not feel engaged 100 per cent in the celebrations. Songs were sung, but

I didn't know the words. All these directors were squeezing me to death in great bear hugs and I didn't know their names. It's not like in England where there are about five directors and you know them reasonably well. Madrid had about forty. When people are excited they jabber, don't they? And they were all jabbering away in Spanish. No one wanted to leave, to lose that great feeling of winning the biggest prize. Then a security man came in and told me a woman was waiting outside for me, which was unthinkable because there were a million security posts and you had to wear badges with boxes crossed out to get access to certain areas. I went out and saw Teresa, the Spanish teacher Chris Robinson had recommended, who'd become a good friend of ours. By some fluky breakdown in security she alone, of all people, had reached the dressing room. She asked me where Victoria was and I said, "I haven't a clue, the security is so intense, she's miles away from this part of the stadium." I asked how on earth she'd got here. She had asked an official where she might find Steve McManaman and got ushered straight to our dressing-room door . . . And the nice thing for me was she stayed chatting for ages until we got shipped onto the bus. We left the stadium in the dark, everyone banging on the windows in time to dreadful Spanish pop music.

'It was 12.30am when we arrived at the celebratory five-course banquet – very intimate it was, just us carrying our medals, and about a thousand other people. It wasn't like we were partying as players, coaching staff and physios and our wives. The club revels in the notion of the Real Madrid family, and the Champions League final is an occasion they turn into a massive reunion with every known long-lost, far-flung branch of the family invited. There were that many people you couldn't get a drink. It was a huge reception, the trophy was put on a stage in a very formal show, the wives came in later, a few at a time, from their different hotels. Karembeu had warned me that the players are in one hotel and the wives and girlfriends get billeted in many and various hotels in different parts of the city. He had booked me a hotel room in the centre of Paris so Victoria and I could stay together after the party. Everyone was scattered around this huge banqueting room; it was a bit weird. As parties go, the Spanish don't celebrate like the English.

'The next day we returned to Madrid to celebrate with our fans in the city. The European Cup had its own seat on the team bus with, I have to say, a great view of the Seine and the Eiffel Tower. We carted it down to the boarding gate as hand luggage. The flight back was a laugh. Raúl, taking the captaincy label a bit far, was on the flight deck. The Iberia pilots had put a Real Madrid flag in the cockpit window. I was enjoying reading a match report under the headline 'El Crack Inglés, Insaciable Real Madrid!'. We came down the steps to an incredible reception on the tarmac. Sanchís and Redondo emerged first with the cup; Del Bosque, Hierro and Raúl got their hands on it too and took it down the steps. An open-top bus was waiting for us on the runway and drove us through crowds of thumbs-up signs, kisses, cheering and applause. White confetti was thrown from bridges; there were hospital workers perching on window ledges, children being held up, champagne bottles popped as the bus drove us right round the city and down the Castellana to the Cibeles fountain. Sergio García, the golfer, joined us on the bus. It was my first experience of the traditional Cibeles celebration – the water had been cut off, the fountain was dry, and we all clambered up bits of chariot and lion. Raúl and Morientes shimmied up to tie a Real Madrid scarf around the goddess's neck and kiss her cheek. Roberto Carlos sat, straddling a lion's head, holding the trophy up above his head, and we all sang the repertoire of traditional songs. I had to mouth words because I hadn't a clue what we were singing. That's fine for a bit, but then you feel a bit uncomfortable. You don't feel genuine, especially if you've grown up in a football hotbed like Kirkdale, where everybody knows all the words to all the footie songs. Slowly our bus inched back through the crowds to the Bernabéu, where they had organised a huge ceremony with troupes of dancing girls and spectacular fireworks. A giant No. 8 had been emblazoned dramatically on the pitch. They announced our names individually and we ran out in a bizarre combination of suit trousers and team shirts. When they called Redondo, Raúl and me it was very razzmatazz – billowing smoke and dry ice – and as the crowd roared and applauded, you had to jog along a white carpet up onto this big platform. Raúl did the matador thing with the Spanish flag. Your name went up in lights on the big scoreboards, next to another huge No. 8 and gradually we all lined up on the platform with some singers. Real Madrid are good at the flash stuff. They must have been planning it for yonks. The trophy was suspended from a crane and gradually cranked down on a wire, the fireworks went off, every seat in the stadium was full as if for a game, a dewy-eyed Del Bosque raised a victorious fist . . . then, with "Hala Madrid!" ringing in my ears, it was straight back home to pack, ready to meet up with England.

'The following day we had another victory parade, which took in the town hall and the cathedral where there was a short mass, attended by all the squad and directors, to have the trophy blessed and offer the title to the Virgin Mary. I couldn't wait to get home to see my family and show people my medal. They'd all called to say they'd had a ball, enjoying themselves in Paris, and what was our celebration like. "It was crap," I said! My phone was clogged with messages: Jamie Redknapp, Robbie choking up, saying, "Your mother would've been proud," you know, Growler getting all emotional. I had two days in Liverpool and then met up with England to go straight into Euro 2000. I left Spain on a high, and then I couldn't wait to get down to see all the England lads.

'The line in the press was that this team were younger than the one who won *la séptima*, that we were the base for a ninth European Cup, for a glorious dominant Real Madrid team. It was a fantastic way to end my first season. I had never, not for a minute, questioned my decision to come to Spain, even in my loneliest moment. We had played eighty games, often three a week. We stayed in a hotel the night before home games, even though they don't start until 9pm. We'd eaten mound after mound of the same spaghetti in a hundred hotels. I'd hardly been at home to draw breath, but I remember thinking, "I'll enjoy it more the longer I'm here."'

* * *

How many fathers introduce their child to a sport and watch them grow up to fulfil the ultimate fantasy? How many hear their own surname announced to capacity crowds at the world's biggest football clubs? A decent amateur himself, David McManaman had introduced his little boy to football, recognising from the age of three or four that young Steven had 'that bit more' than other kids.

'The bigger lads would call on him to play out in the streets, and were competitive about getting him in their teams. At school, when he was seven, he was in an Under-11 team; when he was eleven, he was in the Under-15s. He just kept progressing,' he recalls. 'But he was very, very small and slight. One day I went to watch him and something had happened. He'd go an hour before me to get changed. I started watching the game and thought, "Oh, Steven's not playing," and then a few minutes in I saw this long, thin lad with legs flying down the pitch. Jesus, he looked like a young foal. I didn't recognise him, he'd grown overnight. That was his first growing spurt.

'I've always enjoyed watching him. It was nice going out and seeing him play well, and play with the right attitude. I never worried about whether he'd make it or not. I just enjoyed seeing that talent in him.'

In that day trip back to Liverpool, before joining up with the England camp, David McManaman's eldest son soaked up the Scouse banter and wisecracks as he shared his European Cup winner's medal with pride. 'There was a lot of gratification for everyone my dad and myself had grown up with, two generations if you like,' says Steve. 'Kirkdale was a hotbed of football talent. Forty years ago, there wasn't the accessibility to football clubs that's developed since I was growing up and playing as a schoolboy. We had a lot of great players living in the streets in our area who played in the local teams. When I was four, five, six, seven, I used to go and watch my dad and his mates play football on a Saturday and Sunday. I adored football and they played a very good standard of local football. They wouldn't go on to play for Everton or Liverpool because there weren't the scouts, but many of them played semi-professional, or played for local teams. Whereas now there are a hundred scouts looking at a hundred games all over the place, signing up six- and seven-year-olds, back then there was no such organisation. I'd watch them, and then as I climbed through the ranks all my dad's Saturday and Sunday teammates took a big interest in what I did. Everyone was thrilled to bits for one person to make it, and make it big out of Kirkdale. It wasn't just my dad, but also his mates, because it was like they all owned me. They'd all kicked a ball around with me.

'I grew up an Evertonian because my dad's Evertonian. It wasn't a family thing, it was a dad thing, because his brother supports Liverpool. I remember going to Everton with him very early on, he used to carry me over the turnstiles. My mum's family are not so football-oriented. When I was very young, five or six, I had a Duncan McKenzie shirt. I idolised it, I did. Long sleeves, No. 10, plain blue, EFC – the most wonderful thing in the world. Then my mother dried it on a clothes horse in front of the fire, burnt the sleeves, cut the sleeves off and made it into a short-sleeved shirt. It was never the same. I missed all the stitching and the cuffs. I was distraught. I used to wear that going to watch the football, and then the whole Everton thing grew into more of an obsession when I started playing more. I had team posters on the wall. I bought an Everton song on record. I joined the Junior Evertonians. It's in Gladwys Street and if you were under a certain age you paid cheaper prices. Adult admission was £3, and a Junior Evertonian paid £1.50. You went into the Junior Evertonian pen, you didn't have to queue up at the turnstiles with the adults, you simply showed your little pink card, paid your £1.50 and went in. I was really lucky, really lucky, because I got to see the glory years of Everton. In '84 I went to Wembley with my dad, when they beat Watford 2–0, and had a wonderful time. They won the European Cup-Winners cup, they won the league twice, and they seemed to fly with Peter Reid, Paul Bracewell and Trevor Steven. It was fantastic.

'Football was the be-all and end-all. I collected football cards, I played with a ball every spare second in the day. I'd be walking down the road from an early age and if there was a can on the floor I'd boot it. Other kids would step over it. My life was football, football,

football, but there were other demands on my time. I was a very good cross-country runner and I was in the school quiz team. I remember I was doing something every single night after school. I'd have to: I was the main person in each event. One night I'd have to play football for the third years, the next night for the fourth years, and the night after that I'd be running, and on Sundays I played for the local-league team. It was just bosh, bosh, bosh, but I loved it. The way I grew up, football was a passion. You hear about the organised life in football academies for youngsters who've been spotted at an early age and you wonder if it's not a bit institutionalised. I loved finding my own way with my game. I loved the camaraderie, the independence at a young age, travelling on the bus with the school team . . . they'd supply us with a Saveaway bus pass for the day. We'd sit on the bus together having a laugh . . . I loved it. Football was my thing.

'When I was about fourteen, playing for the City of Liverpool Schoolboys, this army of scouts from different clubs started wanting to take you out, treat you, and get you to sign for their club. You'd go and watch Oldham, for instance, and have a meal and they'd try to impress you. I remember an invitation to go to Everton before a game. They showed me around Goodison. I always remember being ushered into the Everton dressing room and seeing Gary Lineker sitting in the bath.'

Everton offered only a one-year schoolboy contract. At this stage McManaman Sr. shrewdly steered his son to Liverpool. 'The Liverpool scout, Jim Aspinall, a lovely fella who died in early 2004, always used to say to me, "I know Steven's such a good Evertonian, I won't bother you, Dave." And that was true. I had told him he only wanted to sign for Everton. We went to talk to Everton and they offered him a year as a schoolboy. Now Steven at fifteen was very small. I spoke to Steven about it and I said, "I don't think you'll do it in one year, son, because you're very small and you'll be playing against pros who are coming back from injury, grown men." He was very, very tiny. You wouldn't believe it now that he's six foot. I thought one year was not enough. He needed a couple of years. He agreed because he's quite sensible.

'You'd think it would break his heart considering alternatives to Everton, but Steven was very sensible. The next time I saw Jim Aspinall I said, "Jim, do you still want Steve?" And he couldn't believe it. I told him the situation. Jim invited us to come up and see Kenny Dalglish, so we went up and met him. Dalglish just went, "I'll give him two, three years, whatever he wants."'

Steve recalls the interest of both clubs. 'But Liverpool said they wanted me to sign one year as a schoolboy and then when I'd left school I could join them as a YTS for two years. That meant when I left school I knew I had a job, a two-year apprenticeship, learning a trade. A lot of clubs offered me that, but Everton – the club I absolutely adored – said they'd offer me a year of schoolboy forms but nothing after that. We said, "I've been offered this and this by numerous other clubs," and they said, "Well, we don't do that at Everton," which was fair enough. Their attitude was, "If you're good enough then, we'll want you to sign." My dad even applied a bit of emotional blackmail, you know, "*Liverpool* have offered him this, but he loves Everton. Couldn't you offer the same?" They said they'd let us know and three or four days later I opened this letter which spelt out, "No, we don't do that at Everton." I told my Dad it wasn't a problem and I signed for Liverpool.

'It was easy to accept, because the decision had been made for me. A lot of the lads who'd played for City of Liverpool Schoolboys also joined Liverpool so it was a continuation of my football life. And I knew I'd be earning £27.35 a week on the government YTS.

'Subsequently Everton changed their tactics – but before they did, they missed out on so many players, all mad Evertonians: me, Robbie Fowler, Michael Owen, Jamie Carragher, Dominic Matteo . . . And my dad was right, because until the age of sixteen I was still very small. Then somewhere between sixteen and eighteen I had another growing spurt and shot up overnight.

'I remember going to see Liverpool like it was yesterday. I sat in the office with Kenny Dalglish and couldn't keep my eyes from darting towards this pair of football boots by his desk – the best football boots in the whole wide world. Liverpool had just come back from Japan, from the Intercontinental Club Cup, and he'd got these

Pumas that weren't on sale yet . . . they were a size seven, and I was only a five. He said I could have them. I used to wear them all the time even though they were huge on me, just because they were these super boots.

'I've still got that letter from Ray Minshull, Everton's youth development officer, in the drawer upstairs in my bedroom. In my heart I'll always be an Everton supporter, but I'll always have an allegiance to Liverpool because of the people there, people I grew up with. David Moores is a lovely bloke, the greatest chairman. He kept on investing in the club, never got in the manager's way. I'd love Liverpool to be successful again for him, likewise for a lot of the directors, the receptionists and the people upstairs who are still there. But the fact that I was born an Everton fan, and my dad is . . . hopefully if I have children, I'll take them to watch Everton.'

What a moment, then, when David McManaman turned to hug Victoria in the sixty-sixth minute of the Champions League final in the Stade de France. In the euphoria he would not have recalled it, but that decision he helped Steve make at the age of fifteen was a turning point in his career. 'It was,' he agrees later, 'because above all else, Liverpool played his type of football. And Steven struggled his first year . . . well, when I say struggled, he didn't excel because he was so very small. In his second year he took off. So I felt I was right in advising him not to go to Everton. And then, of course, he never looked back.'

Season Two

2000–2001

Football is full of surprises, not always nice ones . . .
It is never wise to look too far ahead.

—Luis Figo

No elite footballer could fail to recognize that the Bernabéu is the place where the true standards are set. Players come to Madrid if they want to stand in the hottest crucible, face the ultimate test.

—Paul Hayward, Daily Telegraph

Rarely, if ever, has there been a time when you thought, 'Steve McManaman? He's got some bottle . . .' Yet watching him at Elland Road I was tinged with a new emotion, one of sheer respect for the Thinking Man's Scally.

—Paul McCarthy, Sunday People

'I'll enjoy it more . . . *the longer I'm here.*' Steve's words gather a momentum and a thorny determination he had not contemplated when he uttered them at the end of his first season in Spain.

During the summer of 2000, everything changed at Real Madrid. The revolution began on 30 June when Florentino Pérez, a small, bespectacled and quietly spoken engineer, whose company Actividades de Construcción y Servicios (ACS) is the largest construction company in Spain, and third largest in Europe, announced his candidacy in Real Madrid's presidential elections against the incumbent Lorenzo Sanz. Scrupulous, driven, respectable – an ex-Madrid councillor for the centre-right *Unión de Centro Democrático*, a personal friend of the Madrid-supporting Prime Minister José María Aznar, and said to be worth €600m – Pérez had stood against Sanz in 1995 and failed pitifully. Now he set himself up against the man who had delivered two European Cups in three years. What was he thinking?

He had, it transpired, been thinking shrewdly. According to Sid Lowe, writing in *FourFourTwo* magazine in March 2003, Pérez, 'the man with *enchufes* – those vital connections that make the Spanish world go round', had commissioned a study that concluded Luis Figo, the darling of Barcelona, was the footballer Madrid fans craved to see in the white shirt more than any other. Pérez had become aware that Figo's contract negotiations with Barcelona were going up and down cul-de-sacs like a taxi driver lost in La Moraleja. Figo later explained how the situation deteriorated: 'We'd had such excellent results at Barcelona in my time there that we needed to renew the details on my contract. I expected them to make an offer that would show they were interested in having me at the club, but they ignored me, my talents, my role in their titles, and they said I would receive no recognition for my efforts.' On 6 July, the very day Lorenzo Sanz was giving his daughter Malula away in marriage to his right-back Míchel Salgado, an extraordinary story broke. Florentino Pérez had paid the disaffected Luis Figo to sign a deal. If Pérez won the election, the Portugal and Barcelona winger would sign for Madrid. If he did not join, Pérez offered to refund the cost of season tickets to all holders. (And if Pérez did not win, Figo remained at Barça, pocketing a non-returnable £1.6m secret agreement fee and no one need be the wiser.) From Figo's point of view, it was money for nothing. Pérez was never going to win, was he? The deal may have been cooked up privately by the player's agent, José Veiga, because Figo, somewhat ambiguously, denies there was a secret agreement: 'It is nonsense. I did all I could to stay with Barcelona, but while Barcelona did not make enough effort to show me they wanted me, Real and the president did everything to make me feel valued. They kept their word and offered me a decent deal. Whenever I gave my word to someone, I kept it.'

During that week Pérez deposited 10,000 million pesetas (£38m) with the Spanish Football Federation. The sum represented Luis Figo's *cláusula de rescisión*. Under Spanish transfer rules, every player has an official value at which his club are obliged to sell. They are rarely invoked, because they are prohibitively high (Zidane's is €180m) and never apply when a sale is agreed. Barcelona would never agree to the sale of Figo. He was the greatest winger in the world. Signed by Johan Cruyff to replace the revered Michael Laudrup, Figo immediately won over Barça fans with his sprints along the flank, his pinpoint crosses and his sublime skills in teasing defenders with his trickery and almost magnetic ball-on-boot dribbling ability. With Barcelona, Figo the 'Lion King' became the embodiment of Catalunyan style, credo and panache – and not merely by wearing the shirt. He and his wife, Swedish model Helene Svedin, who had met in 1995 at a Joaquín Cortés concert in Barcelona, had privately resolved to settle forever in the city they loved (she is unsettled by the attention in Portugal, where Figo is a national institution, and the restrictions it puts on a normal life for their daughters Daniela and Martina; he finds the Swedish climate too cold – Barcelona, by the sea, was a happy compromise). As a consummate contributor to Barcelona, Figo's value was immeasurable. In five years he helped the Blaugranas claim the Spanish Super Cup, two Copa del Rey triumphs, back-to-back Liga championships in 1998 and 1999, a European Cup-Winners' Cup and a UEFA Super Cup. He was the lynchpin of the future, a permanent fixture on the right wing, poised to leave defences in tatters with his feints and flashes of brilliance. They would never ever think of selling him, let alone to those provokers of animosity, Real Madrid.

On 16 July, buoyed by the Figo effect, the unthinkable became fact: Florentino Pérez won the presidential election. Having shrewdly campaigned for postal ballots, he triumphantly outmanoeuvred Sanz, who he blamed for the club's immense debts and chaotic administration. On 24 July, Luis Filipe Madeira Caeiro 'Figo' was unveiled as a white-shirted Madrid player. The adored hero who had celebrated his last success with Barcelona by dying his hair red and blue and chanting from a balcony above the Plaça Sant Jaume, 'White cry-babies, salute the champions!', cost a world record €65m (£38m). More galling still for Barça, Figo was handed the famous white shirt by Alfredo di Stéfano. The legendary Argentine had been snatched from under the noses of Barcelona by Real Madrid in 1953, allegedly with the assistance of former dictator Francisco Franco.

No one foresaw the full impact of this sleight of presidential hand, but the new man in power had set out his stall. The Pérez Revolution was underway. He set out to modernise the club, to clear the debts, run the club as a profit-making business and promote the Real Madrid brand worldwide. The club was no longer to be *cutre* – like an old lady without make-up, as Sky Sports' Guillem Balague put it – but catwalk-glamorous and fashionable. Pérez, growing up in Madrid in the 1950s, had been seduced by the Real side who won five European Cups. The architect of that glittering domination was Santiago Bernabéu, president from 1943 to 1978, who provided Alfredo di Stéfano with a new world-class teammate every year: Puskás, Kopa, Didi et al. The acquisition of each contributed to

Real's aura of invincibility. In the summer of 2000, Pérez set out to emulate his illustrious predecessor by signing a star a season. He would revive the glamour of history, appointing the elderly di Stéfano as honorary president, and other illustrious old boys – the urbane former manager, Jorge Valdano, and the cherubic former striker Emilio Butragueño – as sporting directors. Poaching Figo was Stage One, a move to subdue Barcelona, the domestic enemy, and to wrest glamour from the Catalunyan club. From now on, the world's best players would be Madrid-bound, and the images of the superstars in the white shirts were destined for big-time global commercial sales. Luis Figo became the first player to sell 50% of his image rights to the club.

'I was on holiday in Italy and I kept ringing Michael Robinson, who slipped me information,' recalls Steve. 'But no one in their right mind expected Lorenzo Sanz to lose the presidency. In footballing terms, Florentino Pérez was a nonentity. No one had heard of this bloke. Everyone's reaction was: "He's a high-powered businessman, but it's impossible he'll take over because Lorenzo Sanz has won two European Cups. What more do you want of a president?" When he did win the election, it was all change. New president, new directors, new everyone. All those directors we'd bear-hugged in Paris, gone! And Luis Figo was coming. That was great news: we'd won the European Cup with the players we already had *and* we get Figo – brilliant, because he's an absolutely wonderful player.

'But the next minute we hear the new president has sold Fernando Redondo, the Champions League player of the year who everybody adored. That was all I heard in Italy. Of course the Italian newspapers were full of "Redondo to AC Milan" headlines . . . I phoned Robbo to see what was happening. The Spanish are a people who take to the streets to express their emotions, and he told me people were crying all over Madrid, it was such a terrible shock. The new president had made enemies from minute one. There was horrible graffiti on the stadium and at the training ground. He came in, looked at the club's legendary debts and set about recouping money. No one knows the true story of how much the club were in debt – one figure was £170m. In retrospect you can see he was applying ruthless, twenty-first-century business logic to the rambling old gentleman's club of Real Madrid and football. But at the time he seemed to be swinging a demolition ball to the club as everyone knew and loved it.

'That change in presidency was very uncomfortable for a lot of players. During the candidacy stage, Redondo, who was a powerful figure in the dressing room, had come out publicly and supported Sanz, and other players did too, like Hierro and Salgado, and therefore made enemies instantly with the new president. I didn't say anything because I'd only been there a year and didn't know the personalities. It wasn't my place to speak out about politics. You can imagine players being asked about the prospects of this new guy no one had heard of and them giving a supportive quote about the current president, their employer effectively. We'd just won the Champions League and we'd dunked Sanz in the bath in our dressing room. No one imagined he would go. But he did, and certain players were on the back foot from then onwards. They were "old guard" and that was to hang over them.

'Change is hard for fans, but the sale of Redondo turned out to be shrewd. His market value was high. He was not young, at thirty-one, and Pérez sold him for £12m. Both parties were happy, the sale went through and that pre-season Fernando suffered an injury and was out for two years. He put on weight and found it very difficult to return to form. He never came back to haunt Real Madrid in an opposition shirt. Pérez was lucky in that.

'Then the news broke that I was top of a new For Sale list. Figo was not the sole purchase. The other new arrivals were all midfielders, and included Santiago Solari from Atlético Madrid, Albert Celades from Barcelona, Flavio Conçeicão for £15m from Deportivo and Claude Makelele from Celta Vigo . . . All hell broke loose. Nobody called me in to explain my situation. It wasn't like they said, "You have to go, let's sort out a deal." But I knew what the score was. Contractually, they couldn't tell me to go, so they suggested it'd be "better" if I looked elsewhere. But I wasn't going anywhere. It had taken a while, it had been tough, but I was happy in Spain. Del Bosque and Real Madrid's general manager José Martínez Pirri both told me the club had bought new players, and I might not play as much as last year. I said, "That's not a problem, I'll fight for my place." The rest was gossip. Perhaps the club were dropping bits of information to the press, that is their way. To this day I don't know. It was pre-season and there were pages to fill. I was linked with every club under the sun. The Redondo sale had caused an outcry, a genuine anger, because he was seen to be the orchestrator of our Champions League success. Some of that anger was channelled into my situation. The press sensed a massive story if I went too. They made it sound like I was arguing with the club when that wasn't the case. I was silent. My Spanish was not that refined! All I said, repeatedly and resolutely, was that I didn't want to leave. I didn't shout or moan. I just got on with it.

'Once it got translated back to England, though, and bounced back over the Continent again, it turned into a situation totally detached from reality. There'd be an interpretation of it in various English papers, which would get picked up by the Spanish . . . and people were talking about me as if I'd been locked in a cupboard without a number or role, with the key thrown away until I agreed to be sold. The one lowpoint came when I wasn't required to travel to Monaco for the Super Cup on August 25 – and I said then that I felt I deserved some respect and needed an explanation – but it was rubbish that I was not training or that I hadn't been given a squad number. We sort out numbers in pre-season. Typically we'll be having dinner and the captain – it was Manolo Sanchís then – walks around saying, "OK, who's number two? Míchel Salgado. Three? Roberto Carlos, Raúl, you want to go seven again, Macca eight," and the new guy says, "I'll go fourteen." And that had happened. It isn't a big doling out of numbers from the president to his favoured men. All that time, I had my No. 8.

'The fans were fantastic. I couldn't walk in the city centre without being stopped every few seconds by supporters begging me to stay. They were all saying, "What's going on? Why is this? This is not what we're used to. This is not football, this is media football, money football." The players were great too. Hierro said, "Don't worry about it. It's crazy at the moment. It always happens." Hand on heart, it never bothered me in the slightest. It was more difficult for Victoria and my family. The speculation in the Spanish press had turned into melodramatic nonsense in the English papers so we'd get frantic calls from home. To me it was simple: I had a five-year contract. I was one year into it. If they wanted me to go, they could have said that to me, but they never, ever did.'

Victoria had established herself happily in a job teaching English law to final-year students at Madrid University and at the Colegio de Abogados, the Law Society. Disruption was not welcome. 'We had gone away on holiday thinking, "This is fantastic, what an amazing year it's been." For Steven, professionally, it couldn't have been better, and on a personal level it had been a make-or-break year for us. It was the first time we had lived together, which is a big test anyway, but especially living in a foreign country with all the frustrations that a language barrier poses. But it had gone really, really well. It definitely cemented our relationship. Then while we were away in Italy the presidency changed, and it's "Oh, we're going to sell McManaman." It was very stressful. I am more of a worrier than Steven and I just could not believe it. How can you reach such heights one minute and then be reduced to this level the next minute, because someone takes a new look at the club's financial situation? But Steven is so laid-back, he's got such belief in his own ability. He reads situations well and he has an incredible strength of character. He sat it out, and I was saying, "But are we going?" The thought of moving all our things out again! I was thinking about all the practicalities and he was saying, "No, no, it's going to be fine, don't worry."

'I can see a player with a different make-up would take these things to heart, it would be a nightmare. The whole scenario is potentially soul-destroying. But the response from the players was phenomenal. Real Madrid are a club where people come and go and people don't blink at it – Nicolas Anelka came for £23m and went without a whisper of complaint – but for all the players to unite and stand up for Steven when he had only been there one year, to me, was a fantastic accolade.'

According to Iván Campo, Steve was the first in the dressing room to sense when another player was down and needed an encouraging slap on the back. 'However, you could never tell when he needed a lift. He carried on smiling and joking,' Campo said. Míchel Salgado, son-in-law of the outgoing president, was instrumental in voicing dressing-room protest. 'We all agreed that the treatment was unfair and that Macca's response was honourable,' he recalls more than three years later. 'He carried on training and acting as if he was just another member of the team. A different player might have got much more wound up, confronted the club, the manager or whoever, or maybe done something absurd and something much worse could have happened as a result. But Steve's attitude was important in gaining everyone's respect. I did what I had to do. I said publicly what I felt needed saying: that I thought the treatment of Macca was totally unjust. I threatened to write a letter to the press, signed by all the players, but in the end I didn't need to. Macca started the season as a member of the squad, and he ended up back in the team after a couple of months, when he immediately proved as influential as he had the previous year. I think the support was important for him, too. It's not easy, especially in a team like Real Madrid, for your team-mates to stick their necks on the line for you, but lots did that for Macca. That helped his confidence. And everything went back to how it was.'

'The club's tactic is to leave you out so that you get so frustrated, you go and plead for a transfer,' continues Steve. 'But it reached a point where they could see I wasn't doing that. I'd had a hell of a lot of support and Real Madrid started to look very bad. It's that old cliche, you are only as good as your last game, and my last game was the Champions League final in which I'd scored and been nominated by some people as Man of the Match. The situation lingered. Hierro, Salgado and the senior players went to the coach, and to the president, and complained about the way I was being treated. They were very vocal in the press. And then it all blew over. In the end I was called in by Valdano – "Dr Death" as he came to be known because he was in charge of hiring and firing. He said, "We want you to stay, we think you're fantastic," and words to that effect. And that was about it.'

An extraordinary late-blossoming camaraderie had won the club their eighth European Cup victory in Paris. That same spirit now protected one of the core players in that triumph. 'The previous season, 1999–2000, was our best year in terms of the group of players,' insists Helguera four years, another European Cup, two league championships and an embarrassment of riches later. 'Everyone got on exceptionally well – and that was the key to us winning the eighth European Cup. In terms of team spirit it was the best year I have experienced at Real Madrid. For example, after training Manuel Sanchís would come and make a paella at my house and the whole team would come round. We had an unbelievable spirit, a great bond. But with the new president, the club's policy on the pitch changed. When Redondo went, they wanted Flavio and Claude Makelele in central midfield, a different type of player. And of course when they signed Figo it was far harder for Macca to get a game playing on the right, which is roughly where he had been playing. They thought Macca didn't have a place in the team and they knew they could get a lot of money for him. For the players it was tough to see him go through that. Whenever one of us came to speak to the press we made a point of saying that we would love it if Macca continued. First of all, you have to look at him as a person and, as I said, Macca is fun, kind, a good guy. Whatever you need, any favour you could ask for, Macca's there. He is the best person to have in your dressing room and it hurt us to discover that he could be going. The thing that counted against him was the fact he came on a free, when the football market was on the up, when there was lots of money about and he had a very high salary. The club wanted to rid themselves of that salary. It ended up being a really big factor against him.'

Steve was buoyed, not just by the loyalty of his teammates, but support in the press. Diego Torres, of *El País*, argued that Paris had proved to fans and commentators that the Englishman had a great tactical mind. 'He can manage the Real Madrid shirt because he can read the game so well. It would be difficult to have him on the bench because he is so appreciated by his teammates; they all want him to play. They respect him. They know he can defend as well as attack. In a world of stars he is an incredibly unselfish player.' As Salgado vouches: 'There was only ever one thought in his mind – play for the team. That was Macca's main virtue. You could see that not just in the matches but in training sessions as well. He didn't just dribble for the sake of it. He always chose the best option, he'd give the ball to the best-placed player on the pitch – and that's not as easy as he made it seem.'

After the *octava* in Paris, people found all sorts of ways to find celebratory significance in facts, binding everyone closer together. Del Bosque, for instance, had relished expressing a strong link with McManaman. 'In 1981 I'd played in the European Cup final with Real Madrid where we lost, also in Paris, against Liverpool to a goal by Alan Kennedy. I was marking Ray Kennedy. So it was all very symbolic, Paris, Liverpool, our eighth European Cup, and then Macca scoring for Madrid, a former Liverpool man wearing No. 8 in Paris!' But suddenly Del Bosque had been forced to quash that basic instinct of sentimentality and play the detached manager of a club who had decided Steve could not be part of his plans. Del Bosque did not play El Héroe Inglés – as he had been billed after Paris – at all until he brought him on as a substitute in the last game of the pre-season campaign, the Santiago Bernabéu Trophy, against Santos of Brazil on 5 September. Real Madrid won 2–0, but the evening was most notable for the crowd's emotions. Vociferous pockets of the crowd chanted 'Redondo, Redondo.' When, at half-time, McManaman came on for Figo, the stadium erupted in a spontaneous outburst. 'That was the first time I played after all the rubbish. I remember the crowd getting excited as I warmed up, but I didn't think it was for me. Then I ran out, and they just went bananas. It was very emotional.'

He was back in the squad, but not in the team. He did not make a league appearance until November. Every time he ran on in Cup and two Champions League games, he was greeted with rousing applause. The greatest ovation came, on 25 October, when McManaman came on for forty minutes against Sporting Lisbon when Luis Figo was taken off. Michael Robinson describes the moment his compatriot's ostracism seemed to be over: 'I was at the Bernabéu, televising the game, when Steven finally came on as a sub. My hair stood on end. Almost a hundred thousand people stood up to applaud Steven McManaman because they knew what he'd gone through. He had been a fundamental member of the team who gave us our eighth European Cup, and he scored a goal. The *madridistas* don't forget that. He was given an amazing standing ovation because he had never moaned, never had a go at anybody, always smiled and said he just wanted to play for Real Madrid. The club wanted to palm him off everywhere, not because he wasn't a good football player, just because Florentino Pérez arrived at Real Madrid's doors inheriting an enormous debt. I remember Florentino turned around to me in the directors' box that night and said, "There's no way that guy would go. He must be a bigger *madridista* than me. That guy will always be welcome in my football club." He defied gravity, Steven.'

Steve's situation had made him a cause célèbre. On 10 November, *Marca* ran a sardonic headline: 'McManaman has not died'. It summarised the bald facts: 'Macca has played 40 per cent of games, and not one minute of pre-season . . . He came back from Munich, Murcia and Alicante without starting . . . It was a grave situation . . . He deserved respect, needed an explanation . . . He knew how to put himself above adversity, he did not raise his voice in his suffering [the word used was 'Calvary'] . . . He worked hard and silently. Little by little, the situation turned around . . . He participated in six of fifteen official games in the league or Champions League. He debuted in Malaga for twenty-two minutes . . . playing right-back. He played half an hour against Spartak Moscow at left midfield; he replaced Figo on the right wing for thirty minutes against Sporting Lisbon. He played next to Makelele in central midfield against Mallorca.'

'I played bloody everywhere!' Steve exclaims in recollection.

'Then,' *Marca* triumphantly concluded, '164 days after the European Cup final, he started against Numancia in Soria – and normal service resumed.'

'It was an uncomfortable time for all of us,' Del Bosque recalls ruefully from his table in the shadows at Helen's cafe bar. 'The club had quite contrasting thoughts on Macca the footballer in relation to his salary. There was a further difficulty caused by the president and his board of directors wanting to drive down costs, and this in turn had "on the field" implications, too. It is important to remember this situation arose after the arrival of Florentino Pérez. All the president did was to look at what Macca was earning, look at a balance sheet with all the salaries, and then try to find a way to get Steve transferred. Steve stood his ground; he was told what the club were trying to do, but he respectfully and politely maintained his stance of not wanting to leave Real Madrid. I've experienced similar situations in a dressing room in my playing days. It doesn't mean that you have something against a player, or that there's any animosity, or that you dislike someone. On the contrary, it's something that comes with the job. As a player you are an employee, and this was all about someone upstairs consolidating the playing side with the financial side of the club. At that time the president was obsessed with the financial aspects. It was all to do with an obsession with what Macca earned. Macca always understood this so there was never a problem.

'What I've always felt strongly about, however, is that, putting aside any employment issue, Real Madrid must always be straight with all the players in the squad, and conduct themselves in a manner that befits the club. Whenever there's any kind of dispute, irrespective of whether or not it's resolved, Real Madrid need to behave properly and shouldn't freeze out anyone. The "club" may have been trying to freeze Steve out, but in our day-to-day dealings with him, the management team, his teammates, the whole dressing room behaved in a manner worthy of Real Madrid. The fans always had a lot of affection for Steve. I have to admit, from the outside, it didn't look as if we were perfect in our treatment of him. I'm sure there were occasions where we let him down, or we didn't quite do everything as we should have, but in a big dressing room of twenty-four players, all of them with glowing CVs, it's not always easy to attend to their every need.

'As a manager you have some players who, because of their honesty and personality, it's much tougher to leave out, or let down in that way, compared to other players who are more aloof or conceited. Steve was such an honest, down-to-earth person that it hurt me leaving him out. It might seem that talking about these things in the highly professional world of football doesn't sound too good. That's why I was talking about how important it was to encourage positive relations, a good-natured atmosphere, and also that "humanisation" I mentioned earlier. Perhaps all that sounds a little strange in today's dehumanised world.'

In the press, the year ends on a familiar note: Macca in a hat! Political correctness, or even general good taste, is not something the Spanish tabloids are noted for. Two years later, for instance, when Real Madrid were due to fly to the Far East, Ronaldo was asked to pose for a photograph wearing a Chinese coolie hat and to pull the skin at the corner of his eyes towards his ears to create a slit-eyed expression. Hats had become Steve's leitmotif in *Marca*. When he first arrived the photographers asked him to pose in a policeman's Bobby hat, then a bowler hat (before playing Manchester United), a sombrero (to indicate he suits Spanish life), a fez (before a trip to Turkey), a beanie hat . . . and so on. Whatever the occasion, they produced a themed hat. On 27 December 2000, *Marca* publish a photograph of McManaman in a Father Christmas hat, giving a thumbs-up sign, under the headline: 'Macca, finally a happier year at Madrid . . . The white club declare him *intransferible*, untransferable, and will not listen to offers for him.' And Steve decided that was enough hats.

In the meantime Luis Figo had arrived. The name that launched a thousand incendiary headlines between Catalunya and Castilla walked into Madrid's underwhelming Ciudad Deportiva training facilities, with a holdall containing his boots, shin pads, trainers and wash bag, like any other squad member at the start of pre-season preparation. Except, being the new boy, and a stickler for efficiency anyway, he was probably there scrupulously on time. There was nothing incongruous about his entrance. Notwithstanding his five years of stellar service for Barça, could there be a player of more emblematic Real style than the Portuguese winger? Charged with providing the ammunition for the out-and-out goal-scorers, his artistry – sometimes exquisite, sometimes petulant – would be a key addition to the armoury of the club whose stadium on the Castillana boulevard stands nearly opposite, in every sense, the Ministry of Defence.

Figo's debut came in the Bayern Munich centenary tournament, in which Madrid finished third, losing 1–0 to Manchester United, then beating Galatasaray 3–2 – 'Not for Real Madrid, pre-season fixtures against Mansfield Town or the Girl Guides,' quips Steve. Diplomatically, Figo made the winner for Raúl.

At the season's start, Morientes was injured and Raúl out for two spells. The call for cover for the strikers, initiated by Toshack, repeated by Del Bosque, had still not been answered. (Never mind the call for a centre half.) Out of Madrid's crowd of attacking options, Guti and Roberto Carlos stepped forward on the scoring front, with four goals apiece in the first six games. Of the team's first nine goals, the world-record signing laid on five. Figo was set to make a massive impact, as Guti was quick to recognise: 'Nobody crosses the ball like Luis. His assists are worth half a goal: all the rest of us have to do is push the ball over the line.'

After such a thunder-clap transfer, how did he fit in to Del Bosque's humanised dressing room? 'In Spain they ask what Michael Owen is like, as if he has a supernatural aura off the pitch. I say he's a nice lad,' says McManaman simply. 'In answer to the same question about Luis, I have to say I regard him first and foremost as a very nice bloke I go to work with. Like many high-profile players, he's become wary of journalists. They think he's grumpy and miserable, but in private he's relaxed, good company and a loyal friend. He's typical of players with children, in that he's always one of the early ones in for training. After dropping the kids at school, Luis, like Hierro, always went and had a coffee in the cafeteria first, and then went in for a massage and a stretch. He trains very well, and enjoys a laugh and a joke on the training field. He isn't as intense as someone like Míchel Salgado, who is brutally competitive at all times. Míchel fouls and pulls people back, pinches you – he's a pain in the arse to play against. Luis's ball skills, his control, his trickery, his whole repertoire is mesmerising, but, as with Roberto Carlos, what stands out even in a casual training session is his appetite for playing, for always trying, for expressing himself with a football. He never, ever stands still . . . and then he finishes by going into the gym. He's keen on his rippling muscles!

'Luis is quiet, but he has a massive presence in the dressing room. I'd say he is unteasable. He was such a star at Barcelona, and then so easy-going but self-contained when he arrived in Madrid, he was never the butt of jokes. He has a natural air of seniority. He's tidy and well organised. He likes to dress well and "does" his hair, but he's low-key and consistent in the way he looks. He's not experimental like Helguera or Guti, who get skitted for their outlandish clothes. And he's not one of the noisy lads. Like most of us, he finds the perpetual travel wearing, but he'd be well prepared. On away trips, he would come with this big bag full of books, music, a portable mini-DVD player. He reads a lot and speaks very good English – his Swedish wife Helene, a lovely lady, speaks perfect English too. They try to spend as much time as possible together as a family. Their oldest daughter Daniela is a tomboy, and very friendly with Raúl's son Jorge. You would sometimes see them mucking about together in the car park after training. Victoria says they clamber over the chairs together during games. As couples, we became very good friends with Luis and Helene from the minute he joined – again the linguistic common ground helped – and we remained so until the minute I left. Victoria introduced them to kir royales – cassis and champagne – and they're always saying, "Oh, we had your drink the other night." We often went out to dinner after games – with them it's *always* Chinese or Thai – and I still talk to him a lot over the phone.'

Del Bosque had changed the formation back to 4–4–2, but it was a nominal thing, not a straitjacket for his flamboyant individualists. 'The team invariably went wherever they wanted anyway,' laughs Steve. 'Whether he plays in a back five or four, Roberto Carlos goes where he goes. The same with Míchel Salgado. We bought these two sitting midfielders to be defensive lynchpins and let the game flow forward from them. When we played, it was so fluent and free-flowing. It was never a case of being pigeonholed by your position. I never thought, "Oh no, he's put me there, I might not get a kick." You were in one position at kick-off, and you tried to get into that position if we lost the ball, but it didn't make much of a difference.'

Florentino Pérez had been shrewd in his appraisal of the Portuguese star. One of the strongest men in world football, physically and psychologically, Figo was never daunted by the pressure to perform after such a move. An only child, he grew up worshipping Maradona, Marco van Basten and Michael Laudrup in a modest Lisbon household; his father owned a bar, his mother earned money as a seamstress. Spotted as a potential superstar at a very young age – he represented Portugal at virtually all youth levels – he exhibits basic psychology's profile of an only child in his innate desire to please, to fulfil all expectations placed upon him. As a perfectionist, he dwells on things that didn't, rather than did, work on the pitch. His motto is 'a good player makes his teammate stand out'. He has high standards and no false modesty. When he won the Ballon d'Or in 2000 he was asked who he would have voted for and replied, 'To answer sincerely, myself.' Away from football, he takes his role-model status earnestly, having set up a foundation for underprivileged children. He also works as an ambassador for UNICEF. If you meet him in a social context, through friends he trusts, his curiosity about others makes him warm and friendly beyond the cliche. If he hadn't played football, he says he would have liked to have trained as a psychologist.

Of the challenge in joining Pérez's vision for Real Madrid, José

Carlos Freites, the former Portugal team press officer, says Figo's *amor propio*, his self-love, is key. 'He was a big fish at Barça, a bigger fish in the sense that the goals, the play, the action revolved around him. But, for him, it is a challenge to play in a team of big stars. He likes to test himself at the highest level.'

By mid-October, with Real Madrid top of the league, after beating erstwhile leaders Deportivo La Coruña 3–0, and having earned early qualification for the next phase of the Champions League after a thrilling 5–3 goalfest against Bayer Leverkusen, Figo prepared for his greatest test yet – the first return to Barcelona.

Even without the Figo factor, the game on 22 October was still the *gran clásico*. Since last winning in the Nou Camp in 1983, Real Madrid had won seven league titles, two Champions Leagues and a World Club Cup, but they remained incapable of winning in the Catalan capital. Mutual enmity intensified by the year. Now Real Madrid were returning with the idol who had been the heart and soul of Barça's ambitions. Michael Laudrup, the player Figo had been bought to replace at the Nou Camp, had made the same switch of shirts, and the same 'traitor's' return. He described that day in 1995 playing against his former team as the worst of his life. Jorge Valdano substituted him after sixty-six anguished minutes.

Figo, with nice sarcasm, was to describe his return as 'one of the richest experiences of my life'. Ever since the news of his transfer stunned two sun-baked cities that July, an underground industry in Barcelona had beavered away to create huge copies of the 5,000 peseta note emblazoned with Figo's face and the line *Figo, pesetero*, money-grabber. For Barça fans, the very sight of him returning to compete against Catalunya, wearing the detested white shirt, was an affront to their soul. Taunts of 'Judas' were accompanied by extreme, absurd comparisons: Figo was rhetorically invited to consider the courage of Catholic martyrs who, at pain of death, refused to renounce their faith no matter what temptation – *as if* a player, a contracted employee of a football club, is on a spiritual par with fans whose sole involvement in their club is a fidelity issue. Or, as one fan sought to explain melodramatically on television: 'Real Madrid are seen as the royal team, Barcelona are the team of the people. Figo has become Marie Antoinette.' *Figo: te van a calentar la oreja*, Figo, they're going to make your ears burn, ran the provocative headline in *Marca*. The fans did not need the prompt, especially as Figo himself was not shirking. He had put his face to a nationwide merchant bank's advertising campaign, mouthing the slogan: 'Change is always good – if it's for the better'.

How was 'the traitor' who had incited such public loathing in one pocket of Spain considered in the dressing room? 'We thought it was a laugh. What other reaction can you have?' grins Steve. 'The television cameras replay his Barça celebrations all the time, him rejoicing in a Barça shirt with all the trophies, shouting abuse about Real Madrid, Catalans v. Castilians, at their town hall. "You white cry-babies, you shit-houses" – in Barcelona they're very scatological. It's so embarrassing, isn't it? But as a player you think it's comical . . . it's a bit like those clips of famous pop stars in their early years with dodgy clothes and hair looking like an idiot . . . you laugh. Players see it in a different context to fans. We're performers in that we represent the club – the shirt and the badge – on the pitch. As a team, we're desperate to win. Individually, we're all as competitive as it gets. Part of performing is directing all your energy and ambitions towards glory, but it is also sharing the glory with the people who urge you on, the fans. No matter how much you love the club you play for – the place, the people, the supporters – you move on. No matter how much you love your football, it is also your trade, your means of earning a living over a relatively short period. It is the fans who invest their team with the romanticism and glamour; we, the players, who, on good days, provide it. Fans expect players to have the same value system as them, but theirs is a pantomime expression of heroism and villainy, isn't it? The Figo thing was the explosive example, but that same season Santiago Solari came to us from Atlético Madrid – he'd scored against us memorably in the local derby the year before, and went crazy celebrating in front of the fans – I can see him now, hair down his back, bandanna, going mad. He joins us, and gets totally slaughtered every time he goes back to Atlético. And he always seems to score against them.

'No one in the dressing room knew the details of the Figo transfer. We heard all these rumours about what deals were struck – like if Pérez lost the election Figo kept the money he was promised – but no one, apart from Luis and the president, know the small print of that deal. I certainly wouldn't bloody ask him, and he's one of my best friends at the club. If it was, as the general consensus has it, that he was effectively given a deal for nothing, great for Luis . . . but then Pérez does get in, and it still turns out to be the best thing Luis Figo could have done. It's not as if he came here and didn't win anything. Luis came to Real Madrid and now he's won the European Cup, he's won the league twice, and he's a whole lot wealthier. At Barcelona he certainly didn't win the European Cup. He left a team who struggled for a few years afterwards.

'That night of his first return was murder. They absolutely slaughtered him. None of us wanted to sit next to him on the bus going into the stadium! That journey is an assault on all fronts even when there's no obvious extra aggravating factor. Stones, firecrackers, drum-beats, piercing taunts, it's all hurled at you – and that's just on the bus on the way in. We'd have armed police running alongside the bus, but even so, the windows would be shattered. The captains never need to rouse the players. The adrenalin is on full-force. The police horses rear up and seem close to bolting as they hold back the Barça contingent. I remember the stadium was literally wallpapered with banners and those big specially printed notes of money with Luis's face on it. The noise! It was torture to your eardrums. Luis had taken twenty-three of twenty-nine corners that season, but he didn't take corners that first visit back, because the corner flags are close to the crowd. He didn't venture wide down the wing, either. They threw everything and the kitchen sink at him. We're used to the hostility of the fixture, and so was he, of course, but beforehand I did wonder how he was going to take it. It didn't bother him outwardly at all. He must have been churning inside with trepidation; he, of all people, understands the passion of Barça fans. It wasn't a case of him wondering idly what kind of reception he might get; he knew what was coming his way, but he takes his responsibility as a player and a teammate seriously. He didn't want to let himself, or anyone, down. That's what he's like: an incredibly conscientious teammate and proud professional.'

Figo, the Lion King, famed for the consistency of his prowling, majestic attacking play, wore the haunted look of cornered prey that night. He completed the ninety minutes but his contribution was negligible. In what became the template for every subsequent return, the crowds screamed, 'Figo die,' hurled gestures of contempt and pelted him with symbolic objects (hard items, designed to hurt; rubbish, to suggest that's what he was). According to the referee's meticulous report, Figo's 'welcome back' presents included three mobile phones, several half bricks, a bicycle chain and a shower of coins. The Nou Camp was a cauldron of emotions. 'We hate you so much because we loved you so much,' read one poignant banner. To intensify the emotional maelstrom, at the final whistle, the Barça players rushed to hug and kiss Figo like a long-lost brother.

'The rest of the team thought it would have been better if Luis had not played simply because there was so much pressure on him, but he always wants to play in every single game,' recalls Campo. 'Canal Plus television had installed a noise-measuring device. When we ran out and Figo's name was announced, the intensity of the shouts and boos and whistles broke all kinds of records. I swear it was the loudest noise I have ever experienced.'

Real Madrid lost 2–0, dropping to equal third in the league behind Valencia and Barcelona. 'A horrible night,' recalls Roberto Carlos, who had once been sent off in the *gran clásico* clash for trying to tackle Figo around the neck. 'I remember spending the ninety minutes worrying about being hit by flying objects. All we wanted to do was get out of Barcelona alive.' However, Figo was better at maintaining a bold composure off the pitch than on it: 'There's been too much talk about the atmosphere and about us being afraid. If we'd been afraid we'd have stayed at home. We played badly, it's as simple as that. The last thing I want is for people to be sorry for me. The only thing I'm sorry about is the result. Now I'm more determined than ever to triumph at Real Madrid. Scores are not settled until the end of the season.'

'Vicente Del Bosque had said early on that his goal was to emulate Manchester United and start the next phase of the Champions League with our Spanish league position under control,' recalls Steve. 'You need to be up there by January, to be "winter champions". It's not an official title, more a symbolic base-level of confidence because once the Champions League restarts, with all the travelling that involves, you are liable to drop points in the league. To be as many points clear as possible is the aim. Figo's stature was such that his body language changed the perception of the team. Everyone suddenly started talking about how Real Madrid were now playing with a sleeves-rolled-up attitude, but that was a misconception. The year before – because of the turmoil we went through, we came back from Brazil seventeenth in the league – we must have battled and won games because we ended up fifth in the league. We had great battlers in our team: Hierro, Salgado, Roberto Carlos, Helguera, and Redondo's defensive qualities were always picked out for praise. The season Figo arrived we started on a high, as European champions, and we were always at the top of the table, we were more consistent and so it looked as if we were working harder, but the players we had are the type who can do both.

'We were there or thereabouts from the beginning of the season. We didn't have a blip at all. We topped the table early on, were never out of the top four, were "winter champions" and clear by three points in January and were never less than five points clear thereafter. The end-of-season statistics were impressive. Overall, Real Madrid had most wins (24), fewest losses (6), highest points per game (2.10), most goals scored (81), highest goals scored average (2.13) and highest goal difference (41), longest winning sequence (8), longest undefeated sequence (12), you name it.

'As a result, very few league games stand out because none were invested with tension or anxiety. Players would talk about games in terms of geography as much as anything else, as in we're visiting the Basque country or Catalonia, Galícia or Andalucía. They're very conscious of the distinct cultural identities. We don't have that in the Premiership. I never think, "Oh, it's Birmingham City, we're going to the Black Country where they speak with a Brummie accent." For me, visiting Spanish stadiums for a second time meant the whirl of impressions from my first season was becoming more concrete: when I saw Deportivo La Coruña next on the fixture list, I could visualise the old sea-front Riazor stadium, with its mosaic walls in the Jacuzzi and showers, and think of their flair players, and Brazilian tradition; Valencia I now knew to be the legendary old Mestalla stadium, crap inside, dressing rooms falling to pieces, a treat to arrive in after a hostile, snail-paced journey into the ground – the traffic there is murder; Bilbao – a weird place, where a lot of police wear black balaclavas and everyone is obsessed with the fact that, for me, San Mamés must seem very English, being a square stadium with top and bottom which was originally laid with English turf in 1913. In the south, I knew a 5pm kick-off in June or September could be horrific in the heat, whether in Sevilla's huge Sánchez Pizjuán stadium where Davor Suker was such a hero before he moved to Madrid or Betis's very friendly ground on the other side of the Guadalquivir River. Across town, at the Vicente Calderón, I knew Atlético play in clouds of fumes from the Mahou brewery. Overall, facilities in la Liga teams are not as good as in the Premiership: no executive boxes, players' lounges and often the most basic of dressing rooms. That was an eye-opener when I first arrived. Like a fan, I'd invested the Spanish league with an aura of glamour that you don't find behind the scenes.

'As defending champions, priority number one was to win the Champions League again. League games became fixtures to get out of the way. An exception was the game against Oviedo on January 14, 2001, when Luis Figo received the European Ballon d'Or at the Bernabéu. In a ceremony before the game, Luis received his award on the pitch in front of a host of dignitaries. It was a good game to make a mark in! Luis scored in the first half, and then in the second half we could've been winning about 10–0, honestly we were on another plane. It was fantastic football – to play, to watch, to commentate on. On the television Michael Robinson was saying, "This is the best forty-five minutes of football I've *ever* seen." We were winning 3–0 and the game culminated in me scoring with five minutes to go. I leapt very high and somehow got my boot on the end of a Roberto Carlos cross and the volley rocketed into the top right-hand corner of the net. It was pure instinct. I remember being swallowed up in a hug from Hierro, Karanka and the others, and when I emerged the whole stadium had changed colour. They'd all got their little white handkerchiefs out. It was funny, because I hadn't a clue what that was all about! They had to tell me later in the dressing room that the white hankies, or *pañuelos*, is an expression of extreme emotion borrowed from bull-fighting. It means the worst, the worst, the worst or the best, the best, the best – and it was a very rare reaction. Everyone was laughing, really enjoying themselves. After much celebrating, we all went off home, and the next morning there were so many press at my bloody house wanting me to comment on it . . . *AS* said I had "leapt like a gazelle" and apparently *Marca* had an animated cartoon of my leap on their website, but, because we were off, and no one was at the training ground to give a quote, they needed to fill the following day's pages with a follow-up. They came to my house at nine o'clock in the morning, finger permanently on the buzzer, and I said, "It's my day off. I won't get out of my bed." I never sleep after night games, my mind is buzzing, the adrenalin is still coursing. It's only at dawn that I start falling into a deep sleep . . . and a few hours later the buzzer started going manically.

'So then I'm in the street outside my house, and they're going, "How did you kick it?" I said, "I kicked it like this" – and they started taking photos of my feet, in normal shoes, to recreate the goal second by second. I was like, "Is that it now?" And someone else came up clutching a video and asked to come into the house so we could watch the goal together. I must have grimaced, and he said,

"Please, please, please, please, I'll get the sack, I'll get my head chopped off." So I invited him in and he took hundreds of pictures of me watching my goal over and over again – as if that's what I would be doing, glued to the telly watching myself! "Never again am I scoring good goals!" I said. "That's it, from now on I'm going to score tap-ins."

'Looking back on the 2000–01 season, our domestic dominance was assured from the start, which was a heavy tick on the president's wish list. But the Champions League is the biggest buzz. In the previous year, we had struggled in our groups and then won the whole competition. Our victory required more suspension of disbelief than a James Bond film. But this season we flew, earning early qualification after both group stages with games to spare. Our aim was to be the first team to defend the title since the European Cup was restyled the UEFA Champions League. Everything compounded the feeling we were indomitable. After 3–2 and 5–3 victories over Bayer Leverkusen, two 1–0 wins against Spartak Moscow, we thrashed Sporting Lisbon 4–0 to seal first place in Group A. The opening goal, scored by Guti, was the club's five hundredth in European competition – the next best tally was Bayern Munich's 293.

'In the second group stage, we had Leeds, Anderlecht and Lazio (managed by Sven-Göran Eriksson), and again topped the group with points to spare. The weekend before the first game against Leeds, on November 21, we had celebrated Del Bosque's first year as coach with a victory over Villarreal. I created the goal for our 1–0 victory. The press made a lot of the anniversary, and the stability the coach had brought. Ever unfazed, Del Bosque made me laugh when he was asked by the press to comment on his milestone. He said: "Nobody, least of all me, could have imagined I would last this long. It is very difficult to last a year here; people try to undermine the coach's image even if results are good." You'd never hear an English manager say that, would you?'

A few days later – only a few weeks after being re-embraced as a first-team player – Steve was dismantling a misshapen and under-strength Leeds team at Elland Road. David O'Leary's side, later to grow in strength and belief in defying the odds and reaching the semi-finals, were without Harry Kewell, Nigel Martyn, David Batty, Rio Ferdinand and Olivier Dacourt and were thoroughly outmanoeuvred, at times mesmerised, by the movement and passing of the Spanish giants. The scoreline hardly reflected the comprehensive nature of the defeat, and the evident gulf in class was neatly encapsulated by a fifty-yard volleyed pass by the regal Hierro straight to the feet of his intended. This, one felt, was unlikely to be repeated by Danny Mills.

'It was one of the few games I remember feeling apprehension because on the rare occasions Real Madrid came across English teams, I always felt I had to justify myself, even though I'd won a European Cup. I was fired up to go there, to play very well, and win. I'll never forget it because Leeds had come a long way fast at the time, and when we arrived there you could sense in people an awe of Real Madrid we don't experience in Spain – at our hotel, Oulton Hall, even at the training ground where the Leeds kitman, by all accounts a notorious pest, kept bothering me for players' clothes. I remember, we won 2–0 and people were coming into our dressing room and picking anything up off the floor, socks, shorts, et cetera, saying, "Can we swap these? Can we take these?" Everyone wanted a piece of Real Madrid.

'Leeds, with their injuries, weren't as strong as they could have been. We won at a canter and looked very classy against them, our big stars played well, but what struck me was the difference in fitness levels between the two sides. Leeds huffed and puffed. The Spanish lads are brought up to eat well and look after their bodies, fitness is assumed. Everyone clapped us off. Afterwards all our lads spent hours signing autographs. It was a good feeling, totally outclassing them and flying off to Tokyo right after the game to the Intercontinental Cup.'

Despite – or perhaps because of – his apprehension, Steve's return to home soil prompted a performance that had seasoned observers of European football noting him as a player of calmness and intelligence, transformed by the *calidad*, the quality of technique, around him. 'It will be interesting to see where McManaman ends up in the European Footballer of the Year ballot . . . at club level he has surpassed the likes of David Beckham this past 12 months,' mused Keir Radnedge in *World Soccer*.

How many people in Britain were in a position to see that? Perceptions of Steve have always been many and varied. His happy-go-lucky exterior and languid body language are famously hard to read, if not blatantly misunderstood. Just ask Terry Venables, who will admit that McManaman is the only player, ever, he has had to ask another player about. 'When he came into his first England training session with me, I said to John Barnes, "He's not giving me much of a buzz. His head goes down. Is he not bothered? Just give me a clue about him." And Barnes said, "He *is* bothered. You'll find him fine" – and of course I did.' Liverpool fans knew him to be a player of intelligence who could adapt his game to what was required on the day, but the rest of the nation had him pigeonholed as a dribbler, courtesy of various headlines celebrating that aspect of his game.

'He started out as a winger, but that wasn't really him,' argues Jim Burns, who watched Steve's emergence and development at Liverpool. 'He never had that absolutely explosive pace of Ryan Giggs or the raw power of John Barnes. He wasn't a shadow striker or central midfielder either. Rather Macca played the game his own way. He would work out an opposition's weakness, and then attack it. In this way he soon had a more flexible role in the Liverpool team. He was a skilful player, but not enough to be a classic playmaker. Even so, he made Liverpool play. It is really difficult to describe. He sees the game in a unique manner. People often say about a player, "Yes, not much upstairs but he has a wonderful 'football brain'." Well, Steve clearly has a brain full stop.

'This leads to a very unconventional style. His role at Liverpool, England and Real Madrid was very rarely the same from game to game. The one constant is his dribbling, but sometimes this is cross-field to create a passing angle, sometimes it is directed straight at a defence and sometimes (and most interestingly) it is away and into space in the opposition's half, thus relieving pressure on his beleaguered teammates. Steve is very rare in that he actually adapts to his own team as well as the opposition. Throughout his career you see he forms very strong playing relationships with world-class players, like Paul Gascoigne, Robbie Fowler, Fernando Redondo, Roberto Carlos and so on, because he quickly understands what they need to play well and gives it to them. It is sheer intelligence that defines him as a player.

'That and his exceptional stamina. Because he always seems to work out the weakness both of his marker and the opposition team as a whole, and because he has the endurance of a marathon runner, he often comes into his own in the second half as his tactical and physical attributes come into the ascendant. He also has a happy knack of scoring goals that are both spectacular and important at the same time. Think FA Cup final against Sunderland, Celtic, Celta Vigo, and, of course, the Champions League final.'

That is the view of a Liverpool supporter who watched him week in, week out. But, to the British public, when Steve went to Spain he was literally 'out of sight, out of mind'. Newspapers reported his 'high' – the 2000 European Cup final – and his 'low', the 'hero-to-zero' headlines prompted by Florentino Pérez's initial determination to sell him. Reports appeared in the English press on the same principle as the *pañuelos* show of white hankies: at moments of extreme emotion. This may be hard to recall since the move to Madrid of David Beckham, who attracts his very own bespoke press corps, relaying information 24/7, even broadcasting live his medical ('a chimps' tea party', muttered Bayern Munich general manager Uli Hoeness) and his pre-season games, but before Beckham there was no culture of following an England player abroad in the Spanish league. McManaman's European Cup goal signalled to a wider audience that English players *can* travel, and brought the European transfer scene full circle, but that had not yet happened at media level. As Venables knows well: 'Spaniards know about our cup finals and Premier League titles going back years. They're so knowledgeable about our players, it's incredible,' he says. 'But up until very recently in England we've had this attitude of "It only happens here." We never knew about the rest of European football for a long time. You couldn't even find the results. That's only just started to turn around with Beckham.'

Back in the spring of 2001, Steve was inked in on Del Bosque's regular starting line-up. Since his league return in November he had played every game on the left and he was playing well. He was known as 'Míster golazos', and even had his own song, 'McManaman Mix', a rap-style dance made by a radio station to commemorate the Oviedo *golazo* (great goal) which followed his Champions League final *golazo*. Lyrics, as follows: *'MC MAN A MAN MAN/MC MAN A MAN/MC MAN A MAN/He shoots and it's saved/GOLAZO!/What a ball, what a pass/PELIGRO! [Danger]'* and so on via phrases that mention Chinese food (he was known to like it) and concern he might be hungry (because of his skinny frame). In mid-February his name topped a *Marca Digital* poll for *el nuevo ídolo*, the new Bernabéu idol. But in England he was pigeonholed by the last 'Out of Real's reckoning' headlines. 'Since October, I've played in every bloody game, but no one at home realises,' he exclaimed at the time. 'I've been playing very well, but they think I'm struggling to get a game.' And 'they' appeared to include Sven-Göran Eriksson.

'The trip to Japan and the failure to win the Intercontinental Cup in Tokyo counted as a blip in our campaign to collect international trophies,' recalls Steve. 'When we lost 2–1 to Boca Juniors, the South American champions, Pérez thundered, "How are we ever to conquer the Asian market with performances like that?" People forget the president expressed his commercial ambition right from the start. After Figo was voted World Player of the Year, he was quick to emphasise, "Figo is good business for Real Madrid, not just in sporting terms, but also for economic reasons."'

The season is watermarked with the image of Luis Figo, but

Steve scored twice against Luxembourg, his first goals in an England shirt. Here with former Liverpool teammate and great friend, Robbie Fowler.

John Toshack with Steve. The former Liverpool striker was Steve's first manager at Real Madrid.

Steve enjoying the predictable response from an Old Trafford crowd after the former Liverpool star had orchestrated Real Madrid's stunning defeat of Manchester United in the Champions League quarter-final on 19 April 2000.

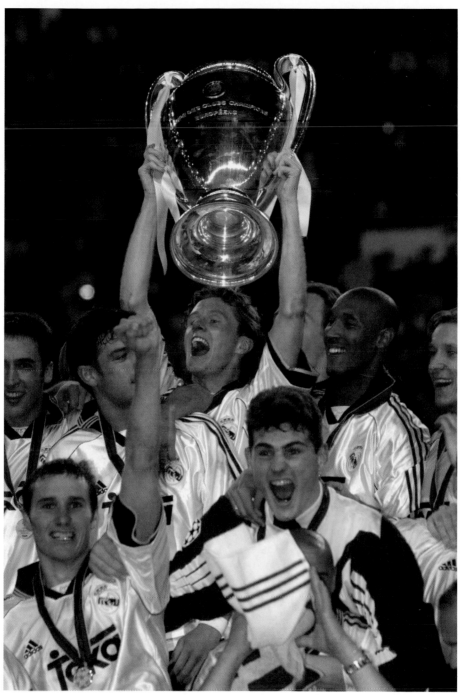

A jubilant Steve holds aloft the trophy with (clockwise from top left)
Raúl, Fernando Morientes, Nicolas Anelka, Míchel Salgado,
Iker Casillas and Iván Helguera.

The goal in the Stade de France that made a fairy-tale of a first season abroad: Steve's volley against Valencia in the Champions League final, 25 May 2000.

Vicente Del Bosque is given the bumps by his victorious first team squad.

The picture that began the revolution: incoming president Florentino Pérez with
Luis Figo and Alfredo di Stéfano after the unveiling of the Portuguese star.

The team that won La Liga title 2000/1: back row, from left to right – Iker Casillas,
Fernando Hierro, Steve McManaman, Guti, Savio, Aitor Karanka.
Front row – Claude Makelele, Míchel Salgado, Roberto Carlos, Raúl and Manolo Sanchís.

Luis Figo, Raúl, Iván Campo, Fernando Hierro and Steve link hands on the run-up to a celebratory dive.

Steve and Santi Solari hold the cup after winning La Liga in 2001. In the background (from left to right) is Míchel Salgado, Manuel Sanchís who retired at the end of the season, Iker Casillas, Fernando Hierro and goalkeeper César Sánchez.

Steve, flanked by Iván Campo and Victoria, shows how beer should be downed in the 2001 league championship celebration dinner.

Steve chips Barcelona goalkeeper Bonano for a crucial Champions League semi-final goal at the Nou Camp on 23 April 2002.

From left to right: R. Carlos, F. Conceiçao, Figo, Guti, I. Helguera, Hierro, Makelele and Morientes.

From left to right: Pavón, Raúl, Ronaldo, M. Salgado, Solari, Zidane, Casillas and César.

Teammate solidarity: Salgado, Guti, Roberto Carlos, Ronaldo, Steve,
Figo and Zidane celebrate Ronaldo's goal against Manchester United.

Hierro triumphantly brandishes the European Cup at Hampden Park, May 2002,
after Real claim their 9th victory.

Inside the dressing room at Hampden Park – Steve with Fernando Morientes.

Roberto Carlos and Steve with his nephew Luke.

Celebration at the statue of Cibeles.

Steve displays the European Cup for the fans gathered outside the town hall
in the Puerta del Sol.

The Real Madrid squad is presented to their biggest fan, King Juan Carlos, during the club's centenary-year celebrations.

The Real Madrid squad lines up to meet His Holiness Pope John Paul II.

Mr and Mrs McManaman walk down the aisle of Palma cathedral,
in Mallorca on 6 July 2002.

Portillo, Luis Figo, Ronaldo and Macca celebrate Intercontinental Cup victory.

Steve in the dressing room celebrating the Intercontinental Cup victory.

Left to right: Helguera, Macca, Flavio, Cambiasso, César, Roberto Carlos, Raúl, Zidane and Ronaldo.

June 2003, the victory parade to Los Cibeles after beating Athletic Bilbao to win a record 29th league championship. Robbie Fowler and his cousin joined Steve and his teammates on the bus.

Claude Makelele established himself quietly as a player of consequence for his new club. Deceptively small and slight, the Congo-born French international undertook the unglamorous fetching and carrying role. 'From day one it was obvious to the players he was a crucial feature of the team, but because he doesn't score twenty goals or do anything visibly fantastic, like beat six men, pass, collect and score, he'll never get the credit he deserves,' says Steve. 'It's like when he moved to Chelsea in September 2003, people said, "He's invisible, he doesn't do anything," but Frank Lampard had a fantastic season and a lot of that was to do with Claude winning the ball and passing it neatly to him. He's an unfussy, effective, horrible-to-play-against engine-room player. When we trained, his reading of the game was so good, you couldn't get past him. Pass the ball and he'd be in the way of it every time. He knew where we were all likely to pass, he had us all taped. His role is to break things up. He is very, very appreciated by the players. It is impossible to overstate his importance. He was a central cog, keeping everything safe and tight behind his ever-adventurous teammates.'

More flamboyantly, this was the season of re-emergence for local boy José María Gutiérrez Hernández, or Guti. The baby-faced blond with a sublime left foot had made his debut at the age of nineteen, courtesy of Jorge Valdano, when an injury to Fernando Morientes gave the slight, floppy-haired teenager his first-team opportunity. In the role of makeshift striker, he scored ten goals in his first fifteen games. However, in between that run – notable for *el dandy* and *el crack* nominations – and the beginning of the 2000–01 season, Guti's reputation had undergone as many transformations as his hair. On paper, his honours included two Champions League victories (1998 and 2000), a Spanish League title (1997), a World Club Cup (1998) and an international debut (in May 1999, against Croatia). In the papers, however, he was ridiculed for his catwalk outings, for having previously been out with an actress who used to be an actor, for being a talent said to be as gifted, if not more gifted, than Raúl, but . . . and here commentators would metaphorically tap their temple with a forefinger and shake their head. The Bernabéu crowd, unconvinced about his commitment, regularly booed him off the field. He was too much of a dilettante. In the controversial annual report filed by Real Madrid technical director Pirri, and leaked prior to the 2000–01 season, the verdict on Guti was emphatic: 'Guti's behaviour is unbecoming of a Madrid player. He has a bad attitude . . . and is not focused on his profession. For sale.' (Steve, however, was one of only five players that Pirri said should not be sold.)

In Steve's view, Guti has suffered because of his versatility. 'When he has the ball he's very skilful, very clever, a great passer of the ball. Sometimes you don't get the credit you deserve when you play in so many positions and you do them very well. He's always been a good goal-scorer when called upon to play further forward, but he considers himself a midfielder. From early on, he's played left midfield, centre midfield, behind the front two. He's done incredibly well. When Beckham came three years later he became a sitting midfield player in the centre, but he can play up front and score goals too.

'Mentally, Guti is all right. The problem for him is that the benchmark among his peers is Raúl, who is quiet and conservative, and has no known enthusiasms beyond football. Rául had a wild party-going year or two when he first emerged but he "reformed" his ways drastically. They're different characters. You see from the way Guti dresses, he's more flamboyant and outward-looking. He's not known as the Becks of Spain for nothing – they're the only two footballers on the planet known to have worn sarongs. He's always sporting some new hair style and his friends are colourful characters. People seize upon that, whereas there isn't that side of Raúl even to contemplate. What speaks volumes for Guti today is that Figo, Zidane and Beckham arrived and he's still playing in midfield.'

'Reaching the Champions League quarter-finals is not an occasion to celebrate for Real Madrid. It is unthinkable that the club would not be in the last eight, or even four. The players' bonus system only kicks in then whereas other teams tend to get bonuses for every game or point won in the group phases. We wouldn't get anything until we reached the quarter-finals. If we'd been knocked out in the qualifying stages, we would have been disgraced. Everyone would have gone ballistic. But there we were, up against Galatasaray. They were a strong team. All the talk about the first leg was, "Oh, it's going to be horrible, very intimidatory," but the trip to Istanbul was fine. We're a pampered lot, footballers; we're insulated in nice hotels, surrounded by security. Apart from the odd coach journey into the Nou Camp, with stones smashing the glass of the windows, I have never felt truly threatened. The Ali Sami Yen stadium certainly provides the full surround-sound experience in terms of swirling noise, firecracker flashes and tangible partisanship, but that's what it's all about, isn't it? The crazy crowd are miles behind the goal. It's not as if they're breathing down your neck.

'We made life difficult for ourselves there. Helguera and Makelele had scored to ensure we went in at half time 2–0 up and playing fantastically well. In the second half we simply capitulated. Jardel started to cause problems in the air for us, and in a flash it seemed they had won 3–2. Umit Davala scored from the penalty spot. Hasan and Jardel added two more. In the space of twenty-eight minutes, we let them score three. Suddenly we faced a tricky second leg.

'That home leg was predictably volatile. People were fighting, arguing, being given their marching orders, but we hammered them 3–0 in the first half, Raúl scoring twice and Helguera again contributing a vital goal. I set up two of the goals with good passes and earned the *el dandy* award in *Marca* the next day, which is always pleasing. And that was that. On to the semi-finals.

'Our preparation for Champions League games differed from the domestic competitions. For Galatasaray, for instance, we'd be gathered as a team to watch fifteen minutes of one of their recent games. The video was never edited down into specific people to watch or typical set-piece options. The coach would stick it in the machine, press Play, and we'd watch fifteen minutes from kick-off to get the gist of their style. That was it. We wouldn't go through free kicks and corners and study them . . . No way, because the players get bored sitting down and watching the telly. If you had a meeting for longer than half an hour with a video, they'd go up the wall. Del Bosque knew that. We saw ourselves as the best, so we wouldn't study potential dangers posed by the opposition. We were always confident enough in what we could do to outplay another team. The overriding belief around the club was that we were the best. Talent will out.

'Were we *over*confident going into the Champions League semi-finals against Bayern Munich? It's a charge that can easily be levelled against Real Madrid, when we fail to reach targets, with all the overblown hype about us being the best team in the world, blah, blah. Certainly we travelled with all guns blazing, very assured, having beaten them at the same stage the year before. In hindsight, maybe we were. It's a fine balance, isn't it? Two years later, in 2002–03, we would be knocked out in a similar vein when we were beaten by Juventus. On both occasions we were extremely confident, whereas in the ultimately successful 1999–2000 season we had struggled to get past Rosenberg, and then had to play Manchester United, who were swimming along. We knew then we were in for a hard game, we weren't as confident. The following year, we were very confident flying to Munich and it wasn't to be . . . Knock-out competitions are great like that, aren't they?

'The hype was amazing after the previous year. Bayern Munich always have the same gameplan: defend, defend, defend and try to hit us on the break. In that first leg, their tactic came off perfectly. We conceded an awful goal ten minutes into the second half which left them with a 1–0 lead to defend at their home in the second leg. It was a mistake by Iker Casillas, one of those things. A timid long-range shot from Giovane Elber somehow sneaked past him. When it happened it was such a shock, because he is remarkable for his concentration and reactions. It wasn't a blatant mistake, but he's saved us that many times he would have been annoyed with himself. We always feel confident that we can score, so no one would have been secretly cursing him. When you're beaten at home, and ultimately knocked out after two legs, everyone remembers it, though, don't they?

'I've slightly blotted out the details of the second game because it was so deeply disappointing. In Spain there is an expression about football being a small blanket, meaning the game is so exciting because one area of the pitch is always exposed. Playing Bayern Munich, when they're defending a lead in a Champions League semi-final, is like being suffocated by a kingsize, winter-weight duvet. You're stifled. They're disciplined, keep their shape and work hard in being unerringly defensive. It's horrible. I remember Guti saying he was surprised to see a Bayern side play such rudimentary football in the European Cup – it was somehow an insult to the spirit of the competition. Elber popped up again to score in the seventh minute. The referee, Milton Nielsen, awarded us a penalty eleven minutes later. Figo scored, so we were 1–1 and knew we could go through on away goals if we got one more, but well before half-time Jeremies scored again from a free kick. Then we had to score two more, so everyone got forward and you could sense the desperation rising. Del Bosque put Morientes on for Karanka, Hierro's partner in central defence, and Savio came on for me. We had as many forwards on the pitch as possible, but nothing worked. We were smothered 2–1.

'When you get knocked out after an away game the anguish continues for hours. We were in Germany, bombarded on all sides by jubilant Munich fans. It's not as if you can get in your car and go home to drown your sorrows. The captains were quite vocal in their frustration in the dressing room. It's unspecific anger, no one wants to be blaming people. Valdano came in, and said something mollifying. At that stage there's no point in kicking and shouting and moaning at people. Then the dressing room falls into an unnatural silence. You can't get out of it quick enough. It's a case of "Let's get back to Madrid as soon as possible".

'When you've won that Champions League trophy once, you just want to win it again and again. It becomes the benchmark, and of course it's been the benchmark for Real Madrid since the fifties. I analysed both games intensely in my mind on the coach to the airport, on the plane, the next day. The frustrating thing was to lose

1–0 at home. We had played so well there, but not beaten an inspired Oliver Kahn, and then conceded a weak goal. We really, really should have won at the Bernabéu. If you are at home in the first leg, and you win without them getting away goals, you're nigh-on through to the final. You don't have to push the game, chase for the result. Even if we had drawn 0–0 at home, we could've drawn 1–1 away, but we were always pushing and that leaves us – almost legendarily – vulnerable at the back. I remember it being very, very upsetting, but the thing about football is we'll have had that disappointment on the Wednesday, and then we'll have played a league game on the weekend. We were top of the table by a six-point margin so the result was not too consequential. Still, when we played Espanyol that Sunday, you could tell our spirits were dented. We were 2–0 up, but ended up drawing 2–2. The crowd were not impressed.'

Some players are closet stattos, with phenomenal recall of every assist, goal and crucial tackle made in their career. Not McManaman, who values skill as a means to an end. He puts everything in the context of winning. For instance, Redondo's sublime outwitting of Henning Berg at Old Trafford the previous season he saw as 'magical, because after the ball had gone through Berg's legs, Redondo ran along and just passed it in front of an open goal to Raúl, who scored, made it 3–0, and got the game over and done with.' He can scarcely recall his own tremendous performance in the first leg of that Bayern Munich tie when two shots on target were somehow turned away with the very tips of Kahn's gloves. 'I played very well, but when you get beaten it doesn't matter, does it?' Well, it does if you are a supporter, and prone to 'what if . . .' musings. And, in retrospect, many McManaman observers see that as a defining game in his career in Spain.

'He had what I consider to be one of his finest games in a Real Madrid shirt,' says David Maddock of the *Mirror*, an old friend. 'With men like Figo, Raúl and Stefan Effenberg on the pitch, he dominated the game. Bayern tied Real's star names up in knots, but they couldn't deal with Steve. He created chances for others, and crucially, two glorious opportunities for himself, as the Spanish team dominated on their home ground. On both occasions, as Steve shot, the entire Bernabéu crowd stood in celebration, only for Oliver Kahn, having the game of his life, to twice pull off not good saves, but miraculous ones. Even now, I wonder how they didn't go in. Had they done so, of course, then Real would have been in another final, and Steve's name would have been written in legend, after a season of heroic commitment to the Madrid cause when, with the new president, it looked as though he couldn't possibly survive the politics of Luis Figo's arrival. There is little doubt he would have remained a central character at the club for years to come. Instead, in direct contrast with Kahn, Casillas chucked one in at the other end, Real lost the match, and with it the tie.

'In the second leg, when Steve was unjustly criticised by none other than Alfredo di Stéfano, there was a strong suspicion he was put up to it by the president, who was still annoyed that the fans had stopped him pursuing his agenda at the start of the season. It was after that semi-final first leg that Pérez decided to extend his policy of buying huge stars to excite the fans, and soon after a deal was mooted to bring Zinedine Zidane to the club. With the arrival of another must-play star midfielder Steve's position at the club would change irrevocably. He would still show his ability to score important goals in important games – no more beautifully portrayed than in the semi-final against Barcelona the following season, when he scored perhaps his best goal for the club – but the fact remains, for all he achieved in his final two seasons, Steve's Madrid career changed under the floodlights on May 1, 2001. Had not Oliver Kahn produced two moments of genius, Steve's time in Spain could have proved even more glorious, but he was never again to be a central figure.'

'May 26, 2000. If we beat Alavés, we would win the league, and we did 5–0. The ease of the result summed up our league campaign: the ever-consistent Raúl scored twice, Guti – arguably the season's most-improved player – bagged another. Hierro ended his twelfth year at the club with his one hundredth league goal and Figo's three direct assists took his year's tally to seventeen. On the day everyone was full of expectation. We had woken up to a perfect Madrid day – blue skies and warm sunshine. When the Bernabéu is full, it's frightening. We're almost unbeatable with the crowd behind us. There was not a minute of nervousness, never any tension or worry. After scoring two in two minutes, we trooped in at half-time feeling we'd as good as won the league. We scored the third on fifty-one minutes. We spent the rest of the second half knocking the ball around, having fun. At the final whistle, the stadium turned electric. The celebrations were incredible, almost as intense in the city as the year before. Real Madrid had claimed the league championship for the first time in four years – a triumphal conclusion to the uncertainty at the start when Redondo disappeared, sold, overnight by a president no one then knew.

'I'd never won a league championship, ever, despite all my dreams at Liverpool. For me it was absolutely brilliant, and to win it in such a strong league. We'd celebrated our Champions League win in 2000 in a dressing room at the Stade de France, but this time we were in our own stadium, with our own people. The celebrations with the fans felt more intimate. The whole winning process restored our spirits after being knocked out by Bayern Munich. It seems a bit churlish to win a league championship and then see it only in context of the title we had failed to defend, but that defeat haunted us all. It made us think, and tinker around a bit, so in a way it helped us prepare for the following year. We knew we should've beaten Bayern Munich, and then when you saw the final, which wasn't a classic, with Bayern beating Valencia on penalties, we still felt convinced the best team in the competition was us and we'd missed a huge opportunity. Del Bosque's first full season ended with a league title. I remember Raúl saying Real Madrid had been "reborn because of his serenity", and he deserved the plaudit. Luis Figo, too, felt gratified. His controversial move was justified straightaway. It was not as if Barcelona had won the Champions League; by the end of the season, his former club was no longer a dominant force.

'Securing the league title early allowed the club time to organise formal celebrations – the on-pitch razzmatazz they're so good at. On the last day of the season, June 17, we played Valladollid at home and received the trophy afterwards. Usually you receive it at the beginning of the following season, but the premature handing-over enabled the club to give Manolo Sanchís the sort of send-off every professional would dream of. Manolo, thirty-six, had played a remarkable eighteen seasons in the first team for Real Madrid, having graduated through the youth section. His father, also Manolo, had played for Real Madrid and his portrait hangs in the distinguished players' gallery in the trophy room. Back in November, when we lost 1–0 to Spartak Moscow, he reached a landmark hundred European games (one more than Gento). He played fifty-eight European Cup and Champions League matches, thirty-five in the UEFA Cup, six in the Cup Winners' Cup and one in the European Super Cup. In total, he played 522 league games for Real Madrid, having made his debut on December 14, 1983 – when Iker Casillas, at eighteen months old, was still in nappies – and hung up his boots having played more than 700 games for the team in official competitions. His record is awesome: eight league titles, two Copa del Rey winners' medals, one League Cup, five Spanish Super Cups, two European Cups, two UEFA Cups and one Intercontinental Cup as well as thirty-seven other minor trophies. He was photographed once sitting on the floor, surrounded by all the trophies he'd won and you could hardly see him for silver handles, knobs and ornate decorations. The Teresa Herrera trophy, for instance, awarded for a pre-season tournament, is five foot tall and wrought like a medieval Tuscan town's tower. The Trofeo Colombino is like a giant galleon. There was another that looked like an elaborately worked silver birdbath. Sanchís was like a giant in a sterling silver Legoland.

'They put on an amazing farewell for him. A polystyrene replica of the Cibeles fountain was lowered onto the pitch. We all had commemorative T-shirts. Naturally there was a gleaming white open-topped bus saying "Campeones 28" – with the image of Figo emblazoned on the side, pointing the way forward with one arm raised, while the rest of us were in a celebratory huddle over the rear-wheel hub. It is always a magical moment when you clamber aboard the bus in the dark, and it creeps slowly through ecstatic throngs of people on our way to the Cibeles fountain.

'The next day's headlines could have been very different. Two of us nearly didn't reach the destination: around one corner, the bus lurched and Santi Solari fell backwards over the railing on the top deck, grabbing on to the nearest thing – me – and we nearly landed head first on the kerb. Somehow we were caught by others just as we'd reached that classic high-jumper's pose going over the bar . . .'

And so, a second year ended with the dignified retirement of a loyal club servant, one whose departure indicated the end of a link with another era. The grinning, heavy-browed Sanchís was the last member of the Quinta del Buitre, the five local lads whose own blossoming coincided with that of their city – a liberal, post-Franco cultural revival in which Madrid finally rivalled the more naturally expressive Barcelona. Together they had graduated from the youth team in which they had played together – Emilio Butragueño, Michel, Miguel Pardeza, Martin Vázquez, and Manolo Sanchís, the last to hang up his boots, who was now sitting on the goddess's chariot for one last time, an algae-green stain on his socks matching the intricate bits of stonework on the fountain, waving goodbye to the fans for whom he had been a model of consistency for nearly two decades.

Settling In

I can't stress enough that the main reason for a player not doing well on the field is for not adapting well enough to a different way of life off it. It's appropriate here to talk in terms of couples because players do not settle when their partner is unable to adapt. Steve and Victoria are a couple who soak up and enjoy their new surroundings, and that has definitely helped Steve feel so much at ease here.

—Jorge Valdano

I wasn't at all surprised that Steve McManaman took to Spain because he's a very outgoing guy. He likes being out in the street, during the day and the night-time. That was one of the questions I always used to get in Spain: 'Are you a day person or a night person?' I'd say, 'Does it have to be one or the other?' And he's intelligent. Some players don't want to learn things, they close their minds, but I've always felt I got on well with Steve in Euro 96 because he's prepared to do something different. His attitude is, 'I'm up for it, whatever you want, I'll have a go,' which is warming for a coach. You get so many who say, 'But I don't do that, I'm this sort of player.' He knows his own mind; he's one of those guys who could turn off if what you were suggesting felt like nonsense, but his initial attitude is responsive. It's a bold step moving abroad, and when he arrived in Spain he was inquisitive enough to say, 'I like this, I want to know more about this . . .'

—Terry Venables

When can you call yourself 'settled' in Spain? When you have learnt the language, subjunctives, passive voice, slang and all? Or when you have judged the assimilation process finely enough to enable you to live and work freely within the different cultural landscape with minimum effort? When you not only learn to love olive oil, red wine and *jamón ibérico*, but also know where to seek out *percebes*, Galician delicacies perilously harvested from below the water level on jagged shores?

Victoria felt quickly at home in Spain beyond the team connection, thanks to her legal work and independent forays into her new neighbourhood. 'Little things, like going to the gym, or having Spanish lessons, meeting people through work – you increase your circle of friends,' she says. 'I've never felt part of the Real Madrid team because that's not something they cultivate. When we first came I kept asking Steven when the pre-season dinner would be. At Liverpool there was always a dinner for the players and their wives or girlfriends, which is a great way of integrating new people. When Real Madrid eventually had one, it was men only. Of course! Rob Jones and his wife Sue were staying, so Rob went with Steven and they both ended up having to make a speech.' ('I stood up and was abusive to everyone, you know, saying it was crazy to be here with all you muppets. Then Rob got up and said the same, which everyone thought was hilarious,' recalls Steve.)

'The funny thing was the next year,' continues Victoria, 'when they had another dinner, Rob and Sue by chance were staying again, so Rob went along with Steven. The other players must think they live with us!

'The men have a great team spirit, and occasionally Steven and I went out to dinner with other players and their wives, but it was important to make a life for myself away from football and make Spain our home. For me, it was difficult to meet people and feel part of the club because of the lack of facilities for families. In the first year, it was positively unfriendly. Wives, girlfriends, family, friends, often little children, used to have to wait for the players after the game in this area next to the car park. I called it the "Pig Pen". It was four sides of corrugated iron, with one door to get in. Nobody spoke, nobody communicated. There was no players' lounge to relax in as there was in England. We'd stand out there freezing to death in January. If the player you were waiting for needed physiotherapy or a massage or had to provide a sample for a drugs test, you could be standing out there for hours.

'Nobody would speak. It was really, really bizarre. In Steven's first season the only wife who said a single word to me was Marie Eugenia, who was married to Julio César. She had just arrived from Mexico and was in the same situation as me, feeling slightly lonely in Madrid. We stuck together at games despite the fact we couldn't understand a word the other said! When we went to Paris, for the Champions League final, I thought it would be a great opportunity to mix. In England all the women travel together and have fun. But, again, it was a huge trip formally planned by the club. There were hundreds and hundreds on the official Real Madrid party so we were all put in different hotels.

'Then, with the new president, came Jorge Valdano and Emilio Butragueño. They had visited Old Trafford and seen the facilities. They asked Steven what could be done to improve things at the Bernabéu to make foreign players feel welcome. I wrote a list of things I thought they should do – have an interpreter, have a support system to include the wives and families, help people find houses, schools, and so on. Steven communicated all this and they agreed. Midway through the second season they put up a small marquee, and straightaway the atmosphere changed. There was somewhere for us to go after the match, have a drink, and everybody was so much more friendly that year. With a glass of wine in hand, everybody started chatting. Roberto Carlos's wife, Alejandra, Iván Campo's partner

Olga, Guti's wife Arantxa – we all had a laugh together. People started bringing their children because there was somewhere comfortable to go. Initially it was a white tent, but heated, with a wooden floor and televisions, and a bar serving drinks and tapas. That was temporary while they built a bigger structure – not the most attractive area, very stainless steel, as if they couldn't quite let go of the original Pig Pen look – but somewhere to socialise until the crowd disappear and you can get to your car easily.

'I said to Steven, "This club is incredible. Don't they realise how important it is to support the family of a foreign player, so that he can settle quickly?" If Steven came home and found me homesick and lonely all the time, he would worry and may think about moving back to England. Later, they eventually organised a box for us, which seated fifteen, for wives and girlfriends so we could sit together and mix. It made such a difference. And they started to plan a proper lounge – a huge box with a bar area, toilets, everything self-contained and very family orientated. But, really, it wasn't until the end of the second year that I started to feel at home at the club.'

For Steve, life in Madrid had settled into a variety of daily routines: home-game days, away-game trips and coveted 'grounding' days at home which punctuated the whirl of a crammed fixture list. By the end of his second season, he had made fifty-six league starts (equal to Míchel Salgado), twelve Champions League and numerous Copa del Rey appearances. His Spanish was good enough to get by, on and off duty, with his guttural Scouse bizarrely lending authenticity to pronunciation. Raúl was impressed how quickly he picked it up. 'Really it was surprising the ease with which he could communicate, maybe not to have a really long conversation, but he immediately learnt the fifteen most important things,' he said. And Steve had long ago stopped baulking at names on official squad lists. 'The Spanish lads . . . you see their names in full and you think, "Who the bloody hell is that?" How they chose the name they're known by seems so arbitrary. With Raúl, it's his first name, and a great name for commentators to draw out when he's scored. With Guti, it's a bit of one of his surnames. He's José María Gutiérrez Hernández in full. Anything goes on your shirt in Spain. I could have had Macca. Savio was always Savio on his shirt, but Bortolini on a team list. When you see Geremi's last name – Ndjitap – you see why he went for his first name.

'Before I came to Spain, you'd think of your typical Spanish player as a lad who ran on to the pitch making the sign of the cross. I was conscious it was a very Catholic country, but, maybe because I am Catholic myself, I didn't find the religious emphasis particularly striking. A lot of lads bless themselves before going out of the dressing room, and then touch the ground and make the sign of the cross when crossing the line. We had one physio, who took us out to warm up, and when the whistle went to start the game you'd see him out of the corner of your eye crossing himself maniacally, four, six, eight times, whatever his lucky number was. Hierro, Raúl, Morientes, all the Spanish lads would cross themselves. On bumpy plane rides – and we did have a few, including two engine fires requiring emergency returns to the airport we'd taken off from, one of them because a bird flew into the engine – the young Spanish lads were terrified, holding their crosses, kissing them, praying out loud and looking up and crossing themselves. Iván Helguera, poor lad, would be in tears. When you go down the tunnel at Barcelona, there are pictures and murals on the walls, and going in and out of the away dressing room, you go past the club chapel. They always say it's for the opposition to pray in because we are supposed to be scared, but the fact that it's there at all! And I suppose it is hard to think of a Premiership equivalent of Madrid's end-of-season tradition of going to La Catedral de Santa María de la Almudena in the city centre to see the priests and give them all the trophies to bless. Mind you, you hear the country-born Brazilians are supposed to be into voodoo, and keeping the spirits happy, but I've spent hours in Roberto Carlos's room watching football and I've never seen severed chicken heads or voodoo dolls of Oliver Kahn with pins in. No, never. He never had anything strange going on!

'I very quickly got into the routine of driving into work. Like any other commuter I would follow the same route every day into training. It took ten minutes, if that. If I had to be at work at nine o'clock it would take me half an hour, but I'd miss the morning rush hour by leaving home around half-ten. I'm very much on autopilot, listening to music, checking messages on my mobile, just going into work. I do call it work. Much as I don't like to swallow the hype, I know I play for the best football team in the world. As much as it's a very enjoyable job that I feel extremely lucky to have, it has its ups and downs like any job. Sometimes it's great, sometimes it's a pain in the neck, as I'm sure everyone finds with their work. I would certainly hate to be in a job that I disliked, but what else can I say? I suppose I could say, "I'm going to training," but I see it as my job and that's what I call it.

'Driving through the gates in the morning can be crazy. You've got fans shouting things depending on the result of the last game, wanting autographs and photographs. And then you've got the press, every day, the same group of thirty who might only want a sentence from you, but they're there. It can be manic, but even then, it gives you a bit of sanity. The whole process of setting the alarm and going in for a fixed time provides necessary structure in a hectic schedule. We have to be in by 11am, and I'm one of those who likes to get in fairly early. Some weeks are mad, you're in a constant state of travelling *somewhere*, to the coach, to the airport, to the hotel, to the coach again, to a ground, back on the coach, to the airport. So, on a morning at home, I'm grateful to be on autopilot subconsciously enjoying the routine. It's grounding.

'Normally I get up at about nine-ish. I have to set an alarm clock or I'd sleep to half two every afternoon. I get up, come straight downstairs and make myself a cup of coffee. I don't eat before training, although it's funny, when I'm away in hotels I always eat a mountain of food. At home I go back up to bed with my coffee and lie there for half an hour watching television – the news, sports news, or the racing news. I can't pretend I'm a morning person. I like my sleep. Once I'm up, and I know I've got training, I'm fine. I leave the house between quarter and half-past ten. The only thing that makes the routine different is whether Victoria has to leave the house before me. As she works, we operate independently in the mornings. It's a bit of a mishmash, and there's a lot of jealousy when one leaves the other in bed.

'In the car I bung on any old music: Oasis, Eminem, dance music that I would never know the name of . . . I have a pile of CDs in the car but I never think, "Right, I'm going to put this on." When I was in England I bought music all the time, always had a favourite album on the go, always knew what I wanted to listen to, but in Spain for some extraordinary reason there are no equivalents of HMV or Virgin record stores. To buy the latest DVDs or CDs seems nigh-on impossible. Thankfully I have friends in the music industry in England who send over batches of CDs. For a long time I had Oasis on – *Heathen Chemistry*.

'A group of ten security guards work at the training ground, and stand at various posts around the complex. They all know us – it would be very embarrassing if one refused a player entry – and when you arrive they wave you down around the fenced-off training pitch at the bottom area where only the footballers are allowed to park. It used to be a Ferrari showroom but that trend died a death a few years ago. Unlike in England, where players tend to be concerned about driving the brand-new whatever, players here aren't bothered. The Spanish come to work in anything. There's a cafe and the basketball players' dressing room, and a place for the younger kids from the second team to change too. Of course the fans are there . . . even when you're bleary-eyed and trying to stagger into the dressing room to get into your kit, they're shouting at you, wanting your autograph, pointing a camera . . . I'd hate to see some of the photos in fans' albums! Though I've never had an embarrassing moment as Ronaldo had, when he drove in one morning in his huge black Hummer – a massive tanklike thing with blacked-out windows – and then couldn't park it because it wouldn't fit in the space.

'You could set your watch by most people's routines. We start training at eleven. The radio's on in the dressing room and the on-the-hour beeps are the key for one of the trainers to come in, say, "Right, come on, lads," and people will stagger out then over the next few minutes. I'm part of the early group – the older lads! We tend to warm up longer, stretching, doing a few weights, having a massage. The exception in our age group is Roberto Carlos, who comes in, throws his kit on and is out in two minutes. Iván Helguera comes running in on the stroke of eleven – I couldn't do that – whereas Zidane is never later than ten fifteen. Santi Solari is always in at exactly ten forty. Training at Ciudad Deportiva is usually open, which means fans are watching the very first steps of our working day. The mood of the last game's result hangs over training. If you've been beaten badly, the fans let you know in no uncertain terms that you performed miserably. They'll shout, "You load of rubbish" or "You lazy things" – nothing terrible. Typically it will last two days, because Real Madrid have always got another high-profile game to concentrate on. If we've been beaten, a lot of players do not go out the night afterwards. It doesn't look good. It's another of the "unwritten rules". More typically, though, we've won and the fans are shouting encouragement. If it's been a very hard game, few people will actually go out and train – so you might have hundreds of people turning up to watch three players jog slowly round the pitch three times and then go back inside. It's surreal.

'If it was one of the players' birthdays, caterers from a restaurant like De María, Txistu or the Asador Donostiarra would have laid out a table with tapas and drinks while we were out training and everyone stayed for a celebratory lunch, which was a great custom. If a birthday fell during one of our trips away, they'd do it the first day we were back. More often than not, though, at the end of the session, you come out and there's a semi free-for-all as we walk to our cars. Journalists ask for an interview or for a sentence, or ask if they can speak to you longer the next day. Every single day. You end up knowing them well, trusting them. I would always say *buenas días* and chat to them away from football. They're not interested in the rubbish. They want to know about the game, and can go into great, great detail about a tiny moment of play. They're frank. If you're not playing well, they'll say so. If you are playing well, they tend to go overboard, but they're not into backbiting and gossip. They don't care about anything other than the football.

'I'd come home and have lunch, often by myself. I was away that often I'd love to get back home. If I went into town for lunch, as I would sometimes, you have to fight your way back home in the traffic. It drove me around the bend. As now, I'll eat anything. I can cook for myself, but I'm also very lazy. I'm not one of those who has to come home and eat pasta with steamed vegetables. I'm lucky I don't have to watch my weight. I'll eat anything to hand, whatever's in the fridge or cupboards – chicken, fish, pasties, beans on toast.

'I was warned that the hours in Spain would be the most disorientating thing to adapt to, but they suit me. Playing late at night, I love all that. I love sleeping. On the day of a game, I'd have gone to bed at 2am, woken up, had coffee, back to bed, then lunch, then back to bed all afternoon, resting or watching telly, relaxing. Then you'd have your pre-match meal and you're off to the game. I really loved playing in the evening . . . it's so relaxing. You get the maximum rest possible.

'For the first three years, we had to spend the night before a home game in a hotel near the stadium – even for a 9pm kick-off. So if you had a home game at the weekend, followed by a mid-week game in Europe and an away game the following weekend, you could be away from home five nights out of seven. I don't know if it was Real Madrid, or Spain, but the travelling experience was not as social as Liverpool or England. Cards aren't a big thing in Spain. Guti would sometimes play cards with the physios. When Ronaldo came we started playing poker . . . I used to take them to the cleaners at poker, I'd hammer them: Guti, Ronaldo, Geremi, Flavio sometimes. But it wouldn't be often. Invariably we'd fly out two days before a Champions League away game, and those trips felt long. You'd try to escape for some fresh air and have a look at the city, but every time you opened a door you were greeted by a deafening cacophony of cheers. If we were playing an away league game, we were imprisoned in the hotel because there were that many people outside waiting for a glimpse of us. We always seemed to be returning to the same cities, Munich, Manchester, Moscow. If you go to Moscow, how many times can you walk around the Kremlin? In between meals, training and the odd team meeting, everyone did their own thing. They could be long, long days. You're in the hotel, out for a light training session, back to the hotel. We always stayed in the same hotel wherever we went: same people, same rooms, same owners, same food, same tradesmen. Each city had its specialist traders who were allowed to get beyond security to flog us local delicacies. The best were the caviar-sellers in Moscow. If you're well equipped with books, music, DVDs, and you have a laugh with your room mate, as I always did with Santi Solari, it's all right. You can rest – and rest and boredom are different things.'

In the summer of 2001, Steve proposed to Victoria while on holiday in Mallorca, and they resolved to marry the following summer, a year to the day, on the island. 'From a sentimental point of view we thought it would be nice to get married there,' recalls Victoria. 'It was a celebration of the fact that we'd moved to Spain, and absolutely loved it. We planned a wedding in the cathedral in Palma, a mixture of Spanish and English traditions with the Roman Catholic bishop and a Church of England priest from the English church there. I had the traditional walk down the aisle in my dress but at the reception afterwards we had flamenco dancers.

'When I look back on our four years in Madrid, I realise how exciting it was to discover a city slowly together. In the first year Marks & Spencer used to have a shop in the city centre so I was able to buy some home comforts. Steven loves an English breakfast, and he didn't like the butter in Spain so visitors used to bring Anchor butter over, it was really ridiculous! But from the start we were adventurous, trying lots of new food. I love things like *jamón ibérico* – I'd never have eaten that before – and olive oil. I hated red wine when I lived in England, I adore it now. In the summer we'd go to the rooftop bar on top of the ABC Centre in Serrano and drink *tinto de verano*, literally "red wine of the summer", which is red wine with a soda-water-like drink called Casera and lots of ice. We'd go to a delicatessen called Embassy (one in La Moraleja and one in Serrano) for *jamón*. It also sells gorgeous cakes – Steven used to love the mini-chocolate eclairs. More French than Spanish, but never mind! La

Frutería, in Calle Hermosilla, has every kind of fruit imaginable and make up beautiful baskets for you.

'The Spanish eat out a lot and tend not to invite you to their houses. They rarely do dinner parties. If they hold a party, it is normally in a restaurant or club. And then you're introduced to all sorts of things you wouldn't pick out of a menu. For instance, when Steven took Rob Jones to that first team dinner, he came back raving about *percebes*, revolting things to look at, like miniature elephants' feet. They are a barnacle that grow on rocks deep below the water on treacherous stretches of rocks in Galicia. When you eat them you get covered in juice, but they're considered a delicacy, and they're delicious. After that, we found restaurants like El Telegrafo or Combarro, specialist fish places which serve *percebes*. Surprisingly for its location, 400km or so from the nearest coast, Madrid has the second largest fish market in the world after Tokyo, so the fish and seafood is fantastic.

'We've ended up with a number of favourite places. If we had something to celebrate, like a birthday or Valentine's Day, we'd go to Zalacain, a Michelin-starred restaurant where they do an amazing hot-chocolate volcano dessert which Steven and I loved, or to Jockey, another top restaurant with a horse-racing theme. If we had friends visiting we'd often take them to Casta Furie, where the waiters are opera singers and burst into song while serving your table. The singing is incredible, and quite stunning when someone breaks into a well-known song in the middle of clearing your plate. If we were shopping in town we'd go to a restaurant called Iroco, which we discovered is like a secret garden in the middle of the city with a beautiful terrace in the summer. Otherwise we'd go to Café Saigon, our favourite of all the Asian restaurants, and run by a friend of Christian Karembeu. After games, we'd always be in De María, where many of the Real Madrid players and staff were at various tables.

'We visited most of the museums and art galleries in the first year, so unless there was a special exhibition on, we tended to let friends and families discover them for themselves. The Prado is just so big.

We prefer the Thyssen or the Reina Sofia if you only have half a day. First-time visitors we'd recommend the usual sites: Plaza Mayor, Puerta del Sol where the statue of the bear is the most central point of Spain, the palace, which is stunning, in a beautiful square called Plaza Oriente. Even if the queues are too off-putting to do a full tour of the palace, you can sit in a lovely cafe outside and soak up the atmosphere. In our last year, one bar was particularly hip – the Ananda, next to Atocha station. It has a real Ibiza feel, the decor is quite Moroccan.

'The Real Madrid physios introduced Steven to Mira Sierra, an estate looking towards the mountains outside Madrid, and the city's best-kept secret. Every once in a while they'd take him for lunch after training, trying out different restaurants in the mountains. In the winter you can go up to the mountains and ski for the day. I went with Michael Robinson's wife, Chris, a couple of times and it's an amazing thing to do. In the summer the mountains are lovely for walking, with stunning scenery. We liked walking near the village of Pedraza de la Sierra, a traditional picturesque Castilian village, and eating suckling pig or baby lamb for Sunday lunch. Other places that leave a deep impression are Ventas La Plaza de Los Toros, the bullring. At any time of the year it is a beautiful building, but it generates an incredible atmosphere during the festival of San Isidro in May. The Easter Processions are very poignant to witness. People in hoods, and gowns, bare feet in chains, walk in silence slowly from all the churches in the old centre.

'Whenever we take any of our friends out at night everybody goes absolutely mad because everything is open until 7am. We tend to be coming back in as it's getting light. José, the driver who helped us so much when we arrived, is so sweet. Whenever we want to have a big night out we phone up José and he drives our car. He's seen our friends the worse for wear! On the way home the car vibrates to the tune of "We love José" as everyone is so grateful. For Steven's thirtieth birthday, as a surprise I organised for his closest friends to fly out from Liverpool, and be hiding in the players' lounge. When he came out, they all jumped on him. That was a really messy weekend, but really good. The nightlife is fantastic here. That's one of the things we'll miss, the fact you can eat and drink and dance until 7am. The days seem so much longer because you're never looking at your watch, there's no time limit here. That took a while to get used to. My parents would be over and we'd ring a restaurant to make a reservation for 8pm, and they'd say, "Sorry, we don't open until 9.30pm." Now we don't think of going out before 11pm. I don't know how we will adapt back to the English way of life.'

Season Three

2001–2002
Real Madrid's Centenary Year

It was a case of, 'OK, who is the best player on the planet? Zidane, by far. Oh, we'll go and get him, then.'

—Steve McManaman on the next big signing

We are sending the image of the twentieth century's greatest club to millions all over the world, over five continents, across languages and cultures, as is only right for Real Madrid, a club that defies frontiers, race and language . . .

—Club statement on the issue of centenary postage stamps

Madrid are celestial, more important than the Holy Spirit. Florentino will appear before us and say, 'Spaniards, we are the glory of the earth and we have a place in heaven,' then he'll pass down the new tablets of Moses. We infidels had better watch out!

—Jesús Gil y Gil, President of cross-town rivals Atlético Madrid

The summer of 2001 was dominated by Florentino Pérez's personal crusade to sign his next superstar. The target? Zinedine Zidane, FIFA World Player of the Year (1998, 2000), the most complete footballer of his generation. Coaches, peers and supporters queue up to cover him in plaudits. Let's take Aimé Jacquet, the French national coach whose team won the 1998 World Cup against Brazil after Zidane scored two goals in the final. 'Zidane has an internal vision,' he told Andrew Hussey, in *Observer Sport Monthly*. 'His control is precise and discreet. He can make the ball do whatever he wants. But it is his drive which takes him forward. He is 100 per cent football.'

Zidane's drive was taking him towards Madrid. As with Figo – and as he would do with Ronaldo in 2002 and David Beckham in 2003 – Real Madrid's president shrewdly ensured the object of his retail desire expressed willingness, indeed determination, to be bought, thus leaving his current employers little choice but to negotiate. The way Pérez invited Zidane to seek re-employment in Madrid is a story as treasurable as Figo's signing – even if it may be a subtle throw of PR dice, perpetuating the notion that Pérez just can't stop the world's best players queueing up at his door. In August 2000, mere weeks after the gleeful capture of Luis Figo, Pérez is said to have caught sight of Zidane at the Champions League Gala. The Monte Carlo Sporting Club, with its retractable planetarium-style star-spangled roof, provided the perfect *mise en scéne* for the act that would bestow his team with the tag '*Los Galácticos*'. Pérez is said to have picked up a napkin and written on it: 'Do you want to play for Real Madrid?' This extravagant gesture – I'm sure the Sporting Club boasts linen, not paper, napkins – gathered pace as the message was passed from hand to hand until it reached Zidane. Without looking up, he found a pen and scribbled something. The napkin was passed back again. Pérez opened it, and beamed. The one-word answer was 'Yes.'

Thus began eleven months of speculation. Real Madrid represented the perfect move for Zidane, both on and off the pitch. The curriculum vitae of France's World Cup winning hero listed under 'club honours' the European Super Cup (1996), the Intercontinental/World Club (1996), the League Super Cup (1997) and Serie A champion (1997, 1998). With Juventus, he twice reached the Champions League final only to lose (to Borussia Dortmund in 1997, and to Real Madrid in 1998). While he saw in Pérez's ambition the best chance to win the ultimate club honours, his wife Véronique, a former dancer of French-Spanish extraction whom he met when playing in Cannes, was said to be increasingly keen to return to her parents' home country to raise their sons. On 3 July, eleven months after the Monte Carlo pass-the-napkin, Florentino Pérez flew to Italy and met Juventus general manager Luciano Moggi to thrash out a deal. Juve demanded £80m. Madrid said no, and mulled theatrically over the names of Gaizka Mendieta and Patrick Vieira instead. Zidane, on holiday in Tahiti, was removed from the wrangling but made his desires known. Juve either had to face keeping a furious player or lowering the asking price. Within days Pérez was flying back from Turin with plans to present a £50m signing to the world's media.

The purchase of Zidane was a presidential declaration of intent. Not for Vicente Del Bosque a quietly arranged 'present' for winning the league in the manner José Luis Nuñez rewarded Terry Venables when he won la Liga in 1985, his first season as coach at Barcelona. 'I went home for a weekend and when I came back the president had bought me, as a surprise, this centre-forward from Zaragoza,' chuckles Venables in recollection. 'I said, "Look, thanks, but he won't play. What are you doing?" It was ludicrous . . . I had a good relationship with Nuñez, he knew his football, but, if anything, today the power a president wields in Spain has got stronger and stronger. How can a manager have no say in signings?'

'Our strategy is clear,' stated Pérez. 'I've always said this club should have the best players in the world. Why? Because they're the most profitable ones. Signing a world-class star means great international projection for Real Madrid and that translates into economic profit. From a financial point of view, Zidane will be a great investment, the same as Figo has been.'

If the capture of Figo was to subdue Madrid's domestic rivals, the presence of Zidane in Pérez's gilded butterfly net was intended to send the Real Madrid image even further abroad. On the calendar for this season, the date 6 March 2002 was circled boldly in red: the hundredth birthday of Real Madrid Club de Futbol. Flaunting the FIFA-designated title of Club of the Twentieth Century, Pérez saw the perfect opportunity to challenge Manchester United's commercial domination. What better way to kickstart that process than to sign the world's greatest talent at a world-record price? Even better, Zidane, proud of his Algerian heritage (he describes himself as 'a non-practising Muslim'), was a French national icon fast becoming the face of young immigrant France. Though he is careful to avoid being used for political ends in the biting crossfire of French racial politics, Zidane's name conjures layers of different cultures. 'Everyday I think about where I come from and I am still proud to be who I am,' he has said. 'First, a Kabyle [from the Berber, the non-Arab people of the Kabylie region of Algeria] from La Castellane [the sensitive immigrant suburb of northern Marseille], then an Algerian from Marseille, and then a Frenchman.' His appeal may transcend the racial, social and religious divides, but these factions represent a market which would now be doused in the spirit of Real Madrid. Duly, more than three hundred newspapers afforded Zidane's transfer front-page status. The club prepared half a million Zidane replica shirts, prioritising the French and Arab markets. The newly set up Real Madrid official website – average a hundred thousand hits per day – went red-hot with eight hundred thousand hits on the day Zidane's signing was announced. Additionally, Pérez acquired a whacking 90 per cent of Zidane's image rights in return for a salary of £4.5m a year after tax.

For the players, centenary year meant the Treble was not so much an unspoken expectation as an obligation. Simple, eh, to win the Copa del Rey, la Liga and a ninth European Cup (venue for the final, Hampden Park, full of historic resonance)? All had to be garnered as part of the grandiose celebrations. For the Copa del Rey, the Spanish Football Federation general secretary Gerardo González confirmed that the final would be played earlier than usual, on 6 March, Real Madrid's birthday, at the Santiago Bernabéu stadium – a decision taken as a 'modest contribution to Real Madrid's centenary celebrations'. Even Luis Figo, who had ended his first season jaded ('I'm not tired of football, but I am sick of so much travelling and so many days stuck in hotels') and who had a World Cup to look forward to by way of a summer break, came up with the requisite club line. 'We believe winning in Glasgow is a sort of destiny,' he said, adding his voice to the chorus of romantics already recalling the heady 1960 goalfest at Hampden Park, when Real Madrid beat Eintracht Frankfurt 7–3 in a display of the most enchanting football ever seen.

While setting the target, Valdano, however, conceded the Treble might be asking too much of players with extra off-pitch, centenary-year commitments. He would be aware, too, that history shows that even the most distinguished Madrid teams rarely achieve a Spanish League and European Cup double. The legendary side who won five European Cups in the fifties only managed it twice. The Emilio Butragueño-led 'Vulture Brigade' won five successive domestic titles between 1986 and 1990, but with three consecutive semi-final defeats fell short of attaining the status of European Cup finalists. The team in which Steve McManaman won his coveted first European Cup winner's medal, in 2000, finished fifth in la Liga.

'We were never told of any specific club aim,' recalls Steve. 'At the same time we know we're expected to win everything every single year. The centenary celebration was built up in the press. The club had organised some event, *every single day*, whether it was teaching kids in a school or opening exhibition centres in the parks of Madrid. The Vuelta de España cycling race, a huge thing around Spain, was due to finish its final leg at the Bernabéu. Magic Johnson came over to play against the basketball team. We were due to meet the Pope, King Juan Carlos, the then Prime Minister of Spain José María Aznar and Kofi Annan at the United Nations. There were homages to di Stéfano, Santiago Bernabéu, concerts with Placido Domingo, exhibitions of all sports in our stadium, you name it. There was even talk of the club making a Hollywood movie starring Antonio Banderas. We knew it was a big year. Subconsciously we're not really bothered about the Copa del Rey . . . we're not. If it falls into our hands we'll be bothered about it, but that year we were bothered about winning it. In the early rounds, we still put the kids out, but once we got to the good teams it was the full line-up every time. The final, which is usually late June/early July, had been dramatically rescheduled to coincide with the club's official birthday at our ground in March. How ridiculous is that?'

For Del Bosque, there was still no new centre-half to rotate-cum-gradually-replace Fernando Hierro. How many times would he fruitlessly request a centre-back from his president only to be attacked later for his team's defensive frailties? There was no cover for the full-backs and still no cover for the injury-prone centre-forward Fernando Morientes. He had Zidane, the world's most consummate football artist, but yet another midfield player, if we reduce him for a minute from maestro status to his technical category. He brought a fantasy package of skills, technique and vision, and an intense determination to win the Champions League. However, with his instinct to move the ball quickly with his first touch, would he be compatible with the more patient style of his teammates? Would he adapt, or would the whole team have to subtly readjust their way to suit him? Pre-season speculation was ready to roll: questions, questions, valid questions. The press were quick to observe that Guti, Raúl, Figo, Savio – and McManaman and Munitis, at a push – were all existing squad members who did, or could, play in the hole behind the forwards. Was Zidane a luxury too far?

'The big question was, where was Del Bosque going to fit him in?' recalls Steve. 'When Zizou played for France and Juventus he seemed to play in a position we didn't have at Real Madrid. He played off the front people. So, would he play behind Raúl? He started off there and didn't settle. It was difficult for him. He had to perform. He had to be £50m worth of player. He could not afford weeks trying to find a place in the team . . . he started behind Raúl, then went centre of midfield, then left midfield, he played all over the place. During the experimentation, Del Bosque at least knew that in Roberto Carlos he had a player who could cover almost the whole of the left side on his own, so it didn't matter much that we lost a conventional left midfielder.' As the manager argued, swatting away early criticism, 'Zidane's arrival may have been inconvenient at first, but it was inconvenient for the opposition, too – his position is difficult to pick up and he's a wonderful player, of course.'

'The significant thing about Zidane's arrival was that it was the start of an unwritten pecking order,' says Steve. If he came off injured, so-and-so went on. There were positions like that all over the park. You sort of knew the scene. You weren't worried about your situation. Zidane is brilliant so everybody was thrilled to bits to have him as a teammate. Would I lose out because of him? Was he the second successive *galáctico* to take my place? I never looked at it that way. The fact we had ten international midfielders is what affected me. I'm lucky in that I play on the right wing, on the left and in the centre, so I'm not vying with any particular player for a position, but then again I was vying with ten.'

With almost comic predictability, pre-season prompted the habitual 'Real Madrid in crisis' headlines. After a two-week warm-up in Switzerland (with McManaman and Solari luxuriantly cool with the sole fan on offer at the Beau Rivage hotel), the squad flew to Egypt for the first of the club's big-earning showcase friendlies. A game against Egypt's top club, Al Ahly, in Cairo, would net £1.5m. The sight of Raúl, Roberto Carlos, Figo and Zidane scrambling up sarcophagus chutes at the pyramids and riding camels in front of the Sphinx provided some striking photo-opportunities for the Arab market (Zidane's roots being maximised, of course). However, the glittering line-up lost 1–0 at the sell-out match ('awful pitch and bizarrely hostile for a friendly', as Steve recalls). It was hardly ideal preparation for a hard season. The squad flew home to participate in the Trofeo Teresa Herrera, the most important of Spain's myriad pre-season tournaments, and finished runners up, losing 2–1 to Deportivo. 'That trophy's a big deal, and even in pre-season games we were slaughtered if we didn't play well.'

So far Zidane had been as quiet a presence on the pitch as he was off it. In the first league game Real Madrid were defeated by Valencia, who during the summer had lost their coach, Héctor Cúper, their captain, Mendieta, and their president, Pedro Cortés. In a horrible introduction to Spanish league football for Zidane, Antonio López Nieto, an experienced referee, signalled fifty-eight fouls in the first forty-eight minutes . . . thirty by Valencia and seven on Zidane. 'Is it always like this?' he discreetly enquired of his teammates after a 1–0 defeat that could have been much heavier but for the brilliance of Iker Casillas.

'Zizou got booted from pillar to post that night,' said Steve. 'Valencia were notorious and suddenly all the games were like that, when the opposition would just defend, defend, defend. In the centenary year people started to loathe us. It went over the top. It was too much. In England, a club would never get away with so much self-congratulation. Can you imagine Liverpool or Man United or Arsenal putting on a year's calendar of events to celebrate their birthday? No. In Spain, we, Real Madrid, became this ostentatiously fantastic team. Down to the last detail. Our kit, for instance, was pure white with a discreet centenary logo, no dirty sponsor's symbol . . . It was very nice to play in plain white kit, but sort of arrogant, too. You know, "We don't need the money and we play the purest game." The players didn't buy into the hype, of course, but that's what started to change public opinion. People were saying, "Who do they think they are?" Well, we were only a football team . . .'

And a football team who managed only one win and five points in the first six league games. Top-seeded in their Champions League group, they had no problem in that forum – as Roma were outclassed in their stadium, and four goals were sent thudding past both Anderlecht and Lokomotiv Moscow (without Zidane, which added fuel to those debates). The Rome game took place on 11 September, despite the horrifying terrorist attacks in New York. 'I was in bed, resting before the game, and had dozed off. The next thing I knew Santi [Solari], who I was rooming with, had come back in and was waking me, asking whether I'd seen what had happened. I hadn't a clue what he was talking about. As he was fingering the remote control, trying to switch on the television, he told me about the planes that had already hit the towers of the World Trade Center, and then we saw they had collapsed. Of course no one, the world over, could absorb the implications of that visual image. Holed up in an anonymous room, in a standard hotel, in a foreign city, it seemed particularly surreal. We were convinced the game would be cancelled, but it wasn't.'

Perilously early in the season, concern had been expressed over the bloated fixture list, the papier-mâché defence and Zidane. 'How many times have we had that?' grins Steve. 'You lose two, three games, it's crisis, crisis, crisis, then bosh, three weeks later you win a game, and they're singing your praises, you're the most brilliant team in the world.'

For Steve, it had been the usual September story of waiting patiently for a regular place while the newly arrived midfielders settled in. (Elvir Baljic, the Bosnian who had arrived in the same summer of 1999 but had been loaned out for eighteen months, told reporters he intended to 'do a Macca', by which he meant fight stoically for his place.) By late September he had claimed his role and Johan Cruyff used his *Marca* column to air the view that McManaman is *el punto de equilibrio en su equipo*, the fulcrum of the team. On 4 November 2001 the Bernabéu was in full, collective song in praise of the Englishman who orchestrated the most ultimately gratifying *madridista* scenario: a 2–0 defeat of Barcelona. 'I started on the left, and Zidane was in the centre. After ten minutes or so, we switched and I played centre midfield. Their lad Xavi was on the ball a lot, causing us problems. I marked him, and ended up having a big say in the game. When you're in the centre, a lot of the play goes through you. The switch freed Zizou to do his stuff, and earned me pleasing headlines the next day. I was declared "the key to unlocking Zidane's potential". Morientes scored the first, midway through the first half. Then, literally on the ninetieth minute, Figo scored against his old team. There was much rejoicing over that one, after the abuse he'd endured at their stadium. Hierro and Rivaldo had their traditional head-butting spat. I like that! That's what it's all about, isn't it? Like most derby matches, there's always a spat somewhere, a few pushes, some handbags. Rivaldo is so mild-mannered, but he always showed a temper against Real Madrid. I admire it when the captain's very hard, very forceful. It shows the way to people – not by doing something stupid that would get you sent off, but by standing up and being counted. That's what it's all about.'

In his regular column in *Marca*, Michel, the former Real Madrid star midfielder, stated it was Madrid's conviction that had settled *el clásico*, while *AS* judged players on a sliding scale from 'perfect' through to 'very bad': *perfecto* – Macca, *fenómenal* – Hierro, *muy bien* – Xavi, *bien* – Pavón, *regular* – Figo, *mediocre* – Coco, *mal* – Rexach, *muy mal* – Rechenback.

Figo's goal was a brief respite. Troubled by poor form and a recurring ankle problem, on a personal level he would write off 2001–02 as a disappointing season. The Spanish press, never knowingly understated, declared him in 'the worst form of his life': his body language was negative, he looked heavy-footed, he couldn't outwit a full-back, let alone deliver a decent cross. McManaman would frequently come on for him, and equally frequently the Spanish press would write, 'and Real Madrid looked like a team again'. But the pecking order had to be maintained. In one press conference, after Steve had come on and again played exceptionally well in replacing Figo, Madrid-based English journalist Sid Lowe said: 'The team looked better with you in it.' Macca modestly laughed it off, making 'I'll pay you later' gestures. He knew the score. It was one of the new 'unwritten rules': the superstars have to play. Fans had to be able to come to games knowing they would see Figo,

Zidane, Raúl and Roberto Carlos. Richard Williams of the *Guardian* makes the apt comparison: 'Pérez shares the philosophy of the old-time Hollywood studio bosses: let's see the money on the screen. In other words, you don't buy stars and leave them on the bench, or even let them take the occasional mid-season break. Starting with their pre-season tour, Real's big names are on display, week in, week out, in every competition available to them.'

On Del Bosque's evident inability to drop or rest Figo, Míchel Salgado conceded: 'There are heavyweights who are untouchable. Touching them can cause even more problems.'

'It was a bit weird,' Steve says. 'Frankly, you shouldn't be out there if you're not properly fit, because there is someone else on the bench who could do the job. Del Bosque didn't think it was fair – at one point he effectively told me his hands were tied. They were the rules set from above. Of course it was frustrating, but less so because I had the support of the press and the fans. I'd be walking in the street and fans would come up and say, "You should be playing, the team's much more fluent with you." In England, people didn't then understand the hierarchy of Pérez's Real Madrid. They do now. But back at home the interpretation of my circumstances was that I wasn't valued as a player. The fact was, Figo had an ankle injury and kept struggling. They kept pushing him back to play. The Figo–Zidane axis was under scrutiny. Once you're struggling and people are starting to get at you, you get frustrated, a bit short-tempered. It wasn't a happy season for Luis. He knew he wasn't playing well. He was even getting whistled off. He couldn't find his form after his injury, and that affected his confidence. Zizou's arrival in itself never caused him problems. People banged on about the team not gelling, but I believe Luis, coincidentally, went through a bad run of form and, as one of our most influential players on the pitch, it had a knock-on effect. How bad was it? He came off in the Champions League final. That says it all. He wasn't happy.'

Off-pitch, a strong case was being aired for McManaman to replace Figo until he recovered form. Within the dressing room, the pair were close. 'It is strange, because normally if you play in the same position as someone else there is a strong competitive element between you,' Figo mused a year later, leaning against the wall of the Madrid players' lounge after a particularly bruising encounter (physically, if not result-wise) against Barcelona. He's dressed in a sleek black leather jacket and jeans, his hair combed back straight from the shower. Much as you don't like to swallow the hype, there is an aura of 'cool' about him, of engaging superiority. You feel like you are talking to the Leader of the Pack.

'Steve was playing on the right side of midfield the year before I came, where I now play, but he is one of the guys who I have a better relationship with in the club. Sometimes it's like that, and sometimes it's more that you fight for the position. I've admired Steve from his earliest Liverpool days. I always kept an eye on Liverpool when I was growing up in the late seventies and early eighties and the English teams were at the peak in Europe. Clubs like Liverpool became my reference point.

'When Steve went to Real Madrid, it was exciting. There was a huge expectation because he came from Liverpool. When I arrived here a year later, I knew he was a great player because I had seen him play great games in his national team, at Liverpool, and he had done a fantastic job in his first year in Madrid. I didn't know him as a person, but he was the one who came forward and helped me a lot in the dressing room, and who I have a close relationship with at the club. We never even joke about our so-called "rivalry" for the same position on the field. For me, he is more versatile than being a right-sided midfielder. He can play on the left, where I think he is best, and he can play inside too. He always puts 100 per cent into helping the team in whatever way he sees they need him.'

Put to Figo the issue of his form, and the fact that McManaman was a viable option Del Bosque was unable to utilise except as a mid- to late-game substitute, and he looks genuinely pained. 'I feel sorry for the other players who work so hard all year and play only sometimes. It's always difficult when you have so much quality in the team and there are players who can't play, because we can't play more than eleven. But our relationship in the dressing room is not affected by that. Honestly, there is no problem with that. It is really important that we have the respect of each other. It is the decision of the coach who plays, but we all know every one of us *could* play. Everyone has something different to contribute towards this team.'

The season had started with Zidane bemoaning his lack of form: 'I'm very much aware that I'm not performing as people and I expected.' But in November, the league campaign swung around and Zidane's contributions became less fitful. He began to enjoy himself. 'Zizou suddenly relaxed,' says Steve. 'It took a while to settle in, find a house. His wife was away a lot with the kids because they couldn't find somewhere suitable to live. It takes time. He was moving countries into a team with a huge amount of pressure on him. He was the sole signing, on a world-record transfer fee. When I came so did lots of others, and I came on a free, whereas others had biggish price tags. The press were diluted in their expectations of us all as individuals at first. But when Zizou came, and he was the best in the world, he was under incredible pressure to perform brilliantly. Luis had set the precedent. He had settled well from day one the year before, and Zizou was expected to do the same. Whenever we played, if he wasn't fantastic, they'd say "Why? What's wrong with him?" But look at him now. No one has a bad word to say about him. Even when he has a bad game, no one even mentions it. He is the best.

'I like the fact he's the best player on the planet, and yet so modest. He's so quiet. On the bus, he sits up at the front by himself, out of the way. He'll read, or he'll have his earphones on, or he'll be watching his DVD. He always wears those socks they give you on planes to stop deep-vein thrombosis. I think all the French players were supplied with them once on international duty. After games he'll always have them on, his feet up, drinking litres of water. He'll look as if he wants to join in, but he doesn't mix. You'd never see him in the players' lounge enjoying a drink after a game. He'd bypass it and go straight home. His wife came to a few games in his first year, but she was pregnant and found the cigar smoke in the crowd distressing. Then, she had three very young boys so it was difficult for them to socialise much. They never came out to dinner after a game. If we were ever given a few days off, most players would go for a break somewhere like Marbella. Zizou would go to a health spa. For every beer Roberto Carlos drank, Zizou would have a litre of mineral water, although he would have a glass of wine with his pre-match meal. He has an iron metabolism disorder and has to drink five litres of water a day.

'At the training ground, he spoke mainly to Claude Makelele, being French of course. Claude is also very quiet. They roomed together but their room wouldn't have been a big party. Makelele could fall asleep anywhere, he'd probably sleep all day, but Zizou didn't sleep much. In a way he's unknowable as a person, but as a teammate you know him very well. Anyone lucky enough to play with him knows he will play intensely hard every time he steps on the pitch. He's so elegant, yet he has a hard side. On the pitch he's very tough, he doesn't mind fouling people. He shouts and moans, he can be dirty when he wants to be, but he's a lovely fella. I remember reading some French rock star saying nobody can work out if Zidane is an angel or a demon because he smiles like Mother Teresa and grimaces like a serial killer.

'Iván Helguera had spent time in Italy and could speak a bit of Italian. He's always loud and friendly anyway, and would integrate Zizou in his craziness. Helguera became mates with him. Would Raúl, as king of the dressing room, make a particular effort? No, in training, Raúl stuck to his own routine. It's not as friendly as it is in England where, for instance, as soon as you finish training you have a meal together in your own facilities. It's always nice to sit down, eat and talk, but in Spain when you finished training, you either went to the gym or got changed and went home until the next day. We never had lunch together unless you arranged it yourself. There would be times when you'd come in for 11am, train, and go home without conversing with anybody. So it could be lonely if you weren't naturally outgoing.'

Míchel Salgado, observing Zidane when he first arrived, concludes both he and Figo are very quiet personalities, but almost diametric opposites. 'Luis is a very strong personality, a special type, but a very private person, while Zizou is very timid, more timid than people would ever think in fact. He doesn't want to be a star. He gets lead-role billing because of what he is – a phenomenon playing football – nothing else. But he doesn't want that, he wants to go by as unnoticed as possible.'

In his difficulty in settling, Zidane epitomised the concerns voiced by Butragueño to Valdano about providing an effective club support system. Zidane became the first foreign player to benefit from the list of helpful suggestions compiled by Steve and Victoria, as Butragueño acknowledges. 'We knew the core of the club is the first team and that you have to provide a perfect environment for them because their domestic happiness directly affects performance,' said Valdano's assistant. 'So [on the strength of McManaman's suggestions] we decided to hire someone to take care of the players. When you sign a player you have to realise it will take time for him to settle, to find a house, a school for the kids, a doctor to register with, whatever. Zidane was the first player in this situation. He was very professional at work but he had problems moving to a new country. A Real Madrid footballer is famous, and fame means money, and people try to take advantage of their situation. They express interest in a house that costs x, and when it's known that Zidane is the person interested, suddenly the house costs three times x. So we set up a system to help our players.'

By the end of 2001 Figo had been declared World Player of the Year, with Raúl, the favourite, coming third. By the beginning of January 2002, Real Madrid topped the league, kicking off the centenary year well with a 3–1 victory over Deportivo La Coruña. Thrillingly for the marketing and financial offices at the Bernabéu, the collective siren call of Raúl, Figo and Zidane had pulled in nine capacity crowds in ten games. With £233m banked from the sale of Ciudad Deportiva, the training-ground complex, the club's £185m of debt was wiped out. Even the captain Fernando Hierro, instinctively resistant to hype, was quoted buying into the glorious dream: 'We've got the raw material to make history.'

History was due to be made on 6 March, but Real Madrid and

their must-be-seen stars began to labour under a heavy workload. In February they played nine games in twenty-five days. 'Playing every three days might not qualify as inhuman, but it's extremely burdensome,' sighed Del Bosque. Expectation weighed heavily. There was little joy in anticipation, merely pressure, pressure, pressure to succeed.

The giant digital calendar beaming from atop the steep-tiered Estadio Santiago Bernabéu had counted down the days to the anniversary of the club's foundation in 1902. 003, 002, 001, kick-off! Bang on the last stroke of midnight, the black flaps bearing red numerals flicked over to 000 – destination date, 6 March 2002.

At 9pm, the white-clad players were unleashed into that legendary Bernabéu atmosphere to commemorate the date with a victory – they more than hoped – over Deportivo La Coruña. For Del Bosque and his team, it was not just a firework extravaganza to celebrate the centenary of a club who had evolved from insalubrious early home grounds (a rubbish dump, fields in the shadows of bullrings) to be granted the royal prefix and become a Spanish institution with a home on the Castellana, the city's central thoroughfare, among the museums, ministries, five-star hotels, landmark fountains and architectural horrors. It was not even just a chance to show that Real continue to uphold their legendary respect for all-out entertaining football and for claiming as their own the primacy of the world's most mesmerising players. No, the ninety-minute confrontation in the presence of King Juan Carlos, the honorary president for the year, was a must-win mission to collect the first of the three trophies Real's sporting director, Jorge Valdano, had set as targets for the 2001–02 season. 'Winning the club's first Treble in our hundred-year history is our grand objective,' he said.

Real have won the Copa del Rey seventeen times, but it has rarely been a priority. 'The year before we were knocked out in the first round by a non-league club and no one made much of it. It was sort of a Worthington Cup scenario for Manchester United or Arsenal,' said Steve. 'This year the Cup's very, very important. We have to win everything. You can't understate it. Everyone's thinking how great it would be to win it and see our name on the cup. Imagine if we don't win it – if we get beaten, at our ground, on our centenary date. It would be a disaster.' Florentino Pérez set the standard with his assertion: 'Madrid winning nothing during its centennial year is a hypothesis I can't contemplate.'

It would indeed be *un día negro*, a black day, as Fernando Hierro declared for a hundred headlines in the Real-drenched sports papers, but the club toasted their 'centenary and a day' with sunny prospects on and off the pitch. A streak of erratic away form had been broken. Following the Champions League win at Porto, the team won their first away league game since early December the previous weekend, against Celta Vigo. Figo was said to be fit again, and McManaman, who had proved over two and a half years to be a veritable big-match magician and committed squad member, had returned to form after a back injury. However, with Zidane ensconced now too, the Englishman was prepared to share a midfield role. 'I'd rather Figo play than not,' he insisted. 'First and foremost we want to win the final. We want all our best players fit. If that means I'm on the bench, so be it.'

Visiting Steve before the game, the talk was not restricted to the game, but of the way Real Madrid were being picked up, dusted down, and redirected by Pérez, at whose instigation the club had taken control of the lucrative image rights of their globally worshipped players and begun exploiting marketing potential. 'The president ordered a type of census to assess how many Real fans there were worldwide and the figure that came back was seventy-five million, compared to twenty-five million Manchester United fans,' he explained. 'This club will never be short of money. The trophy room has silver cups the size of cars. When you look closely you see some of them were for matches against very trivial teams. Everything is big-scale.'

Serious silverware has famously been won down the years. 'But Real have hardly begun to tap into their resources through merchandise. Wait till you see the club shop,' Steve said, as we strolled into the shopping mall attached to the Bernabéu, as workmen painted and varnished the stadium for its big night. Sure enough, in the modest-sized shop with an underwhelming range of goods typical of Continental clubs, he pointed out his image in a range of tacky 3-D pennants. 'I've been here nearly three years and that was done after my first game here, a pre-season friendly. We've had about eleven changes of strip since then. I'm wearing odd boots. I had a huge blister on my toe so one boot was size eight and a half and the other was size ten. And this is a bit rude . . . but everyone laughs at my shorts. Look at the size there. I wish!' he laughed, indicating a 3-D ridge of near-Pyrenean proportions.

Walking on the streets around the Bernabéu, people approached him with cameras, tape recorders, shirts or balls to sign, babies to cuddle, queries about tickets or simply for a general chat. Approaching the club shop, he is clinched in an embrace by a local 'character' known to his four-year-old nephew, Luke, as Stinky Man. Half an hour later, none of those in the company of the Real player can leave the precinct without a further round of embraces. It is like that all the time for Steve, who always obliges with good humour and a chat in Spanish. You would not glean it from the Little England attitude that means McManaman's feats are barely recorded at home, but his lauded presence in Madrid was a symbolic show of confidence for English football. Every day Spaniards approach 'Macca' for a chat about Premiership teams, this distinctive Englishman who shares dressing-room jokes, training travails, airport ennui, dreams of club glory and mutual respect with some of world football's iconic names. How better to cap this than in the glory of a Treble that, according to Pérez, would mark a hundred years full of emotion, effort, sacrifice and success?

'With a team like this, if the football's going well, everything else follows,' Steve replied. 'If the football's going badly, it would be a horrible place to live and work because there's that much pressure, that much history riding on it.'

Suddenly it is 9pm, and kick-off. The scene was set for a party and a sporting triumph: 1902 – 2002 read the freshly painted commemorative stencils along one side of the oddly unregal patchwork pitch. White kite-banners bearing the Real Madrid badge, topped by the royal crest, flew down one side of the pitch, matched by a line of blue and white stripes for Deportivo. The sense of expectancy increased by the second as the stadium filled with giant balloons, banners, drums and flags. A comedy duo worked the crowd of seventy-five thousand, and the pop group Café Quijano played loud enough to drown chants from supporters and sirens from the heavy police presence outside. On came sixteen winners of a television *Pop Idol*-style competition to boom out the Spanish World Cup anthem. Placido Domingo was there. So, too, Alfredo di Stéfano, and FIFA President Sepp Blatter. The players walked out to firecrackers, coloured smoke and a barrage of camera-flashes that left observers with temporary blind spots. Two minutes before kick-off, King Juan Carlos arrived to oversee the final round of competition for his Cup.

If 6 March meant a lot to Real, as a milestone date, it had other connotations. It was also the hundredth final of the Spanish Cup. The celebratory date belonged to Real, but the celebratory competition belonged to the Spanish Football Federation. While this still made Deportivo the underdogs (coach Javier Irureta had suggested a win for Depor would be on a par with Uruguay's shock victory over the hosts, Brazil, in the 1950 World Cup), it did not stop the team from Galicia going all out to party-poop.

The game started explosively. All season the press had waged a pro-Casillas campaign, but 'second-choice' keeper César Sánchez pulled off a brilliant save to rob Diego Tristán in the third minute. However, three minutes later Sergio stunned the Bernabéu into silence with a goal which, followed by a brawl surrounding Raúl, prompted the question: was there too much history riding on a domestic event that, until it became the first hurdle of the centenary Treble, had never been accorded much importance by the club? In all the edginess, it was the Deportivo stylists – the 2000 Liga champions who Real had somewhat arrogantly maintained would lend the occasion credibility – who were preventing Zidane, Figo, Raúl et al from playing their game. In the thirty-eighth minute

Tristán got sweet revenge by striking what would stand as the winning goal, thereby souring Real Madrid's birthday celebrations. (Tristán had been due to join Madrid in the summer of 2000 until the transfer was terminated by incoming president Pérez because he was seen as too much of a party-goer. To which Tristán replied: 'What do you want? A footballer or a priest?')

What did Del Bosque do at half-time to exhort his troops? 'Nothing. Whether we were 5–0 up or 2–0 down his manner was exactly the same. He'd have us all sit down and he would say, quietly, "We need to do this, or that," but he never raised his voice or singled any individuals out for criticism. We'd spend the next twelve minutes checking the time to see when we had to go back out. Sometimes he should have shouted more, of course he should. But he thought it was up to the players to sort themselves out. In the past coaches had screamed at big stars who had gone straight to the president and they were out. He knew his limitations. He had taken over as caretaker manager to steady the ship, and stayed because he brought stability. There were many occasions when I wished he would have a go at people, but his position was weak. There was a long tradition of players holding the power in that dressing room and presidents wielding the power elsewhere.'

Thirteen minutes into the second half, Raúl scored and the atmosphere in the Bernabéu turned white-hot. But the sporting triumph was to be Deportivo's. For the team who had won the Cup only once before, in 1995, also in the Bernabéu, there was mileage to be made as the team who beat Real Madrid on the night that should have been theirs. Depor's fans, cramming the Fonde Norte, sang 'Happy Birthday'. The joy of getting one over Madrid on their hundredth birthday was absolutely immense.

'It was demoralising to lose, and see Deportivo receive the trophy from King Juan Carlos in a near-empty stadium. Our fans had trooped out in dismay or disgust,' recalled Steve. 'Given we were going for the Treble, it was set up for us to lose, wasn't it? For Depor, the motivation to spoil the party was intense. When we win cup finals or Champions League finals, we have pre-printed T-shirts ready to throw on at the final whistle, saying "Champions League winners" or whatever. You can imagine the behind-the-scenes hullabaloo about the hundredth birthday game. The players knew that everyone was getting carried away with it, apart from us. The situation was taken out of our hands . . . it was like we were celebrating before we had to play the game. It was bad psychology. That kind of pressure is sapping. And Depor were an excellent team, while we'd been playing erratically. It could have gone either way. We were desperate to win, but *of course* so were they. Whichever team won would make history. And we didn't play well at all. It was an awful night. We seemed to have lost more than a final. It was as if we couldn't live up to the expectations. You can't simply buy great players and plot to win everything in sight. After all the club's smug self-congratulation and a hundred years of glory, you can imagine people all over Spain were thrilled for that to happen to us on our big night.

'As players we thought the build-up had got out of hand. It was as if the occasion had nothing to do with us, the players and coaching staff. You had musical acts, comic acts, oh yes and a football team will come on for ninety minutes. It was a pity because as players you're desperate to pick up a trophy in March, get it behind you and go on and concentrate on the Champions League and the league with a trophy under your belts. It was a PR disaster, but within the dressing room we kept our confidence. The attitude was: "OK, that's over, let's concentrate on the proper two," But I think the pressure did take its toll. A few weeks later we were top of the league with six games to go. We eventually finished third. *How* on earth did that happen with the players we had?'

As part of the centenary makeover, players were issued with a Welcome to Real Madrid pack, regardless of how long they had been at the club. Each of the blue folders had the individual's name and date of arrival cut out in stencil lettering on the front. Inside was a bog-standard white T-shirt, with a No. 9 embroidered on the back in pale lilac, and the message: 'With this same shirt Alfredo di Stéfano won five European Cups. This shirt represents all the history of Real Madrid. Blood, sweat and tears have spilled over this shirt. We hope that all the magic it contains will help you to achieve glory. *Hala Madrid!*'

There were also three letters. One from di Stéfano, honorary president, describing the 'rectitude, gentlemanliness and honesty' of Santiago Bernabéu, 'which made Real Madrid an example to be followed.' He went on to bid the new generation of players to protect the name and values of the club, particularly its winning spirit. 'Another feature of my team was its winning spirit: never, under any circumstances, did we give up. We always wanted to win, and win again, and I feel that this virtue enabled us to overcome very adverse situations. The renowned line of the poem Martin Fierro – "I am a bull in my corral and a grand bull in an alien field" – remained always in our minds and made us less vulnerable.' Crikey.

The second 'Dear Steve' letter was from Florentino Pérez. 'You now form part of the most prestigious sports club in the world. This must give you great satisfaction as it is a reward for your brilliant career; but you must also see this as an important responsibility. Being a Real Madrid player means defending the pride of millions of fans throughout the world who would give all that they have to wear the club shirt, just once. You represent them and must win their affection and admiration day after day.' And so on.

In case the message still had not registered Jorge Valdano's contribution included a Code of Etiquette, complete with phrases in bold print for the hard of comprehending:

THE MATCHES

We are a winning team. But we must always **WIN WELL**. It does not matter if the match is the final of the Champions League or a pre-season friendly match. Our fans are used to seeing Real Madrid win and this, to a great extent, depends on **your personal and team effort**. Anything else is useless. Do not forget: nothing can take the place of victory.

But you have to **know how to win**. It is not necessary to

humiliate the opponents in order to achieve the most resounding victories. The legend of Real Madrid has been built up on heroic victories that were based on maximum effort and an uncommon desire to win. **When Real Madrid loses, the players shake hands** with their opponents. Protesting to the referee or facing up to opponents leads nowhere, deteriorates our image as a club of gentlemen and is a clear sign of weakness. **Real Madrid does not complain.**

Always bear in mind that a player who plays against Real Madrid is always bent to play the game of his life and win so as to be able to tell his grandchildren, 'I beat Real Madrid'. As far as our rivals are concerned, each game against us is a final.

AT TRAINING

The dressing room is a sacred temple. Nothing that is said there must be aired in public because you and your companions must make up a family on and off the field. The dressing room is the place where you can solve problems which arise when people live together in a group. **Your companions' problems are your problems.**

Fight hard for a place in the first eleven. And if you don't achieve this, fight harder, **but never protest.** Nobody likes to have to sit out the game on the bench, but the manager's decisions must always be accepted by thinking on the fact that he always seeks what is best for the team and that the companion who might substitute you has as much right to play as you have.

WITH THE MEDIA

Each public appearance is followed by **millions of people** all over the world. Your opinions, the way you express yourself and the way you behave will be analysed by all of society, **therefore you must always behave correctly.**

As a basic rule, **no comments are made regarding referees.** This is never done. Neither is criticism brought against any rivals or companions, nor, ever, against the supporters. They may not be gentlemen, but we are.

Elegance, gentlemanly conduct and commitment must underlie each one of your statements. **Remember that each time you speak, people hear Real Madrid.**

IN PUBLIC

Without our fans we are nothing. They fill up the stadium and cheer us on whether we win or lose. All of them deserve our respect and attention.

Being nice in public isn't hard, especially where children are concerned. Everybody would like to have your autograph, but if you are in a hurry, a big smile or a wave will help them feel rewarded.

As regards clothes, the Real Madrid player must not only be elegant in spirit. During trips with the team it is compulsory to wear the official uniform, and on normal days we trust in your good criteria to dress in accordance with what you represent.

IN YOUR PERSONAL LIFE

It is true that your behaviour off the field directly affects the quality of your performance during a game. For a Real Madrid player, **a disciplined life**, with no excesses, helps decisively to achieving the greatest sporting successes.

Follow **the recommendations of the coach, the trainer and the medical services** as regards physical maintenance, nutrition, or the time for rest. This is fundamental for the team to win. And in our club, history demands this.

The emphasis on gentlemanliness, addressed in personal packages to players who had practised the basic principles of sportsmanship all their careers, seemed a tad rich – particularly in view of the growing number of players that would be pushed towards the door, in a very ungentlemanly way, in order to fulfil Pérez's ideal of a cost-effective first team of Zidanes and Pavóns. When the president came in he instituted a policy whereby the club would buy one superstar a year and then rely on homegrown players coming through the youth system. He did not see a need to employ the players in between. 'But kids can't turn into great players overnight,' said Salgado. As well as Steve, Aitor Karanka, Santiago Solari and Fernando Morientes would soon be pushed to leave.

And not because they could not follow the Code of Conduct. Emilio Butragueño positively raved about McManaman's understanding of what it signifies to be a Real Madrid player. 'He very quickly learnt what it means. Maybe because he grew up in that English football culture where the club is very important, he knows how to help the club to fulfil its commitment to society and community. Real Madrid has reached the level it has because of the values represented in the person of Alfredo di Stéfano. They have gone down from generation to generation to players. And Steve understood that from the start. It's like, when you see Mickey Mouse, an association springs to your mind immediately. The same when you see a bottle of Coca-Cola. Well, Real Madrid has become now a brand as well, and there are certain qualities associated with our emblem.'

'It was a weird year,' says Míchel Salgado. 'We had to go to far more events than we really wanted and those appearances were talked about more than the matches themselves. The whole season was odd: seeing the Pope, Magic Johnson, a guy from the NBA who didn't know anything about football [he called the Ultra Sur 'the End Zone Guys']. The problem was there were lots of situations like that. It was a bizarre year, a year with lots of extra pressure. It was tough getting to the Copa del Rey final. We had no sense of enjoyment in reaching a final at all, just relief, and then our defeat was an extremely heavy blow for the team. It was a tough time for everyone, a very, very odd year.'

Success, if not the next dramatic instalment in the centenary year, boiled down to the Champions League. The omens were good after a spotless performance throughout the tournament. Real Madrid, top-seeded in both group stages, finished the first phase top on thirteen points in a group which included Roma, Lokomotiv Moscow and Anderlecht. In the 2–0 victory over Anderlecht in Belgium, on 16 October, Steve scored the second goal after a mesmerising, weblike, quick-touch movement that began with a pass from Hierro to Celades and continued for twenty-four further passes, fifty-one touches, involving eight players in total (Makelele, Guti, Roberto Carlos, Figo and Raúl) – with the ball travelling from Hierro's boot to McManaman's in fifty-eight seconds. In the second phase, they finished top, on sixteen points, above Panathinaikos, Sparta Prague and Porto. Their progress included a coveted, extraordinary win against the 2001 European champions, Bayern Munich, in the quarter-finals.

'This was always going to be an intense encounter after the humiliating defeat at the semi-final stage of the previous season,' recalls Steve. 'The first leg was at the Olympic Stadium in Munich. We had to walk back into that visitors' dressing room we'd left as quickly as possible the previous year. But, as I said, that defeat rankled. I started on the bench, and leapt up with Guti, Morientes, Flavio, Karanka, Pedro Munitis and Iker when Geremi, the novelty of our line-up playing wing-back, scored in the eleventh minute. Late in the seond half César brilliantly saved a penalty from Stefan Effenberg and we thought it would be our night. I came on for Solari for the last fifteen minutes. It's a difficult period to come on for, and I then had the dismaying experience of watching them score twice in the last eight minutes – courtesy of Effenberg and Claudio Pizarro. It meant Bayern could claim a sixth victory over us in the last three seasons. Their coach, Ottmar Hitzfeld, was crowing. "I don't understand all this discussion about Madrid being the best in the world – we always beat them," he said. Goalkeeper Oliver Kahn said: "There's no way they'll put two past me [in the second leg]." *Marca* replied: "One's enough, smarty pants!" The second leg was going to be fiery . . .

'And it was. It was one of those nights when the Bernabéu crackles with tension. We dominated the match from the first minute, but a goal just wouldn't come. We were trailing 2–1 from the first leg. We knew one away goal was enough. We had to be patient. It wasn't until the sixty-ninth minute that Iván Helguera scored, followed by a second from Guti in the eighty-fifth minute. I have rarely heard Del Bosque so thrilled at a result. He was talking in superlatives. "It was a super match, very hard fought, very well played, very tough, very physical but also very tactical – it was exceptional," he raved. Meanwhile Manchester United beat Deportivo La Coruña to set up a semi-final against Bayer Leverkusen. The dream final was still on: Real Madrid, with our historical Glasgow connection, v. Manchester United with Alex Ferguson's personal associations adding particular resonance.'

The draw for the semi-finals resulted in the dreaded all-Spanish fixture against Barcelona, the first meeting of the teams at this stage of the European Cup for forty-two years. 'A semi-final civil war I could do without,' said Del Bosque wryly, amid mumblings that Figo had deliberately got himself booked in the quarter-final to avoid playing against his old club.

'It was a horrible draw,' recalls Steve. 'Anything could happen, it didn't feel like a European contest, just another hostile derby, with form out of the window. The Spanish press – ten times more intense than in England – billed it as the Duel of the Century. On the day of the match *Marca*'s front page headline was "Beyond Words". We had to go to the Nou Camp first, which was potentially tricky. On top of that, the match took place on St George's Day and St George – or Sant Jordi – is the patron saint of Catalonia, so the usual simmering cultural pride scene was massively intensified. But in the fifty-fourth minute Zidane ran into space on the left, took a flick from Raúl and steered a lob that bounced into the far corner of the net. I came on for Guti for the last ten minutes. We were into stoppage time when Flavio passed to me and I saw the chance to chip the goalkeeper.

'I've watched hundreds of replays of my goal and the ball still seems to take an eternity to find the net. The easy thing would have been to whack it in, but I've always tried to do things differently. When I looked up and saw the goalkeeper, Roberto Bonano, off his line I could tell he wasn't expecting to be chipped again, so that's what I went for. I don't score many, but the goals I've scored in the Champions League have been incredibly important. If you score when your team are 3–0, it means nothing to you. It doesn't matter if you beat twenty-six men and curl it in to the corner, you sort of shrug, "Oh, I've just scored," and walk off. The fact was we were winning 1–0 away from home, so for me to score late on and give us that cushion was fantastic. I was ecstatic, the players were jumping all over me, but we were getting that much thrown at us from the crowd – lighters, golf balls, plastic bottles – I was trying to usher them away from the missiles while they kept pinning me to the spot close to the Barça fans as they carried on celebrating.

'To lead 2–0 away from home against Barcelona was crazy. In the dressing room the lads were absolutely thrilled. It was Real Madrid's first win in Barcelona for twenty years. I was just thinking, "We've won with two away goals, we're as good as through to the Champions League final now." But to the Spanish lads it was an immeasurably bigger deal. The Barça factor, how can an outsider truly understand it? It meant so much to them . . . a hell of a lot. For me, primarily, it meant the run-up to the final was lacking that awful tension that hangs over you for a week. We're always confident we can win in that situation at home.

'On a personal level, the Spanish papers went absolutely mad. It is one thing to read about your composure in scoring in the cauldron atmosphere of the Nou Camp, in a match of such high stakes, blah, blah, blah – very nice! – but to have your teammates, the likes of Zidane, Figo, Roberto Carlos, Helguera, Salgado, Morientes and Hierro, buzzing about it for the next few days was fantastic. In retrospect, I think we had all begun to sense the outside world increasingly saw the dressing room in terms of the big stars, the "golden five" they called them before the *galácticos* tag came in, and then the rest of us, who weren't pushed forward as globally marketable players. This was a product of the president's conscious policy, not just a media label, and it undervalued people like Helguera, Makelele and Salgado who were our most consistent performers. After too much bench-warming that season, everyone in the dressing room understood the frustrations I'd endured privately, and were very pleased on my behalf.'

Wednesday 1 May 2002

Steve recalls the deciding leg against Barcelona in a sentence: 'Once Raúl scored at our place, in the second leg, great, brilliant, we're in the Champions League final in Glasgow.' The result was all that mattered. It was played out against a background of high tension. The perimeter of the pitch was guarded by policemen in dark greyish-blue uniforms, topped off by helmets, guns and truncheons hanging from their belts. Two car bombs, laid by the Basque terrorist group ETA, had exploded earlier on the Paseo de la Castellana outside the stadium; the police presence was reassuring, but it also added a symbolic edge. The match was not just the second leg of the 'duel of the century'. By now, Real Madrid had missed out on honours in the first two elements of this season's touted historic Treble – the Copa del Rey and la Liga, conceded after two poor defeats by supposedly inferior teams, a 3–1 drubbing by Osasuna and 3–0 by Real Sociedad, which put Valencia in pole position. Florentino Pérez was said to be so angered by the lacklustre performance – Figo came in for particular criticism – he had considered calling a players' meeting before the tie. On this dark Wednesday night in May the club looked as if they had drafted in the riot police to safeguard the perpetuation of the centenary-year dream of winning the most prestigious element: the European Cup.

After ninety minutes of mesmerising, if not always masterful, play in the cauldron-like festival atmosphere of the Bernabéu, Zidane, Figo, Roberto Carlos, Raúl and co ensured Real's presence at Hampden Park. Steve, who came on for the final thirty minutes to huge cheers of 'Maaa-cca, Maaa-cca' from the crowd, put in a strong ball-winning and energetic performance.

'The players had to cope with too much pressure in the club's special year. The mission was too high. But the Champions League? The players have always considered this the most important honour and they will do their maximum to win it,' said Carlos Sainz, the former world rally champion who plays in the midfield of Real's veterans' side whenever he is at home in Madrid.

The players gave their all. The romantic implication of playing a European Cup final, in the centenary year, in the venue that hosted their most sublime moment of history, was too much to resist. Their achievement in reaching the final against another German team, Bayer Leverkusen, also added another notch in the escalating hatred between Barcelona and Real Madrid, an animosity which sees Real as the Kings of European football (eight European Cups) and Barça as the pretenders with the one European Cup victory, ten years before. In the 1998–99 season, the Catalonian club's centenary year, Barça failed at the semi-final stage to reach the final that was staged in their Nou Camp stadium – much to the glee of the *madridistas*. But Real had progressed to the biggest club stage in their anniversary year; they could claim another feat of one-upmanship.

What would victory on 15 May mean to Madrid? Sainz explained: 'Everybody was expecting Real Madrid to win another European Cup because of the special resonance of this year. Since Florentino Pérez took over as president nearly two years ago, the club have made a big step forward – the organisation is much better, the economics are in order, everything is in place to start a new era of success. The best way to signal that is by winning the European Cup.'

It was a bizarre thought. Unlike most of his players, Florentino Pérez had not yet experienced the joy of winning a European Cup during his time at the Bernabéu.

For Steve, Hampden Park would be a fitting 'home' stage to show the talent and character for which he was renowned after three years in Madrid. 'He is extremely respected because he is very loyal, very professional even when he hasn't always started matches,' said Sainz.

'Whenever the coach asks him to come on and play out of position, he has done it very well. He doesn't make mistakes. The goal he scored in the Nou Camp looked very easy, but technically it was very difficult. He is extremely talented and motivated. Everyone here is surprised the England coach does not include him more.'

Wednesday 15 May 2002

On the day of the Champions League final McManaman's monthly *Telegraph* column appeared, an essay of nervous excitement and anticipation, you would think, on the prospect of winning a second European Cup medal in three years. However, on top of that – for how can you surpass that? – he had to deal with the disappointment of not joining his international teammates for the World Cup finals. On a day that was one of the greatest highlights of his club career, Steve was forced to acknowledge the likely end of his international career.

'I have arrived in Glasgow for tonight's European Cup final to find everyone expecting me to have a right go at Sven-Göran Eriksson for not selecting me in his England squad. What can I say? Of course I think I should be going to the World Cup. Of course I'm confident in my own abilities. Yes, I'm deeply disappointed not to be part of England's Far East campaign, but Eriksson has a job to do. He's chosen the players he thinks will give England their best chance and, unfortunately for me, he's made it clear that I'm not part of his vision.

'If this is the end of my international career then it is a very sad end, just to have a message left on my mobile phone while I was training on the morning the squad was announced.

'I can't say I was completely surprised after not being contacted for any of the last three squads, but then you always hope. First I thought it may be because I was injured, then not playing enough, and then some of the squads seemed very experimental and I reasoned that he knew what I could do. The finality of it is a bit baffling. Sometimes you think you deserve more respect.

'I have always loved meeting up with the England lads. Euro 96 goes down as one of the highlights of my career. The big tournaments are fantastic times, when you're all together as a squad, locked away, living in your own world for three or four weeks. They're the ones you really look forward to. The thing that bothers me among some of the silly reasons bandied around about my exclusion is the impression that I don't care about playing for England. I care passionately. To miss this opportunity of representing my country, as I have done on thirty-seven occasions, hurts a lot, but I'll just have to pick myself up and carry on.

'At least I have tonight's important game at Hampden Park to concentrate on. I don't think I'll start, but I will probably get on for some time. Believe me, though, the last thing I will be trying to do is show everyone what England will be missing in Japan!

'The pressure on Real Madrid to beat Bayer Leverkusen is immense. We are expected to win something every year, but as this is the club's centenary, the aim was to win an unprecedented Treble. Having missed out on the two domestic targets, we have to bring home the big one. Real have won it twice in four years, but to win it three times in five would really put the club into the class of all-time greats. In this era, when there aren't just one or two dominant clubs, but strong clubs from all over Europe, it is really incredible for one club to reach the semi-finals and final so often.

'Before the semi-finals I was among those who had hoped for a Real Madrid v. Manchester United final, because of the strong associations with Glasgow of both Sir Alex Ferguson and Real. The fact that we play a German team, though, adds an historic edge to the occasion. The emphasis in Spain is all on the actual city of Glasgow, as the spiritual home where the great 7–3 demonstration defeat of Eintracht Frankfurt took place in 1960. It should be a corker of a game.'

From the British point of view, the Glasgow football-fest became slightly less gourmet fare once Alex Ferguson's Manchester United team were knocked out. Ferguson had grown up in Govan, a tough, working-class district of Glasgow. As a young man, he had watched

Real Madrid inflict their mesmerising powers over Eintracht Frankfurt in his home city. As a manager, he was still enthralled by their philosophy. 'It's amazing. Their devotion to the trophy is what makes them unique,' he mused. How fitting it would be for him to return to Hampden Park, with his own side, against that standard-bearing opposition. But it was not to be. After a remarkably balanced semi-final – 2–2 at Old Trafford, 1–1 at the Bay Arena – Bayer Leverkusen went through on the Away Goals rule. No one minded in Spain. For Real Madrid were back on that same pitch in Glasgow, against a German team, forty-two years almost to the day since the line-up Pérez sought to emulate staged the most sumptuous club display in football history.

'The fear of failure was huge,' admits Steve in retrospect. 'We were odds-on favourites to win. The pressure was immense, from the historical angle, from the 2001–02 competitive angle. Leverkusen were this tiny team from Germany who were considered "lucky" to have reached the final. But they had developed a winning mentality with their aggressive style, and were a very good side who had knocked out Liverpool in the quarter-finals, Manchester United in the semis. We were on a hiding to nothing straightaway. If we didn't win, we'd have been crucified. With Zidane had come talk that we were less of a team, more of a team built around certain creative individuals. It's true that we rarely went out with a specific gameplan, but with more of a notion that our players are the best and will do something. A lack of team ethic had been blamed for failures in the Copa del Rey and league, but I didn't see it that way. Nevertheless we went on to that pitch with real questions asked of us. Personally, I never dwell on the prospect of losing. I don't go around thinking, "What happens if we get slaughtered?" There's nothing to gain from worrying about it. Victoria was saying, "Oh my God, what happens if you don't win?" But I tried not to consider the possibility. I've lost in finals and it's the worst feeling in the world. I've lost at Liverpool to Manchester United, I've lost that Copa del Rey final, the Champions League semi-finals at Bayern Munich. It's a horrible, horrible feeling, but there's no point in anticipating it. Most footballers can block negative thoughts from their mind. You have to sleep before a big game, and I wouldn't sleep if I was anxious about the outcome of that night's game.

'And so to an outsider, we'd have seemed as pathologically relaxed as ever. We went up to the hotel a couple of days beforehand: a typical Scottish country hotel on the edge of a loch, with tartan up the walls and a lovely golf course. Some of our lads went out to play. I remember Santi Solari and I were in a buggy and César, teeing off somewhere, whacked this ball right through the plastic of the buggy. There was a hole clean through the screen. That was a close shave. Albert Celades was in another buggy, trying to go up a slope, but he couldn't stop it rolling backwards and he and César ended up knee-deep in water in a pond. We were hoping none of these incidents were omens for the game, but César, who was going to start in goal, injured his knee and was hobbling about.

'I don't remember stomach-churning nerves as such on the bus as we drove into Glasgow towards the stadium that night. Glasgow did a wonderful job creating a fantastic atmosphere for such an occasion. You could see the debris of the all-day party as we drove in on the team coach. Everyone I knew who went as a spectator, all my family and friends, kept phoning me saying they were having a ball, a great, great, great laugh. It was then I thought, "I'd love to go and watch me playing."'

Hundreds of silver European Cup-shaped helium balloons went on sale early on match-day morning along Cathcart Road, outside Hampden Park, while in the centre of Glasgow the carnival started in George Square. Bagpipes and steel drums, tartan berets, kilts, Celtic scarves and Braveheart helmets all blended bizarrely with Real Madrid and Bayer Leverkusen colours. The culmination of the world's most prestigious club competition was celebrated with a fervour that was unequivocally welcoming to both Spaniards and Germans.

'Especial Liga de Campeones' read a flier on one side of a news stand; 'Ansgabe zum Verkaus hier' blared the line from the other side. George Square was strewn with piles of Spanish Serrano ham, cheese and (empty) bottles of Rioja as Real Madrid fans picnicked around the statue of William Ewart Gladstone. Their face-painted supporters danced together with their German counterparts on the plinth of the statue of a horseborne Albert, Prince Consort, amicably taking turns to have a singsong in their own language. Outside La Tasca tapas bar on Renfield Street policemen monitoring a rowdy bunch of Spaniards allowed themselves to be draped in scarves and flags for the sake of a photo opportunity. When the crowd burst into 'We are the Champions', with notable Spanish lilt, two elderly Glaswegian women in the bus queue opposite joined in at the top of their voices. And then laughed themselves silly. The atmosphere infected everyone – from the shop assistants and waitresses in official-issue mad hat and T-shirt to ordinary Glaswegians going about their daily business . . . to the streaker who would come on at the start of the second half and nearly score a goal.

Real Madrid claim Glasgow as their spiritual home, as the venue of the famous 7–3 showcase that not only secured their fifth successive European Cup in 1960, but also established the standard for sublime entertaining football. But Leverkusen came to Glasgow determined to feel at home. Never on paper had there been such a one-sided final – given Real's eight previous victories; Leverkusen have never even been champions of the Bundesliga – but, in the spirit of their pragmatic manager, Klaus Toppmoller, the German camp appealed to the Tartan Army in an open letter to lend their support. And so the platform was set for two teams whose vitality had marked the latter stages of their Champions League campaigns. Toppmoller had shown he could motivate his lean, well-organised unit to play entertaining football. Would they live up to their 'Neverkusen' reputation, throwing away this chance as they had so recently their domestic league and cup hopes? Or could they heap the final humiliation on Real Madrid's centenary season? The 'holy trinity' of Raúl, Luis Figo and Zinedine Zidane were supposed to have led the team to a swaggering Treble, but at the 7.45pm kick-off FIFA's Club of the

Twentieth Century were still potentially ninety minutes away from winning nothing in their year of over-indulgent off-pitch celebrations.

'We were in the dressing room a few minutes before we went out when the King, Juan Carlos, came in to shake our hands and wish us luck. It's cool, because he's the King, but it's like, "Hang on, we've got a game." With Real Madrid, pre-match protocol goes out of the window. We weren't in the middle of any mad, crazy rituals to pump ourselves up because we play under pressure all the time. Del Bosque couldn't say, "This team needs to be closeted together for two hours before the game; we can't have our concentration disturbed." So, it was a quick shake of the royal hand and we ran out to warm up.

'I knew I wouldn't be playing unless someone was injured. Of course I wanted to bloody play, but I'd lived with the unwritten rules all season. It wasn't like I'd been dropped for the big game and I was distraught. But I did feel a horrible pang of disappointment when my teammates walked out on to the pitch to that spectacular roar from the crowd, and lined up to sing the anthems – especially when I'd experienced that emotional moment in Paris. Substitutes are not involved in those rites, and I felt numb at missing out on the elements that make a Champions League final special.'

7.59pm – After fourteen minutes the crowd at Hampden had seen two goals; the score was 1–1. For the briefest of periods you could sense a collective desire for a replication of that 7–3 scoreline. It was not to be. History remained intact in two senses. Real Madrid's performance, in which scrappy foul-ridden football was matched with some masterful sequences and touches, did nothing to blur the image of the glorious 1960 triumph, but then it had been absurd to expect it could match a night described by Richard Williams in the *Guardian* as 'Fonteyn and Nureyev, Bob Dylan at the Royal Albert Hall, the first night of *The Rite of Spring*, Olivier at his peak, the Armory Show and the Sydney Opera House rolled into one. Even today,' he wrote, 'the grainy black and white images prove that the legend has not suffered the indignity of exaggeration.'

However, Zidane's fabulous left-footed volley helped bring another European Cup to the Bernabéu's glittering trophy room. His strike, seconds from the whistle for half-time, was a combination of perfect timing and masterful dexterity, which replicated the panache of di Stéfano and Puskás. 'I don't plan those goals; you just have to be ready when the opportunity appears,' Zidane recalled. 'The volley against Leverkusen was a beautiful and unique goal. It was not an easy effort, and I hit it precisely, quickly and just right. It worked. I remember after scoring it that I thought how lucky I was to catch the ball at the right angle and height, because it is a very difficult shot. I am glad it gave us the trophy – it was certainly one of the most important moments of my career.'

'I always thought the game would be a bit nip and tuck,' said Steve. 'They were very gutsy and they never stopped believing they could turn the game around. You could see their gameplan from the start. They were going for the stifling tactic of man-marking Raúl, Morientes, Zidane and Figo, while with typical Real Madrid swagger we had no one near their most gifted player, Michael Ballack. We were 1–0 up after nine minutes, Raúl with one of his typical poacher's strikes. Five minutes later Lucio, who had made the error that allowed Raúl to score, made up for it by heading in a free kick. Both goals came from defensive mishaps, not what you like to think of as typical European Cup stuff, but then Zizou came out with that great goal. It's the best goal I've seen to win a final, unbelievable. So, it was 2–1 at half-time.

'At the start of the second half I kept an eye on Toni Grande, the second coach, who would call me to warm up when Del Bosque gave him the signal. At last it came. If you're told to warm up, you're going on. It's not like in England when you see the subs going for a run up and down the sidelines just to keep warm. I couldn't wait to get on. And it wasn't like we had the game sewn up. The tense, nail-biting bit was at the end. We made chances, and they made chances, and it looked as if we were going to win, but in the last five minutes it went completely crazy. After all the purple prose in the papers about Real Madrid's "sublime" football, we were reduced to doing what teams do every Saturday: getting the ball and kicking it as far as we could from our goal. When we had control, we tried to play, but the centenary dream could have gone horribly, horribly wrong. How many times do you see a goalkeeper getting injured in a game? César came off with a foot problem, and Iker Casillas came on and made about five acrobatic saves in four minutes. He was in the air more than he was on the ground. Rarely can a goalkeeper have felt more gratified about his contribution after coming on as a sub. He won us the final, he was named Man of the Match in certain newspapers and he was only on for about twenty minutes. After the match he was on the floor, crying his eyes out, poor lad. He was overcome.'

In the stands, Victoria was sitting next to César's wife, Dolores, who was also in tears, worried about her husband's injury, but also emotional because it was the final and he was no longer able to participate in the big occasion.

'We won only one trophy in our centenary season, but it was the best one. The relief of winning was indescribable,' continued Steve. 'It wasn't a great game. Zizou's goal is all anyone talks about, whereas the Paris final was universally upheld as a great team performance. Because the Glasgow scoreline was 2–1, Zizou's goal was the deciding factor. In Paris, the 3–0 margin reflected a more comprehensive difference between the sides. I don't go along with the theory that a handful of great individual talents ruin the collective team ethos. When Zidane or Luis play, they're very much team players, but ones who stand out because, more often than not, they conjure a bit of magic that turns a game. The *octava*, as it's always referred to by *madridistas*, was a more satisfying win because we'd struggled that year, and it was incredible how we had turned it around. There were no megastars in the team. Yes, we had Redondo, Raúl, Roberto Carlos and Hierro, but they weren't billed in the way Figo and Zidane were. And it wasn't until we'd bought them that Roberto and Raúl were included in the *galácticos* bracket. The back five were not big-name defenders: Karanka, Campo, Salgado in his first year in Madrid. Ditto, Helguera. It was a watershed victory because after that had come the big change.'

Like McManaman (and Anelka) in 2000 and Figo in 2001, the high-profile signing of the season had left an indelible mark in the most important game of his first year in the white shirt. Zidane's strike would represent a clarifying, perhaps unburdening moment, for the Frenchman who had at last won his treasured first European Cup winners' medal. 'He'd had a quiet season, and with that goal, you could almost hear people saying, "Ah, that's why they bought him,"' recalls Steve. It was Luis Figo's first too. For Steve, Helguera, Salgado, Campo, Savio and Casillas, however, it was a prized second medal. For Hierro, Roberto Carlos, Raúl, Karanka and Morientes it was a third. Zidane and Figo – and Florentino Pérez – had some catching up to do.

'With Real Madrid you have to make the most of celebrating on the pitch because it's never a great laugh afterwards. They don't so much party as mark an occasion. You go from twenty or thirty people, the team and support staff, going ballistic celebrating, spraying champagne everywhere, to a three-course banquet at the Hilton with hundreds and hundreds of unfamiliar faces, TV cameras and press everywhere. There's nothing personal about it. I'd won my second European Cup-winner's medal, but I didn't have a wild time. We had a very formal, sit-down meal and speeches. My dad and all our mates were out drinking until dawn, having a fantastic time, but I was on best behaviour at the official banquet. My sister Karen came. She had brought my nephew, Luke, to Glasgow so she wasn't going out with the rest. It was lovely to see them. Victoria's father was with us, and we managed to sneak in a few of her friends too.'

But not until Victoria had arrived horrendously late. 'The organisation for the families was terrible,' she recalls. 'I thought Paris was bad enough, when we stayed at different hotels and had to walk down a motorway after the game to find our coach. But Glasgow was no better. Being so laid-back, Real Madrid had not started making hotel reservations until very late. By that stage Manchester United fans had booked every hotel in and around Glasgow. So we were put up in three hotels in Edinburgh. They suddenly announced to the players that we could move to the team hotel after the game, but no one thought to tell us to pack our belongings. They were outside Glasgow, we were in Edinburgh – you couldn't just pop back to collect your things. I was given an itinerary, which was hilarious. It started with the flight number and times, then stated "Tuesday Morning – free", "Tuesday Afternoon – free", "Wednesday Morning – free", "Wednesday Afternoon – free", "After Game – tba". What was the point?

'When we were dropped off at Hampden Park the driver said he'd meet us back at a certain place after the game. The match finished in torrential rain, and we couldn't find him. The crowd was huge. We all lost each other, and very few of the wives spoke English. It was chaos. You'd think he'd have a huge official placard, but no. We eventually found him, but he charged off so fast through the crowds and the rain, that we lost him again. Eventually we saw the coach . . . parked in a muddy field . . . and we were all in high heels!

'The next day was just the same: no consideration had been taken at all. The plane landed at Madrid airport and pulled over by an embankment with railings. There were thousands of ecstatic fans waiting for the glorious homecoming. All the wives were herded together and put on a coach, which took us to the training ground – why? None of us had cars there! We were dumped in the middle of the day at their training ground while the players were doing their victory parade through the city. There were all these glamorous wives standing on the pavement trying to hail taxis to get home, at a time when most taxi drivers had stopped work to watch the celebrations somewhere on a TV. It was absolutely incredible. Everyone was very annoyed. I arrived home in time to switch on the TV and watch the end of the celebrations. The players had visited Cibeles, the town hall and the cathedral, and had arrived back at the Bernabéu to run onto one of nine podiums sitting on giant stars. I put in a video to record it, and sat there thinking it would have been nice to have been in the stadium to witness the record ninth victory celebrations, but no one had thought of that. Christian Karembeu had said from his experience in 1998 that wives and families are secondary to Real Madrid on these occasions, and four years down the line they still were, despite the new president's modernisation project. A lot of the players expressed annoyance. The players had won the final, but they were worried about the whereabouts of their wives. We were trailing about, not knowing what was going on, while the celebration was geared towards the directors and their individual parties of family and friends who were pampered all the way. It's funny, because people think the life of a footballer's wife is glamorous. The reality is very different, particularly in Spain where chauvinism still prevails in the world of football.'

The focus of the football world soon moved on to the World Cup Finals in the Far East, but not before one absentee had soaked up some gratifying words of appreciation. Steve's appearance on European club football's biggest stage – back in sight, back in mind – earned universal approval in the British newspapers the following morning. Richard Williams, in the *Guardian*, wrote: 'By the time McManaman arrived on the field, in place of the subdued and ineffective Luis Figo, Real Madrid were beginning to concern themselves primarily with holding on to their 2–1 lead. So he ran hard in support of his colleagues, stopped opponents by whatever means necessary, and generally made himself useful. It seems a shame that a man who has so clearly earned the respect of the players and fans of Europe's leading club should not have been able to produce the sort of performances for England that would have persuaded Eriksson of his value.' Matt Dickinson, in *The Times*, referred back to Steve's *Telegraph* column: 'It was only last week that Zidane said how baffled he was that England could afford to ignore Steve McManaman. Roared on to the pitch when he replaced Luis Figo with half an hour to go, the long-haired winger from Liverpool looked at home in such distinguished company. He now has two European Cup medals, which is one more than anyone who will be wearing an England shirt this summer. "Sometimes you think you deserve some respect," McManaman said. He had it in Glasgow last night.'

In the *Sunday Times*, Ian Hawkey's comment echoed the sentiment expressed for much of the second half of the season in Spain: 'Against the slow-motion re-runs of Zidane's extraordinary volley should be set the picture of Luis Figo, formerly the world's most expensive footballer and for the past three months Real's costliest folly. On Wednesday night Figo was replaced by Steve McManaman after an hour, and Real had a midfield again, and a winger who could cross. The substitution improved Real's football.'

At a time when they thought Steve had a chance of joining up with the England camp for the World Cup, the McManamans had decided on 6 July 2002 for their wedding day. In the event of his involvement, that would have left only a few days of honeymoon before Real Madrid's pre-season started. Now there was small consolation in the potential of a long honeymoon before the actual ceremony. 'I watched the World Cup from Barbados, but the time difference was a killer,' said Steve. 'I didn't see all the games. There was no chance I was setting the alarm for 3 or 5am for any old game. I watched all the England games, bar the Nigeria one, and it was tough not to be a part of England's efforts. By the time we had progressed to meet Brazil, though, I was on my way to my stag weekend in New York and the fact I was with my best mates alleviated any lingering disappointments. The flight was at 10am so my friends and I decided to get to Manchester airport by 7am, check in, and watch it in the bar there. The trouble was, everyone with flights that morning had had the same idea. All the seats were taken. We ended up on the floor of the departure lounge having a good laugh, with a lot of travellers having fun when they spotted me, sitting on the floor, surrounded by my mates in stag-night spirits, glued to the telly.'

England

He has been such an exciting influence on the championships and there is no doubt in my mind he has been the player of the tournament. It is clear he will be an amazing talent to watch for the future.

—Pele after Euro 96

There are those who voted him Man of the Tournament and he was certainly up there. He was at his very best for England during Euro 96, showing exactly what he was capable of as a player. And he was a joy to work with.

—Terry Venables

For four seasons Steve played in Madrid with some of the best players in the world. The experience and knowledge he gained in that time should have stood him in good stead for his international career. Not a bit of it. From the moment Sven-Göran Eriksson left the message on his mobile phone informing him his services would not be required for the 2002 World Cup, Steve's England career record stood still. Played 37 – Won 22, Drawn 12, Lost 3.

In chronological order, the three games lost were: 26 June 1996, the European Championship semi-final against Germany at Wembley, when – as few people will need reminding – the game went to penalties with the scores level at 1–1 after extra time; 12 February 1997, a 1–0 defeat at Wembley in a World Cup qualifier against Italy, the night Gianfranco Zola beat Ian Walker at his near post; and 12 June 2000, a 3–2 defeat by Portugal in England's opening game of the European Championship finals. Steve scored early with a stunning half-volley and when he left the pitch, having injured his left knee in a tackle with Rui Costa, England were drawing 2–2. Statistically, then, he can claim an impressive record.

'My win–loss ratio is good, which, to me, is the most important thing,' says Steve. 'I've always maintained that regardless of whether I have had a fantastic game individually, or not, the only thing that gratifies me is a strong team performance and result.'

After fifteen games under Terry Venables – who gave him his senior debut on a cold November night in 1994, motioning him on as a substitute for the injured Rob Lee against Nigeria – Steve had not only participated in strong team performances, culminating in that unforgettable run of games against Scotland, Holland, Spain and Germany in Euro 96, he had also enjoyed individual acclaim. During Euro 96, he was fizzing down the right wing, linking sublimely with

Paul Gascoigne, David Platt, Paul Ince, Teddy Sheringham and Alan Shearer, complementing what Darren Anderton was doing on the left. Football had come home and Steve was heralded as a leading protagonist in the resurgence. At the tournament's end, he was voted one of the top five most influential players in Europe. His image was chosen for the cover of *The Official Football Association Yearbook 1996–97*. He was English football's bright new thing.

How, then, has he now become perceived as suffering from the John Barnes syndrome – a player of great technical gifts and creative verve, who made a tremendous impact at club level, but who would be less fulfilled at international level? Was it a question of being a maverick talent who could not be integrated in the typically conventional way the national team play? As Paul Hayward of the *Daily Telegraph* remarks: 'As a nation, we prefer our workhorses.' Was it a legacy of being seeped in the Liverpool culture of artistry and self-expression? 'John Barnes and Steve McManaman both saw a lot of the ball at Liverpool, and enjoyed more opportunities to impose themselves on the game. Steve was never a long-ball man,' argues Hayward's colleague, Henry Winter. Or was it that, being so versatile, managers tended to use him as a makeshift left winger and so did not play him to his strengths? 'Condemned as a maverick in his own country, he is hailed as the ultimate team player in Madrid. Why ask him to regress by sticking him on the left wing?' wrote Oliver Holt in *The Times*, suggesting that managers persisted in viewing McManaman in a timewarp, as the young Liverpool player who ran at defenders, rather than as the creative midfield fulcrum he had developed into.

Steve went on to play a further twenty-two games under three managers – Glenn Hoddle, Kevin Keegan and Sven-Göran Eriksson – and he is the first to admit he rarely experienced again the heady form and buzz of Euro 96. Always the big-picture man, he maintains a rational view of his England career. 'Between 1990 and late 1993 I won seven caps for the England Under-21 side, and then from 1994 to 2002 I was called up regularly to England squads depending on my fitness. That means I was playing very good, consistent club football over eleven or twelve seasons in order to be considered one of England's best players. Once you are in an England squad, though, other selection criteria come into play. It's out of your hands. The manager may want to play with a particular tactical formation. He may want to use units of players who combine well week in week out for their club. For any number of reasons, when it actually boils down to naming a team of eleven, rather than a squad of twenty-three, you may or you may not be one of the manager's favoured type of players. For some players, selection can be quite random. Every time an England squad convenes, there is a twist to the names on the list – because of injury, or the sudden emergence of a young player, or the blossoming of a player never previously considered, or the loss of form of others. You can have a year when England games come few and far between. I've always said, the time to judge a player is in a big tournament, a European Championship or a World Cup, when players have had time to build up an understanding, a fluency of play and a collective ambition. For me, after Euro 96, there weren't any more opportunities. I went to the 1998 World Cup, but Hoddle gave me seventeen minutes on the pitch. My contribution in Euro 2000 was curtailed by injury five minutes into the second half of the first game. The last time I played three games in a row for England was Euro 96. Since then it's been stop–start all the way. I felt that was always the problem – I never got into a rhythm.

'I remember the thrill of being selected for the Under-21 side before I even played for Liverpool's first team. I got on very well with Lawrie McMenemy. After my debut against Wales, at Tranmere, he said some encouraging things about my international prospects and joked about my physique – "There's more fat on a chip," he quipped. Lawrie once told me I was this far [thumb and forefinger a centimetre apart] from getting a call-up for the senior side while I was still in the Under-21 bracket, but it didn't happen. In those days, the press would clamour for call-ups. They would run campaigns for the manager to give certain players a go. You don't see that so much under Sven-Göran Eriksson when all and sundry seem to have had a call-up.

'I was included in the senior squad for the first time in 1994, and remember joining up as if it were yesterday. Terry Venables always asked everyone – players and staff – to meet at half nine in the bar at Burnham Beeches Hotel. For a new recruit, it was a relaxing way to get to know other players. The manager and his staff, the experienced players, were all very welcoming. On my last few occasions of flying in from Madrid to meet up with England, it was more like checking into a hotel. People would arrive and go straight to their bedrooms and you wouldn't see anyone until the following day. There was no interaction or conversation until you'd gather on the bus the next morning, but then we'd all be sitting down in rows on the way to training. There was no opportunity to talk to new people. I remember reading an interview with Chris Powell of Charlton, who said after his first England call-up how amazed he was when David Beckham greeted him by his first name. That awe-struck tone would never have happened under Venables. With him we used to have a couple of drinks, relax and talk. He had the knack of making everyone feel included. We were all part of his group. In a very subtle way, he instilled in us all the notion that we had a responsibility in representing England, but we were going to have fun in doing it. You never felt, "Oh, I shouldn't be here," or felt nervous. You always thought, "This is going to be enjoyable." He had everyone involved straightaway, everyone at ease, and with Bryan Robson and Ted Buxton, too, both very warm people and great characters, the coaches mingled with the players. They did not remain aloof in their own rooms. Venables was cool. Everyone wanted to do well for him and earn his respect.

'I heard about him asking John Barnes "to explain" me. All my career people have said they can't read my body language. They think I look like I'm not bothered. It's true I'm not a shouter like Stuart Pearce or Tony Adams. I've never been an outwardly emotional person on a football pitch, but inside I'm as competitive as anyone. I was the same at Liverpool, but I got on very well with everyone who got to know me. You just need to get to know me, that's all! Terry did, very quickly. We had several chats about where or how he might play me. He suggested he would try me on the left and I was fine with that. A good modern footballer should be able to play in five or six positions on the park, and if he can't, he's not going to be a top player.

'In the lead-up to Euro 96 I started five out of six games. That gave me a strong indication I would be an integral part of Venables' plans. I was so lucky, because it was a fantastic time to be involved in the England set-up. England were hosting the European Championship. How many players are fortunate enough to experience that stirring build-up for a big tournament on home soil? The nation was so wrapped up in it. The atmosphere had been brewing for months. When we drove from Burnham Beeches to Wembley – a forty-five-minute drive – people lined the streets all the way to wave our bus past. As the momentum built, the excitement and tension and anticipation seemed to explode. It was crazy. The manager was criticised for taking us away on the tour of the Far East, where we played only one official international against China. We also played against a Hong Kong XI. Gazza had a shiner. Everyone could see him on the big screen that night, sitting on the bench, pulling tongues. He had everyone in stitches. It was very relaxed. But that trip was shrewd of Terry. After a long season, it was refreshing to have a short break away from the intensity of the build-up, and even to let off a bit of steam at the very end of the tour, though none of us like seeing those pictures of the infamous dentist's chair incident again, when, on our one night off, we ended up dousing each other in spirits.

'In retrospect, though, the headlines stuck with some of us. People say you never lose the image first stamped on you by a tabloid headline – and I think that is true. Cathay Pacific claimed there had been £5,000 worth of damage done to the jumbo jet we travelled back on. Apparently one of the televisions had been broken, and a table. On the day Robbie Fowler and myself were due to travel down from Liverpool, we woke up to front- and back-page stories about the two of us wrecking the plane. We were livid. It's an unwritten "dressing-room rule" that you don't reveal anything from the inner sanctum, but we were not afraid to disassociate ourselves from that accusation. Hand on heart, we had nothing to do with that behaviour. The newspapers had gone for all of us heavily, of course, after seeing the dentist's chair pictures. Suddenly it was just Robbie and I accused of being Scouse louts, and we were not happy. The players had a meeting, and Robbie and I expressed our anger at getting the blame for something we had absolutely no part in. The management decided to come out and say the entire squad had decided to accept "collective responsibility", but that did nothing to remove the slur against myself and Robbie. So we came out and made our own statement.

'The whole incident sparked off a frenzy in the newspapers about the irresponsible antics of those given the privilege of representing England. That started a strong siege mentality between the players and the press. There was a refusal to talk to the press all the way through the tournament. In a bizarre way it bound us together into a very tight-knit squad. We had a solidarity on and off the pitch. We were a bunch of like-minded people, a lot of strong characters who loved their football, enjoyed a laugh and a joke together – Tony Adams, Stuart Pearce, Alan Shearer, Teddy Sheringham, Gazza, David Seaman, Gareth Southgate, David Platt, Paul Ince, Jamie Redknapp, Darren Anderton, Gary Neville, Nicky Barmby, Robbie . . . the nucleus was great. We had Burnham Beeches to ourselves. Once the tournament kicked off we were relaxed, enjoying our training. It was a great time for the players and staff. After every game we'd go back to the hotel, eat and rest, then meet in the bar for a few drinks, listen to music, and have a singsong to the early hours – all the way through the tournament, really. No one went their separate ways. The gaffer was cool. He'd let you have a drink, everyone was happy. The team who had played would have a simple warm down the next day. The players who hadn't played would have a full training session. Gazza is hyperactive at the best of times, but during that tournament he was mad. Robbie and myself had to take turns looking after him because one person couldn't keep up with him. I'd go with him for a few hours, then I'd go and rest and Robbie would take over. He had to be doing something all the time, playing pool, table tennis, anything. He'd be up early, six or seven in the morning, and go to the gymnasium for two hours, then he would go and train, then he'd want to play tennis, then do this, and all the time he needed someone to play against.

'I've never seen so many St George's flags as on the journey to Wembley for our first game against Switzerland. Of course we hoped for a brilliant display to start the tournament with a bang and bury the bad press, but the game ended in a disappointing 1–1 draw – not the fantastic game we'd wished for, but often the opening game is a bit like that. If we thought there was pressure on the host nation that first game, there was a hell of a lot more by the second, against Scotland. Against Switzerland the manager had suggested I start on the left – which I was up for – but he then put Darren Anderton on the left, so I was on the right. To this day, the bizarre thing is that because I started on the left wing, everyone thinks I played the entire tournament on the left. Again, first impressions hold indelibly.

'Darren and I are both very good runners. We get up and down the field for ninety minutes without fading, and we were both very good on the ball as well, which suited Terry's plan excellently. That was a thrilling element of Euro 96. For each game, there was a different plan to counter the opposition's strengths and play to our own. It sounds so basic, but it is amazing how relaxed some managers can be about sending out their teams without a specific and adaptable tactical plan. Terry Venables gave us all, individually and collectively, a sharp sense of what he expected us to do. That in itself gives you a certain confidence and when it works the satisfaction is overwhelming. Every player who worked with him rates him very highly as a coach. He got the best out of players. We all wanted to play well for him.

'Against Scotland, however, we played well but luck, too, was on our side – David Seaman kept out a certain goal for Gordon Durie, Gary McAllister missed a penalty, and Gazza's extraordinary moment of inspiration. The Holland game was the best example of an overwhelming tactical victory. Terry was confident he had worked out a way to beat a Dutch team of unbelievable talent – Clarence Seedorf, Edgar Davids, Patrick Kluivert, Marc Overmars, Dennis Bergkamp, Frank and Ronald de Boer and so on. I was pushed further up. He had Alan and Teddy up front, with me as a sort of right-sided forward to put pressure on them. Everything came off. The atmosphere was incredible as Alan and Teddy grabbed two goals each and we'd hammered the hyped-up majestic Holland team 4–1. We went into that game thinking, "We're going to win this." I remember going into the players' lounge afterwards, and seeing film stars, pop stars, TV celebrities. Everyone wanted to be a part of it. We saw our families and friends for an hour or so and then went back to the hotel on the coach. There was quite a singsong in the bar that night!

'Over the next four days, the wave of patriotic pride that swept the country was electric. We were on our fourth game into the tournament now, and we were buzzing as we lined up for the quarter-final against Spain. It was the first time I met Fernando Hierro, the captain of Spain and of my future club, who was playing in central midfield. I actually thought we were fortunate to go through. Spain were efficient and organised, and had the edge on us in terms of possession and chances. They scored an excellent goal that was disallowed, and after a hundred and twenty minutes it was goalless. Time for penalties. Hierro was up first for Spain. Unbelievably, he hit the crossbar and we had the psychological advantage. In contrast, Stuart Pearce buried the ghost of Turin in 1990. You could feel the nation hold its breath as he stalked towards the spot and smashed the ball into the back of the net, his face set like a gargoyle in relief.

'That was it: through to a semi-final against Germany. And we all know what happened. Penalties again. You'd never imagine you'd score five out of five penalties and still get beaten, would you? We lost – my first loss in an England shirt – but we didn't lose anything in defeat. It was the weirdest kind of disappointment. We all had difficulty accepting it, especially as the final was very disappointing, with Germany winning on the Golden Goal rule. After enjoying such camaraderie, it was odd for us to go our own ways for the summer.

That tournament stands out in my memory. There is nothing better than playing a major tournament, locked away with the same lads for five or six weeks, being enveloped by an us-against-everyone-else mentality. You discover what the lads are really like playing games every three or four days in a knock-out competition. The great thing about that squad was that there was no nucleus from one club. We came from everywhere, and there was a good mix of old ones and young ones, mad ones, quiet ones or insomniacs like me. Being at home staved off the isolation factor in that we could go for a walk to the shops near Burnham Beeches or into Windsor. When we were in France for the World Cup two years later, and Belgium for the 2000 European Championship, the place was so boring that occupying spare time became a problem.'

Venables's verdict on McManaman? 'He has the capacity to do most things and he has the open mind that is the mark of an intelligent player. He was always saying to me, "Whatever you want, I'll have a go." I felt he needed encouragement to show just how much he could do and in Euro 96 he showed it. He was really, really one of our best players.

'He and Anderton have the build of marathon runners and both could run all day. Steve played on the left wing in the first game and then I swapped him over and put Anderton on the left. Then other managers came in and played Steve on the left. I think if he's playing on the right he can pop over to the left and do well, but I think he's best as a central or a right midfielder. He gets trapped on the left. Funnily enough, in training, I said to him, "I hope you can kick the ball with your left foot," and boom, he did. But the last thing you learn is the first thing you forget under pressure. He was game enough to have a go, but I moved him where he was more comfortable. And it worked well, it was fantastic. I played him in the centre and gave him the freedom to go both ways. To get the best from Steve you need to tap his endurance. When he was always put on the left, he'd look as if he was worried and people would say he wasn't trying. Of course he was trying. There was a reason why he had problems: he was trying hard to play where he wasn't comfortable. His running then becomes negative, purposeless, because he's not sure of himself. In that European Cup final [in 2000], where he was my Man of the Match, Del Bosque played him to his strengths. He was doing his running, and kept getting in the box. That's what enabled him to score his goal.

'Maybe his England career suffered later in moving to Spain. Out of sight, out of mind. There is a bit of that. He was great for me. I don't know how much other managers went to see him. It is important to do your own work about your players. I went quite a few times to see Gascoigne at Lazio. You're talking two hours on a plane. It can take as long as that to get to Newcastle! I don't understand people saying it would be a wasted journey to go out and find he was on the bench. You can't guarantee a player will start in most of the big European teams . . . and a night in Madrid! How can that be a wasted trip?'

With each of the four England coaches who selected Steve for England squads, there were grounds for empathy. Venables shared a conviviality and view of how the game should be played. After Glenn Hoddle, Kevin Keegan understood the ramifications of being one of few England players to have a successful club stint abroad. And with Eriksson, again, there was potential empathy in being a football person plying a trade in a foreign country. With Hoddle, who replaced Venables, there was – for external observers – valid reason why he, as a so-called footballing free spirit, would be keen to accommodate a player like McManaman in a conventional England side.

'I've never seen myself – as others seem to – as an idiosyncratic player,' says Steve. 'I just knew that after the glory of Euro 96 I had – very gratifyingly – become billed as the young player to build future sides around. But Hoddle was not the sort of character to have relationships with his players. In total contrast to Venables, he was detached and distant. John Gorman, his assistant, was always very good with us, but Glenn was always a step further back. The atmosphere in the England camp changed overnight: we stopped having the same interaction with the head coach that we'd enjoyed before.

'I played in three games that season – two World Cup qualifiers against Poland and Italy, and in a friendly against Mexico. By late spring of 1997 it was clear I needed to have an operation on my left knee. I'd dislocated it a few times, and had a lot of trouble with it all season. Roy Evans was keen for me to get it done straightaway so I had time to recover fully before the next season. That meant Liverpool said I was unavailable to join up with England for Le Tournoi in the summer [where Roberto Carlos would score that famous Exocet of a bending thirty-five-yard free kick against France]. As a player you are torn. You really want to play for England – as I said, the tournaments are the best times with England – but you also understand that they are an absolute nuisance if you're a club manager. I had had a long, hard season playing well in a very good Liverpool side. Euro 96 had dominated the previous summer. I knew I had to have an operation and as much as I wanted to play for England, you have to be sensible when it comes to your body. Glenn Hoddle didn't see it that way at all. People said it was an affront to his control-freakery because, unfortunately, the fax from Roy Evans withdrawing myself and Robbie, who needed an operation on his nose, reached his hand two hours after he had named us in his squad. He was livid, and wondered out loud to the national press whether either of us would feature again in the World Cup qualifiers. "As one door shuts, another door opens for players coming in," he said. "Robbie and Steve know that. And that's the sad thing for those players and a good thing for other players who are going on this trip. We're virtually together for three and a half weeks. We've got time to work with these players, and get to know them."

'Whether Hoddle held that as a long-term grudge, I don't know. Other factors emerged to make my fight for a place harder. In my absence, England won Le Tournoi with victories over France and Italy, and defeat by only a single goal to Brazil in the final match. David Beckham and Paul Scholes emerged as precocious young midfield talents. During the following season I played three or four more games, including a game against Cameroon in November, which Geremi later claimed had made me "famous in Cameroon", and a World Cup warm-up against Morocco in Casablanca, when I felt I played very well. Certainly, the following day, there were comments in the press saying it was my best game for a while and praising my creative influence. The highlight of our 1–0 win, of course, was my club mate Michael Owen's scorching first goal at the age of eighteen years and one hundred and sixty-four days. I played the ball to him and he set off on the run that launched a thousand headlines the next day.

'After that run-in to the tournament, it was a surprise to say the least that Hoddle ignored me during the 1998 World Cup. I ended up playing seventeen minutes in the entire tournament, coming on late in the 2–0 win over Colombia as a substitute for Scholes. Hoddle was intent on being his own man. He had earned ridicule for claiming Michael Owen was not a natural goal-scorer. He dropped Beckham for the first game against Tunisia in Marseille, saying he was "not focused" and "vague" coming into the tournament, which prompted a public row with Alex Ferguson. He certainly didn't have the man-management skills of Venables. A lot of the players resented the way he spoke to us like children. He knew everything. He would pick out an individual and in front of everyone else, he would say he shouldn't be doing it like that. Then he'd show that player how it ought to be done. At that level, that is an insult to a player's intelligence. There is a way of saying what he wanted to say without sounding so condescending. A lot of us were playing at the highest level with our clubs. Instead of giving us confidence, encouragement, and the will to do well for him, he ended up losing the dressing room. It was his attitude. The way he dealt with people. He did nothing to foster camaraderie or confidence. He was very full of himself. Some players called him "chocolate" because he'd eat himself if he could, and he came across like that, to be honest.

'There had been the predictable jokes about Hod the God when he brought in his friend Eileen Drewery, the former Essex pub landlady turned faith healer. Many players had seen her privately before she became involved with the England set-up. A lot of them felt she was very good. The fact she was available to consult was fine by me. If I had an injury, and I wasn't confident it was going to clear up by conventional medical treatments, I'd try a witch doctor in Africa if it would help. When my mother was sick, I would have tried absolutely anything to help her. It wasn't the fact that Eileen Drewery was a faith healer that was the problem. Glenn introduced her to the players and we all thought she was a very nice woman, and her husband Phil was a nice bloke as well. What put us players in a difficult situation was the pressure we were under to go and see her even if we didn't think we needed to. Robbie Fowler said Glenn forced him go to see her. He lasted two minutes in there. She said there was nothing she could do for him. He had three demons. And Robbie came out saying, "I'm not worried because I've heard Gazza has five." He asked me on numerous occasions to visit her but I didn't feel I needed to. I had a slight injury that was healing well. One of the other players came and spoke to me and said Hoddle had had a word with him, and I really should go. That was the thing. You were made to feel you ought to go as it might undermine your chances of being in the team if you didn't. When you look at it in retrospect, the fact that Eileen was part of the official staff in the hotel with the England players was a small thing, really. But it turned into a big issue because Glenn didn't have the press on his side either.

'It was at La Manga, when Hoddle narrowed down a large squad into his World Cup party, that he completely lost our respect. The experience was strange, weird, horrible actually. He was going to tell us personally whether we had made it, but he did it in the most impersonal way. A board was put up listing time slots for each player: 10am David Seaman, 10.30 Alan Shearer, and so on. We were waiting around nervously to go and have our allotted time with him. I was very near the end . . . and of course various meetings ran over time so a silent queue of players formed outside his room. A player would walk out and you would judge by his face whether he was in or out of the squad. If you were out, you had forty-five minutes to return to your room, pack and be sent off to catch a specially arranged private jet so that the rejected players could get home before the press found out their names. It was absolutely horrific. I was one of the last to go in, which initially was nerve-racking because with all the waiting you'd try and read things in the order he wanted to see us. But when I went in, the six who had to go had already been told. So I thought I must be in the squad. I went in a bit more relaxed. He just said, "You're in my squad. I'm very happy with how things are working out. Let's go and have a good World Cup." But Gazza, who's a very good friend of mine, was in hysterics. He was so nervous and wound up beforehand, he's that type of person. He couldn't handle the way it was done. He couldn't sleep without knowing whether he was going or not. He ended up having a drink to calm himself down before he went in. At the time, he wasn't playing well, there was a lot of media debate about whether he was worth taking because, with his talent, he might just be able to turn it on at the crucial moment. Then there was Phil Neville and Ian Walker . . . The way Hoddle handled it was appalling, I thought. I would have been mortified if I hadn't been included in the squad. You weren't allowed to talk to anyone. You had to pack and go, without saying ta-ra to any of the lads. You've been with them away in Morocco and at the training camp in Spain – and then to be told like that, "Pack your bags, there's a minibus to take you to the airport, to fly you secretly out of Spain. When you get to Birmingham airport, there are going to be cars on the tarmac to take you home." It was like, "Thanks very much, are we leaving in shame?" A huge amount of respect was lost on that day. How can someone who is touchy-feely enough to be into faith-healing handle his players like that? Going into that World Cup was very strange. He did not endear himself at all. We were in a lovely place in France, but it was such a contrast to the way Venables organised things. It was very regimented. I think there is a time and a place to trust your players. If you trust them on the pitch, you trust them off it, and vice versa. These were guys at the top of the game, playing professionally for the best clubs in the country.

'He also created a huge divide in the squad. The team who played were treated one way, and the substitutes another way. There is a time when you have to focus on the starting eleven, but not to the extent that you treat them as two separate entities. His starting eleven would train in one area, and the substitutes would be right over at the far end of the pitch. A lot of the substitutes were not happy. We would be training by ourselves. No one was bothering with us, and that hardly engenders a good team spirit. There are ways of keeping a squad together, making everyone feel they have a value, but Martin Keown, Les Ferdinand, Michael Owen to begin with, me . . . we were out on a limb.

'Did we have a drink and a singsong in the bar with Glenn Hoddle? God, no. There were times when we'd be told to go to bed. I'm a bit of a night owl. Whether that's gone against me, I don't know. After training, and lunch, you'd sleep of an afternoon. Athletes' rest, as other sports call it. Therefore in the evening you don't feel tired. By 10pm there is no chance I'm going to sleep so I would go to the physios for a massage, or a coffee and a chat. I got on very well with the physios because they'd be working all the hours in the day, and their time off came late at night. I forged very good friendships with them through doing that.

'Of the five games England played I stayed on the bench for four. It was frustrating as hell. David Batty and Paul Merson were Hoddle's preferred midfield options and I would never say I should have been playing instead of *x* or instead of *y*. Merson had been flying for Arsenal that season. Hoddle also liked wing-backs, which required more defence-minded players like Phil Neville and Graeme Le Saux. But Hoddle's selection seemed arbitrary. Michael missed the first game and turned out to be the star of the show against Argentina. Becks missed the first game, came back against Colombia, scored his first goal, a stunning free kick. People were just coming in and out. I'm not one to say of a manager, "Oh, he didn't understand how to play me." There have been times when I've not played well in an England shirt, I would never deny that. There are times when I've played left midfield, or right midfield, and the game's been hard, and I've had a bad day. That happens sometimes, as anyone who plays football at any level knows. Then I understand I haven't deserved to be in the team the next time, and would be in the squad, and not get on. There have been times when I would get an injury before the next call-up and the coach would give someone else a chance who has done well. I would never come up with excuses for not being appreciated by a manager. But I think what players found maddening with Hoddle was the fact he didn't want to be in the group with his players. We weren't all in it together. He was secretive and distant. I could not work out his attitude towards me.

'When Kevin Keegan took over, we had a convivial manager again. He tried to be friendly with the lads and make things relaxed. We used to have race nights where we would all sit together in front of a big screen showing tapes of horse racing. Keegan or Alan Shearer would be the bookmaker. It was fun and you wouldn't be stuck in your bedrooms, going through the television channels just to alleviate boredom. He liked getting the lads together, having a laugh and a joke with us in training.'

Of course, after a year in Spain, unable to speak freely with teammates because of the language barrier, the fun of meeting up with the England lads was evident to all. When that included Robbie Fowler, it meant a comprehensive review of the Macca & Growler string of horses, and racing in general. Henry Winter recalls a lovely crisp morning during Euro 2000 when he received frantic calls from the England team hotel. 'Kevin Keegan's secretary was saying, 'We're having a massive panic here." I thought the hotel had burnt down, or some other drama had struck the players, but no. "*Macca and Fowler haven't got their Racing Post*," she screeched. They needed the form guide faxed through.'

Steve: 'Keegan had selected me for two games when I was still at Liverpool, against Poland and Hungary. I flew back from Spain, having been at my new club for only a pre-season and a few games, for the game against Luxembourg at Wembley where I broke my international duck, scoring two goals, including an extremely rare header! I played once more against Poland in Warsaw, before enduring my longest spell out with injury. All of that first season in Madrid, I was really looking forward to Euro 2000, and coming in after the jubilation of winning the Champions League and scoring in the final, I was on a huge high. I had congratulations from all directions. The England lads wanted to know everything about Real Madrid and my first year playing abroad. The press suddenly remembered there was this English lad playing in Spain. We were due to play Portugal, a high-profile team, in our first game. There was a great deal of pressure to do well, but that's what it's all about. I scored early on, feeling great and then in a tackle with Rui Costa my left knee went. It was a twisted kneecap. It was so sad, such a contrast to the weeks that had gone before the Champions League final, when the excitement had been building up and up, with Euro 2000 something equally challenging to look forward to. The worst thing about being under heavy treatment in a tournament is that you become detached from the rest of the squad. That was it then.

'I had to spend hours in a hospital having X-rays and scans, then hours waiting for the results and the prognosis, then hours receiving treatment in the hotel. From then on, I always felt on the periphery. People have questioned me about Keegan's tactical preparation but I've never been in a position to judge that. I was nowhere near the white boards and marker pens. I couldn't train, and when I started to train lightly I was under the physio's supervision, so I wasn't involved with the lads. I travelled around with everyone, but they were long boring days for me. I came back and sat on the bench for the last game, but I wasn't really fit. It was the game against Romania, when we were knocked out, and I wanted to be there in case I could come on and help.

'On one level I felt sorry for Kevin Keegan. With England you know you are always under ten times more scrutiny than at any other period of your football career. That means you can pretty much dilute some of the wild stories to a tenth of their strength, and you may get a truer picture. The tales of card schools and gambling under Keegan were so exaggerated. The amounts mentioned were ridiculous. All he did was to come in and try to endear himself to the players, to make it a campaign we were all in together. He wanted to build up team spirit and foster camaraderie and, as a player, you can only commend that. It is pretty boring being holed up in an isolated hotel in Belgium.'

Keegan clearly had belief in Steve as a player, signing him for Manchester City on a free transfer three years after he resigned as England coach. 'Stevie was a gem for me,' he says. 'I had a problem in the team, in that I didn't have a left-sided player, but Stevie would have a go. It wasn't his natural first-choice position but he was clever enough to do a job for me. I can't think of many others who were fit enough or good enough to take on that role. He is a great lad to have around. He's bubbly, he mixes well, he very quickly finds a level to talk to anyone. He's great with young players. He had an air of magic about him because he was with Real Madrid, not always the best but certainly the biggest club in the world. The other lads would always ask him about life in Spain, what the players were like. When he turned up for Euro 2000 after winning the Champions League final and scoring that goal, his presence had a fantastic effect on the squad. It was just very sad he picked up that injury in our first game. Football has a habit of knocking you down when things are going well or catapulting you somewhere when you're at your lowest.

'People who know him, know he's got it all in his locker. He can play in three or four positions very comfortably. In fact he can play any position other than centre half or goalkeeper, and you can't say that about many players. He's very relaxed but you have to know him to understand him. His attitude is, "I am what I am. This is me." He is not someone who makes you think he is trying hard to impress you. He wouldn't come on for the last 10 minutes and make sure everyone took notice of what they'd been missing. Some of us would do that. But not Steve. That's not his way, it never has been. You can't change someone's personality. He plays like he trains, as if it doesn't mean anything to him other than that he's enjoying himself. His skills and fitness come so easily. That relaxed confidence means he can coolly control a game with his passing and running, but when the game is going against us, it is not a good manner to have. It can look like it doesn't mean enough to him. People who know him understand that is not the case.'

During the 1998 World Cup and Euro 2000 the press contingent were treated to the entertainment of watching Steve and Martin Keown clashing in training. 'McManaman represents everything Martin Keown isn't,' recalls Henry Winter. 'Martin took his training *so* seriously. We would watch him home in with some brutal tackles on Macca, diving, giving 100 per cent. And Macca would walk away with a marvellous look of complete disdain.'

Where would that leave the incoming foreign coach, Sven-Göran Eriksson? If Terry Venables and Kevin Keegan both acknowledge the difficulty of reading Steve's demeanour, what hope for him? Not much, according to Michael Robinson. 'The England manager is under amazing pressure and Steven is very easy-going. If you're Eriksson, a Swedish geezer, who arrives as the first foreign coach to run the England team, and you see this happy-go-lucky guy who seems to play things down, you might translate his attitude as "he doesn't care". That's what he did, and that was a misinterpretation of Steven's character, an error of Sven-Göran Eriksson.'

Steve says, 'I found Eriksson all right. He knew he could trust the players. I was injured for his first game against Spain at Villa Park, but I was in the starting line-up for his second and third games, against Finland at Anfield, which we won 2–1 with Michael Owen and David Beckham scoring, and against Albania away. I suffered a kick midway through the first half of that game in Tirana and came off for treatment at half-time. After that I was used only as a substitute, coming on to replace Emile Heskey, Nick Barmby (twice) and Ashley Cole, against Greece, Germany, Albania and Greece.

'When you come on for ten minutes at the end of a game it's always difficult. You can't come on and start putting on a fantastic show-off display of your skills. You have to adapt to the way the game has gone and what is required to get the result. I came on for the last twenty-five minutes against Germany in Munich when we were winning 3–1. We eventually won 5–1. Fantastic. It was good to come on and play a little part, but in the whole scheme of things your twenty-five-minute supporting, steadying role gets forgotten because you came on as a sub when the game was as good as won. No one would mention I played well there, but six months later against Albania, where we won 2–0, they couldn't stop banging on about the fact I was messing about, taping up a ring on my finger. I would never worry about most of the press talk and speculation. I would never want to come out and moan that a manager never knew how to play me. I was happy to play wherever I was asked: centre, left, right midfield . . . The huge difference is that when you play for your club side, and you train with the same people, day in day out, you know how your teammates play like the back of your hand. You can play by pure instinct. When I was in the England team with my Liverpool club-mates Rob Jones, Jamie Redknapp and Robbie Fowler, we wanted to play a certain kind of football. With England it was different. With the exception of Euro 96, I always played better football with my club side than I did with England – as in "on-the-floor, nice, attractive football". When we played Holland and won 4–1 we played fantastic football, but we had the likes of Gazza, Teddy Sheringham, people with great football brains, who could really, really play, and Terry Venables had a familiarity of spirit going that was as good as a club side.

'I didn't expect to play during the Albania game at St James's Park. After the triumphant Germany game four days earlier I assumed Eriksson would stick to his original starting line-up. You get a sense from a coach whether he wants to put his trust in you or not (with Del Bosque, for instance, even though he was not always free to play me, I knew he knew I would never let him down). I was beginning to sense over those few days I did not figure large in Eriksson's plans. I was motioned on about twenty minutes after half-time. I did have to tape up my ring, and maybe the camera lingered on me sorting that out, which sort of projected the whole scenario, but there is no way it would have taken longer than a minute or two. I do remember I slipped over about sixteen times, which got on my nerves, but I came on at 1–0 and we won 2–0 after Robbie scored on eighty-eight minutes. The game hardly needed me to come on and charge up and down for the last fifteen minutes with an exaggerated British bulldog spirit, risking giving the ball away. My role was to maintain the momentum, not disturb it. I certainly wasn't in a huff at being on the bench. As I've said, when you come on late as a substitute your role is limited. You have to look beyond yourself as an individual and contribute to the big picture. I did what I thought needed to be done to help preserve the winning score. I didn't come off thinking of it in terms of a disaster or a star performance.

'I've heard stories that Robbie and I shocked Mr Eriksson by leaving the dressing room to drive straight off into the nearest nightclub. How ridiculous is that? We all celebrated in the dressing room after the game, we all changed. Then I stayed longer for treatment. I had ice on my Achilles and a session with the physios. No, we didn't go to the players' lounge for hours to mix with our family and friends because we didn't have anybody there. Yes, we did leave together, because the plan was to drive the three hours back to Liverpool so I could quickly see my family before flying back to Spain, but we didn't go as quickly as we possibly could because there were fifty thousand bloody people leaving the stadium. How could you possibly get in a car and then join a traffic jam for an hour? Please!

'The Macca and Robbie thing, it's easy, isn't it? "Oh, look, they're enjoying themselves . . . This is going to be trouble." "He's not in bed by ten o'clock – he's a troublemaker." "They're a pair of Scouse scallies." There was an incident at La Manga, too, when Robbie and I were late for dinner, and it was blown out of all proportion. We had all been given a day off and there was an optional round of golf in the afternoon. Robbie and I teed off slightly late because we had to wait for golf clubs. Normally dinner was served at 7pm. By then we were coming to the end of our game. I was two up, and Robbie was desperate to beat me. Since it was a free day we didn't think it would matter if we were twenty minutes late. We went to dinner and there did not appear to be a problem. Months later, the press rumoured that we had been in big trouble and made it into a huge scandal. However nothing was said to us at the time or since and I cannot think why such a minor thing would be held against me. I would never go against a manager's instructions. None of my club managers have ever had a problem with me. If someone said to me, "Go to bed at ten o'clock," don't get me wrong, I'm in bed at ten o'clock, but, when we're free to do what we want, I don't mind going for a game of pool late at night, or having a coffee and a chat. On the night before the European Cup final in 2000 I was having a massage at one o'clock in the morning and there were ten or twelve Real Madrid lads sitting on the floor having a drink and chatting. When you sleep all afternoon, your sleep patterns go awry.

'Eriksson never travelled to Madrid to watch me. I heard from people at the FA that he didn't come because he felt he could never be sure I would be starting a game. But I was involved in most of Real Madrid's games that season. I should have been in his World Cup squad. I should have gone to the World Cup. The suggestion that I wasn't playing enough football was absolutely farcical when you see the squad that was getting picked then, and now. A lot of players are rotated in their club squads. They start games as substitutes and are still picked. The way my England involvement petered out, the way Eriksson rang me in the middle of a weekday morning when he knew I'd be training and left a message, that was a bit hurtful. I'd have preferred it if he'd rung me and said, "Look, Macca, I can't have you in the team because I just don't think you give a monkey's," for example. At least then I could have said, "I do give a monkey's," and try to resolve it. Ever since that day, people ask me all the time, "Why weren't you in it? What happened between you and him?" I've been left with that question mark.

'If I appalled him so much in the Albania game, why, when we were 2–1 down against Greece four weeks later, did he bother to call me onto the pitch? What on earth was he doing putting me on the bloody pitch if he didn't rate me, bringing me on at that crucial time when we were losing a game we needed to get a point from?

'Maybe I should have looked like I was overwhelmed by the England set-up, as if I hadn't been able to sleep because I was so excited about the prospect of playing, but that's never been me. I'm very even-keeled. I don't get nervous in big games. I tend to take everything in my stride, and that's served me well in club football.

I'm quite philosophical about the highs and lows of football. Perhaps that has been misinterpreted. To be honest, I've only seen a handful of people who do get visibly pumped up like Stuart Pearce and Tony Adams. For four years I'd played with the biggest and best club in the world and before each game, we were so relaxed, laughing and joking, chatting, up late at night, having a coffee. You can't say they haven't got the passion to win.

'And then look at the way we went out of the 2002 World Cup. We went out with a whimper in the Brazil game. There was no fight. I'd rather you get Martin Keown on and put him up front for the last ten minutes and go out fighting. If we get beaten, I would like to see us going down kicking and screaming. I hate that look of acceptance on people's faces. "Oh, that's it, then," before the final whistle. Once Brazil were 2–1 up, you could see on the England lads' faces a look of resignation. I hate that.

'I consider I have had a good England career, but I am disappointed not to have earned more than my thirty-seven caps. At times I cannot deny I have been very frustrated by injuries or by being kept on the bench, but I am honoured to have played for my country and will treasure the memories.'

At Real Madrid there was silent consternation that Steve could play alongside their stars yet not get a place in the England squad. 'I think we were a little to blame for his not being selected, because of his lack of first-team opportunities in his last season at Madrid,' said Del Bosque apologetically. If a militant McManaman supporter had wanted to send a petition to the FA spelling out his worth in that 2002 World Cup squad, they could have counted on the signatures of Figo, Hierro, Roberto Carlos, Raúl, Helguera, Salgado, Solari, César, Campo and David Beckham. 'It is difficult because it is not down to me,' said the England captain eighteen months later. 'Steve is a great player, a player who people like to watch. He's got a way about him. It looks a lazy way. He walks with the ball and he'll do a trick and all of a sudden he's off. And I think people like those sorts of players. He's exciting. He runs at players and takes players on, he crosses the ball, he scores goals. Personally, I think he should have had more games for England. It's not down to the players, but, to be honest, yes, he should have had more caps. Of course he should.'

When the question mark is left, all sorts of gossipy theories are put forward . . . that Steve represented the boy at the back of the classroom where Eriksson likes his front-row swots; that like Graeme Le Saux, or even Gareth Southgate (who has had to fight for every game he's played under Eriksson), Steve was over a certain age barrier; that one Scouser in the squad is fine, but more than one spells trouble. It could be, as Matt Lawton of the *Daily Mail* suggests, that he and Fowler are hangovers from a previous era. 'They grew up in the Gazza era. They were both so good when they were young that they've been unlucky enough to end up falling between two eras of management style. Gazza's stories from the 1990 World Cup are outrageous, the opposite of everything Eriksson preaches, and yet England reached the World Cup semi-finals with that. In the same culture England did very well in Euro 96 with Terry Venables.'

Few England managers played Steve to his strengths, and his pass-and-move style and dribbling is not suited to the long-ball midfield service favoured by Eriksson and operated by Steven Gerrard and David Beckham. Tord Grip, Eriksson's No. 2, insists McManaman's omission from the World Cup squad was tactical: 'It was tricky because when I saw him play in Madrid, most of the time he was on the bench. When he came on, he did play rather well. With so many big midfield stars like Figo, Zidane and Makelele, it was not easy for anyone to get into that team, but he was very popular in Madrid. For us, when it came to a decision about the best midfield for England, we made a tactical decision. We had started to play with a diamond, with Steven Gerrard, Nicky Butt and Paul Scholes as the type of players we felt performed well in that formation.'

Quite unexpectedly Grip added: 'And for Euro 2004, he has suffered from a combination of injuries and from his club not doing well . . .'

So he could still earn more caps?

'Why not?' said Grip.

Season Four

2002–2003

If you were to meet Her Majesty the Queen, you would greet her with a 'Good afternoon, Your Majesty.' If you were meeting Ena Sharples in the Rovers Return, you'd probably go, 'Hiya, Ena.' It's a question of adapting yourself to whatever's in front of you. For me, as a football observer, Steven's skill was in interpreting the role he had to play. People win Oscars for being the best supporting actor. That role is fundamental. Steven's role was the Oscar for the best supporting actor in the most wonderful film I've seen in a long time.

—*Michael Robinson*

From the cool comfort of his hotel room in Barbados, Steve watched his teammates flounder in an intriguing World Cup. There was Zidane, a forlorn figure, leaving the pitch with a heavily strapped left thigh, the same limb that weeks before had swung to glorious effect in Glasgow. Incredibly, France, the holders, failed to qualify for the knock-out stages. For Figo, too, it was a dismal end to an inconsistent season as Portugal also failed to emerge from the group stage. Ditto Argentina, while Spain, yet again, could not fulfil the perennial punters' prediction of the tournament's 'dark horses', losing on penalties in the quarter-finals to South Korea. The burgeoning teams of the Far East shook the global balance of soccer power: the world had come within a couple of goals of a Turkey v. South Korea World Cup final. However, in the familiar old-order Brazil v. Germany confrontation, Roberto Carlos – the closest thing on earth to a one-man football team – returned to Real Madrid duty with another elite winner's medal.

Valdano had stifled summer speculation by announcing there would be no other Figo, no other Zidane, the party was over. 'But inevitably, Ronaldo, after his wonderful World Cup, became the president's next target in his policy of signing a star a season,' said McManaman. 'All the talk was of that – the big picture – but there were several technical issues concerning Vicente Del Bosque. In the previous season, César and Casillas had both proved themselves great goalkeepers to the extent that both managed to play in the European Cup final. Which one would he decree first choice, and how would he keep the other happy? After the sale of Aitor Karanka, and the loan to Bolton of Iván Campo, how was he going to fortify a back line who for three years had been described as "papier-mâché thin"? By this stage Claude Makelele, considered by Zidane to be the most crucial player on the pitch, was unsettled. He knew his value to his teammates but he felt under-appreciated by the club who paid him only €1.2m salary. And with no Ronaldo yet, would Javier Portillo fulfil his promise?

'No chance. When the centenary year kicked in, the marketing machine kicked in to overdrive too with the *galácticos* tag and, with it, the trumpeting of president Pérez's "Zidanes y Pavones" policy. The amazing thing, in retrospect, is how little questioning there was of that policy – only Diego Torres in *El País* and Sid Lowe in *FourFourTwo*. From an accountant's view, it's a smart way of trying to cut the wages. The *galácticos*' salaries are cancelled out by the money their image rights make on shirt sales and endorsements, and the young lads don't have to be paid much. In the centenary year, Zidane, Figo and Raúl had superstar billing, with Roberto Carlos sort of roped in, too. In the club shop only their shirts were on display. The club identified itself exclusively with the big stars. The rest of us were not considered *mediáticos*, not worth marketing as stars, basically. The press would ask how you felt about that. All these issues did not directly affect the football, but were starting to creep into the training ground. Del Bosque was not accountable for the personnel situation. Everyone understood his position. But it was potentially divisive. It was obvious that in the grand scheme of things, some of us mattered, some of us didn't. One person would start to feel miffed, then another, and it snowballed. The *galácticos* thing did not affect players with each other, it was an external label. All the players got on remarkably well, but the likes of Helguera, doing a big job for the team – drafted in as a central defender when he considered himself most effective as a central midfielder – he is thinking, "How undervalued am I, then?" Fernando Morientes, a loyal *madridista* who had grown up in the team with, but in the shadow of, Raúl, and who had never let the club down on the pitch, he was to suffer from Ronaldo's arrival [a Zidane] and Portillo's presence [a Pavón]. A whole group of players would soon become known as "the middle class" after Solari's astute comment to *El País*: "The problem with Zidanes y Pavones is that it tends towards the extinction of the middle class."

'Portillo's first-team record was good, but others would play for Real Madrid in the B-team league or the C-team league, score a hundred goals and they're the next best thing. They get put in with the big boys and find it is harder to be consistent. Maybe the club became carried away after the likes of Raúl, Guti and Casillas emerged through the ranks, but look at the ages of Portillo, Pavón, Raúl Bravo, Rubén, all these youth-team players, and all great guys, but to play in a Real Madrid team on a regular basis you need a lot more experience from an early age. The preparation in the B and C leagues is not competitive enough. They're twenty-two, twenty-three, twenty-four. Really, if they're going to play alongside Zidane, Figo and Ronaldo, they should have made it much earlier.'

Florentino Pérez was having a tough time prising Ronaldo from Inter president Massimo Moratti. Given his injury history, the Brazilian was a risky purchase. Yet an irresistible one. The manner in which Ronaldo had raced into position to slide home Rivaldo's rebounding shot, adding the second of two goals that helped his country win the World Cup, dispelled doubts that his physical rehabilitation would be complete. After four injury-plagued seasons, the buck-toothed, chubby-cheeked Brazilian had made the fairytale comeback and Moratti did not want to let him go. But Ronie wanted Real Madrid. He had fallen out with manager Héctor Cúper. Zidane-like, he said the style of football did not suit him. Italian gossips suggested he and his wife, Milène Domingues (world keepie-uppie record holder with 55,187 touches in nine hours and six minutes), were having problems. It was a good time to leave.

As Ronaldo had already said he wanted to go, Moratti's refusal to countenance a deal turned the press against the player. To this day, Ronaldo speaks warmly of the president, as a man 'with vision, heart, common sense and a great soul', and has given his word not to reveal the details of their talks. However, it was clearly a difficult time. 'No one ever asks how my family and I coped during this period in Milan,' he said. 'To start with, I wasn't able to train with the other players. Soon after that, I could not leave my house. I could not enjoy the pleasure of being world champion. I could not even say goodbye to people at Inter, my colleagues. I had to listen to people trying to destroy my image. It was easy to attack me and paint me as the villain. Overnight I became the worst person in the world – the anger was incredible, people decided to show no respect. It was totally out of proportion, but I could not explain myself because of the agreement I had with Moratti. I was depicted to Inter fans as someone who did not care for the club, and that is a lie – I cried like a baby when we did not win the league the previous year.'

Moratti negotiated hard. Every day in August there was a new he-will, he-won't twist leaked to the press. Enter Barcelona president Joan Gaspart – still bitter about Pérez's snaring of Figo – for the stinging dénouement. Sid Lowe told the story well in *FourFourTwo*: 'A couple of days before the August 31 transfer deadline, Gaspart tabled a £10m bid for Madrid striker Fernando Morientes. Pérez, searching for a way to meet Inter's demands, was delighted. FC Barcelona were helping Madrid buy a Nou Camp icon. It seemed too good to be true. At 10pm on deadline day, Gaspart reneged, "accidentally" leaving Madrid cashless and, therefore, Ronaldo-less. Brilliantly dastardly it may have been, but it merely saved Madrid £10m. Sure that the deal was going ahead, Inter had already bought Ronaldo's replacement, Hernan Crespo, and feared being lumbered with both players and no cash. Their price came tumbling – a deal that had been bouncing back and forth all summer was suddenly struck in a matter of minutes. Inter had little choice but to accept Pérez's final bid. Madrid paid €35m (£23.3m) and gave Inter the option, when the transfer window opened in January, of taking an extra €10m (£6.6m) or a similarly valued player of their choice, McManaman or Solari. Neither Steve nor Solari wanted to go. Almost two years later Madrid were ordered to pay Inter €8m to complete this deal. In September, Ronaldo touched down at the Torrejón airbase in a private jet laid on by the club. The next day, smiling awkwardly and performing the obligatory kick-ups (though not as well as his wife, obviously), Ronaldo became the latest crack wheeled before the world's press. His signature, along with those of Zidane and Figo, gave Madrid the most exceptional team in history – at a cost of £120m.'

On the eve of the transfer deadline, on the last Saturday in August, Real Madrid travelled to Monaco as European champions to contest the Super Cup against Feyenoord. The trophy, never won by Los Blancos, was on the president's Must-Win list. Pérez's mind, however, was still whirling with the latest complication in the Ronaldo negotiations. Morientes, told from on high that he was set to go to Barcelona via Inter in order to pay for Ronaldo, had made it clear he did not want to leave. (Later, Emilio Butragueño tells me Morientes' agent had helped set up the agreement.)

'Morientes was part of a triangular deal, but he was emphatic he didn't want to be,' recalls Steve. 'Out of the blue, he was dropped from the squad. When word came down that he wasn't to be included, we were thinking, "What the bloody hell is going on? We're supposed to be playing a football match." Morientes travelled with us, but had to sit in the stands in a suit. The fans chanted his name. It had become a big, public melodrama. In the dressing room we all saw Raúl had a Morientes shirt under his own, ready to reveal it if he scored . . . He said it was a gesture of solidarity for a friend. He didn't score, but God knows what the repercussions would have been if he had!

'We won the game, 3–1, which was fantastic, but the meal afterwards was very subdued. Hierro and Raúl had strong words with the president. As a foreign player I wasn't party to all that was being whispered, but the gist was they told him players could not be treated like currency. The club said they needed money to stop the Ronaldo deal being scuppered, but did that give them leave to shunt Morientes off here, there and everywhere, against his will? None of his friends thought so – and he had powerful friends in the dressing room.'

Later Raúl tells me his intention. 'If I had scored, yes, I would have shown Morientes' shirt as a gesture of friendship. I did what I thought was right at the time and I don't regret it. But the situation did not arise, so all that matters is that we won the Super Cup and took it home to Madrid. Even if I had shown the shirt, nothing would have happened. Aggro here only ever lasts a week.' He laughed nervously.

Morientes stayed. The season had started, as it would end even more tumultuously in the Txistu restaurant, with players driven to confronting their president.

'Ronaldo arrived and everyone's thrilled,' grins Steve. 'You don't know the geezer, but you know he's a nice bloke. He's infectious. Lots of people knew him from doing the Nike ads. Luis, who'd played with him at Barcelona, said he was fantastic. Zidane knew him from the Italian league, and the Brazilians obviously knew him very well. No one had a bad word to say about him, and everyone knew what kind of player he was.

'I'd met him in 1997, on September 6 – Victoria's birthday – in a casino in Monaco. It was the day of the funeral of Diana, Princess of Wales. Football-wise, it was international week and I was injured, so had four days off. I said to Victoria, "If you stay in England, you'll have the most depressing birthday ever," so we flew to Nice, and stayed in St Jean Cap Ferrat. On her actual birthday we went over to Monaco, to the casino, and bumped into Ronaldo. He was under twenty-one so he wasn't allowed in the big boys' casino. He was playing on a little horsey game where you bet on mechanical horses. We recognised each other and said "hello". Neither could speak each other's language so it was one of those smile, thumbs-up sign, back-slapping, OK, OK, conversations. He must have popped down from Milan because it's only a two-hour drive along the motorway. He was just sitting there, happy as a sandboy, playing on this machine with a friend of his.'

A year after he became a Real Madrid player, I meet Ronaldo in the incongruous setting of an isolated health farm near Ashby de la Zouch, the base for the Brazil team before an international against

Jamaica at the Walkers Stadium in Leicester. It is the sort of establishment where eerie chill-out music is piped throughout to a regular clientele of jaded souls in shapeless white towelling robes. Beauty therapists stood aghast, marvelling at how such bulky muscle can balloon between Roberto Carlos's small-boned ankles and knees. Ronaldo and his compatriots, all dense-hewn muscle and dazzling smiles, seem to have too much energy for such a fragile atmosphere.

Ronaldo arrives, a green T-shirted torso cutting a monolithic silhouette in the doorway. He is big. His face is welcoming with trademark gap-toothed grin and warm friendly eyes. He shakes hands, and smiles in gratitude at being steered clear of a chair recently vacated by Kaka, who has left it discoloured by a vast pool of sweat. Catching sight of the doorstopper of a Spanish–English dictionary my *Telegraph* colleague Gareth A. Davies has brought to help smooth through any linguistic difficulties, he laughs, wondering whose vocabulary we think is that size. He shows unusual courtesy, removing his mobile phone from a pocket and switching it off. Answering questions, he is the opposite of glib, often standing up to re-enact an incident.

A casino was an apt place to meet Macca, he laughs, explaining his affinity with the English betting mentality. He, the other Brazilians and Steve developed a daily betting repartee – not for money, but for motivation or stimulation in what can often be hours of tedium. There'd be casual bets on anything from the outcome of free kicks, training exercises, to whoever could get the ball through Ronaldo's legs the most during practice. 'In Monaco I recognised Macca first, and then he recognised me. We chatted for a while and then went upstairs, away from the slot machines, to gamble more. We didn't win that night. When I came to Real Madrid, Macca and I always had lots of little bets with each other. He was always putting money on his horses, and whenever he urged me to put money on his horses, I would ask him what would be the best race, the best day, and they always seemed to lose!

'Macca was a very active person in welcoming me to the club. He's very calm, very mellow, very natural and spontaneous with his friendship. He was one of the first players who gave me my space, let me be myself. He's cool. I felt comfortable with him. He was very receptive to me as a person, not just as a teammate. It was an immediate friendship. I was studying English so I would ask him to translate the lyrics of all the rap songs I like. He would write down the words for me, line by line, on many of our journeys to matches. I wanted to know what was going on in these tracks, but it's probably put him off Eminem and Snoop Doggy Dog, forever!'

Ronaldo's debut was always going to be subject to intense scrutiny. 'Poor lad, he wasn't the fittest when he arrived,' said Steve. 'He'd been on holiday with his family because of all the furore in Milan. He needed time to develop his stamina because he hadn't had a pre-season, but as soon as he could run or join in a match he was playing, because of who he was. He had to get involved straightaway, rather than build up his fitness. This was the Year of Ronaldo.'

On Sunday 6 October, he and Steve were both named substitutes for the home league game against Alavés. Zidane scored in the first minute. Figo made it 2–0 from the spot before the Brazilian Mocelin Magno brought Alaves back into the frame in the thirty-seventh minute. In the second half, Del Bosque introduced Ronaldo to the Bernabéu faithful. Madrid's newest *galáctico* remembers it well: 'I was on the bench with Macca, and it was the first time I'd been part of the group, with him and our other teammates on the bench. There is a roof above the dugout. When I came in to sit down before kick-off I didn't realise it was so low. When Del Bosque motioned for me to come on, I leapt up, whack! – straight into the edge of the roof. I banged my head really hard! A great start, I'm thinking, and I looked across and there was Macca bent over double, pissing himself.

'I scored within sixty seconds of coming on. Then Macca was on the field too. I scored my second fifteen minutes later, with Macca creating it. He was going through the centre, Luis Figo to his right, and me to his left, and Macca laid it on for me. It meant a lot to me, because he gave the impression he was choosing me. He knew it was important to have a strong debut.'

'In retrospect it was the worst thing he could have done! Everyone went, "Oh God, he's going to score six in every game," exclaimed

Steve. 'The newspapers went crazy, calling it *debuta madre*, the mother of all debuts – which was a great pun, a play on the slang phrase, *de puta madre* [literally, of a whore mother], which means "bloody brilliant".'

Already Real Madrid had established themselves as the proverbial Jekyll and Hyde side. When they were good (at home), they were very, very entertaining; when they were bad (away), the defence were very, very entertaining. This tendency had become so pronounced that commentators were moved to suggest that this was Real Madrid's way of keeping the playing field level. Give your opponents a head start by conceding a few goals and keep your superstar forwards on their toes.

'When Zidane arrived, teams became very physical with us. With Ronaldo, too, and the *galácticos* billing, more teams came out with seven or eight defenders. The perception was that, having captured the biggest world stars, we were virtually unbeatable. But we were not a big, strong, physical team. Two set-pieces and we could be down. Away, we could be vulnerable, because we were so attack-minded.

'On September 15, we had travelled to Italy to take on AS Roma for our first Champions League game as defending champions. Just when most people were suggesting Real Madrid were the last team in the world to need divine help, our preparation started with a private audience with the Pope, who famously played in goal as a young man in Poland. Nevermind that His Holiness is also a FC Barcelona member of almost twenty years' stnading, all of the squad were invited to his mountain retreat where there was a fantastic, very moving ceremony. Our president gave a speech, then John Paul II addressed us in very good Spanish. We all knelt down individually for a blessing and kissed his hands – apart from Zidane who refused to kiss the Pope's ring – and he presented us with rosary beads. I am a Catholic, and what with all the Spanish, Portuguese and Brazilians, we were predominantly a Catholic team, so it was a very meaningful meeting. We agreed that the nervous sense of occasion you feel before a match like a European Cup final, in front of thousands of people, does not compare to meeting in person a world leader like the Pope. His mind is very alert and his senses acute, even though physically he cuts such a frail figure.

'Two days later we took on Roma and won 3–0, Guti scoring twice either side of one from Raúl. Eight days on and we were thrashing KRC Genk 6–0 in a crowd-thrilling goalfest at home. The first was an own goal from Zokora. Míchel Salgado scored on the stroke of half-time, then in the second half, Figo (from the penalty spot), Guti, Celades and Raúl swept past the goalkeeper, Jan Moons. I was on the bench for that one, but would at least come on in three of those Group Stage 1 games, and started the home encounter with AEK Athens.'

In early September McManaman had the prestige of captaining a Real Madrid side who thumped eight goals past San Sebastian de los Reyes in the Spanish Cup. 'I had been there the longest of everyone named in the side, so I was captain. It boils down to seniority. If you were in a league game and Raúl went off, he'd go over to the person who'd been there longest after him. That's all it is, but to lead out a Real Madrid team felt a great honour, to get them in a huddle and say "Come on!" in Spanish and toss coins with the referee and hope you understand what's he going to say. I'm thinking to myself beforehand, "Heads is *cara* or *cruz*, but what is tails? What if he says blah blah blah and I'm like, 'What?'" In fact he had a coin, green on one side, red on the other . . . and you called a colour. There I was, running through my future tenses, you know, "We *will* kick in this direction, we *will* attack that goal," and the referee just points and nods.

'By the first week of November we had slipped to sixth in the league and dropped five points out of six at home to Roma and Athens in the Champions League. Against Athens, we were winning 2–0 – I scored both of them in the first half – but we drew 2–2. That was a reversal from the norm. We drew 3–3 over there, conceding sloppy goals in a rollercoaster match on an appalling pitch, and played terribly back at home. After that result, the AEK coach Dusan

Bayevic described the result as "historic". Again you got the feeling that the fact we had all these superstar players gave other teams an extra incentive to beat us because they'd outwitted the likes of Figo, Zidane, Raúl and Ronaldo.

'By this stage, my personal season was shaping up to be a strange one. I was always named in the squad. I would start on the bench, come on lateish, score the odd goal, play well enough to consider I might have earned a more regular role in the team, but it was not to be. As every lad on the bench knew in their hearts, it didn't matter how well we played: there was a preordained pecking order. By the end of the season, I was disappointed only to have participated in about thirty games in all competitions. Solari was in exactly the same situation. Morientes suffered worst of all. He was on the bench for thirty games, regularly coming on as substitute for Ronaldo, but his end-of-season total of minutes on the pitch added up to 455 – though he was still named in the national squad. In retrospect, the situation for the likes of us, and Cambiasso, Celades and Miñambres was bleak, but you keep hoping. When you love your training, you are incredibly happy at your club, you are part of a great camaraderie throughout the squad, then, of course, you keep trying to maintain your performance levels. Very, very gradually – and very reluctantly, because we were all essentially happy – a certain group of us lost hope that policy and circumstances would ever change enough to earn us a more fulfilling role again. At one stage, I was very frustrated. One of the backroom staff detected that and encouraged me to go and see Del Bosque about the selection policy, but the manager virtually confirmed his hands were tied behind his back. Tactically, they had started the season with a central midfield pairing of Makelele and Cambiasso. Then Flavio was preferred to Cambiasso, but Guti ended the season playing more often than either of them as the preferred "fourth" midfielder. Figo and Zidane, of course, played almost every game.'

Pressure on Real Madrid mounted because Real Sociedad – a low-cost regenerated side with no household names – were the team who topped the table. Unlike the stuttering, expensively assembled Real

Madrid juggernaut of talent, the team from the Basque country were very consistent, very hard to break down and suffered very few injuries. The name *los galácticos* sounded good when they were winning, but hung sarcastically in the air when the team were suffering one of their increasing string of defeats. To add ignominy, a 2–0 defeat in late October to lowly Racing Santander – and Ronaldo's first ninety-minute outing – had incurred column inches of questions about why Madrid had not managed to stop Pedro Munitis from playing. Munitis, loaned out but still on the Madrid pay-roll, scored against the team with whom he had spent two years – and that very pre-season. 'He was part of our squad yet he could score against us. We had a young lad, Julio Alvarez, out with Rayo Vallecano, who took all the penalties. It's baffling how a member of your staff can be in a position to knock you out of the Cup, send you down, take away crucial points in the championship battle. He's your friend, but he's not. And, of course, he wants to play especially well to prove a point to everyone.' How that scenario, featuring an on-loan Fernando Morientes, and former Madrid striker Samuel Eto'o, spurned signing Gabriel Milito, Luis García (on loan to Murcia) and Valdo, sent on a free transfer to Osasuna, would come back to haunt Real Madrid the following year. It was like a curse.

Increasingly, Ronaldo was subject to criticism. Like Zidane the year before, he was experiencing difficulties settling into consistent form. Unlike Zidane, who is zealous in maintaining his fitness, Ronaldo was caricatured as fat and lazy. On *Noticias del Guiñol*, Spain's version of *Spitting Image*, his puppet caricature was dressed up as a seal. To the Spanish, the seal represents excess weight. Ronaldo's seal was depicted playing perpetual keepie-uppie while Jorge Valdano earnestly declared, 'He looks more agile by the day.' Since his debut, Madrid managed only one win in eight league and Champions League matches, with Ronaldo's name flashing up only once as scorer on the electronic scoreboard. Even Roberto Carlos, his friend, came out with strong comments. 'Now what Ronie is also finding is that at Real Madrid it's not a question of everyone working for his personal benefit – as it was at first at Inter and Barça before that,' he said. 'He has to take responsibility for his own game – like Zidane, Figo, Raúl and myself.' But there were smiles in the Bernabéu's commercial department. More than a hundred and twenty thousand Ronaldo shirts, at almost £50 apiece, had been sold in the first five weeks since his arrival.

'By mid-November, when we drew 0–0 at home with Real Sociedad, Ronaldo was being whistled off. The complaint was, "He looks sluggish",' said Steve. 'He probably didn't work as hard as he could and the fans let him know. But he needed time. This time the previous year everyone was going mad about Zidane's lack of impact, and the season culminated in him scoring the most fantastic goal in the Champions League final. Ronie had only played four or five games. The pressure for us to win every game in an even more spectacular manner had told on him, only because he wasn't fit enough when he arrived to go in all guns blazing. But, of course, being the new big star he had to play as soon as he could kick a ball. He's not bothered by the criticism. He knows how good he is. And the newspapers secretly love him because he has a way with words. He said the Bernabéu crowd was like a woman, and he had to find a new way of pleasing her every day. You don't get lines like that from Luis, Zizou or Raúl. His biggest mistake was scoring two so effortlessly when he came on as a substitute on his debut; the expectation was he would bang them in in every game. Our next league game, against his former club Barcelona, was building up to be a massive game for Ronaldo.'

It would have been . . . except that Ronaldo had to withdraw through illness. 'He has the fever of a dinosaur,' insisted Jorge Valdano, as suspicion grew that Ronie had lost his nerve. Conveniently for his detractors, Ronaldo's illness also prevented him playing in Milan a few days later.

On 24 November, Luis Figo made his second return to Barcelona. To a neutral observer in any seat in the steep-stacked tiers, the spot-the-dot figure on the pitch in the No. 10 shirt, dwarfed by the enormity of structure and circumstance, cut a magnificently unbowed figure. As Steve said, 'Typical Luis, he was even backheeling off the rubbish they pelted him with.' The football was dismal, the collective emotion chilling, but every move Figo made was pure drama.

Consider his stance in taking corners. Through a cacophony of ear-perforating whistles, ominous drumbeats, staccato taunts, smoke bombs and yet another pelting of plastic bottles, lighters and cans, he walked towards the flag to take the corner. Leisurely, almost theatrically, he picked up one hate-propelled missile after another and tossed them off the pitch. Again he tried to take the corner. Further bombardment.

A phalanx of black-helmeted riot police braced themselves in a line in front of the corner who were baiting Figo. He tried again. Roberto Carlos strode over to help clear the debris. Remarkably, given the historic acceptance of Catalan anti-*madridista* passion, Barcelona captain Carlos Puyol was moved to do the same, appealing to the fans to settle.

It was not until his fourth attempt that Figo, having purposefully pushed back his personal security wall to give himself a run-up, whipped in a stinging high cross. He almost scored. The goalie had to palm it over. Another corner.

It was the same scenario on the other side of the Nou Camp's north goal. This time the referee had had enough. So, clearly, had both sets of players, seventy-five minutes into a game in which emotion had long overwhelmed motivation. They hardly needed the order to retreat down the tunnel. The *gran clásico* of Spanish football – the game that boasted a meeting of the world's best players in a historically epic derby that had attracted seven hundred journalists from twenty-six countries and prompted black-market Internet ticket prices of up to €1,000 – was suspended in shame. Sixteen minutes later both sides ran back out to play out the rest of the disappointing, bitter, scrappy match that ended 0–0 and with Barcelona's ground under threat of closure.

'This was a disgrace to Spanish football,' pronounced Valdano afterwards. 'They broke the windows of our coach. The abuse started as soon as we arrived. This has gone beyond the limits of rivalry.'

Figo, for five years a Barcelona favourite, had experienced the wrath of his former worshippers two years ago on his only previous return. Traitor, liar, money-grabber – he had lived with those labels. But what happened this time went beyond sporting or nationalistic rivalry. A severed suckling pig's head was among the gruesome projectiles that underlined an open hatred which had been brewing all week. On Friday, after training, Barcelona coach Louis van Gaal had insisted this would be a game against a Real Madrid team, not Figo alone, and that the mentality of the supporters was one thing, that of his players another. He had emphasised it was a league game, one which the home team were obliged to win after their poor start to the season. To lose points at home would be a killer blow to morale.

For Figo, the passing of two years and the mooted return of Ronaldo to the Nou Camp promised a dilution of hostilities, but the Barcelona faithful insisted the Brazilian was not a target. He had, after all, gone to Inter Milan in between Spanish giants. 'It is all about Figo, because he went direct to Madrid when he said he never would. That caused deep pain,' said one. The absence of Zidane, who had scored on both previous visits to the Nou Camp, followed by the last-minute withdrawal of Ronaldo, effectively turned the clock back to 2000 and the immediacy of Figo's so-called treachery. 'No Zizou, and Ronaldo is out with a high temperature!' exclaimed one fan before kick-off. 'Now we just need Figo to die on the pitch.' He meant it.

The talking point in Madrid had been whether Figo would take corners. In Barcelona, the match-day build-up was obsessive to the point where Barça fans were fed the statistic that on average Figo takes corners every 18.1 minutes. In other words: Be Armed. After the game an imperiously defensive van Gaal, backed up by his president, claimed Figo had been the provoker. In his previous visit Figo had clearly been unnerved by the hostility of his reception. On his second return he remained resolutely unwilting. Even those who had never before taken to him emerged from the cauldron admiring his spirit and strength of character. If provocation was remaining on the pitch, he was guilty.

To think that two hours before kick-off, fans from as far apart as Japan and Blackpool waiting for the arrival of the Real Madrid team bus (which came, speeding, to the accompaniment of smoke bombs, red flares, rearing police horses and hurtling armed security vans) had said: 'It's just a match you have to be at.' As it turned out, the much-anticipated league encounter had still to fulfil its reputation. Rather like Ronaldo.

Two days later Madrid played AC Milan in the first of the Champions League Group Stage 2 games, and lost 1–0 in a typically tight game to a first-half goal from Andriy Shevchenko. Then it was on to Japan, as European champions, to play the South American champions, Olimpia of Paraguay, for the World Club Cup. Two years before they had lost to Boca Juniors, to Pérez's dismay, but goals from Ronaldo and Guti ensured the squad brought home the second trophy of the season. 'Our schedule is in our heads, not written down for us,' said Steve. 'That period was crazy. We had travelled to Barcelona after training on Friday, played Saturday, flew back to Madrid to train on Sunday and Monday, flew late Monday to Milan, played on Tuesday, flew home to train Wednesday and Thursday morning, flew to Tokyo for a week. After that kind of travelling whirl, three hotels, six flights, three games, endless getting on and off coaches, I have to say I love to come home and sit on the sofa, put up my feet and watch TV.'

Wednesday 18 December 2002

The culmination of the club's somewhat long-winded and pompous calendar of centenary-year celebrations was a glamour match that pitted Real Madrid – who boasted five of the last six FIFA World Players of the Year – against a world select team. By official decree, it was supposed to be the only football match scheduled for the day, but, comically, Michael Owen and others could not make it because they were playing in the Worthington Cup. Some Catalan journalists also organised a game as a way of breaking the ban and sticking fingers up at Madrid. Anyway, officially, it promised either an exhibition of skills from a collection of the world's very best players, or an in-house joke: how could a World XI match up to Florentino Pérez's fantasy team?

The previous night, Ronaldo had collected his World Player award at the requisite glitzy ceremony in Madrid's Palacio de Congresos. He was an hour late, which caused Oliver Kahn to develop a mysterious injury that meant he couldn't play the following night. 'It left the World Select XI issuing SOS calls for a goalkeeper, but irritating the reviled Bayern Munich man endeared Ronie to the fans at a time when he needed that,' laughed Steve.

'It was basically a collection of the world's very best players, and the chance to see them on the same pitch at the same time comes once in a blue moon, doesn't it?' he said. McManaman replaced Figo after thirty-one minutes and wore the captain's armband for the last twenty-five. That was an honour in itself, but more starkly he was the only Englishman to participate, following the withdrawal of David Beckham and Michael Owen through club commitments. Birmingham City's Senegalese player Aliou Cissé was the sole Premiership representative. The occasion was not a sell-out; as kick-off approached, the club opened the doors and let people in for free. Ten minutes before there appeared to be a crowd invasion, but the white-topped mob rushing to the centre of the pitch in torrential rain turned out to be the orchestra reclaiming their stands and seats as the weather made Placido Domingo's planned rendition of 'Hala Madrid!' impossible. He performed at half-time instead.

Fervent roars from a nowhere-near-capacity crowd greeted the name of every Real Madrid player – the stadium announcer finding a preposterous number of 'r's to roll in Raúl and Ronaldo. The guest opposition – Cafu, Paolo Maldini, Rivaldo, Michael Ballack, Bixente Lizarazu – walked out as if mesmerised by a dramatically spotlit plinth of Real's recent clutch of trophies: the European Cup,

European Super Cup and the World Club Cup, freshly flown in from Japan.

It was, as Steve had anticipated, 'a relaxed game with no mad, crazy tackles', a farcical number of substitutions to ensure the superstar count – but a good platform for Ronaldo who, despite his clutch of 'player of the year' gongs, still had much to prove to the *madridistas*. However, yet again, the air of expectancy had stifled, not inspired. Like the Copa del Rey final of the previous year, which was supposed to have produced the first trophy of a glorious Treble; the birthday World Select game was a damp squib, failing to produce an entertaining showcase of talent. Rather like the home side on one of their bad days, the glamour was in the billing, not in the action on the pitch. And Madrid only won once the *galácticos* had gone off.

'Back in the league, Real Sociedad continued their unlikely dominance,' said Steve. 'Everyone kept expecting them to slip up because they didn't have a big squad, but their forwards Darko Kovacevic and Nihat Kahveci kept scoring, and their physios remained untroubled. We were under scrutiny. Players' commitment – mainly Ronaldo's – was questioned. There was one unusual incident when a hidden camera in a nightclub caught him earnestly chatting up two girls to no avail, and the press made a big thing of him being unlucky in love. By this stage, it was well known he and his wife had separated. I was with Victoria and some friends in the bar. In the footage you can just see me chatting to two men about football while Guti was filmed taking this almighty drag from a cigarette, incredibly theatrically. But poor Ronie, a lot of mileage was made of a five-second shot. Not that he was bothered.

'The club's "Zidanes and Pavones" policy was starting to look totally unrealistic. We had twenty-three or twenty-four internationals in the squad – it was like Chelsea became in 2003–04. How could Del Bosque integrate juniors into a set-up to gain experience unless he could rotate the squad freely, and rest the big stars? Javier Portillo was about the only one from the academy who kept on being given chances. He scored a very important goal in the ninetieth-minute against Borussia Dortmund, so we drew 1–1 and stopped the Germans from knocking us out on away goals. He kept coming on and scoring goals like a super-sub. He was probably best coming on like that, rather than playing from the start. Del Bosque had spent years at the club working with the youth team. He'd like nothing better than to introduce them – if they were of the same ilk as Raúl, Guti or Casillas. But they weren't. Look at them the following season, 2003–04. They had sold or loaned out fifteen of us experienced players. They put all the young lads on the bench, but will any of them be in Real Madrid's first team in five years' time? If they were good enough, they would have been playing a couple of years ago, full stop. They would have emerged at the ages Raúl, Guti and Iker did.'

In January, Real Sociedad were winter champions, but Real Madrid now lay second, still infuriatingly up and down (being knocked out of the Copa del Rey by Mallorca, for example, 5–1 on aggregate in the quarter-finals). By early March, Madrid led the table by a point, but the newest *galáctico* had still not won people over. 'Ronaldo is the only player who is not integrated in the tasks of the team,' said Del Bosque, uncharacteristically speaking out about a player. Míchel Salgado, too, acknowledged that 'Ronaldo's not at his best and he knows it'. The response was quick. Ronaldo scored a brilliant hat-trick at Alavés on 1 March, which put him second after Deportivo's Roy Makaay in the list of Spain's leading goal-scorers on thirteen.

Ronaldo was a lovely and lovable guy in the dressing room, but from the outside, the perception of him as a lazy superstar who could earn a standing ovation for one single spectacular strike on goal – when the mood took him – exacerbated the difference between the *galácticos* and unheralded workhorses, like Makelele, Helguera, Salgado, even Guti. How infuriating that must have been for Morientes, who had become a resident bench-warmer, first in the pecking order to come on as substitute for Ronaldo. He had started two games – both Champions League fixtures, away to Genk and to AC Milan – but come off in both. The depth of his frustration was there for all to see at the home game against Borussia Dortmund. Del Bosque motioned him to come on for Zidane with nine minutes left to go, and he angrily refused. Solari, the next to get the nod, moved up the pecking order and went on.

'It was weird, that incident,' recalled Steve. 'Television cameras did not capture the incident, but it was leaked to the press so graphically that everyone can visualise it. Morientes wouldn't have leaked it because he comes out of it horribly: he was blatantly rude in what he said. Del Bosque wouldn't have liked to stir anything up. It was typical Real Madrid: everything gets leaked from the dressing room, which is damaging.'

It was clear you had to be psychologically strong to accept the position Morientes, McManaman, Solari, Guti, César, Celades and Cambiasso found themselves in. It was hard not to be wounded by the apparent indifference, as Solari, educated at an American college, explained in his Ivy League English over a cup of coffee after training one day. 'It is difficult. We have five or six players who we know have to be hurt or injured in order for us to even have a chance of playing. Everybody knows that. On the other hand they are the best players of their generation, specialists who will be remembered as the best in history over ten or fifteen years. Sometimes the frustration is so much you feel you *have* to play, but sometimes you see that you are part of a very special team in history,' he said.

'Steven and I have both had prolonged spells as regulars. Steven won the eighth European Cup playing as a regular and scoring in the final. Last year I played as a regular, too, in all the Champions League games and won the ninth European Cup. This season we are not playing regularly, but that doesn't mean we couldn't come on and play. It means this club is so big that they have the luxury to have Steven, Guti, Morientes, César on the bench. César was our goalkeeper in the Champions League last year and he was fantastic. But we are all on the bench. What can you do? Wait for your time and try to do your best when you are handed a chance. The team cannot field more than eleven players. You have to be strong personalities, of course you do. You cannot underestimate the frustration. You have to have a good sense of humour and enjoy being part of the set-up, but it is hard. You know you can *play*, that you can do *great* things on the pitch. It is very, very, very frustrating. What is difficult is trying to accept you are not a regular when you are training every day as if you are, not just for six months, but for three years! So you train hard for three years, sometimes you have a spell in the team, but most of the time it's just odd games. You have to keep trying hard because otherwise you'd kill yourself.

'I think, what we've all come to realise is, you have to feel useful to the team. As long as you feel you have made some individual contribution to the team, and you know you are valued for that, then the achievement, the medals, mean something. It doesn't matter whether you play in sixty games or fifteen, if in those fifteen you did enough to help your team win. I have to play every game I get as if it is a Champions League semi-final. If I score, or put on a good performance, that is a valuable contribution. All the time, though, I know this is a special time in the special history of the club.

'Del Bosque went out of his way to make everyone feel special. He tries, but I think it must be difficult for him as well. We have these star players, these talented players on the bench, and these players from the junior academy and the policy now is that they must come through. So Del Bosque has little leeway. The coach's job is very difficult here.'

Iván Campo, twice a European Cup-winner with Real Madrid, went on loan to Bolton Wanderers during Steve's fourth season. His move to the Reebok was much more of a personal quest than your average transfer: after prolonged spells on the bench, his self-esteem had plummeted drastically. English followers will recall his contribution to Real Madrid's 2000 European Cup campaign, particularly the two quarter-final legs against Manchester United when he was an integral part of a back five – a defensive line cited as the reason behind the Spanish club's successful campaign that year. In the 2001–02 season, however, Campo made only ten league and five Champions League appearances, as the intensity of Madrid's ambitions took its toll. 'The thing is, you've always got at the back of your mind that you're playing for Madrid and in two days' time you've got a game – league, Champions League, the cup. You're under the microscope constantly,' he recalled of his experience. 'If you lose, or play badly, there are repercussions in the press on a huge scale. It's not the easiest environment to work in. One big game after another builds up the pressure. Then, the squad stayed in a hotel the night before home games too. The travelling routine was very intense. You hardly saw your family. If you had kids, you almost never see them, or your wife or girlfriend. You pretty much live football all your life, there is no respite.

'That's a difficult atmosphere for a player who isn't getting a regular run-out with the team: you start questioning why you are doing it. That had a negative effect on me. It was very difficult playing at a club like Madrid. It's a team packed full of stars: Zidane, Raúl, Roberto Carlos, Figo. You've got them on one level, and then you've got the other players who are looked upon in a slightly different manner, let's just say . . . People talk about the egos in that dressing room, but there wasn't a problem. On the contrary, it's a very close-knit atmosphere. Whether you are a star, or slightly less than a star, everyone gets on very well and the coaches don't treat you any differently either.

'What *is* difficult to handle is the attitude that if you are a star you can play at a certain level. You might only be playing at ten per cent of your game, but you're still Raúl, you're still Zidane, you're still Figo, you're still a star. If you're on the superstar level you can live off your reputation whereas we, the other players, have to do more than our best almost, just to get a look-in. Real Madrid is not so much a football club as a PR company now. That's not a criticism because I had a fantastic first two years at Madrid, but as a player you yearn to contribute more week in, week out.'

Of the bench diehards, César explains the survival tactics that evolved. 'Macca, Solari and I had been together three years and we had all played full seasons in the team. We all played in the

Champions League final in Glasgow, but the next season was difficult for us as we were on the bench quite a bit. We'd use our humour to keep our spirits up. We were always having a laugh. One thing Solari and I would do to wind up Macca was to make up expressions in English. We used to spend all day coming up with phrases in English, but not your usual English. There are Spanish phrases that don't translate properly in English, but end up sounding funny. We invented our own English between ourselves. For instance, "I shit in your tooth" is the literal translation of the well-used Spanish expression "*me cago en tus muelas*". It doesn't mean anything in English, but it's funny as a result. There were hundreds of expressions we'd adapt like this. "*Me cago en la leche*" is "I shit on the milk" in English, but we'd even mix up the languages for Macca by throwing in a bit of French to really do his head in, and it'd become "I shit on the *lait*".

'As substitutes, you are not involved with the team in the usual traffic on and off the pitch, the warm-up and half-time, so we found ways of amusing ourselves. Before the game the subs normally get in a circle and, using one touch, keep the ball away from the person in the middle. There'd always be Macca, Solari and me plus two other subs, because you need at least five for this particular practice routine. One day in Mallorca there were only three of us. No worries! Macca, Solari and I would do the same routine. However, it's very difficult with two and one in the middle and only one touch. So we came up with a new rule: the whole pitch counts as in. So there we were, the first player hammers the ball the length of the pitch to the second player with the middle-man chasing after it. It was so funny. The people in the stadium couldn't believe it, they even showed it on TV because it looked so bizarre.

'We spent a lot of time together cooped up in hotels before games, on buses, in planes. We had a brilliant atmosphere between us. At first Macca was my English teacher. I carried my English book, *Essential Grammar in Use*, everywhere and I'd always be saying, "Macca, how do you say . . . ?" Macca would always try and help me, but the problem is, when he speaks English properly, he goes so fast that I can't understand a word. The Liverpool accent is impossible to fathom!'

What emerges from the subs' talk is an astonishingly genuine bond in the dressing room; there is no *galácticos* hierarchy among the players. 'The press certainly always talk about these categories, but for us inside the dressing room it's nothing like that,' argues César. 'For example, I play golf with Ronaldo, as did Macca. We joke with him all day. The press may have us pigeonholed, but it's not a problem for us, we're all of us equal while at the same time we obviously realise that some players earn more than others, some play more often than others, some are more handsome and some are much uglier! None of this is important to us. What's important to me, and was to Macca too, is that I know who I get on well with, who I can and can't joke around with. But it's no problem whatsoever between ourselves that someone is thought to be more important because the press say so or the fans hero-worship him. It's not a big deal for us and I know it wasn't for Macca.'

'We were hovering at the top of the league, when the Champions League reached the serious stages,' recalls Steve. 'The relief of drawing Manchester United in the quarter-finals was fantastic. In the league, teams had been coming out to stifle us. There's nothing worse. It's so negative. But to play Manchester United, we knew, would be fun. There would be space, the game would be free-flowing. Our players *loved* playing against them, because we both liked to attack – and the battle is to establish who is the best at the attacking game.'

And, of course, it was a marketing dream. Such a clash of high-profile teams, both of whom put faith in self-expression, did not need a final to inspire fans, as Valdano agreed. 'It is a huge game,' he nodded enthusiastically, a dapper figure in a dark blue suit, sitting in one of the meeting rooms in the refurbished Bernabéu offices. 'You have the two teams in the world these days who most like to play good football, about to face each other. Manchester's style of play is a bit more predictable, and they like to move the ball around quickly. Ours is a bit more creative and a bit more difficult to work out. Although they are quite similar styles in the sense that we both need possession of the ball in order to impose our superiority, it's true to say that there are also some interesting contrasts, which make it a game without equal. These days football is all about marketing and it would be difficult to find a game with so many big names taking part. What's more, every one of these star names is capable of providing something special. The only miracle with this game is that the two managers are the same as three years ago. The other six quarter-finalists in the Champions League this season have all changed their managers at least twice in the last three years.'

Tuesday 8 April 2003, Estadio Santiago Bernabéu

How Manchester United might turn around the quarter-final in the second leg was under discussion from the moment referee Anders Frisk signalled full-time in Madrid. 'Difficult, but not impossible,' was the verdict of one section of Manchester United fans filing out of the stadium, faces blank with drained expectation after the 3–1 defeat. 'Impossible, because they totally outclassed us. I can see us scoring two goals, but I can't see us keeping a clean sheet,' was the bleaker chorus from the pessimists anticipating part two of the humiliating yet edifying Real Madrid masterclass scheduled for 23 April.

English fans who breakfasted silently in hotels across Madrid – many crawling in from an all-night tour of the bars around the Plaza Mayor – might have taken comfort from the reaction inside the Real camp. Their supporters had jumped in ecstasy at sublime goals from Luis Figo and Raúl, and shaken heads in amazement at Zinedine Zidane's mesmeric repertoire (though that is their fortnightly privilege), but the likes of Guti, Roberto Carlos and Fernando Hierro trickled into the players' lounge from a dressing room described by Steve, who spent the ninety minutes on the bench, as 'very quiet and subdued'.

'No one can believe we allowed them to score that away goal,' he said. 'We totally outplayed them. They looked embarrassed to have to come out for the second half. We should have won by four or five, and the lads know it. We shouldn't have this little bubble hanging over us, this worry that we could be beaten at Old Trafford. No one's happy.'

It stood as a further caveat to United fans: that disappointment ensured Real would arrive in Manchester as much on a mission as at the start of the first foray. While Jorge Valdano accepted congratulatory embraces amid the canapés in the inner sanctum, his amiable assistant, Emilio Butragueño, twitchily observed that Sir Alex Ferguson's team were 'strong' and that the requisite 2–0 scoreline was not unattainable for United at Old Trafford.

Overwhelmingly, though, with the muted sense of vague satisfaction was a feeling of joy for Luis Figo. For the last few weeks he – and, more vulnerably, his family, happily settled in Madrid – had endured rumours of a swap involving David Beckham. How ridiculous that notion seemed as the Portuguese international majestically eclipsed the England captain on the pitch. First, Figo was a totemic symbol of the era ushered in by Pérez at the Bernabéu, given the way he was wooed from arch-rivals Barcelona in 2000 to universal incredulity. Yes, he can cross and do wondrous things with a dead ball, like Beckham, but, as an individual talent in full flow, he seems so much more. His imposing presence is emphasised by the fact that off the pitch he appears surprisingly small.

His goal in the twelfth minute had the crowd clapping, singing and bowing down en masse in reverence to Feee-Go Feee-Go. It also prompted an appraisal by Real's knowledgeable spectators of Beckham. Later – in an interesting cameo of inverted celebrity – Guti's wife, Arantxa, hovered excitedly like a teenager around the United coach with her camera, desperate to snap the England midfielder. However, for fans I was sitting alongside, Beckham was decreed a one-dimensional player. Paul Scholes and Ryan Giggs, a long-standing star for the Spanish, were more admired; only Ruud Van Nistelrooy was afforded the compliment of nervous, negative anticipation whenever he had possession.

Ronaldo still had the home crowd gesturing in frustration. He was booed off when Del Bosque replaced him with Guti with six minutes to go. Real's 2002 summer big acquisition clearly wanted to join in the attack and the teasing demonstration of skill, but he looked less refined than his teammates. Steve had an interesting perspective. 'The press and the fans really like his personality, but there are certain players – a bit like me – who look slightly ungainly on the pitch. Our gait doesn't reflect our work-rate or concentration. It's like Chris Waddle: even when he was working hard, it looked as if he wasn't. It's a body-language thing. On top of that, with Ronaldo, he has a particular attitude about his role. If the ball's over there, he won't go and chase it. He thinks his job is in a certain area, and the fans can see that. He missed pre-season training and that is a big thing when you're trying to settle into a new club. The first few months he was injured, and then suddenly he was right in the action and playing every single week with all the expectations that came with his arrival after the World Cup. But saying all that, he's our leading goal-scorer. I am convinced the best is yet to come from him.'

Not at Old Trafford was the hope of United fans, bruised by the way their players were teased in such embarrassing fashion by the white shirts. 'We certainly don't need him to be on song as well,' as one fan put it wryly.

Two days before the second leg, Real Madrid had that most inconvenient of big home-league fixtures: Barcelona. The fixture had a new emblem to splash across the newspapers, the waxy image of the severed pig's head hurled at Figo in the grim December clash at the Nou Camp. For Barcelona's return, however, the atmosphere was not as militant. As leaders of la Liga and 3–1 up on Manchester United at 'half-time' in their Champions League quarter-final, Real were consciously superior to their Catalan rivals, who were hovering above the relegation zone. A degree of restraint owed much to Madrid being a city that expresses itself with more formality than Barcelona's creative buzz. Its fans have a hauteur instilled by their history. Given, too, the preponderance of peace rainbows and anti-war banners hanging from balconies everywhere from the Plaza Mayor to the well-heeled residential streets, it seemed possible that the humanitarian plight in Iraq had given a different perspective to this ancient footballing enmity. More relevant than anything, perhaps, was the date of the fixture: Easter Saturday. The build-up thus coincided with Holy Week, which annually sees sections of the city closed off for lengthy, often silent, penitential processions in which men and women, hidden by purple hoods and cloaks, walk barefoot, dragging chains, to atone for their sins. Other processions re-enact Christ's suffering en route to crucifixion. 'Judas' taunts aimed at Figo in the Barcelona press rang pathetically hollow.

On a chilly, drizzly evening, the match that Sir Alex Ferguson had his eye on kicked off with no projectiles on the pitch, no armed guards around the perimeter, and with none of the majestic play that so cowed Beckham, Scholes et al. Ronaldo and Luis Enrique scored against their former clubs to eke out a flat 1–1 draw. Since they had danced around United thirteen days earlier, Real Madrid had lost 4–2 to Real Sociedad, beaten an invitation Galician team 3–0 for charity (in which Steve scored the opener with a stunning volley) and been uninspired against Barcelona. Prospects suddenly looked brighter for Ferguson's team who purged their Bernabéu nightmare with an unbelievable 6–2 victory over Newcastle, held Arsenal to a 2–2 draw and beat Blackburn 3–1. Man Utd v. Real Madrid, the decisive leg: a *gran clásico* for sure.

Wednesday 23 April 2003, Old Trafford

'Chendo, the former Real star, tipped me the wink that I'd be starting,' recalls Steve. 'It came out of the blue. I hadn't played very much in the run-up to that game, and it was only the second Champions League game I did start. But Del Bosque knew I'd be desperate to play against United and that I wouldn't disappoint him.

It was a hectic but exciting build-up. As my family only live down the road, people came to the hotel, and we had players like Iván Campo and Geremi coming to catch up with their old teammates. People literally camped out by the hotel to get autographs; the hotel had the reception area cordoned off. You couldn't open a door without walking into a wall of fans, so after breakfast one day, just to escape from the hotel, I took some of the lads into the city centre to do some shopping. We went to Flannels, a shop managed by a friend of mine in Deansgate, which has all the designers under one roof. Guti spent a fortune there, Solari and Makelele came out with huge carrier bags too. We had a car waiting outside to take us back to the hotel because we were all clad in our Real Madrid tracksuits, not exactly inconspicuous – because you travel in your official clothes. We got back and then all the other lads wanted to go to the shop in the afternoon.'

9.30pm. Manchester United 4, Real Madrid 3.
The Spanish side win 6–5 on aggregate

'What a game! What an exciting way to get through to the Champions League semi-finals, after two tremendous games against Manchester United,' said Steve, perilously close to an exclamation for such a laid-back character. 'The noise generated by Old Trafford made a big impression on the Spanish lads. We were knocking Manchester United out of the competition, but the fans never stopped cheering and booing to help their side. And then the home crowd clapped our players off. No one could believe that. They were saying, "The fans here are crackers. This would never happen in Spain. What is going on?"'

What had gone on was a night with layers of fairy-tale elements: a fabulously entertaining tally of goals, United repeatedly coming from behind to beat the European champions on home turf; Beckham's proudly composed riposte not only to starting on the bench, but to being dismissed as 'one-dimensional' after the first leg; Steve starting a game he had charmed at the same stage of the competition three years ago. And more: 23 April 2003 will go down as the night Ronaldo finally earnt a place in *madridista* hearts.

'I'll see you back here on the 28th of May!' came the parting shot of one *madridista* to a United steward manning staircase 22 on the South Stand.

'I think you will. And you'll win the final!' was the jovial response, summing up a night of mutual respect most resonantly felt after sixty-seven minutes when all 66,708 people in Old Trafford rose simultaneously to honour Ronaldo as the Brazilian was taken off minutes after completing a stunning, tie-winning hat-trick. In an idiosyncratic piece of theatre, Steve came off five minutes later to an equally gratifying reception: a chorus of boos from the home crowd as virulent as you'd expect for a former Liverpool player.

In a Continental fug of tobacco smoke, ecstatic away supporters filed out of their designated section in a corner of Old Trafford, a blur of Real Madrid regalia: red and yellow flags with the silhouette of a black bull draped around shoulders, purple and white scarves knotted around wrists, a procession of white replica shirts of Bernabéu goal-scorers past and present – Mijatovic, Suker, Raúl, McManaman, Zidane, Figo, Ronaldo. Some carried *Marca* tucked under their arm; others held banners, now neatly folded, that they had tied carefully on to the railings before kick-off. The chat was all about why Beckham had started on the bench, Ronaldo's hat-trick, Juve in the semi-final and Steve's laughter at the reaction when he was taken off. Even in the revelry of a glorious quarter-final victory, debate charged the night air. Only the undertrodden remnants of the traditional snacks of sunflower seeds and home-made foil-wrapped chorizo sandwiches were lacking to make the visiting fans' section feel genuinely like a microcosm of the Bernabéu atmosphere.

It seemed improbable in retrospect that only fifteen days before the World Player of the Year had been whistled and jeered by his own supporters in the first leg. It was not just that he was the one Real player who had failed to live up to his superstar billing that night, it was a recurring frustration that he had yet to show – or yet to look as if he was even trying to show – his best effort in the famous white shirt. Steve had been adamant the best was yet to come from his mate Ronie. And it was. The chubby-faced Brazilian had gone off on Wednesday night with Spanish fans chanting, 'Ronaldo, Ronaldo,' accompanied by theatrical bows – an image which represented a seismic shift in appreciation. The irony was that it came with mass appreciation of his talent from the opposing fans too.

'It made a huge impression on me,' said Ronaldo. 'It's not very often in your career that you go to an away stadium and you play a great game and you lose the game [but not the tie] and the people who are supporting the team playing against you end up applauding what you've done. And even though the scoreboard shows your team have lost, you leave the field to such applause: this is such a rare thing in football. For me, it was very beautiful. Certainly something I wasn't expecting. The whole scenario took me by surprise.

'My goals? The first one, I don't know who passed to me . . . it was on the counter-attack and I gained speed on Rio Ferdinand, got around him and hit it past the goalkeeper. The second one, Roberto Carlos went on a run and I received the ball from him alone in the goalmouth. The third was a lovely shot from outside the area, passing over Barthez. Without doubt, it was one of the very best games I've played in my entire career.'

After the redemption of the World Cup's Golden Boot came the redemption of England's own Golden Balls. Beckham's appearance was greeted with whispers of excitement among the Spanish fans tantalised, now, by the prospect of his rumoured move to Madrid. His brilliant trademark free kick, and the vigour he brought to United's game, upgraded his reputation.

While the players warmed up before kick-off, the Old Trafford sound system had boomed out the 1992 'Barcelona' Olympic anthem sung by Freddie Mercury and Montserrat Caballé. Was that a subtle taunt to the visitors, an operatic paeon to their bitter Catalan rivals? If so, it was certainly more subtle than any of the pre-tie barbs emanating from Ferguson, who had accused UEFA of rigging the quarter-final draw. Nevertheless, he spoke for everyone present when he said his team and Vicente Del Bosque's men had that night displayed 'football of incredible imagination'.

'Everyone was thrilled for Ronaldo,' said Steve. 'He had taken so much criticism but, with that hat-trick, he showed what he is worth on the biggest stage in a massive game. He now has the signed match ball in his trophy room. That was a funny moment. They don't have the hat-trick match ball custom in Europe. I went to the referee's room and asked for it, and then took it around to be signed by all the players. I wrote "Beautiful!" Ronie thought I was just messing around. In fact most of the players thought I was crackers. They just did their signatures, as if it was for autographs, not messages or congratulations.

'Ronie is a relaxed character, but I could tell his performance meant a lot to him when I saw him at Madrid airport. Even at 5am, there was an overwhelming media reception – with early editions of *Marca* and *AS* so we could see the headlines – and he was picking and choosing who he spoke to. A lot of people had been extremely harsh about him, and there were certain radio journalists he wouldn't speak to even though they were desperate to hear his views on his hour of glory. He made his point.'

Tuedsay 6 May 2003

'We were playing Juventus in the fourth consecutive Champions League semi-final since I'd come to Madrid. A phenomenal achievement for any club, you'd have to say, but it was considered a routine milestone for the club to reach,' said Steve. 'After the thrill of two free-spirited games against Manchester United, we anticipated a tighter, tactical encounter with the leaders of Serie A. The challenging aspect to playing Italian teams was the feeling that there was no distinct home advantage. We were still without Raúl, recovering from appendicitis, and then the big blow on the night was losing Ronaldo who had really started making the difference.'

In the absence of Raúl, the Brazilian had become Real's talismanic Champions League scorer. Early in the second half of the first leg, he followed on from his Old Trafford hat-trick with a typical strike to open the scoring, but, minutes later, hobbled off the Bernabéu pitch with a strained left calf muscle. A preliminary medical examination declared him unlikely to recover in time. It was a significant setback. The combined efforts of Fernando Morientes, Javier Portillo and Guti failed to make an impact. 'Too much this,' said one fan, gesticulating with wide zigzag motions. 'Not enough of that,' up pumped his fist as he made his point emphatically. Mesmerising creativity around the goal, but where was the ruthless finishing?

'We really missed Ronie and Raúl,' admitted Steve. 'Morientes hadn't played for a long while and that showed. Portillo is a young lad, who comes on as a sub. In Spain if you're not in the first team, you don't play football. There are no reserve teams. It was very difficult to ask Portillo to come on and play a certain kind of game against the defensive experience of Juventus.'

Before the match the hard-pressed central defender Iván Helguera had said 'only 6–0 would make me feel comfortable' for the return, but '3–0 would allow me to feel more relaxed'. Steve nevertheless maintained the Real dressing room were pleased with the single-goal advantage. 'When we beat Manchester United 3–1 in the quarter-final first leg, the players were very subdued because we had allowed them that away goal. But we were all much happier with 2–1 against the Italians because of the way they play. This game was never going to be as attack-minded as against Man U. Results against Italian teams show we have a better chance of winning over there. In front of their crowds, they have to open up to be a bit more entertaining, and in doing that they make themselves more vulnerable.'

'The important thing was to win,' agreed Zidane, in brilliant form against his old side. 'The second leg will be tough, but we know we are capable of scoring anywhere.'

Raúl had trained for the first time the day before the game, and was reported to have pleaded hard for a place in the team. His anticipated return would bring back some taut urgency, they presumed, and one uncomfortable fact for Juventus remained: even in the absence of Raúl and Ronaldo, Real had still won the game. No wonder Pérez expressed typical Real swagger. After sitting next to King Juan Carlos, he reported: 'The King's last words as he left were, "See you at Old Trafford."'

Tuesday 13 May 2003

11.30am. After forty-five minutes' delay, Iberia flight 5848 took off with no reported problems.
1.30pm. The Real Madrid squad arrived at Turin airport to a reception of a hundred and fifty supporters. Only Figo and Zidane signed autographs.
2.30pm. The party arrived at the Hotel Meridien Lingotto, constructed on the site of the first Fiat factory in Turin. Greeted by fifty fans. Lunch, light siesta. Raúl and Vicente Del Bosque talked to press. Squad travelled by bus to 7pm training.

Winning the European Cup is a deep-seated expectation for Real Madrid's supporters – *Solo una obsesión*, as a huge Ultra Sur banner depicting the trophy declared. No wonder, then, that the quest for a tenth victory, and the first successful defence for thirteen years, came with the official club website flashing up a running commentary on the minutiae of travel to the penultimate knockout game along with regular updates on the state of Ronaldo's left calf.

'Our lead was fragile. Juventus needed only to win 1–0 at home and we were out,' said Steve, who started on the bench. 'The 3–0 loss they had suffered to Manchester United, early in the campaign, was in fact the only occasion they had failed to score in twenty-two Champions League and Serie A matches. They had Edgar Davids and Alessio Tacchinardi back from suspension to bolster the midfield, plus combative Uruguayan defender Paolo Montero. Ronaldo had been doubtful with a calf problem, and Raúl, despite his desperation to play three weeks after an appendix operation, had clearly still been in pain during light training. I remember hearing an unthinkable line in our dressing room: "We're a bit light up front. Raúl will have to play." We were missing not just Ronaldo, but more crucially Claude Makelele who had a thigh problem. Without his gritty play in central midfield, our defence would be exposed. And so it was.

'No one was in doubt about what was at stake that night. In the Spanish press, Real Madrid against Juventus was presented as good against evil, light against darkness, nasty boring Italians against beautiful Madrid. The backlash after a defeat would be spectacularly vicious. The stadium, which can be lacking in atmosphere, was an incredible sight, throbbing with black-and-white support. A record turnout of 67,229 made the concrete stadium vibrate with energy. The manager surprised everyone by starting with Cambiasso and Flavio. We didn't start well, and looked completely out of sorts. Edgar Davids was racing around and Pavel Nedved was outstanding. Very quickly, it seemed, we were 3–0 down after some "average" defending. Trezeguet scored, then Del Piero. Luis missed a penalty. Nedved scored the third. It was agonising to watch from the bench. In the last twenty minutes we clicked into gear, and had lots of chances. I came on and played well. Zizou scored, but it was too late. If we could have made it 3–2, we'd have gone through, but it wasn't to be. Juve were efficient, dogged and composed. At the final whistle, there was no dramatic slump to the floor, no tears. We simply shook hands and swapped shirts.

'When you've had great success, you take the lows with the highs. It broadens your perspective. You know you can't expect to win every trophy every year, but it was very, very disappointing. It wasn't as if we were beaten by a better team. The feeling was exactly the same as two years earlier, when we were knocked out by Bayern Munich. When we got knocked out, we all walked out thinking we should have won that over two legs. As in 2001, I didn't think we lost it away: we should have wrapped it up at home. There were no excuses. It wasn't as if we were saying, "God, they were good." When you don't win because of your own failings, it's the worst mixture of feelings: massive disappointment, nagging frustration and sickening numbness. There is this terrible silence. Inwardly everyone is calculating whose fault it was. Luis is probably thinking about the penalty he missed. The defenders are probably wondering what they should have done to stop the goals. I never like to blame the defence because the way Real Madrid play, we leave the defence so isolated. We did miss Makelele because he was at the heart of the team for the majority of the season, but we shouldn't have missed him as much as we did. Some of our so-called bigger stars – who normally play at their best in the big games – were very quiet.

'In England, the mentality is to say sorry if you feel you were to blame for a crucial goal or missed goal. I once made a mistake against Villareal away from home. I made a bad back pass, the goalie came out and kicked it to one of their forwards, who scored. We went on to win the game, but at half-time I came in and said, "I'm very sorry for that mistake," and everyone was like, "What are you apologising for?" After the game one of the press fellas said, "I couldn't believe you apologised. Fantastic!" If you transposed our predicament to an English team, there were a few lads who would probably have wanted to hold their hands up in that dressing room in Turin, and say, "Sorry about that, lads, that was a nightmare," and everyone would say, "Don't worry about it." But that isn't the way in Spain. Luis wouldn't come in and apologise for his bad penalty. Hierro wouldn't have said, "Sorry, I had a bad night." We never apportioned blame, especially over two games. Our defeat came about through a combination of injuries, absences, errors and missed chances. Afterwards I kept being asked how I felt for Nedved, who would miss the final thanks to a second yellow card for a foul on me. It was sad for him, but I was feeling much more sad for us at that point! And then, the whole disappointment was compounded by watching the final, that dull, dull encounter between Juventus and AC Milan.'

'After our Champions League exit, we took heavy criticism individually and collectively, but the truly vitriolic attacks were on Del Bosque and Hierro. There was a tide of opinion that argued it was quite possible that we could win nothing. Fans were openly disparaging about us. It wasn't, "Oh they were unlucky." So we had to keep going and hope this season would be the mirror image of 2000–01, my second season, when we lost in the semi-finals to Bayern Munich and went on to win the league. Real Sociedad still hadn't slipped up. First we had to beat Atlético Madrid – a passionate local derby – and hope that Real Sociedad would suffer from a right hard game at Celta Vigo. We hammered Atlético 4–0. We knew from the bench and the crowd what the score was at the other place (Celta had dramatically beaten Sociedad 3–2). Then it boiled down to the last game of the season, against Athletic Bilbao.'

It had been a long, long intense season. There were just a few days left for the players to rally and win the game that would salvage their season. On paper, it was an easy path to redemption, a league game at the Bernabéu – how often did Real Madrid lose those? Privately Del Bosque cited the Atlético game as the one where he thought they had won the title, but, at the same time, sensed a surprising coldness towards him. As he put it: 'As if some people didn't want us to win the league' [because it made sacking him the following week so much harder]. And then the David Beckham bombshell drops. The media furore begins. Players are angry. The papers are full of suggestions of a dressing-room revolt and of angst-ridden references to the Tenerife syndrome. Beckham apologises for the distraction and wishes his future teammates good luck. But was it all about to go horribly wrong?

'The fact they announced his signing before the title-decider was deemed a kick in the teeth,' said Steve. 'The very fact that it was supposed to be a sweetener to keep the fans happy, in case we lost, offended everyone. Would the team with the much-trumpeted trophy players end up without the trophies? God forbid.'

Sunday 22 June 2003. Real Madrid v. Athletic Bilbao, 9pm kick-off

1–0 Ronaldo after nine minutes.
1–1 Alkiza, thirty-six minutes.
2–1 Roberto Carlos, forty-five minutes.
3–1 Ronaldo, sixty-two minutes.

The title was won. The stadium resounded to cheers, applause and, of course, the stirring bars of 'Hala Madrid!' Ronaldo – just as the big signings of 2000, 2001 and 2002, McManaman and Anelka, Figo and Zidane, had done – sealed the season's triumph as the hero.

But two minutes from the final whistle that gave Real Madrid a record twenty-ninth league title, came a signal that the club's history was about to turn another small degree on its axis: Del Bosque motioned for the captain to come off. He did not know it, but for the very last time Fernando Ruiz Hierro walked off the Bernabéu pitch, a dignified figure acknowledging the faithful as they stood up and applauded him with tremendous warmth.

'We were playing for the title and I did think it was a bit weird when Vicente took him off with two minutes left,' recalls Helguera. 'We were ecstatic, full of emotion, because we were on the point of winning the league, we weren't about to stop and contemplate what that action might mean for Hierro. Nobody considered that he could be on the way out. Vicente was very sensitive, very clever in that sense. Hierro had captained a championship-winning team, and Vicente made sure he got a good send-off.'

Del Bosque celebrated the record twenty-ninth title – his second while manager – with the hunch that he was about to become a former Real Madrid coach. 'I could smell it in the air, but I didn't know anything for definite,' he would tell me later.

Salgado maintains everyone feared Del Bosque and Hierro were going to leave. Both were negotiating new deals and, under normal circumstances, should have renewed by then. 'No one said anything because contract situations are private, but we knew something was up because nothing had been announced and we were one game from the end of the season. But their predicaments didn't cause the problems and arguments that were soon to ruin the celebration dinner in Txistu restaurant. That was caused by a series of factors. However I think that the way we reacted was the detonator for what happened to them . . . or maybe it was the justification. For the club to act the way they did, they must have had something in mind anyway.'

What was going on behind closed doors in the Txistu? For an official club line, Emilio Butragueño gives a candid version: 'The news of David Beckham's signing came out, yes, and our players weren't so happy. The news came out that week, not because Manchester United are stockmarket listed [which was the justification given at the time], but because we decided with United that it was impossible to sit on the information for a week. We decided we had to be able to use our channels of communication to announce the news and control the impact of it. Our players weren't so happy, but we went on to win the title so it wasn't serious.

'Real Madrid players have to shoulder many responsibilities. That was the last week of the season. We had been knocked out by Juventus in the semi-finals of the Champions League, which prompted much scrutiny of the team. The last league game of the season was like a final exam at university. When you end it, it's like the air inside a balloon exploding. The Txistu night was difficult for everybody. We had a dinner, which was a little strange. It is very difficult to win a title, no? You achieve that, then you have to celebrate it in the proper way. I would prefer not to speak about all the meetings and discussions in the restaurant that night. It wasn't very agreeable for anybody, but the positive was that we won the title. There are many anecdotes of that night, but life is like that. We are human beings. We are talking about feelings, sentiments, different ways of thinking and looking at things. As time goes by, you realise that all these incidents turn into little anecdotes, and after six months, they are not so important. It's life.'

Helguera was more specific. It wasn't merely the release of end-of-season pressures, more the culmination of a number of grievances over the way club policy was moving, he argued. 'We wanted to make a stand, to make a point that we're here for a reason. We're not here to travel to Asia as was planned for the pre-season, to always do everything the club wants. From that moment the club learnt something. This year [2003–04] the club talks more to players about their views on trips. Up to a point we understand that the club want us to travel, but, for instance, it was ridiculous to consider flying us to play in South Africa between our two Champions League games with Bayern Munich. And the trip was cancelled. The Txistu night was a shout from all the players – *galácticos* and non-*galácticos* – that we have rights within the club. We agree with lots of things the club wants to happen, but it is always, always important for the players to have a collective voice. Not only at Madrid, but at any club. We understand that the club will always carry more weight. They pay us. It is a business, that's normal. If I owned a bar I'd want things done my way, but always knowing that the employees, my collaborators and workers, have rights. It was like a trade union speaking to the bosses, through our *capitanes*. We weren't trying to go against the club. We simply wanted our rights acknowledged, we wanted a right to give our views. And Florentino appears to have learnt from that night. Now he wants the players to be heard. Things went wrong and he's trying to avoid that now.'

Not until the next day did Vicente Del Bosque learn his fate. Nor was the message delivered in the spirit of Santiago. Bernabéu's code of 'rectitude, gentlemanliness and honesty'. 'On the Monday evening I went to do a TV programme and that was when I heard I wouldn't be carrying on,' he said quietly. 'Apparently, the club had said that that was that. I was in the studio of Antena 3, preparing to be interviewed. We were almost live on air with this interview when I was told the news by J. J. Santos, a journalist. A minute after the broadcast ended, our press officer, Joaquín Maroto, who was with me in the TV studio, received a call on his mobile from Jorge Valdano asking me to call in at the stadium. So it was in Valdano's office at about eleven o'clock on the Monday night that the club's decision was confirmed.

'But all of this isn't important! These things happen in life. When I first arrived at the club I met Santiago Bernabéu, then successively I got to know Ramón Mendoza, Ruíz de Carlos, Lorenzo Sanz and Florentino Pérez. Therefore since I've never considered myself to be in any president's camp, I've simply been a Real Madrid man through and through. I think that each president has always wanted what's best for the club. Naturally times have continued to change, but the main thing is that each president has always had the best interests of the club at heart. They've all helped to ensure that the hundred years of the club have been good ones.

'It's true, since I've left I've felt a little awkward and embarrassed at times going to games at the Bernabéu. I don't want to make a big show of turning up but at the same time I shouldn't have to hide either. I would like to go there regularly and feel more like myself. It has been a bit uncomfortable. At the same time I'm clear-headed about it, I've not committed any crime so I shouldn't have to hide away. I go in an executive box where it's calmer, but as time goes on I'd like to be able to go with my wife and children. They're building on the Ciudad Deportiva training ground now. From the window in my house I've videoed what it looked like when it was my place of work. I've videoed it now they're working on the site, and in a year and a half I'm going to record another to show its development. The training ground has turned out to be the financial sustenance of the club. The new one will be tremendous. They've not started building it yet but it's going to be in a really beautiful place. It's not on the Castellana, but you can't have everything!'

Season Five

2003–2004

I admire Real Madrid and I admire Florentino Pérez, but I feel the club have become too Hollywood. Del Bosque had to go because he was fat and had a moustache. To me, he was that attractive wrinkle, that contact with the normal person in society. The last thing Real Madrid need when they have all the great superstars, they dress in the immaculate white, perform in the great Bernabéu and win everything, the last thing they need is an ultra-good-looking manager. It's too much. Everyone wants these brilliant, gorgeous, oversuccessful people to get a fucking good hiding whenever they play. They want them to be human, to suffer, to be hurt. It's too perfect now.

—Michael Robinson

Real Madrid occupy a special place in football, analogous to the status enjoyed by the Scuderia Ferrari in Formula One. Both represent a link with a golden era. Just as Ferrari's heritage stretches back to the dawn of motor racing, so Real's five European Cups came at the right time to make a powerful impression on a generation of post-war schoolboys. During the occasional period of decline, everyone wonders when they are going to start winning again. And when they do, everyone complains about their apparently impregnable hegemony.

—Richard Williams, Guardian

As Steve said before he flew to Mallorca on holiday, 'The sacking of Del Bosque and Hierro was a massive shock. The whole winning-the-league celebration was odd, strangely flat, but what hurt most were the departures. The club had done it right at the end of the season, so we all had four weeks to get our heads around it. We came back and no one mentioned it that much. You know what it's like, the start of a new season, all the build-up, the new signings . . .'

Thursday 24 July 2003

'We reported to the training ground in the morning for our pre-season medical. I arrived about half-past ten to fill the usual ten test tubes of blood and provide a urine sample. I said hello to Becks who had arrived horrendously early, as you do. As the new recruit, he was running on the treadmill, doing more comprehensive tests for the doctors, while the rest of us had a bit of the breakfast that's laid on. They take so much blood out of you, the physios insist you put sugar back into the system, so on the first day back at work there's a breakfast table with cereal, sandwiches, fruit, yoghurt, croissants, juice and coffee. The atmosphere felt different – a new coach had arrived with his staff. There were a lot of new faces, but the lads were all laughing and catching up with each other's holiday news. We were given tour itineraries and collected the new official club uniform, which is all there hanging up for you on the first day. Then we boarded the coach to the airport for the twelve-and-a-half-hour flight to Kunming, China.

'Becks had rung me while I was at my house in Mallorca for some advice about what to take on the tour of Asia. He was asking about what normally happens on pre-season, whether he would have to bring many clothes for free time, did he need trainers, what do you wear on the plane, that sort of thing. Like me, he'd moved to Real Madrid after spending his career at one club, where you know the form inside out. At Madrid your official wardrobe is quite large – suit, tracksuit, casual trousers, shorts, and any number of shirts, formal, T-shirts, white, short-sleeved, whatever – and it's difficult to know what you're expected to wear when. It brought it all back to me, that first-day feeling of wanting to double-check everything to make sure you've got it right. When they tell you what time to be somewhere, they do so in Spanish – although, of course, Carlos Queiroz was there to clarify things with Becks in English. I helped him, but I was in the dark, too, because the whole format of this Far East tour – "The Conquest of Asia", as the club now refer to it – was new to everybody. Previously we had been holed up in glorious isolation in Switzerland. You ran, you sweated, you rested, you got to know your new teammates, you had fun together, no one bothered you. You played strong teams to sharpen you. The coach experimented a bit if he had to and the only press in attendance were the regular Spanish football reporters we all knew well.

'This was altogether different. The itinerary looked daunting. A week in Kunming, in South-East Asia, followed by Beijing, Tokyo, Hong Kong and Bangkok. We knew it was going to be chaotic. Instead of having a pre-season base, we were getting on a plane every three or four days. But everyone was excited. Whatever's happened the season before, there's always that typical new-season buzz. The Spanish lads were a bit wary of Beckham, but I said he was fine, it is only the press attention he brings with him that is horrible. Luis, as an English-speaker, befriended him. He and I chatted to him and the others seemed to accept him straightaway. The best thing he did was on the promotional tour of the Far East he made with his wife, when we'd just signed him. He came out then and said sorry about the fuss, he didn't want the No. 7 because that was Raúl's shirt, and Raúl is the King of the Bernabéu. After that, I think the lads were ninety-five per cent sure he'd be quite normal, but they still weren't completely sure.

'A noisy crowd turned up to see us off at the airport. We were told where to sit on the plane: Raúl sat with Morientes, Zidane with Makclclc, Munitis with Helguera, Raúl Bravo with Portillo, Guti with Ruben, Figo with Salgado, Casillas with Pavón, Roberto Carlos with Ronaldo, César with Celades, Miñambres with Carlos Sánchez, me with Solari, and Beckham with Cambiasso. I could see those two weren't going to be able to communicate at all so I asked Cambiasso if he wanted to swap. Then we had the two Argentines together and the two English – as we would pair up to renew the England v. Argentina rivalry over many a highly charged game of table tennis and pool. We all changed into shorts and flip-flops, read, played cards, listened to music and then slept. It was a hell of a long flight. The captain announced we were flying over Iraq when breakfast was served and the cabin crew asked to have pictures taken next to us. There was quite a queue of air hostesses waiting to be snapped in our row with Becks. Hours later we arrived, groggy, just wanting to have a shower and crash out in a hotel, only to discover Kunming had laid on a reception billed to their four million inhabitants as 'the event of the year'. That wasn't on the itinerary! We were met by lines of Chinese people dressed in national costume or riding on elephants, girls carrying the large version of bright paper cocktail umbrellas, and others who put floral garlands around our necks. An orchestra cranked up and we were then treated to a display of dancers, more elephants and about four million people milling around in the new Real Madrid shirts. The club's website is hilarious. It reports: "The fans displayed four elephants to show Kunming's fondness for Real Madrid. Roberto Carlos, Figo, but above all, Beckham were the most applauded players. Middle-aged men and women burst into tears on catching a first glimpse of England's captain."

'At the start we were all excited, but the number of functions took their toll. Every time we put on our shorts to train, there'd be thousands and thousands in their seats to watch us. Every time we went anywhere there would be wall-to-wall screaming fans. Every single day, there were hundreds and thousands of reporters from all over the world. We were on public show the whole time, under this unrelenting gaze. We'd train in front of people who'd paid to see us jog around a pitch. We'd have to attend functions, shake hands, smile into banks of flashbulbs. It was a circus. We were a troupe of performing seals. We once had to train in one corner of a pitch for twenty minutes so that all footage would show a particular model of a car parked on the running track behind us. Every sponsors' or charity function we went to there'd be massive posters of the six *galácticos* – Raúl, Roberto Carlos, Ronaldo, Luis Figo, Zinedine Zidane and David Beckham – and not a picture or name of anyone else in the team. With the exception of Raúl and Roberto Carlos, those were the players with image-right deals with the club, so those were the images they were pushing to flog shirts, but it was so divisive, the very opposite of the team-building operation a pre-season should be about. We were all carted around Asia, but it was as if players like Makelele, Helguera, Salgado, Solari, Guti, Morientes, César, even Casillas, did not exist. There was no problem between the players, but you can see how the atmosphere changed in certain players' relationships with the club. Last year Makelele, Helguera and Salgado were our best players and incredibly undervalued, and felt it. They'd played consistently very well for three years. The dressing room staff treated us all as equal, but the people above did not. Queiroz was about two days into his job and he already had unhappy players.

'Nor could he consider critical squad issues, such as his defence. Since I arrived in 1999, the club had shed defenders, and never brought in experienced replacements. Campo, Karanka and Geremi had been sold, Sanchís retired, Hierro sacked. Then they suddenly ruled out the signing of the Argentine Gabriel Milito from Independiente. The excuse was that he had failed the medical, that a knee injury had not recovered sufficiently to withstand the rigours of the Spanish league. But that didn't stop Zaragoza signing him three days later (and he went on to have a great season). There was still this notion that defenders aren't glamorous.' ('They would have taken him on if it was going to sell thousands of shirts,' sniped Fernando González, the technical director of would-be sellers,

Independiente of Buenos Aires.) 'We were now alarmingly thin on experienced defenders – and centre half is a specialist position. Helguera, much happier as a central midfielder, was going to have to continue in central defence, partnered with any of the young lads, Raúl Bravo, a left-back, Pavón or the inexperienced Rubén. And that was the first-choice central defence! God forbid if Helguera became injured. Hierro's presence – his experience and his guidance of the young players – was going to be missed more than anyone at the club had anticipated.

'The way Makelele made a stand about his salary, and very swiftly left for Chelsea, was an all too predictable scenario. He went on strike in mid-August complaining that, among "the *galácticos*", he was treated like a second-class citizen on third-class wages. He was hardly spoken about. He was our most important player, in that if he was absent, we suffered – as the Juventus semi-final defeat showed. Zidane always cited his retriever role as the most significant in the team. He'd sweat as much in training, work selflessly hard in matches, but they wouldn't give him a salary he deserves because they wouldn't get the money back from shirt sales. Who wants a Makelele shirt when you can have Ronaldo? But with him going, and Flavio Conçeicão on the way out, who would form the defensive midfield partnership? That tour painted a very clear picture to players. For a start, it had not been finalised until Beckham's signing was confirmed. We were judged not on our worth to the team but on our worth as a marketing tool. Claude was not happy with that, and moved. Míchel and Iván are not that happy now, are they? So many players say they were happier four years ago.

'For players like Figo and Zidane, intensely private individuals and family men, three weeks away with no competitive purpose was torture. As we went from exhibition training session to exhibition game – with the match ball being dropped from helicopters and dry ice billowing from the goals – it was as if the red carpet at a film premiere had turned into a treadmill and we were on it fifteen hours a day for three weeks. Smile fatigue, autograph fatigue, handshake fatigue – we had it. We had fantastic experiences, like visiting the

Forbidden City and being allowed to sit in the chair used by Mao Zedong. Tiananmen Square was emptied "just for the exclusive enjoyment of the Spanish club". Very nice, but we had no idea if there might be political implications in any of that. When we were in Japan and Hong Kong, the way the press zealously trailed us was frightening. We'd be in a car with curtains drawn and there'd be fifteen or twenty paparazzi motorbikes following us. We entered the Peninsula Hotel where you go right up to the top for a drink and there's a famous glass urinal so you have a bird's-eye view of the city while you're having a pee. We'd come out and there was a scrum assembled to commemorate the moment we exited the toilet. How Beckham puts up with the attention he gets, none of us could work out. He seemed embarrassed about it. He's very conscious of the murderous interest in him. The lads were looking at it, saying, "Oh my God." It was crazy, crazy, crazy.

'We'd travel three or four hours by plane, another two hours by coach, arrive somewhere and we'd be expected to trot out on to a training pitch surrounded by thousands of fans who'd paid to see us. We were shattered. We longed for some privacy, some space, to get to a hotel, and maybe go privately to the gym. But we had to go and put on a training show because fifty thousand people had paid to see us train. At the Tokyo Dome we literally went out, jogged around the field a few times and waved to people. Some of the lads then went in, some put on a five-a-side game incorporating as many tricks as possible. We had well and truly morphed into the Harlem Globetrotters of football.

'Back at the hotels we were virtually under armed guard. All our rooms were on one floor and ten great beefy security guards stood outside the lifts and by the stairs, so that no one could get anywhere near us. In Bangkok, the only people allowed through were the traders selling dodgy Louis Vuitton stuff. They'd give you a catalogue, and they'd be back two hours later with a cowboy version of anything you ordered. Some of the young lads were bewildered by the mobs. One night we did go out for an "official" private drink. We had to go up an escalator, but at the top there was a jostling scrum of press – they'd been tipped off, of course. We had to elbow and barge our way through them or we'd all have toppled backwards in a domino effect down the escalator.

'We went from Kunming's Hou Kong National Stadium to Beijing Workers' Stadium to Tokyo's Dome Stadium to Hong Kong and on to the Rajamangal Stadium in Bangkok, and I didn't play a minute in any game. The club had entered contracts with the host cities stipulating that all the superstars would play – against these little teams. With Figo, Zidane and Beckham inked in the midfield, I knew the score. Even though we were playing the China Dragons and the Girl Guides, Queiroz would talk for ages before kick-off, as if to keep up the pretence that these were proper games. Normally in pre-season, the whole squad plays half an hour here, forty-five minutes there. But the big names played all the time. Pre-seasons are notoriously hard: you run, you work hard, you get your body ready. This circus meant we did very little meaningful preparation. You can't flog a dead horse, and everyone was so jaded travelling, making personal appearances, shaking hands, following a guy with a clipboard, you couldn't put on a marathon three-hour training session. Everyone needed to go to bed. It was surreal. I remember in Hong Kong we were all waiting, in our suits, for yet another tediously boring meet-the-ambassador reception, complete with official photos, and I suddenly recognised Jackie Chan. No one told us he was the Ambassador of Hong Kong. He had on this terribly dodgy suit and two pairs of glasses, one pair over his eyes, the other on the top of his head, ready to pull down the minute he stepped outside. After a sword-fighting exhibition, he gave us all T-shirts. That was a light moment, and we had a laugh when Guti lost his passport and had to be left behind in Tokyo, but it didn't alleviate the players' feelings. A lot of them were very unhappy. Everybody hated it. There wasn't one person who would have said, "Oh, that was good, something different." Players like Figo and Zidane are tremendous professionals, and it was terrible preparation for a new season. Every three days we were crossing time zones whereas in Switzerland we'd train, eat and sleep in a quiet town. We'd go to bed early, get up early.

We'd play games against good-standard opposition. This year there was none of that. The teams we played were rubbish, exhibition games.

'I'd spoken to Victoria at the end of the fourth season and said I thought it would be a good time to go. In the Far East, a lot of the lads said they were desperate to leave. They knew it was too much. The Disneyfication of Real Madrid had gone too far. It was getting out of hand. A lot of them said if they could have left then, on the right terms, they'd have gone. A lot of us did go, and a lot of them still want to. But it's leaving at the right time, getting a fair deal. Morientes knew he could be playing well, but Ronaldo would always come back as soon as he's fit enough to kick a ball no matter what. As we knew too well, there were positions like that all over the park.

'Back in Madrid, it was suddenly a whirlwind. One day I was in training. The next day I was in England, touring the City of Manchester Stadium and signing for Manchester City. The day after that I was back in Spain to watch Madrid play in the season-opener against Real Betis. For the last time as a Real Madrid player I went into our dressing room – the huge space with boot room on the right, the low L-shaped wooden benches in the centre and personal lockers, individualized with illuminated full-size posters of ourselves in case we forget who we are! I said my goodbyes to the players and staff. The following day I went into the training ground to pick up my boots and bumped into Hierro and Morientes doing the same thing. I didn't make a big deal of it. People were saying "Ta-ra" as they were going out on to the training pitch. We knew we'd all stay in touch. I was fine because I knew it was the right time to be moving on. It wasn't as if I was going against my will. I'd said to Victoria, "It's going to get crazy . . . I've had four fantastic years here. Now is a good time to go." I wasn't sad, more excited about joining a new football club.'

Steve was philosophical, professionally ready to move on to the next stage of his career. Football is a transient business. Every year at football clubs players come and go. Players are itinerants. Victoria, however, was sentimental about the business of moving.

'Our time was over,' she lamented. 'We'd had the most amazing time. We fell in love with Spain – the people, the way of life, the food and culture. I had never expected it to feel like home, but it did. I was more upset to leave than Steven. It was the end of our Madrid era and I found that desperately sad. If I could, I would have wound the clock back and done it all over again. After four years it was a wrench to leave my work and life in Spain. It was hard saying goodbye to the friends we had made, both in and out of football. There were a few tears shed. However, I knew that it was the right decision for Steven, and that I should look forward to the new challenge ahead.'

Six months after Steve had left for Manchester City, having earned the tag of 'Britain's most successful football export', David Beckham spoke about his former England teammate. A Liverpool lad through and through and a superstar from Manchester United may not have been the likeliest of personal allies, but for six weeks Beckham observed with admiration the role Steve had forged for himself in the Real Madrid dressing room. Sitting on a table in an empty foyer at the Las Rozas training complex, where Madrid were temporary tenants of the Spanish FA as the new place was under construction and the Ciudad Deportiva demolished, Beckham was relaxed and surprisingly open. He was wearing a black jumper with number-motifs on it, combat trousers and white trainers, his long hair tied back and still wet. Next to him was a large white box and a copy of his autobiography. Known by then to be loving the football side of his life in Spain, the England captain – the ultimate pin-up *galáctico* – as yet had experienced only the disappointment of losing the Copa del Rey final to unfancied Zaragoza. But a timebomb was ticking under Florentino Pérez's grand strategy, and under Beckham's personal life. He was swinging his legs on that training-ground foyer table, talking about Macca, three days before the *News of the World* published its account of his alleged affair with a former personal assistant responsible for helping him settle in Madrid.

Steve had broken the tradition of England players failing abroad. Had that made Beckham's own decision to test himself in Spain easier? 'Not really. I felt that I could come here and do well despite what anyone else said. I would have come anyway,' he said.

'But I think what Steve did achieve over here – two European Cups and two league titles – is quite good going. It's not bad! He won a lot of respect from the Spanish people. You see that when he comes back here, the way he's treated. The people love him. He scored some great goals, he won trophies and, the most important thing, he won so much respect. Steve did remarkably well. And I know his family really enjoyed it over here as well.

'Like me, he'd only played with one club before. Leaving Liverpool for another massive club like Real Madrid was always going to be a big step: it's a place he grew up at, and where he left behind the people he'd grown up with. Coming to a different country to play for a different team is tough, definitely, but he made it work. He moved in, learnt the language and enjoyed his time here. I respect him for picking up the language. It's tough. If you set your mind to it and have lessons every day then it will happen, but it's hard to get going with all the games, the training and travelling. He did it, and I respect him a lot for that.

'I remember a couple of years ago, when Steve used to play for England, we were away on a trip and we were both with the physios having a massage at the same time. I was asking all the questions, because when someone plays for Real Madrid you like to ask questions, you like to know what the other players are like, and he just raved about the whole thing. I kept turning round to him saying, "And what's he like?" "And him?" "What's the life like?" And he just loved it . . .

'My move came up so quickly, just like that it was decided [he clicks fingers], so I didn't speak to him until everything had been signed during the summer. It was about three weeks before I actually came over. I called to ask him what I had to do, what I had to bring, things like that. Steve being here helped me a lot. There was someone English to answer my questions. I was able to talk to him, ask him things about the city and the people and the club, and find out the do's and the don'ts. He was there for me if I needed anything. It was reassuring to know that I had someone to talk to about even the minor things, like what suit to wear when we're travelling. It might not sound important, but it helps if you're not worrying about the details. He helped me immensely in the first month.

'I do wish he was still here, because he did really well for me. And all the lads genuinely loved him as well. My first week, when we were away on the tour of Asia, it struck me how well all the players got on and I realised then how much they liked Steve. Later, a friend was in the box at the Bernabéu when Steve came over from Manchester for the game against Valencia. Afterwards my friend said it was obvious from his reception they absolutely love him here. Maybe it was his personality, maybe the way he is . . . but they love him in Spain.

'He was great to me. He warned me that the Spanish hours are the biggest thing to adapt to and that you can't prepare for it. He was right – it was the hardest thing at first, but I like it now. I like the more sociable way they go out for meals.

'But most of all I needed someone who was going to explain to the rest of the players that I am actually quite normal. Steve said so and helped people see that about me. That was the good thing, because if I was on my own and there weren't many people speaking English here and I had come into the team, I think it would have been hard to get know people. But on the tour we teamed up, England versus Argentina, to play table tennis and pool against Solari and Cambiasso. And we beat them. That's the main thing!'

Postscript

Here's one for you. Who is the most successful British footballer ever to play abroad? Any ideas? Well, you can forget about Gary Lineker, Liam Brady or Graeme Souness. You can discount David Platt, Ray Wilkins and Chris Waddle. You can even forget about the great John Charles, such a dazzling success at Juventus in the late fifties.

No, if you're going purely on medals there is only one name to consider. Steve McManaman appeared in no fewer than eleven finals for Real Madrid during four years in the Spanish capital, to earn universal respect as well as an absolute fortune. Among those finals, by the way, were two winning ones in the Champions League, the first of which – against Valencia – included a spectacular volleyed goal.

—*Alan Smith, Daily Telegraph*

On 31 August 2003, Steve signed a two-year contract for Manchester City. 'I've said before, the politics in Spanish football clubs are complex to say the least, and I had accepted the previous season that to move home after four years would be perfect. Not many foreign players last that long at the Bernabéu and I had had a fantastic time. I loved every minute of playing and living in Spain, testing myself at the highest level. I will always feel lucky I had the opportunity to play and be part of such a great club. Having signed for City, I rushed back to Spain to go to the stadium and say some goodbyes – not so much to the players, who I can always call and will stay in touch with, but to the stewards, match-day workers and office staff who helped welcome me to the Bernabéu in 1999. They were all hugging me, and in the players' lounge after the game against Real Betis, I had great continental bearhugs from Jorge Valdano, Emilio Butragueño, the directors and the club's solicitors who had finalised my leaving deal. They said the doors were always open for me, that I was part of the Real Madrid family. It was quite emotional, and I'm glad I went back. It was important to leave on a good note ready to begin the exciting next phase of my career.'

Steve and Victoria packed up their belongings from Christian Panucci's house – things they had shipped out, like the black and white framed photographs of Lennon and McCartney taken by Astrid Kirchherr, girlfriend of Stuart Sutcliffe, the so-called fifth Beatle, as well as objects they had accumulated in four years. Wrapped up carefully was the contents of a large trophy cabinet containing two European Cup-winners' medals, two league championship medals, two Spanish Super Cup-winners' medals, a World Club-winner's and European Super Cup-winner's medal and assorted other medals and accolades. There was a letter from Jorge Valdano to be kept with the dog-eared one from Everton Football Club's youth coach. *'Dear Steve, I enclose the replicas of the league and Supercup trophies that the first-team squad of Real Madrid so brilliantly won in the 2002–03 season. I hope that what you contributed to the club's success and history gets kept as a memento of an unforgettable moment. A warm embrace, Jorge Valdano.'* Also packed were photographs of those distinctive goals in the European Cup final in Paris, and the Champions League semi-final against Barcelona, as well as numerous commemorative gifts – crystal paper weights, letter openers, clocks, mini-replicas of the Cibeles fountain, Egyptian hieroglyphics, trinkets from pre-season games. There were watches bestowed on players for winning the Champions League: one bears a naff Real Madrid logo on the otherwise elegant Franck Muller face; the other is displayed in a box which opens up to play, in distinct ice-cream van tone, 'Hala Madrid!'. There was a plate for being voted the 2001 'Mejor Persona del Vestuario', best dressing room per-sonality of the year, as well as cases of wine, which arrived every Christmas from De María, Txistu and the Asador Donostiarra. These were all mementos that certified Steve had squeezed his nose, jumped off the highest diving board and passed the exam Michael Robinson referred to in his gloriously mixed metaphor.

As well as material goods, the McManamans brought back unquantifiable friendships, memories, enthusiasms and influences. As Steve's great friend Santi Solari said: 'Sometimes, in moving to a new club, it's better to have to adapt to a new country, too, because it challenges you at all levels. In football you have to adapt to a different league, a different style and approach in playing. Away from football, you have to adapt to the language, the food, the hours, a new way of life. That experience makes you grow so much as a person.'

For Real Madrid, *el año de Beckham* ended without trophies. The lunacy of rigid adherence to the 'Zidanes y Pavones' policy and the weaknesses Steve had foreseen were visible early on. A league game away against Seville on 9 November 2003 hinted at imminent implosion. With Míchel Salgado suspended and Roberto Carlos injured, new coach Carlos Queiroz played his centre-halves as full-backs, and paired the inexperienced Rubén with Helguera in the centre. Within seventeen minutes, Madrid conceded three goals. Rúben was hastily taken off and sat on the bench, his cheeks wet with tears. He was subsequently sent out to Germany, to Borussia Mönchengladbach, on loan. On Robinson's programme, *El Día Después*, footage of the puzzled faces of the *galácticos*, 4–0 down, was run over and over again in slow-motion. 'It was one of the most eloquent videos I've ever put on,' Robinson said. 'Nobody spoke. The music helped to show what it feels to be lost on a football pitch. "I'm confused, where do I look? Help. I've got no clothes on. I've no place to hide."'

Despite that result – a foretaste of a collapse to come, brushed away as a one-off – for a few months, the Treble was on . . . until Real Madrid were beaten by lowly Real Zaragoza in the final of the Copa del Rey. It set the pattern for a string of defeats, each of which had a sting in the tail. Man of the Match in the Copa final was one Gabriel Milito, the central defender whom Madrid had all but signed in the summer before suddenly pulling out ('Florentino could not face spending a lot of money on a defender,' admitted one club insider). On 6 April Real Madrid played the second leg of a Champions League quarter-final tie against Monaco, and were eliminated from the competition despite taking a 4–2 advantage into the game and holding a 5–2 advantage at half-time. Fernando Morientes, one of several international players loaned out to reduce salaries, scored the goals that sent the *galácticos* crashing to earth. Real Madrid were paying £30,000 per week of his wages. Casillas called the defeat 'the chronicle of a death foretold'.

Just days before that game, Beckham's private life had hit news-stands all over the world. A selection of slogans at the training ground expressed fans' disgust at the overall state of affairs. 'Less partying, more work.' 'For you, whores and millions; for us, indignation.' 'Menos millones, mas cojones,' 'less millions, more balls,' were a few typical cries.

Zidane and Roberto Carlos both claimed, and displayed, near-terminal fatigue. Real Madrid could not rally themselves in the league. A stumbling 3–0 home defeat at the hands of Osasuna enabled Valencia to snatch the lead in la Liga. Valdo – a Real Madrid player on loan to the Pamplona-based club, scored the first goal and set up the third, destroying Madrid every time he got the ball. There followed the gut-wrenching indignity of a home loss to Barcelona, in which Figo was sent off; and a 2–0 defeat at the rain-lashed home of Deportivo La Coruña during which Zidane was flashed the red card and an angry Beckham was substituted. A week later Madrid lost 3–2 to Mallorca. In Barcelona the Catalan papers spelt out the details from the 1992 and 1993 'síndrome de Tenerife'. Barcelona – eighteen points behind them at Christmas, and fired by the unlikely alliance of Ronaldinho and Edgar Davids – were determined to finish the season above Real Madrid. They only had to wait a week. To universal incredulity, Real Madrid lost to already-relegated Real Murcia, a defeat orchestrated by one John Toshack. This time the *galáctico* to earn the red card is Beckham. Unlike McManaman, Figo, Zidane and Ronaldo, the season's big-name signing did not end the season by stamping heroic authority on a trophy-winning victory. Ironically for a player who cannot yet converse in Spanish, he finished this year by calling the linesman an 'hijo de puta' (son of a bitch). The season ends with a record fifth successive defeat against Real Sociedad, the low-cost team with no household names.

Steve's view was that it was, indeed, a predictable disaster. 'In the four years I was there we won a European Cup or league title every season, but we never did the double or the Treble even with the great squad of players we had,' he reasons. 'So for the club to suddenly get rid of fifteen of us, and say they'll play with the kids . . . They were on a hiding to nothing. And all the players knew that. You have to feel sorry for them. They were the ones who were going to get loads and loads of criticism. From minute one, as soon as they saw the eight internationals who had been on the bench go, they were going, "Oh my God. What on earth are we doing?" And how they have missed Hierro this season. Even if he had been used sparingly to preserve his fitness, what a difference his presence at the training ground and the big matches would have made. Those young defenders would have benefited from his experience; he was so good with the young lads. There is no way the club would have imploded so dramatically if he had been there. He would certainly have prevented the mental collapse.'

Presidential elections loomed in the summer; scapegoats were needed. Queiroz was sacked and José Antonio Camacho appointed new head coach. As a former Real Madrid full-back for sixteen seasons, winning nine league championships, five Copas del Rey and two UEFA Cup medals, he will undoubtedly see the sense in underpinning the team's creative foundations with a stronger defence. As Henry Winter wrote: 'The headline that was never, never, never expected during Pérez's reign – "Real Buy Defender" – is about to roll on to Castilian presses.' In the last week of the 2003–04 season and in the ultimate PR exercise, Real buy a big-name defender – Walter Samuel – from Roma for €22m.

At the season's end, Jorge Valdano resigned. With Queiroz taking the flak, and Valdano stepping down, would the disassociation with the 2003–04 season be enough to win Florentino Pérez a new presidential term in office in the forthcoming elections? The failure to win anything was a significant challenge to Pérez's beliefs, subjecting the club to ridicule. Beliefs once ennobled as an admirable desire to create the best football team the world has seen, with a commitment to the artistic ideal, were seen by a wider audience as plain commercial avarice and vainglorious image-consciousness. A few had always seen it as that. It was hard to give credibility to a policy referred to as 'Zidanes y Pavones' when Francisco Pavón himself, the graduate from *la cantera*, was omitted because of weak performances – even from a 2003–04 squad with precious few defenders to call upon.

Off-pitch, more bad news hit the headlines. The club learnt that the property deal Pérez had organised through his *enchufes* to sell the former training-ground complex to the municipality and simultaneously wipe out the debt Real Madrid had accumulated throughout the 1990s would be under investigation by the European Commission. This was later thrown out. Míchel Salgado was one of several long-time players who understood that Beckham's presence had destabilised the old culture of order and privacy – not that he was critical of him personally. 'We are now a team with players who are very *mediatico*: Figo, Zidane, Ronaldo and especially Beckham. Every one brings with them change, but Beckham's arrival has had the hugest influence. It's opened up the *prensa de corazón*, the gossip media, which is absolutely no good at all for us. Now the press are hanging on our every move. It's a disaster, an authentic disaster.'

Had there been too many changes too soon the previous summer? With Del Bosque and his staff, out went the captain Hierro and fifteen others (Claude Makelele, Geremi, McManaman, Pedro Munitis, Julio César, Tote, Rodrigo, Valdo, Sousa, Fernando Morientes, Flavio Conçeicão, Albert Celades, Congo, Aganzo, Julio Alvarez); out, too, went the familiar, homely surroundings of the Ciudad Deportiva training facilities for temporary residency of the Spanish Football Federation's sterile Las Rozas facilities, situated in a dispiriting urban development thirty-five kilometres north-west of the city. Iván Helguera talks openly of a dilution of spirit when the club turned into a showbiz commodity, when the traditional collective, *los blancos*, turned into five or six *galácticos*. 'With people like Macca and Makelele, happy, open people, it's like thinking you are going to play a game of football in your neighbourhood, with your people. You look forward to it. You know you're going to enjoy it. But then everything changes. You are in a new neighbourhood. Different people turn up to play who are colder – that's their personality and you understand that – but it's like you don't know anyone any more. They may be great players, but they're not *your* great players. That's what's happened a bit. It's not just Macca and Makelele, sixteen people left, others who also represented that openness, that liberty, that happiness we had in our football.

'However much we say so-and-so's a great person and an excellent footballer, it doesn't matter here. If he doesn't sell lots and lots of shirts, he's not a star. I think the club has to realise that there are players like Macca, like Míchel Salgado, Iker Casillas, Claude Makelele, Fernando Morientes, Raúl and Santi Solari who are, or have been, the engine of this team. Raúl, Macca, Míchel, Fernando,

Iker and I together won a European Cup before any of the superstars arrived. We won a league without them. At Juve, who are not a bad side, Zidane never won the European Cup. At Inter, Ronaldo didn't either. We've won it without them. Could they win one without us? They haven't yet. You don't just need individual talents who play wonderfully, you also need the guys who run a lot.'

As Salgado had said in late November 2003: '[In the European Cup final in Paris] we were obliged to function more as a team. At the moment, we don't have to so much – or, more to the point, we can't because there are five players that have to work as a team and five that you can't oblige to do so.' Salgado and Helguera spoke without bitterness. They know, too, that the lure of football is its cyclical nature. The end of one era is the beginning of another. The sacking of a coach introduces the aspirations and ideals of another. The departure of players will lead to the arrival of different talents. Del Bosque has been invited back to run Real Madrid's youth team, but turned down the offer. A Spanish coach has taken over at Liverpool. There was talk that Santiago Cañizares, the goalkeeper Steve outwitted to score his goal in the European Cup final of 2000, may be playing in Liverpool colours in 2004–05. Fernando Hierro is on pre-season trial at Bolton. Claude Makelele, Iván Campo, Geremi and Steve McManaman will continue to rib each other on opposing sides in Premiership games. And Florentino Pérez has won a second term as Real Madrid president.

It may no longer be Hierro stroking that telling, long pass to thrill the Bernabéu; it may not always be Luis Figo running a theatrical dance around defenders, or Roberto Carlos and Míchel Salgado bombing up the wings, or Steve McManaman, the beanpole Scouser, coming up with a stunning volley in the biggest of games; but the free-flowing magical football will continue. There will be more politics, more trophies, more victories, more defeats, more goals, more controversies, more of what Butragueño prefers to call 'anecdote', more victorious renditions of 'Hala Madrid!'.

And, always, always, there will be more people inspired by the skills of the players in the white shirts. Hunter Davies, that wise football appreciator, described in a Sunday newspaper how he was wandering along the Formentor cliffs in Mallorca. At the highest point of the long, rocky headland he stopped to buy a postcard at a tiny kiosk. To his surprise, given the island's more traditional allegiance to Barcelona, the vendor was wearing a Real Madrid shirt. When the man turned slightly, Davies saw the name across the back of his shoulders. McManaman.

'Call me an old fool, sorry, a young fool,' he wrote. 'But, as a football fan, I felt a shiver of pride. That here, on a remote cliff in a foreign land, a British player should be so honoured.'

Summary of Appearances and Goals

| Season | League | | | | | Copa del Rey | | Champions League | |
	Played	Starts	Minutes	Goals	Yellows	Played	Goals	Played	Goals
1999–2000	28	19	1715	3	1	5	0	13	1
2000–2001	28	22	2068	2	3	–	–	11	0
2001–2002	22	12	1976	2	2	4	0	13	2
2002–2003	15	6	581	–	–	6	1	6*	2

* Names in squad: 32; Starts: 2; Appearances as sub: 13

Acknowledgements

Thanks go to everyone who gave generously of their time to be interviewed for this book, particularly players and staff of Real Madrid, past and present: Fernando Hierro, Luis Figo, Ronaldo, Iván Helguera, David Beckham, Míchel Salgado, Raúl, Jorge Valdano, Emilio Butragueño, Santiago Solari, César Sánchez, Iván Campo, John Toshack and Vicente Del Bosque. Also to Steve's former club and national coaches, Graeme Souness, Terry Venables and Kevin Keegan; and to Tord Grip, David McManaman, Michael Robinson of Canal Plus, Chris Robinson, David Barber of the Football Association, Stephen Done of Liverpool FC museum, Carlos Sainz, Julian Henry, Jim Burns and Jonathan Harris.

I am grateful to David Welch, sports editor of the *Daily Telegraph*, for his support, and to Ben Findon, also of the *Telegraph*, for his enthusiasm for Spanish football and loan of his books. I would also like to thank the following journalists and broadcasters for their views, guidance, encouragement at critical moments (and for fielding the odd batty phone call): Henry Winter, Paul Hayward and Kevin Garside of the *Daily Telegraph*, Patrick Barclay of the *Sunday Telegraph*, lan Hawkey of the *Sunday Times*, Richard Williams of the *Guardian*, Matt Dickinson of *The Times*, Guillem Balague of *Sky Sports*, Matt Lawton of the *Daily Mail*, Kaz Mochlinski, Santiago Segurola of *El País*, Xavier Rivoire of *L'Equipe*, and Glenn Moore of the *Independent*.

Several people have been key props and/or sounding boards:

David Luxton, our agent, for his incorrigible support (sorry I never get the jokes); Sid Lowe in Madrid, who undertook research, translation and an eagle-eyed fact-check, and whose feature in *FourFourTwo* March 2003 became a well-thumbed reference point; Martin Smith of the *Daily Telegraph* for his comments and loan of a ton of *World Soccer* magazines; David Maddock of the *Mirror*, Rory Ross, Niall Edworthy, Andrew Baker and Jasper Rees for mutual books-in-progress advice.

For help with logistics and translation I am indebted to Philip Dickinson, Nigel Hack, Oscar Soler Vázquez, Juan Ramón Martin-Portugués, Gareth A. Davies and Olivia Pemberton.

I would like to thank Andrew Gordon and Ian Chapman of Simon & Schuster for their enduring enthusiasm.

The idea and responsibility of co-authoring a book would have remained daunting were it not for three inspirational literary editors I was lucky enough to work for over a period of eight years – Philip Howard of *The Times*, and Nicholas Shakespeare and John Coldstream of the *Daily Telegraph* – and I often wish the late David Cameron and Dick Garrett, former *Telegraph* colleagues, were still around for their genial chats about writing.

For allowing me time to write during school holidays I am extremely grateful to Elizabeth and Patrick Edworthy, Gill and David Ross, Janet Clarke, Euan Edworthy and my husband Rory. And to Isabella, Alexander and Emily – I can now say hand on heart, 'It's finished!'

– SE

Index